1st UK edition

£5

THE FIXER

"What is your name?"

"Yakov Shepsovitch Bok."

"Did you murder this unfortunate child?"

"Never. Why should I kill an innocent child?"

Yakov could not understand why they were asking such a question. He knew he had broken the law by living and working in a part of Kiev forbidden to Jews.

But even so, why should he, a poor fixer, a mere handyman, be accused of ritual murder?

Also by Bernard Malamud

THE NATURAL
THE ASSISTANT
THE MAGIC BARREL
A NEW LIFE
IDIOTS FIRST

THE FIXER
Bernard Malamud

EYRE & SPOTTISWOODE · LONDON

FOR PAUL

Irrational streams of blood are staining the earth . . .
                                        YEATS

O yonge Hugh of Lyncoln – slayn also
With cursed Jewes, as is notable,
For it is but a litel while ago –
Preye eek for us, we synful folk unstable,
. . .   CHAUCER

I

From the small crossed window of his room above the stable in the brickyard, Yakov Bok saw people in their long overcoats running somewhere early that morning, everybody in the same direction. Vey iz mir, he thought uneasily, something bad has happened. The Russians, coming from streets around the cemetery, were hurrying, singly or in groups, in the spring snow in the direction of the caves in the ravine, some running in the middle of the slushy cobblestone streets. Yakov hastily hid the small can in which he saved silver roubles, then rushed down to the yard to find out what the excitement was about. He asked Proshko, the foreman, loitering near the smoky brick-kilns, but Proshko spat and said nothing. Outside the yard a black-shawled, bony-faced peasant woman, thickly dressed, told him the dead body of a child had been found near by. "Where?" Yakov asked. "How old a child?" but she said she didn't know and hurried away. The next day the *Kievlyanin* reported that in a damp cave in a ravine not more than a verst and a half from the brickworks, the body of a murdered Russian boy, Zhenia Golov, twelve years old, had been found by two older boys, both fifteen, Kazimir Selivanov and Ivan Shestinsky. Zhenia, dead more than a week, was covered with stab wounds, his body bled white. After the funeral in the cemetery close by the brick factory, Richter, one of the drivers, brought in a handful of leaflets accusing the Jews of the murder. They had been printed, Yakov saw when he examined one, by the Black Hundreds organizations. Their emblem, the Imperial double-headed eagle, was imprinted on the cover, and under it: SAVE RUSSIA FROM THE JEWS. In his room that night, Yakov, in fascination, read that the boy had been bled to death for religious purposes so that the Jews could collect his blood and deliver it to the synagogue for the making of Passover matzos. Though this was ridiculous he was frightened. He got up, sat down, and got up again. He went to the window, then returned hastily and continued to read the newspaper. He was worried because the brick factory where he worked was in the Lukianovsky District, one in which Jews were forbidden to live. He had been living there for months under an assumed name and without a residence certificate. And he was frightened of the pogrom threatened in the newspaper. His own father had been killed in an incident not more than a year after Yakov's birth – something less than a pogrom, and less than useless: two drunken soldiers shot the first three Jews in their path, his father had been the second. But the son had lived through a pogrom when he was a schoolboy, a three-day Cossack raid. On the third morning when the houses were still smouldering and he was led, with a half-dozen other children, out of a cellar where they had been hiding he saw a black-bearded Jew with a white sausage stuffed into his mouth, lying in the road on a pile of bloody feathers, a peasant's pig devouring his arm.

2

Five months ago, on a mild Friday in early November, before the first snow had snowed on the shtetl, Yakov's father-in-law, a skinny worried man in clothes about to fall apart, who looked as though he had been assembled out of sticks and whipped air, drove up with his skeletal horse and rickety wagon. They sat in the thin cold house – gone to seed two months after Raisl, the faithless wife, had fled – and drank a last glass of tea together. Shmuel, long since sixty, with tousled grey beard, rheumy eyes, and deeply creased forehead – dug into his caftan pocket for half a yellow sugar lump and offered it to Yakov who shook his head. The pedlar – he was his daughter's dowry, had had nothing to give so he gave favours, service if possible – sucked tea through sugar but his son-in-law drank his unsweetened. It tasted bitter and he blamed existence. The old man from time to time commented on life without accusing anyone, or asked harmless questions, but Yakov was silent or short with answers.

After he had sipped through half his glass of tea, Shmuel, sighing, said, "Nobody has to be a Prophet to know you're blaming me for my daughter Raisl." He spoke in sadness, wearing a hard hat he had found in a barrel in a neighbouring town. When he sweated it stuck to his head, but being a religious man he didn't mind. Otherwise he had on a patched and padded caftan from which his skinny hands hung out. And very roomy shoes, not boots, which he ran in, and around in.

"Who said anything? You're blaming yourself for having brought up a whore."

Shmuel, without a word, pulled out a soiled blue handkerchief and wept.

"So why, if you'll excuse me, did you stop sleeping with her for months? Is that a way to treat a wife?"

"It was more like weeks but how long can a man sleep with a barren woman? I got tired of trying."

"Why didn't you go to the rabbi when I begged you?"

"Let him stay out of my business and I'll stay out of his. All in all he's an ignorant man."

"Charity you were always short of," the pedlar said.

Yakov rose, enraged. "Don't talk to me about charity. What have I had all my life? What have I got to give away? I was practically born an orphan – my mother dead ten minutes later, and you know what happened to my poor father. If somebody said Kaddish for them it wasn't me till years later. If they were waiting outside the gates of heaven it was a long cold wait, if they're not still waiting. Throughout my miserable childhood I lived in a stinking orphans' home, barely existing. In my dreams I ate and I ate my dreams. Torah I had little of and Talmud less, though I learned Hebrew because I've got an ear for language. Anyway, I knew the Psalms. They taught me a trade and apprenticed me five minutes after age ten – not that I regret it. So I work – let's call it work – with my hands, and some call me 'common' but the truth of it is few people know who is really common. As for those that look like they got class, take another look. Viskover, the Nogid, is in my eyes a common man. All he's got is roubles and when he opens his mouth you can hear them clink. On my own I studied

12

different subjects, and even before I was taken into the army I taught myself a decent Russian, much better than we pick up from the peasants. What little I know I learned on my own – some history and geography, a little science, arithmetic, and a book or two of Spinoza's. Not much but better than nothing."

"Though most is treyf I give you credit—" said Shmuel.

"Let me finish. I've had to dig with my finger-nails for a living. What can anybody do without capital? What they can do I can do but it's not much. I fix what's broken – except in the heart. In this shtetl everything is falling apart – who bothers with leaks in his roof if he's peeking through the cracks to spy on God? And who can pay to have it fixed let's say he wants it, which he doesn't. If he does, half the time I work for nothing. If I'm lucky, a dish of noodles. Opportunity here is born dead. I'm frankly in a foul mood."

"Opportunity you don't have to tell me about—"

"They conscripted me for the Russo-Japanese War but it was over before I got in. Thank God. When I got sick they booted me out. An asthmatic Jew wasn't worth the trouble. Thank God. When I got back I scraped again with my broken nails. After a long run-around which started when I met her, I married your daughter, who couldn't get pregnant in five and a half years. She bore me no children so who could I look in the eye? And now she runs off with some stranger she met at the inn – a goy I'm positive. So that's enough – who needs more? I don't want people pitying me or wondering what I did to be so cursed. I did nothing. It was a gift. I'm innocent. I've been an orphan too long. All I have to my name after thirty years in this grave-yard is sixteen roubles that I got from selling everything I own. So please don't mention charity because I have no charity to give."

"Charity you can give even when you haven't got. I don't mean money. I meant for my daughter."

"Your daughter deserves nothing."

"She ran from one rabbi to another in every town I took her, but nobody could promise her a child. She ran to the doctors too when she had a rouble, but they told her the same thing. It was cheaper with the rabbis. So she ran away – may God protect her. Even a sinner belongs to Him. She sinned but she was desperate."

"May she run for ever."

"She was a true wife to you for years. She shared your every misfortune."

"What she caused she shared. She was a true wife to the last minute, or the last month, or the month before that, and that makes her untrue, a black cholera on her!"

"God forbid," cried Shmuel, rising. "On you!"

Eyes agitated, he thickly cursed the fixer and fled from the house.

Yakov had sold everything but the clothes on his back which he wore as peasants do – embroidered shirt belted outside his trousers, whose legs were stuffed into wrinkled high boots. And a peasant's worn and patched, brown sheepskin coat, which could, on occasion, smell of sheep. He had kept his tools and a few books: Smirnovsky's *Russian Grammar*, an elementary biology book, *Selections from Spinoza*, and a battered atlas at least twenty-five years old. He had made a small bundle of the books with a piece of knotted twine. The tools were in a flour sack tied at the neck, the crosscut blade protruding. There was also some food in a cone of newspaper. He was leaving behind his few ruined sticks of furniture – a junkman had wanted to be paid to take them – and two sets of cracked dishes, also unsaleable, that Shmuel could do with whatever he wanted – use, axe, or

14

fire – they were worth nothing. Raisl had had two sets for her father's sake, for herself it made not much difference. But in exchange for the horse and wagon the pedlar would get a fairly good cow. He could take over his daughter's little dairy business. It could hardly pay less than peddling. He was the only person Yakov knew who peddled nothing and sold it, in bits and slices, for real kopeks. Sometimes he traded nothing for pig bristles, wool, grain, sugar beets, and then sold the peasants dried fish, soap, kerchiefs, candy, in minute quantities. That was his talent and on it he miraculously lived. "He who gave us teeth will give us bread." Yet his breath smelled of nothing – not bread, not anything.

Yakov, in loose clothes and peaked cap, was an elongated nervous man with large ears, stained hard hands, a broad back and tormented face, lightened a bit by grey eyes and brownish hair. His nose was sometimes Jewish, sometimes not. He had to no one's surprise – after Raisl ran away – shaved off his short beard of reddish cast. "Cut off your beard and you no longer resemble your creator," Shmuel had warned. Since then he had been admonished by more than one Jew that he looked like a goy but it had caused him neither to mourn nor rejoice. He looked young but felt old and for that he blamed nobody, not even his wife; he blamed fate and spared himself. His nervousness showed in his movements. Generally he moved faster than he had to, considering how little there was to do, but he was always doing something. After all, he was a fixer and had to keep his hands busy.

Dumping his things into the open wagon, a rusty water bucket hanging under it between the back wheels, he was displeased with the appearance of the nag, a naked-looking animal with spindly legs, a brown bony body and large stupid eyes, who got along very well with Shmuel. They asked little from each other and lived in peace. The horse did mostly as he pleased and Shmuel indulged him. After all, what difference did a short delay make in a mad world? Tomorrow he would be no richer. The fixer was irritated with himself for acquiring this decrepit beast, but had thought better a lopsided exchange with Shmuel than getting nothing for the cow from a peasant who coveted her. A father-in-law's blood was thicker than water. Although there was no railroad station anywhere around, and the coachman came for travellers only every second week, Yakov could have got to Kiev without taking over the horse and wagon. Shmuel had offered to drive him the thirty or so versts but the fixer preferred to be rid of him and travel alone. He figured that once he got into the city he could sell the beast and apology-for-dray, if not to a butcher, then at least to a junk dealer for a few roubles.

Dvoira, the dark-uddered cow, was out in the field behind the hut, browsing under a leafless poplar tree, and Yakov went out to her. The white cow raised her head and watched him approach. The fixer patted her lean flank. "Good-bye, Dvoira," he said, "and lots of luck. Give what you got left to Shmuel, also a poor man." He wanted to say more but couldn't. Tearing up some limp yellowing grass, he fed it to the cow, then returned to the horse and wagon. Shmuel had reappeared.

Why does he act as though he were the one who had deserted me?

"I didn't come back to fight with anybody," Shmuel said. "What she did I won't defend – she hurt me as much as she did you. Even more, though when the rabbi says she's now dead my voice agrees but not my heart. First of all she's my only child, and since when do we need more dead? I've cursed her more than once but I ask God not to listen."

"Well, I'm leaving," Yakov said, "take care of the cow."

"Don't leave yet," Shmuel said, his eyes miserable. "If you stay Raisl might come back."

"If she does who's interested?"

"If you had been more patient she wouldn't have left you."

"Five years going on six is enough of patience. I've had enough. I might have waited the legal ten, but she danced off with some dirty stranger, so I've had my fill, thanks."

"Who can blame you?" Shmuel sighed sadly. He asked after a while, "Have you got tobacco for a little cigarette, Yakov?"

"My bag is empty."

The pedlar briskly rubbed his dry palms.

"So you haven't, you haven't, but what I don't understand is why you want to bother with Kiev. It's a dangerous city full of churches and anti-Semites."

"I've been cheated from the start," Yakov said bitterly. "What I've been through personally you know already, not to mention living here all my life except for a few months in the army. The shtetl is a prison, no change from the days of Khmelnitsky. It moulders and the Jews moulder in it. Here we're all prisoners, I don't have to tell you, so it's time to try elsewhere I've finally decided. I want to make a living, I want to get acquainted with a bit of the world. I've read a few books in recent years and it's surprising what goes on that none of us knows about. I'm not asking for Tibet but what I saw in St Petersburg interested me. Whoever thought of white nights before, but it's a scientific fact; they have them there. When I left the army I thought I would get out of here as soon as possible, but things caught up with me, including your daughter."

"My daughter wanted to run away from here the minute you got married but you wouldn't go."

"It's true," said Yakov, "it was my fault. I thought it couldn't get worse so it must get better. I was wrong both ways so now enough is enough. I'm on my way at last."

"Outside the Pale only wealthy Jews and the professional classes can get residence certificates. The Tsar doesn't want poor Jews all over his land, and Stolypin, may his lungs collapse, urges him on. Ptu!" Shmuel spat through two fingers.

"Since I can't be a professional on account of lack of education I wouldn't mind being wealthy. As the saying goes, I'd sell my last shirt to be a millionaire. Maybe, by luck, I'll make my fortune in the outside world."

"What's in the world," Shmuel said, "is in the shtetl – people, their trials, worries, circumstances. But here at least God is with us."

"He's with us till the Cossacks come galloping, then he's elsewhere. He's in the outhouse, that's where he is."

The pedlar grimaced but let the remark pass. "Almost fifty thousand Jews live in Kiev," he said, "restricted to a few districts, and all in the way of the first blow that falls if a new pogrom should come. And it will fall faster in the larger places than it falls here. When we hear their cries we will rush into the woods. Why should you walk straight into the hands of the Black Hundreds, may they hang by their tongues?"

"The truth of it is I'm a man full of wants I'll never satisfy, at least not here. It's time to get out and take a chance. Change your place change your luck, people say."

"Since the last year or so, Yakov, you're a different man. What wants are so important?"

"Those that can't sleep and keep me awake for company.

18

I've told you what wants: a full stomach now and then. A job that pays roubles, not noodles. Even some education if I can get it, and I don't mean workmen studying Torah after hours. I've had my share of that. What I want to know is what's going on in the world."

"That's all in the Torah, there's no end to it. Stay away from the wrong books, Yakov, the impure."

"There are no wrong books. What's wrong is the fear of them."

Shmuel unstuck his hat and wiped his brow with his handkerchief.

"Yakov, if you want to go to foreign parts, Turks or no Turks, why not to Palestine where a Jew can see Jewish trees and mountains, and breathe the Jewish air? If I had half a chance there's where I'd go."

"All I've had in this miserable town is a beggarly existence. Now I'll try Kiev. If I can live there decently that's what I'll do. If not, I'll make sacrifices, save up, and head for Amsterdam for a boat to America. To sum it up, I have little but I have plans."

"Plans or none you're looking for trouble."

"I've never had to look," said the fixer. "Well, Shmuel, good luck to you. The morning's gone so I'd better go."

He climbed up on to the wagon and reached for the reins.

"I'll ride with you as far as the windmills." Shmuel got up on the seat on the other side.

Yakov touched the nag with a birch switch the old man kept in the holder, a hole bored into the edge of the seat, but the horse, after an initial startled gallop, stopped short and stood motionless in the road.

"Personally I never use it," the pedlar remarked. "It's there as a warning. If he dawdles I remind him it's there. He seems to like to hear me talk about it."

"If that's the case I'm better off walking."

"Patience." Shmuel smacked his lips. "Gidap, beauty – he's very vain. Whenever you can afford it, Yakov, feed him oats. Too much grass and he's prone to gas."

"If he's prone to gas let him fart." He flicked the reins.

Yakov didn't look back. The nag moved along a crooked road between black ploughed fields with dark round haystacks piled up here and there, the peasant's church visible on the left in the distance; then slowly up the narrow stony cemetery road, a few thin yellow willows amidst the graves, and around a low tombstone-covered hill where Yakov's parents, a man and woman in their early twenties, lay buried. He had considered a visit to their weed-strewn graves but hadn't the heart at the last minute. The past was a wound in the head. He thought of Raisl and felt depressed.

The fixer snapped the rod against the nag's ribs but got no increase of motion.

"I'll get to Kiev by Hanukkah."

"If you don't get there it's because God wills it. You won't miss a thing."

A shnorrer in rags called to the fixer from beside a tilted tombstone. "Hey, there, Yakov, it's Friday. How about a two-kopek piece for a Sabbath blessing? Charity saves from death."

"Death is the last of my worries."

"Lend me a kopek or two, Yakov," said Shmuel.

"A kopek I haven't earned today."

The shnorrer, a man with ugly feet, called him goy, his mouth twisted, eyes lit in anger.

Yakov spat in the road.

Shmuel said a prayer to ward off evil.

The nag began to trot, drawing the rickety wagon with its swinging bucket banging the axle past the cemetery hill, down the winding road. They drove by the poorhouse, a shabby structure with an addition for orphans, which Yakov averted his eyes from, then clop-clopped across a wooden bridge into the populous section of the town. They passed Shmuel's hut, neither of them looking. A blackened bathhouse with boarded windows stood near a narrow stream and the fixer felt suddenly itchy for a bath, thinking of himself in the thick steam, slapping his soapened sides with a twig brush as the attendant poured water on his head. God bless soap and water, Raisl used to say. In a few hours the bathhouse, steaming from its cracks, would be bulging with Jews washing up for Friday night.

They rattled along a rutted dusty street with thatched cottages on one side, open weedy fields on the other. A big-wigged Jewess, sitting on her doorstep, plucked a bloody-necked hen between her knees, as she cursed out a peasant's sow rooting in the remnants of her potato garden. A pool of blood in the ditch marked the passage of the ritual slaughterer. Farther on, a bearded black goat with a twisted horn, tethered to a post, baaed at the horse and charged, but the rope around his neck held and though the post toppled, the goat was thrown on its back. The doors of some of the cottages hung loose, and where there were steps they sagged. Fences buckled and were about to collapse without apparent notice or response, irritating the fixer, who liked things in place and functioning.

Tonight the white candles would gleam from the lit windows. For everybody else.

The horse zigzagged towards the market-place, and now the quality of the houses improved, some large and attractive, with gardens full of flowers in the summertime.

"Leave it to the lousy rich," the fixer muttered.

Shmuel had nothing to say. His mind, he had often said,

had exhausted the subject. He did not envy the rich, all he wanted was to share a little of their wealth – enough to live on while he was working hard to earn a living.

The market, a large open square with wooden houses on two sides, some containing first-floor shops, was crowded with peasant carts laden with grains, vegetables, wood, hides and whatnot. Around the stalls and bins mostly women clustered, shopping for the Sabbath. Though the market was his usual hangout, the fixer waved to no one and no one waved to him.

I leave with no regret, he thought. I should have gone years ago.

"Who have you told?" Shmuel asked.

"Who's there to tell? Practically nobody. It's none of their business anyway. Frankly, my heart is heavy – I'll tell the truth – but I'm sick of this place."

He had said good-bye to his two cronies, Leibish Polikov and Haskel Dembo. The first had shrugged, the other wordlessly embraced him, and that was that. A butcher holding up by its thick yellow feet a squawking hen beating its wings saw the wagon go by and said something witty to his customers. One of these, a young woman who turned to look, called to Yakov, but by then the wagon was out of the market-place, scattering some chickens nesting in the ruts of the road and a flock of jabbering ducks, as it clattered on.

They approached the domed synagogue with its iron weathercock, a pock-marked yellow-walled building with an oak door, for the time being resting in peace. It had been sacked more than once. The courtyard was empty except for a black-hatted Jew sitting on a bench reading a folded newspaper in the sunlight. Yakov had rarely been inside the synagogue in recent years yet he easily remembered the long high-ceilinged room with its brass chandeliers, oval stained windows, and the prayer stands with stools and wooden candleholders, where he had spent, for the most part wasted, so many hours.

"Gidap," he said.

At the other side of the town – a shtetl was an island surrounded by Russia – as they came abreast a windmill, its patched fans turning in slow massive motion, the fixer jerked on the reins and the horse clopped to a stop.

"Here's where we part," he said to the pedlar.

Shmuel drew out of his pocket an embroidered cloth bag.

"Don't forget these," he said embarrassed. "I found them in your drawer before we left."

In the bag was another containing phylacteries. There was also a prayer shawl and a prayer book. Raisl, before they were married, had made the bag out of a piece of her dress and embroidered it with the tablets of the Ten Commandments.

"Thanks." Yakov tossed the bag among his other things in the wagon.

"Yakov," said Shmuel passionately, "don't forget your God!"

"Who forgets who?" the fixer said angrily. "What do I get from him but a bang on the head and a stream of piss in my face. So what's there to be worshipful about?"

"Don't talk like a meshummed. Stay a Jew, Yakov, don't give up our God."

"A meshummed gives up one God for another. I don't want either. We live in a world where the clock ticks fast while he's on his timeless mountain staring in space. He doesn't see us and he doesn't care. Today I want my piece of bread, not in Paradise."

"Listen to me, Yakov, take my advice. I've lived longer than you. There's a shul in the Podol in Kiev. Go on

Shabbos, you'll feel better. 'Blessed are they who put their trust in God.'"

"Where I ought to go is to the Socialist Bund meetings, that's where I should go, not in shul. But the truth of it is I dislike politics, though don't ask me why. What good is it if you're not an activist? I guess it's my nature. I incline towards the philosophical although I don't know much about anything."

"Be careful," Shmuel said, agitated, "we live in the middle of our enemies. The best way to take care is to stay under God's protection. Remember, he's not perfect, neither are we."

They embraced quickly and Shmuel got down from the wagon.

"Good-bye, sweetheart," he called to the horse. "Good-bye, Yakov, I'll think of you when I say the Eighteen Blessings. If you ever see Raisl, tell her her father is waiting."

Shmuel trudged back towards the synagogue. When he was quite far away Yakov felt a pang for having forgotten to slip him a rouble or two.

"Get on now." The nag flicked an ear, roused itself for a short trot, then slowed to a tired walk.

"It'll be some trip," the fixer thought.

The horse stopped abruptly as a field mouse skittered across the road.

"Gidap, goddamit" – but the nag wouldn't move.

A peasant passed by with a long-horned bullock, prodding the animal with a stick.

"A horse understands a whip," he said across the road in Russian.

Yakov belaboured the beast with the birch rod until he drew blood. The nag whinnied but remained tightly immo-

24

bile on the road. The peasant, after watching awhile, moved on.

"You son-of-a-bitch," said the fixer to the horse, "we'll never get to Kiev."

He was at the point of despair when a brown dog rustling through a blanket of dead leaves under some trees came on to the road, yelping at the horse. The nag hurried forward, Yakov barely grabbing the reins. The dog chased them, barking sharply at the horse's hooves, then at a turn in the road, disappeared. But the wagon rolled on, bucket rattling, its wheels wobbling, the nag trotting as fast as it could.

It clip-clopped along the hard dirt road, on one side of which flowed a mild stream below a sloping embankment; and on the other were the scattered log huts of a peasant village, their roofs covered with rotting straw. Despite poverty and the antics of too many pigs the huts looked better than the shtetl cottages. A bearded peasant chopped wood, a woman pumped water from the village well. They both stopped to stare at him. A verst from his town and he was a stranger in the world.

The horse trotted on, Yakov gazing at the fields, some ploughed under, where oats, hay, sugar beets had grown, the haystacks standing dark against the woods. A crow flew slowly over the stubble of a wheatfield. The fixer found himself counting sheep and goats grazing in the communal meadows under lazy thick clouds. It had been a dank and dreary autumn, the dead leaves still hanging on half the trees in the woods around the fields. Last year at this time it had already snowed. Though as a rule he enjoyed the landscape, Yakov felt a weight on him. The buzz and sparkle of summer were gone. In the violet distance the steppe seemed melancholy, endless.

The cut on the horse's flank, though encrusted, still

oozed red droplets and drew fleas he switched away without touching the animal. He thought his spirits would rise once he was out of the shtetl but felt no relief. The fixer was troubled by discontent, a deeper sense that he had had no choice about going than he wanted to admit. His few friends were left behind. His habits, his best memories such as they were, were there. But so was his shame. He was leaving because he had earned a worse living – although he hadn't become a gravedigger – than many he knew with fewer brains and less skill. He was leaving because he was a childless husband – "alive but dead" the Talmud described such a man – as well as an embittered, deserted one. Yet if she had been faithful he would have stayed. Then better she hadn't been. He should be grateful to be escaping from a fruitless life. Still, he was apprehensive of going to a city of strangers – Jews as well as Gentiles, strangers were strangers – in a sense a forbidden place. Holy Kiev, mother of Russian cities! He knew the towns for a dozen versts around but had only once, for a week in summer, been in Kiev. He felt the discontent of strangeness, of not knowing what was where, unable to predict or clearly visualize. All he could think of were the rows of shabby crowded tenements in the Podol. Would he go on in the same useless poverty and drab experience amid masses of Jews as poor as he, or somehow come to a better way of life? How at his age? – already thirty. Jobs for him were always scarce. With just the few roubles in his pocket how long would he last before starving? Why should tomorrow be better than today? Had he earned the privilege?

He had many fears, and since he rarely travelled long distances, had fears of travelling. The soles of his feet itched, which meant, the old wives said: "You will journey to a far-off place." So, good, but would he ever get there? The horse had slowed down again, a black year on its stupid head. Suppose those clouds, grown dark and heavy, cracked open on their undersides and poured snow upon the world. Would the horse make it? He pictured the snow falling thickly, in a few minutes turning the road and fields white so you couldn't see where one ended and the other began, the wagon filling up with snow. The nag would stop. Yakov might switch him till his bones gleamed through the blood but the animal was the type that would quietly lie down in the snow to spite him. "Brother, I'm tired. If you want to go on in this storm, go in good health. But not me. I'll take sleep and if it's sleep for ever, so much the better. At least the snow is warm." The fixer saw himself wandering in drifts until he perished.

But the horse said nothing, and it didn't look like snow – or rain either. It was a brisk day beginning to be windy – it raised the nag's mane – and though the horse moved leisurely it moved steadily. Yet as they went through a grove of black-branched trees, the leafless twigs darkly intertwined high above Yakov's head, the small wood grew gloomy, and the fixer still searching for a change in the weather became actively nervous again. Shading his eyes in the queer light, he peered ahead – a winding road, absolutely snowless. Enough of this, he thought, I'd better eat. As though it had read his mind the nag came to a stop before he pulled the reins. Yakov got down off the seat, and taking hold of the bridle, drew the horse to the side of the road. The horse spread its hind legs and spattered a yellow stream on the road. Yakov urinated on some brown ferns. Feeling better, he tore up several handfuls of dry tussocky grass, and since he could locate no feedbag in the wagon, fed it in fistfuls to the nag. The horse, its sides heaving, chewed with its eroded yellow teeth until the grass foamed.

The fixer's stomach rumbled. He sat under a sunlit tree, raised his sheepskin collar, and opened the food parcel. He ate part of a cold boiled potato, chewing slowly, then half a cucumber sprinkled with coarse salt, with a piece of sour black bread. Ah, for some tea, he thought, or if not that, some sweetened hot water. Yakov fell asleep with his back to the tree, awoke in a hurry, and climbed up on the wagon.

"It's late, goddamit, come on, move."

The nag wouldn't budge. The fixer reached for the switch. On second thought he climbed down, unhitched the rusty bucket and went looking for water. When he found a little stream the pail leaked, but he offered it, half full, to the horse, who wouldn't drink.

"Games I don't play." Yakov poured out the water, hitched the bucket on the hook under the wagon, and stepped up to the seat. He waved the switch till it whistled. The nag, lowering his ears, moved forward, if one could call it movement. At least it wasn't where it had been before. The fixer again whistled the air with the switch, and the horse, after an indecisive minute, began to trot. The wagon rattled on.

They had gone on a while when the wagon caught up with an old woman, a pilgrim walking slowly in the road, leaning on her long staff, a heavy peasant in black, wearing men's shoes and carrying a knapsack, a thick shawl wrapped around her head.

He drew over to the side to pass her but as he did Yakov called out, "A ride, granny?"

"May Jesus bless you." She had three grey teeth.

Jesus he didn't need. Bad luck, he thought. Yakov helped pull her up to the wagon seat and touched the nag with the birch whip. To his surprise the horse took up his trot. Then as the road turned, the right wheel struck a rock and broke with a crunch. The wagon teetered and sagged at the rear, the left wheel tilted inward.

The old woman crossed herself, slowly climbed down to the road, and walked on with her heavy stick. She did not look back.

Yakov cursed Shmuel for wishing the wagon on him. Jumping to the ground he examined the broken wheel. Its worn metal ring had come off. The wooden rim had caved in, splintering two spokes. The split hub leaked axle grease. He groaned.

After five minutes of stunned emptiness he got his tool sack out of the wagon, untied it and spread out the tools on the road. But with hatchet, saw, plane, tinsmith's shears, tri-square, putty, wire, pointed knife and two awls, the fixer couldn't fix what was broken. Under the best conditions it would take him a day to repair the wheel. He thought of buying one from a peasant if he could get one that fitted, or nearly fitted, but if so where was the peasant? When you didn't need them they were in your beard. Yakov tossed the pieces of broken wheel into the wagon. He tied up his tools and drearily waited for someone to come. Nobody came. He considered returning to the shtetl but remembered he had had enough. The wind was colder, sharper, got under his coat and between the shoulder-blades. The sun was setting, the sky turning dark.

If I go slow maybe I can make it on three wheels to the next village.

He tried it, sitting lightly as far to the left on the seat as he could, and begged the nag to take it easy. To his relief they went forward, the back wheel squeaking, for half a verst. He had caught up with the pilgrim and was about to say she couldn't ride when the other rear wheel, grinding thickly against the axle, collapsed, the back of the wagon hitting the road with a crashing thud, the bucket crushed. The horse lurched forward, snorted and reared. The fixer, his body tipped at a perilous angle, was paralysed.

Eventually he got down off the seat. "Who invented my life?" Behind him was the empty treeless steppe, ahead the old woman. She had stopped before a huge wooden crucifix at the side of the road, crossed herself, and then slowly sinking to her knees, began to hit her head against the hard ground. She banged it until Yakov had a headache. The darkening steppe was here uninhabited. He feared fog and a raging wind. Unhitching the horse and drawing him out from under the wooden yoke, Yakov gathered together the reins. He backed the nag to the wagon seat, and climbing up on it, mounted the animal. No sooner up than down. The fixer placed his tool bag, book bundle, and parcels on the tilted seat, wound the reins around him, and remounted the horse. He slung the tools over his shoulder, and with his left hand held the other things as they rested on the horse's back, his right hand grasping the reins. The horse galloped forward. To Yakov's surprise he did not fall off.

They skirted the old woman, prostrate at the cross. He felt foolish and uncertain on the horse but hung on. The nag had slowed to a trot, then to a dejected walk. It stood stock still. Yakov cursed it into eternity and eventually it came to life, once more inching forward. When they were on the move, the fixer, who had never sat on a horse before – he couldn't think why except that he had never had a horse – dreamed of good fortune, accomplishment, affluence. He had a comfortable home, good business – maybe a small factory of some kind – a faithful wife, dark-haired, pretty, and three healthy children, God bless them. But when he was becalmed on the nag he thought blackly of his father-in-law, beat the beast with his fist, and foresaw for himself a useless future. Yakov pleaded with the animal to make haste – it was dark and the steppe wind cut keenly, but freed of the wagon the horse examined the world. He also stopped to crop grass, tearing it audibly with his eroded teeth, and wandering from one side of the road to the other. Once in a while he turned and trotted back a few steps. Yakov, frantic, threatened the switch, but they both knew he had none. In desperation he kicked the beast with his heels. The nag bucked and for a perilous few minutes it was like being in a rowboat on a stormy sea. Having barely survived, Yakov stopped kicking. He considered ditching his goods, hoping the lightened load might speed things up, but didn't dare.

"I'm a bitter man, you bastard horse. Come to your senses or you'll suffer."

It availed him nothing.

By then it was pitch dark. The wind boomed. The steppe was a black sea full of strange voices. Here nobody spoke Yiddish, and the nag, maybe feeling the strangeness of it, began to trot and soon came close to flight. Though the fixer was not a superstitious man he had been a superstitious boy, and he recalled Lilith, Queen of Evil Spirits, and the Fish-witch who tickled travellers to death or otherwise made herself helpful. Ghosts rose like smoke in the Ukraine. From time to time he felt a presence at his back but would not turn. Then a yellow moon rose like a flower growing and lit the empty steppe deep into the shadowy distance. The distance glowed. It'll be a long night, the fixer thought. They galloped through a peasant village, its long-steepled church yellow in moonlight, the squat thatched huts dark, no lights anywhere. Though he smelled woodsmoke he saw none. Yakov considered dismounting, knocking on a strange door and begging for a night's lodging. But he felt that if he got off the horse he would never get back on. He was afraid he might be robbed of his few roubles, so he stayed put and made uncertain progress. The sky was thick with stars, the wind blowing cold in his face. Once he slept momentarily and woke in shivering sweat from a nightmare. He thought he was irretrievably lost, but to his amazement, before him in the distance rose a vast height glowing in dim moonlight and sprinkled sparsely with lights, at the foot of which ran a broad dark river reflecting the half-hidden moon. The nag stopped jogging and it took them an almost endless hour to make the last half verst to the water.

3

It was freezing cold but the wind was down on the Dnieper. There was no ferry, the boatman said, "Closed down. Closed. Shut." He waved his arms as though talking to a foreigner although Yakov had spoken to him in Russian. That the ferry had stopped running sharpened the fixer's desire to get across the river. He hoped to rent a bed at an inn and wake early to look for work.

"I'll row you across for a rouble," the boatman said.

"Too much," Yakov answered, though deadly tired. "Which way to the bridge?"

"Six or eight versts. A long way for the same thing."

"A rouble," the fixer groaned. "Who's got that much money?"

"You can take it or leave it. It's no easy thing rowing across a dangerous river on a pitch-black night. We might both drown."

"What would I do with my horse?" The fixer spoke more to himself.

"That's none of my business." The boatman, his shoulders like a tree-trunk, and wearing a shaggy grizzled beard, blew out one full nostril on a rock, then the other. The white of his right eye was streaked with blood.

"Look, mate, why do you make more trouble than it's worth? Even if I could haul it across, which I can't, the beast will die on you. It doesn't take a long look to see he's on his last legs. Look at him trembling. Listen to him breathing like a gored bull."

"I was hoping to sell him in Kiev."

"What fool would buy a bag of old bones?"

"I thought maybe a horse butcher or someone – at least the skin."

"I say the horse is dead," said the boatman, "but you can save a rouble if you're smart. I'll take him for the cost of the trip. It's a bother to me and I'll be lucky to get fifty kopeks for the carcass, but I'll do you the favour, seeing you're a stranger."

He's only given me trouble, the fixer thought.

He stepped into the rowboat with his bag of tools, books, and other parcels. The boatman untied the boat, dipped both oars into the water and they were off.

The nag, tethered to a paling, watched from the moonlit shore.

Like an old Jew he looks, thought the fixer.

The horse whinnied, and when that proved useless, farted loudly.

"I don't recognize the accent you speak," said the boatman, pulling the oars. "It's Russian but from what province?"

"I've lived in Latvia as well as other places," the fixer muttered.

"At first I thought you were a goddam Pole. Pan whosis,

a

Pani whatsis." The boatman laughed, then snickered. "Or maybe a motherfucking Jew. But though you're dressed like a Russian you look more like a German, may the devil destroy them all, excepting yourself and yours of course."

"Latvian," said Yakov.

"Anyway, God save us all from the bloody Jews," the boatman said as he rowed, "those long-nosed, pock-marked, cheating, bloodsucking parasites. They'd rob us of daylight if they could. They foul up earth and air with their body stink and garlic breaths, and Russia will be done to death by the diseases they spread unless we make an end to it. A Jew's a devil – it's a known fact – and if you ever watch one peel off his stinking boot you'll see a split hoof, it's true. I know, for as the Lord is my witness, I saw one with my own eyes. He thought nobody was looking, but I saw his hoof as plain as day."

He stared at Yakov with the bloody eye. The fixer's foot itched but he didn't touch it.

Let him talk, he thought, yet he shivered.

"Day after day they crap up the Motherland," the boat-man went on monotonously, "and the only way to save our-selves is to wipe them out. I don't mean kill a Zhid now and then with a blow of the fist or kick in the head, but wipe them all out, which we've sometimes tried but never done as it should be done. I say we ought to call our menfolk to-gether, armed with guns, knives, pitchforks, clubs – any-thing that will kill a Jew – and when the church bells begin to ring we move on the Zhidy quarter, which you can tell by the stink, routing them out of wherever they're hiding – in attics, cellars, or ratholes – bashing in their brains, stabbing their herring-filled guts, shooting off their snotty noses, no exception made for young or old, because if you spare any they breed like rats and then the job's to do all over again.

34

"And then when we've slaughtered the whole cursed tribe of them – and the same is done in every province throughout Russia, wherever we can smoke them out – though we've got most of them nice and bunched up in the Pale – we'll pile up the corpses and soak them with benzine and light fires that people will enjoy all over the world. Then when that's done we hose the stinking ashes away and divide the roubles and jewels and silver and furs and all the other loot they stole, or give it back to the poor who it rightfully belongs to anyway. You can take my word – the time's not far off when everything I say, we will do, because our Lord, who they crucified, wants his rightful revenge."

He dropped an oar and crossed himself.

Yakov fought an impulse to do the same. His bag of prayer things fell with a plop into the Dnieper and sank like lead.

II

Where do you go if you had been nowhere? He hid at first in the Jewish quarter, emerging stealthily from time to time to see what there was to see in the world, exploring, trying the firmness of the earth. Kiev, "the Jerusalem of Russia", still awed and disquieted him. He had been there for a few hot summer days after being conscripted into the army, and now, again, he saw it with half the self – the other half worried about his worries. Still, as he wandered from street to street, the colours were light and pretty. A golden haze hung in the air in the late afternoons. The busy avenues were full of people, among them Ukrainian peasants in their native dress, gypsies, soldiers, priests. At night the white gas globes glowed in the streets and there were thick mists on the river. Kiev stood on three hills, and he remembered his first trembling sight of the city from the Nicholas Bridge – dotted with white houses with green roofs, churches and monasteries, their gold and silver domes floating above the green foliage. He wasn't without an eye for a pretty scene, though that added nothing to his living. Still, a man was more than a workhorse, or so they said.

The other way, across the glassy brown river – the way he had come on a dying horse – the steppe stretched out into the vast green distance. Only thirty versts and the shtetl was invisible, gone – poof! – lost, maybe expired. Though he felt homesick he knew he would never return, yet what would it come to? More than once Raisl had accused him of being afraid to leave and maybe it was true but at last it wasn't. So I left, he thought, what good will it do me? Was she back? he wondered. He cursed her when he thought of her.

He went where he had not been before, speaking in Russian to anyone who spoke to him – testing himself, he explained it to himself. Why should a man be afraid of the world? Because he was, if for no other reason. Numb with fear that he would be recognized as a Jew and ordered out, he stealthily watched from the gallery of a church as the peasants, some with knapsacks on their backs, knelt and prayed at the altar before a tall gold crucifix and a jewelled ikon of the Madonna, as the priest, a huge man in rich thick vestments, chanted the Orthodox service. The fixer had the shivers as he looked, and the strange odour of incense increased his nervousness. He almost rose out of his boots as he was touched on the arm and saw at his side a black-bearded hunchback who pointed to the peasants below smacking their heads against the flagstone floor and kissing it passionately. "Go thou and do likewise! Eat salted bread and listen to the truth!" The fixer quickly left.

Stupefied that he dared the adventure, he afterwards descended to the Lavra catacombs – under the old monastery on the Pechersky hill overlooking the Dnieper – amid a group of frightened, pasty-faced peasants holding lit candles. They moved in a loose line along low, damp-smelling passages, where through barred windows he caught glimpses of the saints of the Orthodox Church lying in open coffins, covered with shabby cloths of red and gold. Small red lamps glowed in the walls under their ikons. In a candle-lit cell, as the line moved on, a monk with rat-tail hair to his shoulders held out a relic of "the hand of St Andrew" for the faithful to kiss, and each knelt to touch the parchmented hand to his lips. But though Yakov had considered a quick kiss of the bony fingers, when his time came to kneel, he blew out his candle and groped his way on in the dark.

Outside there was a crowd of beggars, some of them armless and legless cripples from the late war. Three were blind. One rolled his eyes inward. One bulged his so that they looked like fish eyes. And one read sonorously "by divine inspiration" from a book of gospels which he held in his hands. He stared at Yakov and Yakov stared at him.

2

He lived in the heart of the Jewish quarter in the Podol District in a teeming tenement hung with mattresses airing and rags of clothing drying, above a courtyard crowded with wooden workshops where everyone was busy but no one earned much of anything. They stayed alive. The fixer wanted better, at least better than he had had, too much of nothing. For a while, during the cold rains of late autumn, he confined himself to the Jewish section, but after the first snowfall in the city – about a month after he had arrived –

he began to edge out again, looking for work. With his tool sack slung over his shoulder he trudged from street to street through the Podol and Plossky, the flat commercial districts reaching to the river, and went up the hills into neighbourhoods forbidden to Jews to work in. He sought, he continued to say to himself, opportunities, though in seeking them he sometimes felt like a spy behind enemy lines. The Jewish quarter, unchanged in ages, swarmed and smelled. Its worldly goods were spiritual goods; all that was lacking was prosperity. The fixer, having left the shtetl, resented the lack. He had tried working for a brushmaker, a man with a foaming beard who had promised to teach him the business. The wages were soup. So he had gone back to being a fixer and it came also to nothing, sometimes soup. If a window was broken they stuffed it with rags and said a blessing. He offered to replace it for a pittance, and when he had done the work they gave him thanks, blessings, a plate of noodle soup. He lived frugally in a low-ceilinged cubicle, in a printer's assistant's flat – Aaron Latke's, sleeping on a bench covered with a burlap sack; the flat was crowded with children and smelly feather beds, and the fixer, as he parted with kopeks and earned none, grew increasingly anxious. He must go where he could make a living or change his craft, maybe both. Among the goyim his luck might be better, it couldn't be worse. Besides, what choice has a man who doesn't know what his choices are? He meant in the world. So he walked out of the ghetto when no one was looking. In the snow he felt anonymous, in a sense unseen in his Russian cap and coat – any unemployed worker. Russians passed him without looking at him and he passed them. Having been told he did not look Jewish he now believed it. Yakov trudged in the snow up the hill to the Kreshchatik, the broad main street, trying kiosks, shops, public buildings, but finding little to do, a few odd jobs, payment in greenish coppers. At night in his cubicle, a glass of hot tea cupped in his reddened hands, when he thought of returning to the shtetl he thought of death.

Latke, when the fixer said this aloud, looked at him in popeyed horror. He was a man with arthritic hands and eight half-starving children. The pain hindered his work but not his labour.

"For God's sake, patience," he said. "You're not without brains and that's the beginning of luck. Afterwards, as they say, your ox will calve."

"To have luck you need it. I've had little luck."

"You've just come green from the country, so at least be patient till you know where you are."

So the fixer went looking for luck.

One desperate evening, the gas lamps casting a greenish glow on the snow, Yakov, trudging at twilight in the Plossky District, came upon a man lying with his face in the trodden snow. He hesitated a minute before turning him over, afraid to be involved in trouble. The man was a fattish, bald-headed Russian of about sixty-five, his fur cap in the snow, his heavy face splotched a whitish red and blue, snow on his moustache. He was breathing and reeked of drink. The fixer at once noticed the black and white button pinned to his coat, the two-headed eagle of the Black Hundreds. Let him shift for himself, he thought. Frightened, he ran to the corner, then ran back. Grabbing the anti-Semite under the arms he began to drag him to the doorway of the house in front of which he had fallen, when he heard a cry down the street. A girl wearing a green shawl over a green dress was running crookedly towards them. At first he thought she was a crippled child but then saw she was a young woman with a crippled leg.

She knelt, brushed the snow from the fat man's face, shook him and said breathlessly, "Papa, get up! Papa, this can't go on."

"I ought to have gone for him," she said to Yakov, cracking her knuckles against her breast. "This is the second time this month he's fallen in the street. When he drinks in the tavern it becomes an impossible situation. Kindly help me get him home, sir. We live only a few doors from here."

"Take his legs," said Yakov.

With the girl's help he half carried, half dragged the fat Russian up the street to the three-storey yellow brick house with a wrought-iron awning above the door. The girl called the porter, and he and the fixer, she hobbling up after them, carried her father up the stairs into a large-roomed, well-furnished flat on the first floor. They laid him on a leather couch near the tile stove in the bedroom. A Pekinese began to yelp, then growled at the fixer. The girl picked the dog up, deposited it in another room, and at once returned. The dog barked shrilly through the door.

As the porter removed the man's wet shoes he stirred and groaned.

"With God's help," he muttered.

"Papa," said his daughter, "we owe thanks to this good man for assisting you after your accident. He found you face down in the snow. If not for him you would have smothered."

Her father opened his humid eyes. "Glory be to God." He crossed himself and began quietly to cry. She crossed herself and dabbed at her eyes with a handkerchief.

As she was unbuttoning her father's overcoat, Yakov, after staying for a last deep breath of the warmth, left the flat and went down the stairs, relieved to be out.

The girl called to him in a tight high voice from the top of the stairs and quickly hobbled down after him, holding to the banister. Her face was sharp, her green eyes searching, hungry. She seemed about twenty-five, slightly built, her torso long, with thick honey-coloured hair that she wore loose around the shoulders. She wasn't pretty but she wasn't plain, and although he was sorry for her crippled leg he felt for her a strange momentary revulsion.

She asked him who he was, not quite looking at him, her eyes lowered, then shifting to a direct glance. She stared at the sack of tools on his shoulder.

He told her little: he was a stranger, recently from the provinces. It occurred to him then to remove his cap.

"Please come back tomorrow," she said. "Papa says he would like to thank you when he is in a better frame of mind, but I will tell you frankly you may expect something more than mere thanks. My father is Nikolai Maximovitch Lebedev – semi-retired – he was already retired but had to take over his brother's business affairs at his death – and I am Zinaida Nikolaevna. Please call on us in the morning when Papa is himself. He's usually at his best then, though never at his very best since my poor mother's death."

Yakov, without giving his name, said he would return in the morning and left.

Back in his cubicle in Aaron Latke's flat, he wondered what was "more than mere thanks". Obviously the girl meant some sort of reward, possibly a rouble or two, and with luck, five. But he had doubts whether to go back there. Should he take a reward from a self-advertised Jew hater? He hadn't for a minute been comfortable in his presence, or the girl's. Then either better not go, or tell the old man who he was indebted to and leave. But that wasn't what he wanted to do. Yakov sweated in his thoughts, the drunkard's two-headed eagle staring him in both eyes. He slept badly and woke with a new thought. Why not a rouble or two if it kept a Jew alive? What better service from an anti-Semite? He recalled a Russian saying: "A fearful wolf should stay out of the forest," but decided to go anyway, take a chance, or how would he know what went on in the world?

So he returned to the house in the Plossky without his bag of tools, though he could not dress up, nor did he want to. Zinaida Nikolaevna, wearing an embroidered peasant blouse and skirt, with two green ribbons plaited into her hair and some strings of yellow glass beads at her throat, led him to her father's bedroom. Nikolai Maximovitch, in a loose wadded robe with a fur collar, sat at a table by a curtained window, a huge book open before him. On the wall behind hung a large chart in the form of a tree showing by way of white printed slots on its thickest black branches the descent of Nicholas II from Adam. A framed portrait of the Tsar sitting with the pale-faced Tsarevitch hung above that. The house was overheated. The little dog snarled at the fixer and had to be carried out of the room by the cook.

Nikolai Maximovitch rose slowly, an old man with wrinkled, red-rimmed, wet melancholy eyes, and welcomed Yakov without embarrassment. The fixer, thinking of his Black Hundreds button felt for him contempt, and a portion of the same for himself. His throat tightened. Though he wasn't trembling he felt he might be.

"Nikolai Maximovitch Lebedev," the fat Russian said, offering his soft pudgy hand. A thick gold watchchain hung on his paunch, and his vest was dusty with snuff grains.

Yakov, after a slight hesitation, shook hands, answering as he had planned, "Yakov Ivanovitch Dologushev." To have given his name might have finished off the reward. Yet he felt ashamed and sweaty.

Zinaida Nikolaevna busied herself with the samovar. Her father indicated a chair for the fixer.

"I have a good deal to thank you for, Yakov Ivanovitch," he said, resuming his seat. "I lost my footing in the snow, no doubt there was ice under it. You were very kind to assist me – not everyone would have. Once, under quite different circumstances – I began to drink only after the death of my beloved wife, a woman of exceptional qualities – Zina will affirm the truth of what I am saying – I fainted from illness on Fundukleyevsky Street, in front of a coffee shop, and lay on the pavement with a gash in my head for an unconscionable time before anyone – in this case a woman who had lost a son at Port Arthur – bothered to come to my assistance. Nowadays people are far less concerned about their fellow-humans than in times past. Religious feeling has shrunk in the world and kindness is rare. Very rare indeed."

Yakov, waiting for him to come to the reward, sat tightly in the chair.

Nikolai Maximovitch regarded the fixer's worn sheepskin coat. He took out his snuff-box, inserted a pinch in both nostrils, blew his nose vigorously in a large white handkerchief, sneezed twice, then after a few futile attempts, succeeded in thrusting the box back into his robe pocket.

"My daughter informs me you were carrying a bag of tools yesterday. What is your trade, if I may ask?"

"Repairs, et cetera, of all kinds," Yakov answered. "I do carpentering, also painting, and roofing."

"Is that so? Are you presently employed?"

The fixer, without thought, said he wasn't.

"Where are you from if you don't mind saying?" said Nikolai Maximovitch. "I ask because I have a curious nature."

"From the provinces," Yakov answered, after a moment's hesitation.

"Ach – really? – a country boy? – and a good thing, may I say. The country virtues are not to be denied. I'm from the region of Kursk myself. I've pitched hay in my time. Do you come to Kiev as a pilgrim?"

"No, I came for work." He paused. "Also, if possible, for a little education."

"Excellent. You speak well although with a provincial accent. But grammatically. Have you had some schooling?"

Blast his questions, the fixer thought.

"I've read a little on my own."

The girl was watching him through lowered eyelids.

"Do you also read in the Holy Scriptures?" asked Nikolai Maximovitch. "I presume you do?"

"I know the Psalms."

"Wonderful. Did you hear, Zina? – the Psalms, wonderful. The Old Testament is admirable, the true prophecy of Christ's coming and his redemption of us through death. However, it is in no way equal to the preachings and parables of Our Lord, in the New Testament. I have just been rereading this." Nikolai Maximovitch glanced down at the open book and read aloud: "'Blessed are the poor in spirit; for theirs is the kingdom of heaven.'"

Yakov, grown pale, nodded.

Nikolai Maximovitch's eyes were humid. He had again to blow his nose.

"He always cries when he reads the Sermon on the Mount," said Zinaida Nikolaevna.

"I always cry." Clearing his throat, Nikolai Maximovitch read on: "'Blessed are the merciful; for they shall obtain mercy.'"

Mercy, the fixer thought, it makes him cry.

"'Blessed are they which are persecuted for righteousness sake; for theirs is the kingdom of heaven.'"

Come already to the reward, thought Yakov.

"Ah, this is most moving," Nikolai Maximovitch said, having to wipe his eyes again. "You know, Yakov Ivanovitch, I am in some ways a miserable man, melancholic, a heavy drinker, yet something more than that although I recently set my clothes on fire while smoking a cigarette when a piece of hot ash fell on my trousers, and if Zina had not alertly poured a pitcher of water over me, I would now be a burnt corpse. I drink because I happen to be more sensitive than most – I feel much too keenly the sorrows of life. My daughter will attest to that."

"It's true," she said. "He is a man of more than ordinary feeling. When our former little dog Pasha died of a distemper, Papa couldn't eat for weeks."

"When Zina was a child, after her severe illness I wept every night over her poor crippled leg."

"It's true," she said, her eyes moist.

"I tell you this so that you may know the kind of person I am," Nikolai Maximovitch said to Yakov. "Zina, please serve the tea."

She brought the tea to the marble-top table on a thick silver tray, with two clay pots of whole-fruit jam, raspberry and peach; and Viennese rolls, and butter.

It's mad, I know, Yakov thought. Tea with rich goyim. Yet he ate hungrily.

Nikolai Maximovitch poured a little milk into his tea and ate a buttered roll. He ate with gulping noises, as though drinking what he ate. Then he sipped again from the hot glass and set it down, patting his snuff-swollen lips with a linen napkin.

"I would like to offer you a modest reward for your timely assistance."

Yakov hastily put down his glass and rose.

"I ask for nothing. Thanks for the tea and I'd better be off."

"Spoken like a Christian, but please sit down and listen to what I have to say. Zina, fill Yakov Ivanovitch's glass and put plenty of butter and conserves on his roll. Yakov Ivanovitch, what I have to say is this. I have an empty flat on the next story, recently vacated – the tenants proved entirely unsuitable – four fine rooms that need painting and re-papering. If you care to undertake the task I offer forty roubles, which is more than I would ordinarily pay, considering the fact that I furnish the paint and other materials; but the circumstances in this case are different. It is, of course, a matter of gratitude, but wouldn't you rather work than peremptorily receive from me some silver coins? Is money ever valuable if it is come by without labour? An offer of work is an appreciation of merit. Notwithstanding you did me the greatest of favours – I might have suffocated in the snow, as Zina points out – isn't my offer of work a more estimable reward than a mere payment of money?" He looked eagerly at Yakov. "Therefore will you accept?"

"In the way you put it, yes," said Yakov. He got up quickly, said he had to be going, and after stumbling into a closet on his way out, hurriedly left the apartment.

Though he worried what he was getting into and changed his mind every half hour as he lay restlessly on his bed-bench that night, the next morning he went back. He returned for the same reason he had gone the first time – to collect his reward. What he earned for his work in this case was the reward. Who could afford to say no to forty roubles – a tremendous sum? Therefore why worry about returning?

Go, do the job quickly, collect the money, and when you have it in your pocket, leave the place once and for all and forget it. After all it's only a job, I'm not selling my soul. When I'm finished I'll wash up and go. They're not bad people. The girl's direct and honest in her way, though she makes me uneasy, and as for the old man, maybe I misjudged him. How many goyim have I known in my life? Maybe someone stuck that Black Hundreds pin on his coat when he was drunk in the tavern. Still, if it's really his own I'd like to ask him straight out, "Nikolai Maximovitch, will you please explain how you can cry for a dead dog yet belong to a society of fanatics that urges death on human beings who happen to be Jews? Explain to me the logic of it." Then let him answer that.

What also troubled the fixer was that once he went to work, even though the "reward" made it different from work though not less than work, he might be asked to produce his passport, a document stamped "Religious Denomination: Judaic," which would at once tell Nikolai Maximovitch what he was hiding from him. He chewed his lips over that but decided that if the passport was asked for he would say the police in the Podol had it; and if Nikolai Maximovitch insisted he must produce it, that was the time to quit or there would be serious trouble. It was therefore a gamble, but if you were against gambling, stop playing cards. He guessed the Russian was probably too muddled to ask for the passport although he was required to by law. Still, after all, it was a reward, maybe he wouldn't. Yakov was now somewhat sorry he hadn't at once identified himself as a Jew by birth. If that had killed off the reward, at least there would be no self-contempt. The more one hides the more one has to.

He did an expert job on the flat – scraped the walls clean

of paper, and the ceilings of flakes and loose patches. He plastered where he had to, then thickly calcimined the ceilings – nothing but the best for Nikolai Maximovitch. And he pasted the wallpaper neatly though his experience with papering was limited – in the shtetl only Viskover, the Nogid, was that fancy. Yakov worked all day and into the night by yellow gaslight to get the job done, collect his roubles, and disappear. The landlord, stopping now and then to catch his breath, laboured up the stairs each morning to see how the work was progressing, and expressed himself as most pleased. In the afternoon he got out his vodka bottle, into which he had cut strips of orange peel, and by sunset was drunk. Zina, unseen during the day, sent up the cook, Lidya, with a snack at lunch-time – a fish pie, bowl of borscht, or some meat dumplings so delicious it seemed to the fixer he would have done the job for the food alone.

One night Zina limped up the stairs, expressing surprise he was working so late. She asked Yakov if he had eaten since lunch, and when he said he was not hungry she suggested, nervously laughing, that he eat supper with her, Papa having already retired and she liking company. The fixer, greatly surprised by the invitation, begged off. He had, he explained, too much to do, and apologized for his clothes. Zina said not to mind that. "Clothes can be shed in a minute, Yakov Ivanovitch, but whether they are or not cannot change a man's nature. He's either kind or he isn't, with or without clothes. Besides I don't care for excessive formality." He thanked her but said he couldn't take the time off from work. There were two more rooms to do. The next evening she came up again and somewhat agitatedly confessed she was lonely; so they ate together in the kitchen downstairs. She had dismissed Lidya and throughout the

50

meal talked constantly, mostly of her childhood, the young ladies' school she had attended, and the pleasures of Kiev in the summertime.

"Days are long and hot, but nights are languorous and starlit. People refresh themselves in their flower gardens and some walk in the parks, drink kvass and lemonade, and listen to the symphonies. Have you ever heard *Pagliacci*, Yakov Ivanovitch? I think you would love Marinsky Park."

He said he did not mind parks.

"The Contract Fair opens in the spring, it's most entertaining. Or if you like there's a cinematograph to go to on the Kreshchatik."

Her eyes darted glances as she spoke and when he looked at her she glanced away. Afterwards the fixer, made nervous by her chatter, excused himself to go back to work, but Zina followed him up the stairs to watch him paste on the wallpaper she had selected, bunches of blue roses. She sat on a kitchen chair with her legs crossed, the good one over the crippled, and cracked and ate dried sunflower seeds, rhythmically swinging her leg as she watched him work.

Then she lit and awkwardly smoked a cigarette.

"You know, Yakov Ivanovitch, I couldn't possibly treat you as an ordinary common labourer for the simple reason that you aren't one. Certainly not in my eyes. Really you are a guest who happens to be working here because of Papa's idiosyncratic ways. I hope you realize that?"

"If you don't work you don't eat."

"Quite true, but you are more intelligent and even genteel – at any rate, sensitive – please don't shake your head over that – than the average Russian labourer. I can't tell you how exasperating they can be, particularly Ukrainians, and really we dread having repairs or improvements made.

51

No, please don't deny it, anyone can sense you are different. And you told Papa you believe in the necessity of an education and would like to further your own. I heard you say that and approve very much. I too love to read, and not only romances. I'm sure you'll find excellent opportunities for yourself in the future, and if you are alert may some day be as comfortably off as Papa."

Yakov went on papering.

"Poor Papa suffers dreadfully from melancholia. He gets quite drunk by nightfall and has no appetite, to speak of, for supper. He usually falls asleep in his chair, Lidya removes his shoes, and with Alexei's help we get him to bed. At night he awakes and says his prayers. Sometimes he undresses himself, and it's almost impossible to find his clothes in the morning. Once he put his socks under the rug, and I found his drawers, all wet, in the water closet. Usually he isn't awake till mid-morning. It's hard on me, of course, but I can't complain because Papa's had a difficult life. And there's no one to keep me company in the evening but Lidya and at times Alexei when he happens to be fixing something, but quite frankly, Yakov Ivanovitch, neither of them has an idea in his head. Alexei sleeps in the basement, and Lidya's small room is at the back of the flat off the terrace beyond Papa's bedroom; and since I would rather read at night than listen to her go on and on, I dismiss her early. Sometimes it gives me pleasure to be the only one up in the house at night. It's very cosy. I light the samovar, read, write letters to old friends and crochet. Papa says I make the most remarkable lace doilies. He marvels at the intricacy of the patterns. But most of the time," she sighed, "to tell the truth, it can be dreadfully lonely."

She chewed a sunflower seed disconsolately, then remarked that although she had been crippled through illness as a child, she had always been considered attractive by the opposite sex and had had more than one admirer.

"I don't say this to flaunt myself or be brazen but because I don't want you to think of me as being at a disadvantage with regard to the normal experiences of life. I am nothing of the sort. I have a quite attractive figure and many men notice me, especially when I'm dressed up. Once in a restaurant a man ogled me so insistently Papa went over to him and demanded an explanation. The man humbly apologized and do you know, Yakov Ivanovitch, when I got back home I broke into sobs."

Gentlemen called on her of course, Zina went on, but unfortunately not always the most sensitive or worthy, a situation more than one of her friends had to put up with. Sensitive, dependable men were rare, although such persons could be found in all classes, not necessarily gentry.

He listened with one ear, aware that her glance traced his every move. Why does she bother? he asked himself. What can she see in a man like me whose advantages are all disadvantages if I have it right? I have little wit in Russian, it's a heavy language for me. And if I said "Jew" aloud she'd run in six directions. Yet she often entered his thoughts. He had been a long time without a woman and wondered what it would be like to be in bed with her. He had never had a Russian woman, though Haskel Dembo had slept with a peasant girl and said it was the same as with any Jewess. The crippled leg, Yakov thought, would not bother him.

He finished papering the fourth room that night and except for the woodwork the job was done. Two days later when it was all but finished, Nikolai Maximovitch unsteadily ascended the stairs to inspect the flat. He went from room to room, running his fingers over the wallpaper, looking up at the ceilings.

"Outstanding," he said. "Quite outstanding. An honest and attractive piece of work, Yakov Ivanovitch. I congratulate you."

Later he said as though in afterthought, "You must excuse me for asking, but what are your political predilections? Surely you're not a Socialist? I ask in the strictest confidence without attempting to pry, and not in the least accusatorily. I ask, in a word, because I am interested in your future."

"I am not a political person," Yakov answered. "The world's full of it but it's not for me. Politics is not in my nature."

"Very good, indeed. Neither am I, and much better off in the bargain if anyone should ask. Yakov Ivanovitch, don't think I will soon forget the quality of your craftsmanship. If you should care to go on working for me, though in another, and may I say, advanced capacity, I would be more than happy to employ you. The truth of the matter is that I am the owner of a small brickworks near by, although in a contiguous district. I inherited it from my elder brother, a lifelong bachelor who went to his final reward half a year ago after suffering from an incurable disease. I tried to sell the factory but the offers were so disgraceful that, although I have little heart or, at this time of my life, head for business, I have kept it going, although, I confess, barely profitably. My foreman Proshko is in charge, an excellent technical person who is otherwise an ignorant man, and confidentially, the drivers who work under him have not been accounting for every brick that leaves the yard. I would like you to go in as a sort of overseer to handle accounts and, on the whole, look after my interests. My brother was involved in every phase of the operations, but I have little patience with bricks."

54

Yakov, though he had listened with excitement to the proposition, confessed he was without experience in business. "I know nothing about bookkeeping."

"Common sense is what's needed in business once honesty is assured," said Nikolai Maximovitch. "What there is to learn you will learn as you go along. I usually visit for an hour one or two mornings a week, and what you don't know I'll try to help you with, though I frankly confess my knowledge is limited. There's no need to protest, Yakov Ivanovitch. My daughter, whose judgement in these matters I respect, has the highest opinion of your merit, and you may believe me, I thoroughly share it. She considers you a man of sobriety and sound sense, and I am confident that after you have mastered the fundamentals you will do a responsible and effective job. During the period of your – ah – apprenticeship I will pay you forty-five roubles monthly. I hope that's satisfactory. But there is another advantage for you that I should mention, frankly one that will work to our mutual benefit. My brother converted part of a loft over the brickyard stable into a warm and comfortable room, and you may live there without payment of rent if you accept my offer."

The forty-five roubles astounded and tempted the fixer.

"What is it an overseer does? Excuse the question, but I'm not a man of the world."

"Worldliness is vanity, it doesn't appeal to me. The overseer manages the business end of the enterprise. We manufacture about two thousand bricks daily – many fewer than we used to – a thousand or so more during the building season, not quite so many this time of the year; and it has been fewer lately although we have a contract with the Kiev Municipal Council for several thousands of bricks. The Tsar himself has given orders for civic improvements to be

55

made before the Romanov Jubilee, and the Municipality is tearing up wooden walks and laying down entire streets of brick sidewalk, though this is done of course when the weather permits, not in the winter snow. And we also hold a small contract for bricks for the restoration of certain fortifications above the Dnieper. Yes, I would expect you to keep track of orders received and, to be sure, of the exact number of bricks manufactured as well as those carted out. These figures you will get from Proshko, but there are ways of checking. You will also send out statements requesting payment and enter payments received in the ledger. Once or twice weekly you will turn over bank drafts and other monies to me, and in the meantime keep them safe in the strongbox. Proshko will of course retain the responsibilities of the technical foreman, and I will tell him I expect him to place all orders for supplies through you. You will also make out the wages inventory and pay the workers at the end of the month."

Though beset by self-doubt and every kind of fear, Yakov was thinking this might be his important chance. A few months' experience at this kind of work and other opportunities might open up for him. "I'll think it over carefully," he said, but before Nikolai Maximovitch had descended the stairs, he had accepted.

The landlord returned with a vodka bottle to wet the bargain. Yakov had two drinks and his uneasiness wore off. He was preparing himself for a better future, he told himself. He slept for a while on the floor and later finished the last of the woodwork, once more uneasy.

It was nightfall. After he had swept and cleaned up, soaked the paintbrushes in turpentine, and washed, he heard Zina limping up the stairs. She was wearing a dress of blue silk, her hair up and encircled with a white ribbon, her

56

cheeks and lips delicately rouged. She invited Yakov to eat
with her again. "In celebration of the completion of your
fine work, and most of all, to your future relationship with
Papa, though he has already retired and we shall be alone."

He had the old excuses, was even a little irritated by the
invitation and wanted to escape, but she would not hear of
it. "Come, Yakov Ivanovitch, there's more to life than
work."

It was news to him. Still, he thought, the job's done here
and this is the last I'll see of her. So what's wrong with
farewell?

On the kitchen table Zina had laid out a feast, even some
food he had never seen before. There were stuffed cucumbers, raw Danube herring, fat sausages, pickled sturgeon
with mushrooms, assorted meats, wine, cakes and cherry
brandy. The fixer, overwhelmed by the spread, felt at first
self-conscious. If you've had nothing you're afraid of too
much. But he swept that aside and ate hungrily those things
he had eaten before. He sucked the red wine through delicious chunks of white bread.

Zina, open and happy, and looking more attractive than
he had ever seen, picked here and there at sweet and spicy
things and filled her wineglass often. Her sharp face was
flushed, she talked about herself and laughed at nothing at
all. Although he tried to think of her as possibly a friend she
remained strange to him. He was strange to himself. Once,
staring at the white tablecloth, he thought of Raisl but put
her out of his mind. He finished the meal – he had never
in his life eaten so much – with two glasses of brandy, and
only then began to enjoy the "party".

When she cleared the table Zina's breath was heavy. She
brought out a guitar, plucked it, and in a high thin voice
sang, "Ech, my pack is heavy." It was a sad song and filled

57

him with mild melancholy. He had thought of getting up to leave, but the kitchen was warm and it was pleasant to sit there listening to the guitar. Then she sang, "Come on, come on, my darling angel, come and dance with me." When she put down her guitar, Zina looked at him in a way she never had before. Yakov understood at once where they were. Excitement and foreboding flowed into one feeling. No, he thought, it's a Russian woman. If she slept with me and found out who I was she'd cut her throat. Then he thought, it's not always so, there are some who wouldn't mind. For himself he was willing to experience what there was to experience. But let her lead.

"Yakov Ivanovitch," Zina said, pouring herself another glassful of wine which she at once drank down, "do you believe in romantic love? I ask because I think you guard yourself against it."

"Whether I do or don't it doesn't come easily to me."

"I heartily agree that it oughtn't to come too easily," Zina said, "but it seems to me that those who are serious about life – perhaps too serious – are slow to respond to certain changes in the climate of feeling. What I mean to say, Yakov Ivanovitch, is that it's possible to let love fly by like a cloud in a windy sky if one is too timid, or perhaps unable to believe he is entitled to good fortune."

"It's possible," he said.

"Do you love me – just a little, Yakov Ivanovitch?" she asked quickly. "I've sometimes noticed you looking at me as though you might. For instance, you smiled at me quite delightfully a few minutes ago, and it warmed my heart. I dare ask because you yourself are very modest and tend to be conscious – overconscious, I would say – that we are from different classes, though I believe much alike as people."

58

"No," he said. "I can't say I love you."

Zina flushed. Her eyelids fluttered. After a long minute she sighed and said in a smaller voice, "Very well, then, do you like me at all?"

"Yes, you have been kind to me."

"And I like you too, indeed I do. I think you are serious and a well-informed person."

"No, I am half an ignoramus."

She poured herself some cherry brandy, sipped from the glass and put it down.

"Oh, Yakov Ivanovitch, please for a moment let up on your seriousness and kiss me. I dare you to kiss me."

They got up and kissed. She groped for him, her body clinging tightly to his. He felt for an instant an anguished pity for her.

"Shall we stay here longer?" she whispered, breathing heavily, "or would you care to visit my room? You've seen Papa's but not mine."

She looked him full in the face, her green eyes lit dark, her body hot, still clinging. She seemed to him an older woman, possibly twenty-eight or nine, someone used to looking out for herself.

"Whatever you say."

"What do *you* say, Yakov Ivanovitch?"

"Zinaida Nikolaevna," he said, "excuse me for asking you this question but I don't want to make a serious mistake. I've made my share of them – every kind you can think of – but there are some I don't want to make again. If you are innocent," he said awkwardly, "it would be better not to go any further. I say this out of respect for you."

Zina reddened, then shrugged and said frankly, "I'm as innocent as most, no more nor less. There's nothing to worry about in that regard." Then she laughed self-consciously and said, "I see you're an old-fashioned person and I like that, although your question to me was hardly discreet."

"If one why not another? What about your father? What I mean to ask is, is it likely he might find out if we go to your room?"

"He never has," she said. He was momentarily surprised at her answer and then accepted it without another question. Why wrestle with a fact?

They went silently along the corridor, Zina hobbling, Yakov tiptoeing behind her, to her perfumed bedroom. The Pekinese, lying on the bed, looked at the fixer and yawned. Zina picked it up and went again down the hall to lock it in the kitchen.

Her room was full of knick-knacks on numerous small tables, and pictures of kerchiefed girls on the wall. Peacock feathers stuck out from behind the frame of a mirror. In the corner of the room hung an ikon of the Holy Mother with a small red oil lamp lighted before it.

Should I stay or should I go? Yakov thought. On the one hand it's been a long season without rain. A man is not a man for nothing. What do the Hasidim say? "Hide not from thine own flesh." On the other hand what does this mean to me? At my age it's nothing new. It means nothing.

When she returned he was sitting on the bed. He had taken off his shirt and undershirt.

Yakov watched uneasily as Zina, after removing her shoes, knelt at the ikon, crossed herself, and for a moment prayed.

"Are you a believer?" she asked.

"No."

"I wish you were, Yakov Ivanovitch," she sighed.

60

Then she rose and asked him to undress in the lavatory while she got ready in the bedroom.

It's her leg, he thought. She'll be under covers when I come in. Better that way.

He removed his clothes in the lavatory. His hands still stank of paint and turpentine, and he soaped them twice with her pink bar of perfumed soap. He smelled them again but now they stank of the perfume. If there's a mistake to make I'll make it, he thought.

Seeing himself naked in the mirror he was at first uneasy, then sickened by what he was about to do.

Things are bad enough, so why make them worse? This isn't for me, I'm not the type, and the sooner I tell her the better. He went into the bedroom, carrying his clothes.

Zina had braided her hair. She stood naked, her bosom full, sponging herself from a white bowl, in the gaslight. He saw a dribble of bright blood run down her crippled leg and said, stupefied. "But you are unclean!"

"Yakov! – You startled me." She covered herself with the wet cloth. "I thought you would wait till I called you."

"I didn't know your condition. Excuse me, I had no idea. You didn't mention it, though I realize it's personal."

"But surely you know this is the safest time?" Zina said. "And there's no inconvenience to speak of, the flow stops the minute we begin."

"Excuse me, some can but I can't."

He was thinking of his wife's modesty during her period and until she had been to the baths, but could not say that to Zina.

"Excuse me, I'd better be going."

"I'm a lonely woman, Yakov Ivanovitch," she cried, "have mercy a little!" but he was already dressing and soon left.

3

One night in the dead of winter, in the cold thick dark at 4 a.m., after the drivers Serdiuk and Richter had come for two teams of horses – leaving six horses in the stalls – and he had heard them clomp out of the stable and clack dully across the snow-covered cobblestones, Yakov, who had been two days in the brickyard, got quickly out of bed, lit a short candle and hurriedly dressed. He sneaked down the outer stairs from his room above the stable and went along the fence of palings, past the squat brick-kilns to the cooling shed. Motionless in the wet cold, he watched the drivers and their helpers, in steaming sheepskins, the horses' flanks steaming, loading the straw-covered long wagon-trucks with large heavy yellow bricks. The work progressed slowly, helper tossing a brick to helper, who tossed it to the driver on the wagon, who laid it in place. After what seemed to him an endless time standing in the dark, blowing on his hands and trying soundlessly to stamp the cold out of his boots, Yakov had counted three hundred and forty bricks loaded into one wagon, and four hundred and three into another. Three other wagons at the shed went unused. But in the morning when Proshko, the foreman, presented him with the voucher in the stuffy low-ceilinged shack where Yakov sat at a table stacked with ledgers and bundles of useless papers from the past, the badly written numbers scrawled on a torn piece of wrapping paper came to a total of six hundred and ten bricks, instead of seven hundred and forty-three, and the fixer ground his teeth in anger at the cold-blooded nerve of the thievery.

Though Yakov was desperately eager for work, he had reluctantly accepted Nikolai Maximovitch's offer, at the last minute almost in panic trying to back out when he learned that the Lukianovsky, where the brickyard was located – near a cemetery, with a few houses and trees scattered around and beyond it, more heavily on the far-off side about half a tombstoned verst away – and where he was expected to live, was a district forbidden to Jews to reside in. He had then told the owner of the brickworks that he would not take the job because he had many doubts he could do the work as it should be done. But Nikolai Maximovitch, advising him not to be hasty, had pooh-poohed his doubts.

"Nonsense, you will do better than you suppose. You must learn to have confidence in your natural abilities, Yakov Ivanovitch. Just follow my late brother's method with the ledger – old-fashioned but accurate – and you will master the system as you go along." Yet puzzled somewhat, he raised his offer by three roubles a month, and Yakov, trying every way to convince himself to take the job, then suggested it would be more convenient for him if he could go on living in the Podol – he never said where in the district – and come to work very early each morning. It wasn't too far a walk from where he lived. The electric trolley, which stopped close by the brickyard, did not run after dark.

"Unfortunately you won't be of much use to me living in the Podol," said Nikolai Maximovitch. They were talking in the brickyard on a cloudy end-of-January day – a pall of black smoke hung over the kilns – and Nikolai Maximovitch still wore his Black Hundreds button on his coat, which Yakov, when speaking to him – he saw himself unable to detach his eye if once he stared at it – had to ignore or look around, for the button loomed large and unsettling.

"It is not what goes on here during the workday that worries me so much," the anti-Semite said, "although I

63

assure you that worries me too; but I am deeply concerned with what happens in the early morning hours when the wagons are being loaded for the first deliveries. Daylight is too strong for a thief. It's in the dark when the ghosts are flying and good people are lying abed that he does his dirty work. My late-lamented brother, who had little respect for sleep – one must respect it or it will not respect him – was here at 3 a.m. in every weather to oversee each and every wagonload. I am not asking you to do the same, Yakov Ivanovitch. That sort of dedication to a business enterprise is fanatic and in his case led, I am convinced, to my brother's early death." Nikolai Maximovitch crossed himself with eyes shut. "But if you were to look in on them in the early morning hours, and also unexpectedly during other loadings, counting off aloud a close estimate of the number of bricks in the trucks, it might tempt them not to overdo it. I expect some thievery – humans are humans – but of necessity there has to be a limit. It would be impossible for me to get a reasonably just price for this factory if it should go bankrupt."

"How do they steal?" the fixer had asked.

"I suspect the drivers under Proshko's supervision or connivance. They take out more than they account for."

"Then why don't you give him the boot?"

"More easily said than done, my dear boy. If I did I would have to shut down the plant. He is an excellent technical man – one of the best, my brother used to say. I confess it is not my purpose to catch him thieving. As a religious person I want to keep him from it. And wouldn't you say it was the more sensible as well as charitable thing? No, let's arrange it as I say. Take the room above the stable, Yakov Ivanovitch. It's yours without a single kopek of rent."

Since he had not mentioned the fixer's papers – neither the passport necessary for new employment, nor the residence certificate he would need, Yakov uneasily took the chance and accepted the job. He had for a fleeting minute again considered saying he was a Jew – just quietly informing Nikolai Maximovitch: "Well, you ought to know what the situation is. You say you like me; you know I'm an honest worker and don't waste the boss's time, then maybe it won't surprise you to hear I was born Jewish and for that reason can't live in this district." But that was of course impossible. Even supposing – a fantastic suppose – that Nikolai Maximovitch, two-headed eagle button and all, overlooked the confession in his own interests, still the Lukianovsky was not for Jews, with certain unusual exceptions, and if a poor fixer were exposed as one living there he would be in serious trouble. It was all too complicated. For the first week Yakov was daily on the verge of leaving, escaping from the place, but he stayed on because he had heard from Aaron Latke that counterfeit papers of various kinds were available to prospective buyers at a certain printing establishment in the Podol, for not too large a sum, and though the thought of acquiring such papers gave him severe sweats, he decided he ought to keep it in mind.

When Proshko brought in the voucher the morning after Yakov had spied on the drivers loading the wagons, though the fixer's heart beat loudly when he saw the false figure on the paper, he informed the foreman that Nikolai Maximovitch had told him to be present at night when the wagons were loaded, and since it was his responsibility, he would be there from now on. Proshko, a burly, thick-eared man with a rough beard, who wore high rubber boots muddy with yellow clay and a long dirty leather apron, gazed at the fixer with intense small eyes.

"What do you think goes on in the wagons at night? Are the drivers on their knees fucking their mothers?"

"What goes on goes on," said Yakov nervously, "but the number of bricks that you loaded last night and this figure on your paper don't agree, if you'll excuse me for saying so."

He then wished he had said it differently, though how was it possible to say it differently to a thief?

"How would you know how many bricks were loaded?"

"I stood near the shed last night, counting them, according to Nikolai Maximovitch's direction. In other words, I did as he told me." His voice was thick with emotion, as though the bricks belonged to him, although the strange thing was they belonged to an anti-Semitic Russian.

"Then you counted wrong," Proshko said, "this is the number we loaded." He tapped a thick finger on the paper on the table. "Listen, my friend, when a dog puts his nose into shit, he gets it dirty. You have a long nose, Dologushev. If you don't believe me look in a mirror. A man with a nose like that ought to be careful where he puts it."

He left the shack but returned in the afternoon. "What about your papers," he said, "have you registered them yet? If not, hand them over here and I'll have them stamped by the District Police."

"I'm obliged to you," Yakov said, "but that's already been seen to and done. Nikolai Maximovitch took care of it. You don't have to trouble yourself."

"Tell me, Dologushev," said Proshko, "why is it you talk Russian like a Turk?"

"And what if I am a Turk?" The fixer smiled crookedly.

"He who runs too fast raises the wind against him." Lifting his leg Proshko farted.

Afterwards Yakov felt too uneasy to eat supper. I'm the

66

wrong man to be a policeman, he thought. It's a job for a goy.

Yet he did what he was asked to. He appeared in the shed every morning in the 4 a.m. cold and counted the bricks in the wagons. And when he looked out the shack window and saw them loading up during the daylight hours, he went outside to watch. He did it openly, preventing the thieves from their thievery. When Yakov appeared at the shed, no one spoke but the drivers sometimes stopped their work to stare at him.

Proshko no longer turned in vouchers each morning, so Yakov wrote his own. The bookkeeping was not so difficult as he had thought – he had caught on to the system, and besides there wasn't that much business. Once a week Nikolai Maximovitch, more drearily melancholic, arrived by sledge for receipts to be deposited in his bank, and after a month Yakov received a long congratulatory letter from him. "Your work is diligent and effective, as I foresaw, and I shall continue to vest in you my utmost confidence. Zinaida Nikolaevna sends her regards. She too applauds your efforts." But no one else did. Neither the drivers nor their helpers paid any attention to him, even when he tried to make conversation. Richter, the heavy-faced German, spat in the snow at his approach, and Serdiuk, a tall Ukrainian who smelled of horse sweat and hay, watched him, breathing heavily. Proshko, passing the fixer in the yard, muttered, "Bastard stool pigeon!" Yakov pretended not to hear. If he heard "Jew" he would dive into the sky.

Except for these he was on more or less decent terms with the other workers in the yard – he paid them on time, about fifty left from almost two hundred employed when the yard had turned out six or seven thousand bricks a day – and this was so despite the fact that Proshko was spreading nasty stories about him; one that Skobeliev, the yardkeeper, had told him was that the fixer had once done time as a convicted thief. But no one sought him out as friend or kept him company when the brickyard was closed, so he was mostly alone. After work Yakov stayed in his room. He read by lamplight – though Nikolai Maximovitch had promised to install an electric bulb – for hours each night. His reading in the past was what he had accidentally come across; he now read what he wanted to know. He continued to study Russian, wrote out long grammatical exercises and read them aloud. And he devoured two newspapers every day, though they often gave him the shivers, both things reported as fact, and things hinted at; for instance, Rasputin and the Empress, new plots of terrorists, threats of pogroms, and the possibility of a Balkan war. So much was new to him, how is one to know all he ought to know? He began then to haunt the bookshops in the Podol in his free time, searching for inexpensive books. He bought a *Life of Spinoza* to read during the lonely nights in his stable room. Was it possible to learn from another's life? And Russian history fascinated him. He went through stacks of pamphlets on the shelves in the rear of the shops. He read some on serfdom, the Siberian penal system – a terrifying account he had found in a bushel the bookseller had winked at. He read about the revolt and destruction of the Decembrists, and a fascinating account of Narodniki, idealists of the 1870's who had devoted themselves to the peasants in an impulsive attempt to stir them to social revolution, were rebuffed by them, and turned from peasant-mysticism to terrorism. Yakov also read a short biography of Peter the Great, and after that a horrifying account of the bloody destruction of Novgorod by Ivan the Terrible. It had entered the madman's head that the city intended treason to him, so he had ordered a wooden wall

68

built around it to prevent escape. Then he marched in with his army, and after putting his subjects through the cruellest tortures, daily slaughtered thousands of them. This went on in increasing savagery, the sound of horror rising to the sky as the wailing mothers watched their children being roasted alive and thrown to wild dogs. At the end of five weeks, sixty thousand people, maimed, torn, broken apart, lay dead in the foul-smelling streets as disease spread. Yakov was sickened. Like a pogrom – the very worst. The Russians make pogroms against the Russians – it went on throughout their history. What a sad country, he thought, amazed by what he had read, every possible combination of experiences, where black was white and black was black; and if the Russians, too, were massacred by their own rulers and died like flies, who were then the Chosen People? Fatigued by history, he went back to Spinoza, rereading chapters on biblical criticism, superstition, and miracles which he knew almost by heart. If there was a God, after reading Spinoza he had closed up his shop and become an idea.

When he wasn't reading, Yakov was composing little essays on a variety of subjects – "I am in history," he wrote, "yet not in it. In a way of speaking I'm far out, it passes me by. Is this good, or is something lacking in my character? What a question! Of course lacking but what can I do about it? And besides is this really such a great worry? Best to stay where one is, unless he has something to give to history, like for instance Spinoza, as I read in his life. He understood history, and also because he had ideas to give it. Nobody can burn an idea even if they burn the man. On the other hand there was the activist Jan De Witt, Spinoza's friend and benefactor, a good and great man who was torn to pieces by a Dutch mob when they got suspicious of him although he was innocent. Who needs such a fate?" Some of the little essays were criticisms of "Certain Conditions" as he had read about them in the newspapers. He read these over and burned them in the stove. He also burned the pamphlets he could not resell.

Something that unexpectedly bothered him was that he was no longer using his tools. He had built himself a bed, table, and chair, also some shelves on the wall, but this was done in the first few days after he had come to the brickyard. He was afraid that if he didn't go on carpentering he might forget how and thought he had better not. Then he got another letter, this from Zina, her handwriting full of surprising thick black strokes, inviting him – with her father's permission – to call on her. "You are a sensitive person, Yakov Ivanovitch," she wrote, "and I respect your ideals and mode of behaviour; however, please don't worry about your clothes, although I am sure you can purchase new ones with the improved salary you are earning." He had sat down to reply but couldn't think what to say to her, so he didn't answer the letter.

In February he went through a period of severe nervousness. He blamed it on his worries. He had visited the place where he could get counterfeit papers, had found they were not impossibly expensive although they were not inexpensive, and he was thinking of having a passport and residence certificate made out under his assumed name. When he awoke, hours before he had to, to check the number of bricks in the trucks his muscles were tight, his chest constricted, breathing sometimes painful, and he was uneasy when he dealt with Proshko. Even to ask him the most routine questions troubled the fixer. He was irritable all day and cursed himself for trifling mistakes in his accounts, a matter of a kopek or two. Once, at nightfall, he drove two boys out of the brickyard. He knew them as troublemakers, one a pale-faced pimply boy of about twelve, the other like a peasant with a head of hair like hay, about the same age. They came into the yard after school, in the late afternoon, and pitched balls of clay at each other, broke good bricks, and hooted at the horses in the stable. Yakov had warned them to stay out of the yard. This time he caught sight of them through the shack window. They had sneaked into the yard with their book satchels and threw rocks at the smoke curling up from the kilns. Then they hit the chimneys with pieces of brick. Yakov had rushed out of the shack, warning them to leave, but they wouldn't move. He ran towards them to scare them. Seeing him coming, the boys hooted, touched their genitals, and clutching their satchels, sped past the supply sheds and scrambled up a pile of broken bricks at the fence. They tossed their book satchels over the fence and hopped over it.

"Little bastards!" Yakov shouted, shaking his fist.

Returning to the shack, he noticed Skobeliev watching him slyly. Then the yardkeeper hurried with his stick to light the gas lamps. After a while they glowed in the dusk like green candles.

Proshko, standing at the door of the cooling shed, had also been looking on. "You run like a ruptured pig, Dologushev."

The next morning a police inspector visited the fixer to ask if anyone in the brick factory was suspected of political unreliability. The fixer said no one was. The official asked him a few more questions and left. Yakov was not able to concentrate on his reading that night.

Since he was sleeping badly he tried going to bed just after he had eaten. He fell asleep quickly enough but awoke before midnight, totally alert, with a sense of being imperilled. In the dark he feared calamities he only occasionally thought of during the day – the stable in flames, burning down with him in it, bound hand and foot unable to move; and the maddened horses destroying themselves. Or dying of consumption, or syphilis, coughing up or pissing blood. And he dreaded what worried him most – to be unmasked as a hidden Jew. "Gevalt!" he shouted, then listened in fright for sounds in the stable to tell him whether the drivers were there and had heard him cry out. Once he dreamed that Richter, carrying a huge black bag on his back, was following him down the road by the graveyard. When the fixer turned to confront the German and asked him what he was carrying in the bag, the driver winked and said, "You." So Yakov ordered and paid for the counterfeit papers, though weeks went by and he did not claim them. Then for no reason he could think of he began to feel better.

He went through a more confident period, when for the first time in his life he spent money as though it was nothing more than money. He bought more books, paper to write on, tobacco, a pair of shoes to relieve him from boots, a luxurious jar of strawberry jam, and a kilo of flour to bake bread with. The bread did not rise but he baked it and ate it as biscuit. He also bought a pair of socks, a set of drawers and undershirt, and an inexpensive blouse, only what was necessary. One night, feeling an overwhelming hunger for sweets, he entered a candy store to sip cocoa and eat cakes. And he bought himself a thick bar of chocolate. When he counted his roubles later, he had spent more than he had bargained for and it worried him. So he returned to frugality. He lived on black bread, sour cream and boiled potatoes, an occasional egg, and when he was tempted, a small piece of halvah. He repaired his socks and patched his old shirts until there was nowhere he hadn't made a stitch. He saved every kopek. "Let the groats accumulate," he muttered. He had serious plans.

72

One night in April when the thick ice of the Dnieper was cracking, and Yakov – after selling the books he had recently bought and afterwards wandering in the Plossky District – was returning late to the brickyard, it began to snow unexpectedly. Coming up the hill approaching the cemetery, he saw some boys attacking an old man and scattered them with a shout. They ran like frightened rabbits through the graveyard. The old man was a Jew, a Hasid wearing a caftan to his ankles, a round rabbinic hat with a fur brim, and long white stockings. He slowly bent and retrieved from the snow a small black satchel tied with brown twine. He had been hurt on the temple and the blood dripped down his hairy cheek into his tousled two-forked grey beard. His eyes were dazed. "What happened to you, grandfather?" the fixer said in Russian. The Hasid, frightened, backed off, but Yakov waited and the old man replied in halting Russian that he had come from Minsk to see a sick brother in the Jewish quarter and had got lost. Then some boys had attacked him with snowballs embedded with sharp stones.

The streetcars were no longer running, and the snow was falling in thick wet flakes. Yakov was uneasily worried but thought he could take the old man into the brickyard, let him rest while he applied some cold water to his wound, then get him out before the drivers and their helpers came in.

"Come with me, grandfather."

"Where are you taking me?" said the Hasid.

"We'll wipe the blood off you, and when the snow stops I'll show you which way to the Jewish quarter in the Podol."

He led the Hasid into the brickyard and up the stairs to his room above the stable. After lighting the lamp, Yakov tore up his most tattered shirt, wet it, and wiped the blood

73

off the old man's beard. The wound was still bleeding but it didn't bother the Hasid. He sat in Yakov's chair with his eyes shut, breathing as though he were whispering. Yakov offered him bread and a glass of sweetened tea but the Hasid would not accept food. He was a dignified man with long earlocks and asked the fixer for some water. Pouring a little over his fingers over a bowl, he then withdrew a small packet from his caftan pocket, some matzo pieces wrapped in a handkerchief. He said the blessing for matzos, and sighing, munched a piece. It came as a surprise to the fixer that it was Passover. He was moved by a strong emotion and had to turn away till it had gone.

When he looked out the window the snow was still falling but there were signs of a moon, a circle of dim light within the falling snow. It'll soon stop, he thought, but it didn't. The glow disappeared and once more it was dark and snowy. Yakov thought he would wait till the drivers arrived, quickly count the bricks, and when the snow stopped, sneak the old man out after the wagons had left and before Proshko came. If the snow didn't stop, the old man would have to leave anyway.

The Hasid slept in the chair, woke, stared at the lamp, then at the window and slept again. When the drivers opened the stable door he awoke and looked at Yakov, but the fixer made a sign for silence and left to go down to the shed. He had offered the Hasid his bed but when he returned the old man was sitting up awake. The drivers had loaded the wagons and were waiting in the shed for daylight. They had wrapped chains around the horses' hooves but Serdiuk had said if the snow got deeper they would not leave the yard. Now Yakov was worried.

In his room, huddled in his sheepskin coat, he stood watching the snow, then rolled and smoked a cigarette and

74

made himself a glass of tepid tea. He drank a little, fell asleep on his bed, and dreamed he had encountered the Hasid in the graveyard. The Hasid had asked, "Why are you hiding here?" and the fixer had struck him a blow on the head with a hammer. It was a terrible dream and gave him a headache.

He awoke to find the old man staring at him, and his nervousness returned.

"What's wrong?" he asked.

"What's wrong is wrong," said the old man. "But now the snow has stopped."

"Did I say anything in my sleep?"

"I wasn't listening."

The sky had lightened and it was time to go, but the Hasid dipped the tips of his fingers into water, then unknotted the twine around his satchel, opened it, and removed a large striped prayer shawl. From the pocket of his caftan he took out a phylactery bag.

"Where is the east?" asked the old man.

Yakov impatiently indicated the wall with the window. Saying the blessing for phylacteries, the Hasid slowly wound one around his left arm, the other on his brow, binding the strap gently over the crusting wound.

He covered his head with the capacious prayer shawl, blessing it, then prayed at the wall, rocking back and forth. The fixer waited with his eyes shut. When the old man had said his morning prayers, he removed the shawl, folded it carefully and put it away. He unbound the phylacteries, kissed them, and packed them away.

"May God reward you," he said to Yakov.

"I'm much obliged but let's move on." The fixer was sweating in his cold clothes.

Asking the old man to wait a minute, he went down the

75

snow-laden stairs and walked around the stable. The yard was white and still, the roofs of the kilns covered with snow. But the wagons, though loaded with bricks, had not yet left and the drivers were still in the shed. Yakov hurried up the stairs and got the Hasid and his satchel. They hastened through the spring snow to the gate. He led the old Hasid down the hill to the streetcar stop, but while they were waiting a sledge with tinkling bells drove by. Yakov hailed it and the sleepy driver promised he would take the Jew to his street in the Podol. When Yakov got back to the brickyard he felt he had been through a long night. He felt out of sorts and unreasonably depressed. On the way to the stable he met Proshko in high spirits.

When he entered his room Yakov had the sudden feeling that someone had been in it while he was out with the Hasid. He had the impression things had been moved, then set back not exactly in place. He suspected the foreman. The smell of horse manure and rotting hay seeped up from the stable. He hastily searched among his few possessions but could find nothing missing, neither household articles, his few books, nor roubles in the tin can. He was glad he had sold some of the books and burned the pamphlets; they were about history but some history was dangerous. The next day he heard that a body had been found in a cave near-by, then he read with fascinated horror a newspaper account of the terrible murder of a twelve-year-old boy who had lived in one of the wooden houses near the cemetery. The body was found in a sitting position, the boy's hands tied behind his back. He was clad in his underwear, without shoes, one black stocking hanging on his left foot; scattered near-by were a bloodstained blouse, a schoolboy's cap, a belt, and several pencil-smeared copy books. Both the *Kievlyanin* and *Kievskaya Mysl* carried a picture of him, Zhenia Golov, and Yakov recognized the pimply-faced boy he had chased out of the yard with his friend. One newspaper said the boy had been dead for a week, the other said two. When the Police Inspector had examined his swollen face and shrunken mutilated body, he had counted thirty-seven wounds made by a thin pointed instrument. The boy, according to Professor Y. A. Cherpunov of the Kiev Anatomical Institute, had been stabbed to death and bled white, "possibly for religious purposes". Marfa Vladimirovna Golov, the bereaved mother, a widow, had claimed the body of her son. There was a picture of her in both newspapers, pressing the boy's poor head to her grief-stricken bosom, crying desolately, "Tell me, Zheniushka, who did this to my baby?"

That night the river overflowed its banks, flooding the lower reaches of the city. Two days later the boy was buried in the cemetery, a few short steps from his home. Yakov could see from the window of his stable the trees still powdered with April snow, and wandering amid them and the thin tombstones, the black crowd, among them some pilgrims with staves. When the coffin was lowered into the grave, hundreds of leaflets exploded into the air: WE ACCUSE THE JEWS. A week later the Kiev Union of Russian People, together with members of the Society of the Double-headed Eagle, placed a huge wooden cross on the grave of the boy – Yakov watching from afar – at the same time calling on all good Christians, according to the newspapers that night, to preach a new crusade against the Israelitic enemies. "They want nothing less than our lives and country! People of Russia! Have pity on your children! Avenge the unfortunate martyrs!" This is terrible, Yakov thought, they want to start a pogrom. In the brickyard Proshko sported a Black Hundreds button on his leather apron. Very early the next morning the fixer hurried to the printer's for his counterfeit papers but when he arrived he found the place had burned down. He ran back to the stable and hastily counted his roubles to see if he had enough to get to Amsterdam and possibly New York. Wrapping up his few things, and slinging his bag of tools on to his shoulder, he was on his way down the stairs when a man who identified himself as Colonel I. P. Bodyansky, the red-moustached head of the Secret Police in Kiev, with several other officials, fifteen gendarmes wearing white looped cords across the breasts of their uniforms, a detachment of police, several plainclothes detectives, and two representatives of the Office of the Chief Prosecuting Attorney of the District Superior Court, about thirty in all, rushed up the stairs with drawn pistols and swords, confronting the fleeing Yakov.

"In the name of His Majesty Nicholas the Second," said the red-headed colonel, "I arrest you. Resist and you are dead."

The fixer readily confessed he was a Jew. Otherwise he was innocent.

III

In a long, high-ceilinged cell under the District Courthouse, a dismal faded stucco structure in the commercial section of the Plossky a few versts from the brickyard in the Lukianovsky, Yakov, in a state of unrelieved distress, could not blot out the sight of himself marching manacled between two tall columns of gendarmes on horses, their sabres drawn and spurs clinking as they hurried him along snowy streets tracked slushy by sledge runners.

He had begged the colonel to let him walk on the sidewalk to lessen his embarrassment, but was forced into the wet centre of the street, and people on their way to work had stopped to watch. They gazed at first quietly, then in deep silence, broken by whispers, muttering and a few jeers. Most seemed to wonder what the parade was about, but then a uniformed schoolboy in a blue cap and silver-buttoned coat, poking his fingers up like horns over his head, danced in the snow behind the prisoner, chanting,

"Zhid, Zhid", and that awoke murmurs, hoots, mockery. A small crowd, including some women, began to follow them, jeering at the fixer, calling him dirty names, "murdering Jew". He wanted to break and run but didn't dare. Someone flung a block of wood at him but it struck a horse that broke into a wild gallop, kicking up snow and running two squares before it was controlled. Then the colonel, a huge man in a fur cap, raised his sabre and the crowd scattered.

He delivered the prisoner first to Secret Police Head-quarters, a one-storey brown building in a side-street; then after a long annoyed telephone conversation, fragments of which the frightened prisoner sitting on a bench in an ante-room surrounded by gendarmes, overheard, the colonel escorted Yakov directly to an underground cell in the District Courthouse, leaving behind two gendarmes who patrolled the corridor with naked sabres. Yakov, alone in the cell, wringing his hands, cried out, "My God, what have I done to myself? I'm in the hands of enemies!" He hit his chest with his fist, bewailed his fate, envisioned terrible things happening to him, ending by being torn apart by a mob. Yet there were also moments of sudden hope when he felt that if he only *explained* why he had done what he had done, he would be at once released. He had stupidly pre-tended to be somebody he wasn't, hoping it would create "opportunities", had learned otherwise – the wrong oppor-tunities – and was paying for learning. If they let him go now he had suffered enough. He blamed also egotism and foolish ambition, considering who he was, and promised himself it would be different in the future. He had learned his lesson – again. Then he jumped up and cried aloud, "What future?" but nobody answered. When an orderly brought in tea and black bread, he could not eat though he had eaten nothing that day. As the day wore on he groaned often, tore his hair with both fists, and knocked his head repeatedly against the wall. A gendarme saw him and strictly forbade it.

Towards evening, the prisoner, sitting immobile on a thin mattress on the floor, heard footsteps in the corridor other than the measured tread of the armed guard who had replaced the two gendarmes. Yakov scrambled to his feet. A man of medium height carrying a black hat and fur coat hurried along the dimly lit corridor to the dark cell. He ordered the guard to open the cell door, lock him in with the prisoner, and leave. The guard hesitated. The man waited patiently.

"I was ordered not to leave, if it's all the same to your honour," said the guard. "The Prosecuting Attorney said not to let the Jew out of my sight because it's a most important case. That's what I was told by his assistant."

"I am here on official business and will call you when I need you. Wait outside the corridor door."

The guard reluctantly opened the cell, locked the man in with Yakov and left. The man watched till the guard had gone, then took a candle-stub out of his coat pocket, lit it and set it in some drops of wet wax in a saucer. He held the saucer in his hand, studying Yakov for a long moment, then put it down on the table in the cell. Seeing his cold breath in the light he drew on his fur coat. "I am subject to lingering colds." He wore a darkish beard, pince-nez, and a thick scarf wrapped around his neck. Facing the fixer, who was standing stiffly at attention, inwardly trembling, he introduced himself in a quiet resonant voice.

"I am B. A. Bibikov, Investigating Magistrate for Cases of Extraordinary Importance. Please kindly identify yourself."

"Yakov Shepsovitch Bok, your honour, though there's nothing extraordinary about my foolish mistakes."

"You are not Yakov Ivanovitch Dologushev?"

"That was a stupid deception. I admit it at once."

Bibikov adjusted his glasses and looked at him in silence. He lifted the candle to light a cigarette, then changed his mind, set it down, and thrust the cigarette into his pocket.

"Tell me truly," said the Investigating Magistrate in a severe voice, "did you murder that unfortunate child?"

A fog of blackness rose before Yakov's eyes.

"Never! Never!" he cried hoarsely. "Why would I kill an innocent child? How could I have done it? For years I wanted a child but my luck was bad and my wife couldn't have one. If in no other way at least in my heart I'm a father. And if that's so how could I kill an innocent child? I couldn't think of such a thing, I'd rather be dead."

"How long have you been married?"

"Five years going on six, though I'm not really married now because my wife left me."

"Is that so? Why did she leave you?"

"To make it short and simple she was unfaithful. She ran off with an unknown party and that's why I'm in jail now. If she hadn't done that I would have stayed where I belonged, which means where I was born. This very minute I'd be sitting down to supper, such as it was, but it could have been worse. When the sun went down, whether I had earned a kopek or not, I headed straight for my hut. It wasn't such a bad place to be, now that I think of it."

"You're not from Kiev?"

"Not the city, the province. I left my village a few months after my wife left me and I've been here since November. I was ashamed to stay on there with things as they were.

There were other reasons but that was what bothered me most."

"What other reasons?"

"I was fed up with my work – no work at all. And I hoped, with a bit of luck, to get myself a little education. They say in America there are schools where a grown man can study at night."

"You were thinking of emigrating to America?"

"It was one of my thoughts, your honour, though I've had many such and they've all come to nothing. Still in all, I'm a loyal subject of the Tsar."

The Investigating Magistrate found the cigarette in his pocket and lit it. He smoked silently, standing on the other side of the table, still studying Yakov's tormented face in the candlelight.

"I saw among your possessions when you were arrested a few books, among others a volume of selected chapters from the work of the philosopher Spinoza."

"That's right, your honour. Could I get them back? I'm also worried about my tools."

"In due course, if you are not indicted. Are you familiar with his writings?"

"Only in a way of speaking," said the fixer, worried by the question. "Although I've read the book I don't understand it all."

"What is its appeal to you? First let me ask you what brought you to Spinoza? Is it that he was a Jew?"

"No, your honour. I didn't know who or what he was when I first came across the book – they don't exactly love him in the synagogue, if you've read the story of his life. I found it in a junkyard in a near-by town, paid a kopek and left cursing myself for wasting money hard to come by. Later I read through a few pages and kept on going as though there were a whirlwind at my back. As I say, I didn't understand every word but when you're dealing with such ideas you feel as though you were taking a witch's ride. After that I wasn't the same man. That's in a manner of speaking of course, because I've changed little since my youth."

Though he had answered freely, talking about a book with a Russian official frightened the fixer. He's testing me, he thought. Still when all's said and done, better questions about a book than a murdered child. I'll tell the truth but speak slowly.

"Would you mind explaining what you think Spinoza's work means? In other words if it's a philosophy what does it state?"

"That's not so easy to say," Yakov answered apologetically. "The truth is I'm a half-ignorant man. The other half is half-educated. There's a lot I miss even when I pay the strictest attention."

"I will tell you why I ask. I ask because Spinoza is among my favourite philosophers and I am interested in his effect on others."

"In that case," said the fixer, partly relieved, "I'll tell you that the book means different things according to the subject of the chapters, though it's all united underneath. But what I think it means is that he was out to make a free man out of himself – as much as one can according to his philosophy, if you understand my meaning – by thinking things through and connecting everything up, if you'll go along with that, your honour."

"That isn't a bad approach," said Bibikov, "through the man rather than the work. But you ought to explain the philosophy a little."

"Who knows if I can," the fixer said. "Maybe it's that

God and Nature are one and the same, and so is man, or some such thing, whether he's poor or rich. If you understand that a man's mind is part of God, then you understand it as well as I. In that way you're free, if you're in the mind of God. If you're there you know it. At the same time the trouble is that you are bound down by Nature, though that's not true for God who is Nature anyway. There's also something called Necessity, which is always there though nobody wants it, that one has to push against. In the shtetl God goes running around with the Law in both hands, but this other God, though he fills up more space, has less to do altogether. Whoever you end up believing in, nothing has changed much in the world if you're without work. So much for Necessity. I also figure it means that life is life and there's no sense kicking it into the grave. Either that or I don't understand it as well as it's said."

"If a man is bound to Necessity where does freedom come from?"

"That's in your thought, your honour, if your thought is in God. That's if you believe in this kind of God; that's if you reason it out. It's as though a man flies over his own head on the wings of reason, or some such thing. You join the universe and forget your worries."

"Do you believe that one can be free that way?"

"Up to a point," Yakov sighed. "It sounds fine but my experience is limited. I haven't lived much outside the small towns."

The magistrate smiled.

Yakov snickered but caught himself and stopped.

"Is such a thing as you describe it, true freedom, would you say, or cannot one be free without being politically free?"

Here's where I'd better watch my step, the fixer thought.

Politics is politics. No use fanning up hot coals when you have to walk across them.

"I wouldn't know for sure, your honour. It's partly one and partly the other."

"True enough. One might say there is more than one conception of freedom in Spinoza's mind – in Necessity, philosophically speaking; and practically, in the state, that is to say within the realm of politics and political action. Spinoza conceded a certain freedom of political choice, similar to the freedom of electing to think, if it were possible to make these choices. At least it is possible to think them. He perhaps felt that the purpose of the state – the government – was the security and comparative freedom of rational man. This was to permit man to think as best he could. He also thought man was freer when he participated in the life of society than when he lived in solitude as he himself did. He thought that a free man in society had a positive interest in promoting the happiness and intellectual emancipation of his neighbours."

"I guess that's true, your honour, if you say so," said Yakov, "but as far as I myself am concerned what you said is something to think about, though if you're poor your time is taken up with other things that I don't have to mention. You let those who can, worry about the ins and outs of politics."

"Ah," Bibikov sighed. He puffed on his cigarette without speaking. For a moment there was no sound in the cell.

Did I say something wrong? Yakov thought wildly. There are times it doesn't pay to open your mouth.

When the magistrate spoke again he sounded once more like an investigating official, his tone dry, objective.

"Have you ever heard the expression 'historical necessity'?"

86

"Not that I remember. I don't think so though maybe I could guess what it means."

"Are you sure? You've not read Hegel?"

"I don't know his name."

"Or Karl Marx? He too was a Jew, though not exactly happy to be one."

"Not him either."

"Would you say you have a 'philosophy' of your own? If so what is it?"

"If I have it's all skin and bones. I've only just come to a little reading, your honour," he apologized. "If I have any philosophy, if you don't mind me saying so, it's that life could be better than it is."

"Yet how can it be made better if not in politics or through it?"

That's a sure trap, Yakov thought. "Maybe by more jobs and work," he faltered. "Not to forget good will among men. We all have to be reasonable or what's bad gets worse."

"Well, that's at least a beginning," the magistrate said quietly. "You must read and reflect further."

"I will just as soon as I get out of here."

Bibikov seemed embarrassed. The fixer felt as though he had disappointed him, although he was not sure why. Probably too much incxact talk. It's hard to make sense when you're in trouble, considering also your other natural disadvantages.

The magistrate after a while absently asked, "How did you bruise your head?"

"In the dark, in desperation."

Bibikov reached into his pocket and offered the fixer his cigarette-box. "Have one, they're Turkish."

Yakov smoked in order not to affront the man, though he could not taste the cigarette.

Taking a folded paper and pencil-stub out of his suit coat pocket the magistrate placed them on the table, saying, "I leave this questionnaire with you. We will have to know more biographical details since you have no police record. When you have answered each question and signed your name, call the guard and give him the paper. Be accurate in everything you say. I'll leave the candle with you."

Yakov stared at the paper.

"I have to hurry now. My boy has a fever. My wife gets frantic." The Investigating Magistrate buttoned his fur coat and put on a wide-brimmed black fedora that looked large for his head.

Nodding to the prisoner, he said quietly, "Whatever happens you must have fortitude."

"My God, what can happen? I'm an innocent man."

Bibikov shrugged. "It's a touchy thing."

"Have mercy, your honour; I've had little in my life."

"Mercy is for God, I depend on the law. The law will protect you."

He called the guard and left the cell. As the door was being locked he hurried away in the dimly lit corridor.

The fixer felt at once a sense of intense loss.

"When will you come back?" he shouted after him.

"Tomorrow." A distant door shut. The footsteps were gone.

"It's a long tomorrow," said the guard.

2

The next morning a new guard unlocked the cell, searched Yakov thoroughly for the third time since he had awakened, manacled him tightly with heavy handcuffs attached by a short thick chain, and in the presence of two other armed guards, one of whom cursed the prisoner and prodded him with his pistol, escorted Yakov, about as dead as he was alive, up two flights of narrow booming wooden stairs into the Investigating Magistrate's office. In the large anteroom some clerks in uniform sat at long tables scratching on paper with wet pens. They gazed at him with intense interest, then looked at each other. Yakov was led into a brown-walled smaller office. Bibikov was standing at an open window, waving his hand back and forth to thin out the cigarette smoke. As Yakov entered he quickly shut the window and seated himself in a chair at the head of a long table. The room contained a bulky desk, several shelves of thick books, two large green-shaded lamps, and a small ikon in the corner; on the wall hung a large sepia portrait of Tsar Nicholas II, bemedalled and immaculately barbered, staring critically at the fixer. The picture added to his discomfort.

The only other person in the room was Bibikov's assistant, a pimply-faced man in his thirties, with a thin beard through which his small chin was visible. He was sitting next to the magistrate at the short end of the table, and Yakov was told to take his seat at the other end. The three escorting guards at the magistrate's request waited in the antechamber. He, after barely glancing at the prisoner – almost distastefully the fixer thought – fished among some official documents in a pile before him and drew forth a thick one whose pages he thumbed through. He whispered something to the assistant, who filled a heavy fountain-pen from a large bottle of black ink, wiped the nib with an ink-stained rag, and began to write quickly in a notebook.

Bibikov, looking ill-at-ease and tired, seemed changed

89

from last night, and for a moment Yakov nervously wondered if it was the same man. His head was large, with a broad forehead and a pelt of dark greying hair. As he read he nibbled on his thin underlip; then he put down the paper, blew at his pince-nez, adjusted them with care and sipped from a glass of water. He spoke in a voice without warmth, addressing the fixer across the table: "I will now read you a portion of the deposition of Nikolai Maximovitch Lebedev, factory owner of the Lukianovsky District; that is, his factory is in the Lukianovsky—" Then his official voice changed and he said quietly, "Yakov Shepsovitch Bok, you are in a difficult situation and we must straighten things out. Listen first to a statement of the witness Lebedev. He says it was your intent from the outset to deceive him."

"It isn't true, your honour!"

"Just one minute. Please contain yourself."

Bibikov took up the document, turned to an inside page and read aloud:

"'N. Lebedev: He whom I knew as Yakov Ivanovitch Dologushev, although he did me, by chance, a personal favour of some magnitude, for which I generously rewarded him, and my daughter treated him most considerately, was a less than honest man – more accurately, a deceitful one. He concealed from me, for reasons that are obvious – and well he might for I would never have employed him had I known what I do now – that he was in truth, although he attempted to hide it, a member of the Jewish Nation. I confess I felt a tremor of suspicion when I observed his discomfiture at a query I addressed him concerning the Holy Scriptures. In response to my question whether he had made it a habit to read the Holy Bible, he replied he was familiar only with the Old Testament, and blanched greatly when I proceeded

90

to read him some telling verses from the New Testament, in particular from the Sermon on the Mount.'

"'Investigating Magistrate: Anything else?'

"'N. Lebedev: I also noticed an odd hesitancy, a sort of bumbling when he spoke his name for the first time, that is to say the assumed name, which he was as yet unfamiliar with. It did not, need I say, your honour, fit his Jewish tongue. Furthermore, for an ostensibly poor man he showed extreme reluctance – perhaps this is to his credit – to accept my generous offer of a position in my brickworks, and my suspicions were further aroused because he seemed uneasy when I had broached the matter of his living in the room above the stable on the factory grounds. He wanted to work for me and yet he was afraid to, naturally enough. He was troubled and nervous, constantly wetting his lips and averting his eyes. Since I am somewhat incapacitated in health – my liver gives me trouble and I suffer a marked shortness of breath – I had need of an overseer who would live on the premises and see that my affairs were kept in order. However, since the Jew had helped me when I became suddenly ill and collapsed in the snow, my suspicions were not long lasting, and I offered him the position. I believe he knew full well, when he accepted my unwitting offer, that the Lukianovsky District is sacred territory and forbidden to Jews for residence, except, as I understand it, for exceptional services to the Crown; and I take that to be the reason he made no attempt to turn over to me his papers so that I might deliver them to the District Police.'

"'Investigating Magistrate: Did you ask for them?'

"'N. Lebedev: Not directly. Yes, perhaps I did once and he made me some sort of fishy Jewish excuse or other, and then as I was having trouble with my health I neglected to remind him again. Had I done that and he refused my request, I would at once have ordered him off my property. I am a generous and lenient man, your honour, but I would never have tolerated a Jew in my employ. Please note, if you will, the sigillum on my coat lapel. I consider it a mark of this man's insolence that he was not quailed by it in my presence. For your information I am a former recording secretary of the Society of the Double-headed Eagle.'"

The magistrate laid down the paper, removed his glasses and rubbed his eyes.

"You have heard the deposition," he said to Yakov. "I have also read your questionnaire and am familiar with the responses, but I must now ask you to comment on the remarks of the witness Lebedev. Is the substance of them correct? Be careful in your reply. This, though not a trial, is a police investigation to see if an Act of Indictment is warranted."

Yakov rose in excitement. "Please, your honour, I don't know much about the law, and it isn't always simple to say yes and no in the right place. Would you let me speak to a lawyer for advice? I might even have a few roubles to pay if the police will return my money to me."

"Yes and no take care of themselves if a man tells the truth. As for consulting a lawyer, that is not possible at this stage. In our legal system the indictment comes first. After the preliminary examination the Investigating Magistrate and Prosecuting Attorney consult, and if both believe the suspect to be guilty, an Act of Indictment is drawn up and sent to the District Court, where it is either confirmed or disapproved by the judges. The defence may begin after the accused is informed that the indictment has been voted, and he is then given a copy of it. Within a week or so, possibly a bit more, the accused may select his counsel and inform the court."

"Your honour," Yakov said in alarm, "suppose a man is innocent of what they say he did? What's it all about is a confusion in my mind. One minute I think it's as clear as daylight and the crime we're talking about is a small one, no more than a mistake you might say, and the next minute you say things that make me shiver. For my little sin why should anybody accuse me of a big one? If I gave a false name to someone does that mean there's bound to be an indictment?"

"We will know in due course what is bound to be."

The fixer, sighing heavily, sat down, his manacled hands twitching in his lap.

"I have asked you to comment on the witness Lebedev's remarks," Bibikov said.

"Your honour, I give you my word I meant no harm. What I did wrong – even Nikolai Maximovitch admits it – I did with reluctance, against my will. The truth is I found him drunk in the snow. As a reward he offered me a job I didn't ask for. I could've refused it and I did once or twice, but my money was going fast, I had rent to pay and et cetera. I was getting desperate for work – my hands complain when they have nothing to do – so I finally took what he offered me. He was satisfied with the paint and the papering job I first did, and he also told me I was a good overseer in the brickworks. I used to get up at half past three every night to inspect the loading of the wagons. If he said it once he said it more than once. Ask him yourself, your honour."

"True, but didn't you give him a false name as your own? In effect, a gentile name? That was no accident I take it? That was your intent, wasn't it?"

The magistrate had forcefully thrust his face forward. Was this the man who said he admired Spinoza?

"It's my mistake, I admit it," said Yakov. "I gave him the first name that popped into my head. I wasn't thinking, your honour, and that's how a man comes to grief. When you're faced with a worrisome situation it's not so easy to keep your mind on what comes next. Dologushev is a one-eyed peasant near my village who slaughters pigs. But the truth of it is I really didn't want to live on the factory grounds. It got so I couldn't sleep from worrying so much. Nikolai Maximovitch mentions that I was afraid to take his offer to live in the stable. He says so himself in this paper you just read to me. I asked him if I could live in the Podol instead and walk to the job, but he said no, I had to live there. In other words it wasn't my idea in the first place. And he's mistaken if he thinks he asked for my passport. Maybe he thought he did but he didn't. He's a melancholy man and sometimes vague in his thoughts. I swear he never asked me. If he had, that would have ended it then and there. I would have thought the jig's up and gone home. It would have saved me a lot of misery."

"Still, you did live in the Lukianovsky, though fully aware it was illegal for you to do so?"

"That's as you say, your honour, but I didn't want to lose the job. I was hoping for a better life than I had." His voice had begun to plead, but noticing the magistrate's compressed lips and stern gaze, Yakov stopped speaking and inspected his hands.

"In the questionnaire," said Bibikov, snapping on his glasses and consulting another paper, "you state you are a Jew 'by birth and nationality'. Do I sense a reservation, and if so what is it?"

The fixer sat silent a minute, then looked up uncomfortably. "What I meant by that is I'm not a religious man. I was when I was young but lost my belief. I thought I mentioned that when we talked last night, but maybe I didn't. That's all I meant by that."

"How did it happen? I refer to your loss of religion."

"I guess there's more than one reason even though I don't recall them all. In my life, the way that it's turned out, I've had a lot to think about. One thought breeds another. Give me an idea and in two minutes there's a second pushing out the first. Also I've been reading a little here and there, as I mentioned to you, your honour, and have picked up a few things I never knew before. It all adds up."

The magistrate leaned back in his chair. "You haven't by some chance been baptized along the way? It might be convenient if you had."

"Oh, no, your honour, nothing at all like that. What I mean to say is I'm a freethinker."

"I understand that, though to be a freethinker assumes one would know how to think."

"I try my best," said Yakov.

"What do you think freethinker means?"

"A man who decides for himself if he wants to believe in religion. Maybe an agnostic also. Some do and some don't."

"Do you think it adds to your stature to be irreligious?"

My God, what have I said? the fixer thought. I'd better keep this simple and small or I'll dig my grave and they'll lay me in it.

He said hastily, "It's as you say, your honour, yes and no fall into place if you tell the truth. I'm telling the truth."

"Let's not complicate matters unnecessarily." Bibikov sipped from his water glass. "Legally you are a Jew. The Imperial Government considers you one even though you twist and squirm. You are so recorded on your passport.

95

Our laws concerning Jews apply to you. However, if you are ashamed of your people, why don't you leave the faith officially?"

"I'm not ashamed, your honour. Maybe I don't always like what I see – there are Jews of all sorts, as the saying goes, but if I'm going to be ashamed of anyone, it might as well be myself." As he said this his colour heightened.

Bibikov listened with interest. He glanced down at his notes, then looked up with eyes narrowed. Ivan Semyon-ovitch, the assistant, who reacted quickly to his remarks, often taking on the same facial expression as the magistrate, glancing at the notes from where he sat, leaned forward intently.

"The absolute truth, please," said the Investigating Magistrate sternly. " – Are you a revolutionary, either as a theorist or activist?"

Yakov felt the force of his pounding heart.

"Does it say that anywhere in your papers, your honour?"

"Please answer my question."

"No, I'm not. God forbid. That's beyond me, if you know what I mean. It's not my nature. If I'm anything I'm a peaceful man. 'Yakov,' I used to say to myself, 'there's too much violence in the world and if you're smart you'll stay out of it.' It isn't for me, your honour."

"A Socialist or member of any Socialist parties?"

The fixer hesitated. "No."

"Are you certain?"

"I give you my earnest word."

"Are you a Zionist?"

"No."

"Do you belong to any political party whatsoever? That would include Jewish parties."

"To none at all, your honour."

96

"Very well. Have you noted the responses, Ivan Semyonovitch?"

"Every word, sir. I have it all," said the pimply assistant.

"Good," said Bibikov, absently scratching his beard. "Now there is another matter I wish to question you about. Wait till I find the paper."

"Excuse me, I don't mean to interrupt," Yakov said, "but I would like you to know that my passport was stamped 'Permission Granted' when I left my village. And when I got to Kiev, the very next day after my arrival which happened late at night – the next day I brought it to the passport section of the Police Station of the Podol District. It was also stamped there, your honour."

"That is already noted. I've examined the passport and your remarks are substantially correct. However, that isn't the matter I was about to bring up."

"It was only in the Lukianovsky, if you'll excuse me, your honour, that I didn't register. That was where I made a mistake."

"That is also noted."

"If you don't mind, I'd like to mention that I served for a short time in the Russian Army."

"Noted. A very short time, less than a year. You were discharged for illness, were you not?"

"Also because the war was over. There was no use for any more soldiers at that time."

"What was the illness?"

"Attacks of asthma, on and off. I would never know when they would hit me next."

"Are you still troubled with this ailment?" the magistrate said conversationally. "I ask because my son has asthma."

"Mostly it's cleared up though sometimes on a windy day I find it hard to draw a breath."

"I'm glad it's cleared up. Now permit me to go on to the next item. I will read from the deposition of Zinaida Nikolaevna Lebedev, spinster, age thirty."

This is terrible, the fixer thought, squeezing his hands. Where will it all end?

The door opened. The magistrate and his assistant looked up as two officials strode into the room. One, in a red and blue uniform with gold epaulets, was the officer who had arrested Yakov, Colonel Bodyansky, a heavy man with a cropped red moustache. The other was the Prosecuting Attorney Grubeshov, Procurator of the Kiev Superior Court. He had that morning gone down to stare at the fixer in his cell without addressing a word to him. Yakov had stood frozen against the wall. Five minutes later the prosecutor had walked away, leaving him in a sweaty state of unrest.

Grubeshov placed on the table a worn portfolio with straps. He was a stoutish man with a fleshy face, side-whiskers, thick eyebrows and hawklike eyes. A roll of flesh on the neck hung over his stiff collar, the tabs of which were bent over a black bow tie. He wore a dark suit with a soiled yellow vest and seemed to be repressing excitement. Yakov was again apprehensive.

Bibikov's assistant had at once arisen and bowed. At a warning glance from the magistrate, the fixer hastily got up and remained standing.

"Good morning, Vladislav Grigorievitch," said Bibikov, a little flustered. "Good morning, Colonel Bodyansky, I am examining the suspect. Kindly be seated. Ivan Semyonovitch, please shut the door."

The colonel brushed his fingers over his moustache, and the Prosecuting Attorney, smiling slightly at nothing in particular, nodded. Yakov, at the magistrate's signal, shakily resumed his seat. Both officials studied him, the Prosecuting Attorney, once more intently, almost as though appraising the fixer's health, weight, stamina, sending chills down his back; or as though he were a new animal in the zoo. But the colonel looked through him as though he did not exist.

He wearily wished he didn't.

Bibikov read part way down the typewritten first page of the paper in his hand, then flipped through several more pages before he glanced up.

"Ah, I have it here," he said, clearing his throat. "This is the key statement: 'Z. N. Lebedev: I felt from the first he was different or odd in some way but could not guess how basically so, or I would never have had anything to do with him, you may believe me. He seemed to me somewhat foreign, but I explained to myself that he was from the provinces and obviously lacking in education and cultivation. I can only say I was on the whole uncomfortable in his presence, although of course truly grateful that he had assisted Papa that time he slipped in the snow. Afterwards I detested him because he tried to assault me. I told him firmly I never wished to see him again –'"

"It's not true, I didn't assault her," Yakov said, half rising. "It's not true at all."

"Please," said Bibikov, staring at him in astonishment.

"Silence," said Colonel Bodyansky, pounding his fist on the table. "Sit down at once!"

Grubeshov drummed with his finger-tips.

Yakov quickly sat down. Bibikov glanced at the colonel in embarrassment. To the fixer he said firmly, "You will please control yourself, this is a legal investigation. I shall continue to read: 'Investigating Magistrate: Are you charging sexual assault?'

"'Z. N. Lebedev: I'm sure he intended to assault me. By this time I had begun to suspect he might be a Jew but when I saw for certain I screamed loudly.'

"'Investigating Magistrate: Explain what you mean that you saw "for certain".'

"'Z. N. Lebedev: He – I saw he was cut in the manner of Jewish males. I could not help seeing.'

"'Investigating Magistrate: Go on, Zinaida Nikolaevna, after you have calmed yourself. You may be embarrassed but it is best to speak the truth.'

"'Z. N. Lebedev: He realized I would not tolerate his advances and left the room. That was the last I saw of him, and I thank God.'

"'Investigating Magistrate: Then there was no assault in the true sense of the word, if you will pardon me? He did not touch you or attempt to?'

"'Z. N. Lebedev: You may say that but the fact remains he undressed himself and his intentions were to have relations with a Russian woman. That's what he hoped for, or he wouldn't have undressed and appeared naked. I'm sure you wouldn't approve of that, your honour.'

"'Investigating Magistrate: There is no approval expressed or implied either of his conduct or yours, Zinaida Nikolaevna. Did you afterwards inform your father, Nikolai Maximovitch, of this incident?'

"'Z. N. Lebedev: My father is not well and hasn't been in good health or spirits since the death of my poor mother. And his only brother died a year ago of a lingering illness, so I didn't wish to upset him further. He would have wanted to horsewhip the Jew.'"

"It is noted that at this point the witness wept copiously."

Bibikov laid down the paper.

"Will you say now," he asked Yakov, "whether you attempted to force yourself upon Zinaida Nikolaevna?"

Ivan Semyonovitch filled the magistrate's water glass from a porcelain pitcher on the table.

'Absolutely not, your honour," Yakov said hastily. "We ate together twice on her invitation while I was working in the upstairs flat, and the last night – the night I finished painting – she afterwards invited me to her bedroom. Maybe I shouldn't have gone – that's obvious now – but it's not such a hard thing to do when you consider a man's nature. Anyway, I had doubts and the minute I saw she was unclean, if you'll excuse me for saying so, your honour, I left. That's the honest truth and I could try from now to the Day of Judgement and not make it truer."

"What do you mean 'unclean'?"

The fixer was distraught. "I'm sorry to mention such things but if a man is in trouble he has to explain himself. The truth of it is she was having her monthlies."

He lifted his manacled hands to wipe his face.

"Any Jew who approaches a Russian woman ought to be strung up," said Colonel Bodyansky.

"Did she state such was her condition?" Grubeshov spoke with a slight thickness of speech.

"I saw the blood, your honour, if you'll excuse me, while she was washing herself with a cloth."

"You saw the blood?" the Prosecuting Attorney said sarcastically. "Did that have some religious meaning to you as a Jew? Do you know that in the Middle Ages Jewish men were said to menstruate?"

Yakov looked at him in surprise and fright.

"I don't know anything about that, your honour, although I don't see how it could be. But getting back to Zinaida Nikolaevna Lebedev, what her condition meant to me was that it wouldn't do either of us any good, and I was a fool to agree to go to her room in the first place. I should have gone home the minute I finished my work and not be tempted by a table full of all kinds of food."

"Relate what happened in the bedroom," Bibikov said. "And please confine yourself to the question at hand."

"Nothing happened, your honour, I swear it with my whole heart. It's as I said before – and also the young lady in the paper you just read – I got dressed as quickly as I could and left. I assure you of that, and it was the last I saw of her. Believe me, I'm sorry it happened."

"I do believe you," said Bibikov.

Grubeshov, sharply startled, stared at the Investigating Magistrate. Colonel Bodyansky shifted uncomfortably in his chair.

Bibikov, as though justifying himself, said, "We found two letters, both identified by the witnesses as written in their hand. One was from Nikolai Maximovitch addressed to Yakov Ivanovitch Dologushev, praising his diligence as an overseer of the Lebedev Brickworks, and the other was from the daughter, Zinaida Nikolaevna, on a sheet of perfumed blue letter paper, inviting the suspect to call on her at her home and expressly stating in the letter that she was writing it with the permission of her father. I have both letters in my files. They were turned over to me by Captain Korimzin of the Kiev City Police, who found them in the office of the brickworks."

The colonel and Prosecuting Attorney sat like statues.

Again addressing Yakov, the magistrate said, "I gather from the date that the letter from the young lady was written after the incident already described?"

"That's right, your honour. I was working in the brickworks then."

"You did not write her as she requested?"

"I didn't answer the letter. I figured I was born with a lot more trouble than I needed and there was no sense searching for more. If you're afraid of a flood stay away from the water."

"Her later remarks to me though of informal nature," the magistrate said, "affirm your statement. Therefore, considering the circumstances – this does not mean that I admire your behaviour, Yakov Bok – I will recommend to the Prosecuting Attorney that you not be charged with attempted sexual assault."

He turned to his assistant, who, nodding, wrote hastily.

The Prosecuting Attorney, flushing through his sidewhiskers, picked up his portfolio, pushed back his chair and got up noisily. Colonel Bodyansky also arose. Bibikov reaching for the water glass, knocked it over. Jumping up, he dabbed at the spilled water on the table with his handkerchief, assisted by Ivan Semyonovitch, who in dismay quickly gathered up the papers and began to dry those that had got wet.

Grubeshov and Colonel Bodyansky, neither speaking a word, strode sullenly out of the room.

When he had blotted up the water, the Investigating Magistrate sat down, waited till Ivan Semyonovitch had dried and sorted the papers, and though embarrassed at the incident, picked up his notes, and clearing his throat, once more addressed the fixer in his resonant voice.

"We have laws, Yakov Bok," he said grimly, "directed against any member of your faith, orthodox or heretic, who assumes or counterfeits a name other than that entered in his official birth records, which is to say for the purpose of one sort of deception or another; but since there are no forged or counterfeited documents involved in this case, and since there is at present no record of similar previous offences by you, I shall be lenient this time and not press this charge, although I personally feel, as I have already informed you, that your deception was repugnant and it is only by the greatest good fortune that it did not become an even more reprehensible situation —"

"I thank you kindly, your honour —" The fixer wiped his eyes with his fingers.

The magistrate went on. "I shall, however, ask the court to charge you for taking up residence in a district forbidden to Jews, except under certain circumstances which do not in any way appertain in your case. In this regard you have disobeyed the law. It is not a capital crime but you will be charged and sentenced for a misdemeanour."

"Will I be sent to jail, your honour?"

"I am afraid so."

"Ach. But how long in jail?"

"Not very long – a month at least, possibly less, depending on the magistrate who sentences you. It will teach you a lesson you are apparently in need of."

"Will I have to wear prison clothes?"

"You will be treated the same as other prisoners."

There was a knock on the door and a uniformed messenger entered. He handed an envelope to Ivan Semyonovitch, who quickly passed it to Bibikov.

The Investigating Magistrate, his hand trembling a little, tore it open, read the handwritten note, slowly cleaned his glasses, and hastened out of the room.

Though he knew he could expect trouble – although he had half hoped he would be let off with a warning or even a severe dressing down and sent running back to the Jewish quarter – oh, with what pleasure he would run! – Yakov, after his first disappointment, felt relief that things weren't a lot worse. A month in jail is not a year, and three weeks are less; besides, if you wanted to look at it that way, rent was free. After his manacled march through the snowy streets, the mutterings of the crowd, and the terrible question the Investigating Magistrate had put to him last night in his cell, he had expected a calamity if not worse. Now things had calmed down. Practically, there was only this minor charge, and perhaps a lawyer could get the sentence reduced to maybe a week or nothing at all? It meant, of course, good-bye to some roubles from his savings – surely the police would return them to him – but a rouble he could earn, if not in a day, then in a week or month. Better a month spent grubbing for one than a month in prison. It didn't pay to worry over roubles. The main thing was to be free, and once they freed him, Yakov Bok would be less foolish in his dealings with the law.

The magistrate's assistant had hesitantly reached over to read the note that Bibikov had crumpled up and left on the table. After glancing at it he smiled vaguely; but when the fixer attempted a smile in return, the assistant vigorously blew his nose.

Then the Investigating Magistrate returned, breathing through his mouth, his face drawn and grim, followed into the room by Grubeshov and Colonel Bodyansky. Once more they seated themselves at the table, the Prosecuting Attorney again unstrapping his portfolio. Ivan Semyono-vitch gazed at them with concern, but neither of the officials spoke. The assistant tested his pen, and held it ready to write. Grubeshov's smile was gone, his lips set. The colonel's expression was deadly serious. One look at them and a vast fear again surged through Yakov. Cold sweat prickled his back. Once more he expected the worst. At least almost the worst.

"The Prosecuting Attorney will now ask you a few questions," Bibikov said quietly though hoarsely. He sat back and fiddled with his pince-nez string.

"If you please, first my question," said the colonel, nodding to Grubeshov, who was peering into the compartments of his portfolio. The Prosecuting Attorney, looking up, assented.

"Will the prisoner state," Colonel Bodyansky's voice boomed out in the room, "whether he is a member of certain political organizations I shall now name: Social Democrats, Socialist-Revolutionists, or any other groups including the Jewish Bund, Zionists of whatever ilk or stripe, Seymists, or Volkspartei?"

"I've already gone into that," Bibikov said with a touch of impatience.

The colonel turned on him. "Mr Investigating Magistrate, the task of protecting the Crown from its enemies is under the jurisdiction of the Secret Political Police. Already there has been too much interference in our affairs."

"Not at all, colonel, we are investigating a civil offence —"

"Even a civil offence may be *lèse majesté*. I ask you not to intrude on my questions and I won't interfere with yours. Tell me," he said, turning to Yakov, "are you a member of any of those so-called political parties I have just named, or of any secret terroristic or nihilistic organizations? Answer truthfully or I will send you to the Petropavelsky Fortress."

"No, sir, none, not one," Yakov replied hastily. "I've never belonged to a political party or any secret organizations such as you just mentioned. To tell the truth I don't know one from the other. If I were a better educated man I might, but as it is now whatever you ask me about them I can tell you very little."

"You will be severely punished if you are lying."

"Who's lying, your honour? As a former soldier, I swear I am not lying."

"Save your breath," said the colonel in disgust, "I've never met a Jew I could call a soldier."

Yakov's face turned a fiery red.

The colonel wrote furiously on a slip of paper, thrust it into his tunic pocket and nodded to the Prosecuting Attorney.

Grubeshov had drawn a black oilskin-covered notebook out of his portfolio and was, with arched brows, studying one of its closely handwritten pages. Then he put the notebook down, and though he stared at the fixer, seemed to be in a pleasant state of mind as he remarked in a dry but slightly thick voice, "Well, we have been amusing ourselves, Mr. Yakov Shepsovitch Bok, alias Dologushev, alias I know not what else, but I now have some serious questions to put to you and I request that you give them your most serious attention. By your own admission you are guilty of certain flagrant violations of Russian law. You have confessed to certain crimes and there is good reason – excellent reason – to suspect others, one of so serious a nature that I shall not name it until we have further sifted the evidence, which I propose to continue to do now, with the permission of my colleagues."

He bowed to Bibikov, who, smoking, gravely nodded in return.

"Oh, my God," groaned Yakov, "I swear to you I am innocent of any serious crime. No, sir, the worst I am guilty of is stupidity – of living in the Lukianovsky without permission, that the Investigating Magistrate says I can get a month in prison for – but certainly not of any serious crimes."

God forgive me, he thought in terror. I'm in a bad spot

now, worse than quicksand. That's what one gets for not knowing which way he's running, to begin with.

"Answer this question precisely," said Grubeshov, referring to his notebook. "Are you a 'Hasid' or 'Misnogid'? Please take down his answers with extreme accuracy, Ivan Semyonovitch."

"Neither. I'm neither one nor the other," said Yakov. "As I told his other honour – if I'm anything at all it's a freethinker. I say this to let you know I'm not a religious man."

"That won't do you any good," said the prosecutor, suddenly irritable. "I was expecting just such a response, and of course it's nothing more than an attempt to divert the questioning. Now answer me directly, you are a circumcised Jew, aren't you?"

"I'm a Jew, your honour, I'll admit to that and the rest is personal."

"I've already gone through all this, Vladislav Grigorievitch," said Bibikov. "It's all in the notes of the testimony. Read it to him, Ivan Semyonovitch, it will save time."

"I must ask the Investigating Magistrate not to interrupt," Grubeshov said testily. "I have no interest in saving time. Time is immaterial to me. Please let me go on without useless interruption."

Bibikov lifted the pitcher to pour himself a glass of water but it was empty.

"Shall I refill it, your honour?" whispered Ivan Semyonovitch.

"No," said Bibikov, "I'm not thirsty."

"What's this freethinker business about?" said the colonel.

"Not now, Colonel Bodyansky, I beg you," said Grubeshov. "It is not a political party."

Colonel Bodyansky lit a cigarette.

Grubeshov addressed Yakov, reading aloud certain words from his notebook and pronouncing them slowly.

"There are those among you – are there not? – Jews who are called 'tzadikim'? When a Jew wishes to harm a Christian, or as you call him, 'goyim', he goes to the 'tzadik' and gives him a 'pidion', which is a fee of some sort, and the 'tzadik' uses the power of the word, in magical incantations, to bring misfortune on the Christian. Isn't that a true fact? Answer me."

"Please," said Yakov, "I don't understand what you want of me. What have I to do with such things?"

"You'll find out, if you don't already know, only too soon," said Grubeshov, flushing. "In the meantime answer me truthfully and directly without vomiting a mouthful of irrelevant questions in return. Tell me now, what do you Jews mean by 'afikomen? I want the truth without varnish."

"But what has this got to do with me?" Yakov said. "What do I know about these things you're asking me? If they're strange to you they're strange to me."

"Once more I will direct you to limit yourself to my questions. I will tell you patiently for the last time that I am not interested in your personal comments. Keep in mind that you are already in very serious trouble and curb your tongue."

"I am not positive," said the fixer, disheartened, "but it's a matzo of some kind that's used in the Passover ceremony for protection against evil spirits and evil men."

"Write that all down, Ivan Semyonovitch. Is it magic?"

"To my way of thinking it's superstition, your honour."

"But you say it's the same as matzos?"

"Practically the same, I think. I'm not an expert in these

things. If you want to know the truth I haven't much use for such matters. I have nothing against those who want to follow the customary ways, but for myself I'm interested in what's new in the world."

He glanced at the Investigating Magistrate, but Bibikov was looking out the window.

Grubeshov slid his fingers into the portfolio and withdrew something covered with a handkerchief. He slowly peeled the four corners of the handkerchief and triumphantly held up a triangle of broken matzo.

"This was found in your habitat in the stable at the brick factory. What have you to say now?"

"What can I say, your honour? Nothing. It's matzo. It's not mine."

"Is it 'matzo shmuro'?"

"I wouldn't know if it was or wasn't."

"I understand that 'matzo shmuro' is eaten by very religious Jews."

"I think so."

"How does it differ from ordinary matzo?"

"Don't ask me, your honour. I don't really know."

"I'll ask what I please. I'll ask until your eyes pop out. Do you understand that?"

"Yes, sir."

"Did you bake this matzo?"

"No."

"Then how did it get into your habitat? That's where the police found it."

"It was brought in by an old man, a stranger to me. I give you my earnest word. He was lost one night near the cemetery and I took him in till it stopped snowing. Some boys had hit him with rocks. He was frightened."

"Near the cemetery in the Lukianovsky this occurred?"

"Where the brickworks is."

"Was he a 'tzadik'?"

"Even suppose he was, what has that got to do with me?"

"Answer with respect!" The Prosecuting Attorney struck the table with his palm. The piece of matzo fell to the floor. Ivan Semyonovitch hastily retrieved it. He held it up for all to see, it had not broken. Bibikov wet his dry lips. "Answer courteously," he said.

Yakov, in a dull state, nodded.

Grubeshov again bowed to the magistrate. "My deepest thanks." He paused as though to say more, then changed his mind. "Did your friend the 'tzadik' come often to the stable?" he asked Yakov.

"He came that once. He was a stranger to me. I never saw him again."

"That was because you were arrested not long after his departure."

Yakov could not argue the point.

"Is it true that you hid other Jews in the stable and trafficked with them in stolen goods?"

"No."

"Did you steal systematically from your employer, Niko-lai Maximovitch Lebedev?"

"As God is my judge, never a single kopek."

"Are you certain you did not yourself bake this matzo? A half bag of flour was found in your habitat."

"With respect, your honour, it's the wrong flour. Also I'm not a baker. I once tried to bake bread to save a kopek or two but it didn't rise and came out like a rock. The flour was wasted. Baking isn't one of my skills. I work as carpenter or painter most of the time – I hope nothing has happened to my tools, they're all I've got in the world – but generally I'm a fixer, never a matzo baker. What there is to fix I fix though it pays little and generally my luck in jobs has been bad. But I'm not a criminal, your honour."

Grubeshov listened impatiently. "Answer strictly to the point. Did the 'tzadik' bake the matzos?"

"If so not in my house. Who knows if elsewhere, he didn't tell me but I don't think so."

"Then some other Jew did?"

"It's probably true."

"It's more than probable," said the Prosecuting Attorney, glaring at him. "It's the truth of God."

When Yakov saw him peering again into his evil portfolio, he wrung his manacled hands under the table.

Grubeshov now slowly drew forth a long, stained rag.

"Have you seen this before?" He danced the stained rag over the table with his fingers.

Bibikov watched the dancing rag, absently polishing his glasses; Ivan Semyonovitch stared at it in fascination.

"I will describe it to you," said the Prosecuting Attorney. "It is part of a peasant's blouse similar to the one you are presently affecting. Was this rag, by some chance, formerly a possession of yours?"

"I don't know," said Yakov wearily.

"I advise you to think more carefully, Yakov Bok. If you've eaten no garlic your breath won't stink."

"Yes, your honour," Yakov said desperately, "it's mine more or less, although that's nothing to worry about. The old man I mentioned to you was hit on the head by a rock, and I used part of an old shirt I was no longer wearing – it fell apart on my back – to wipe the blood away. That's God's own truth and all there is to it, I swear."

"So you admit it's bloodstained," shouted the Prosecuting Attorney.

Yakov felt his tongue turn to dust.

112

"Did you ever chase any children in the brickworks yard in the vicinity of the kilns, in particular a twelve-year lad by the name of Zhenia Golov?"

The fixer was unable to reply.

Grubeshov, after glancing at Bibikov, smiled broadly as he mincingly asked the fixer, "Tell me Yankel Jew, why are you trembling?"

3

Why does a man tremble?

When he was locked in the cell again there were three filthy straw pallets on the floor. One was his – what a misery that he could think of it as his; and two new prisoners were lying on the others. One was a hairy man in rags, the other a living skeleton. Both stank across the room, of dirt and poverty. Though neither paid any attention to him, the ragged one blinking at the wall, the other snoring, the fixer kept to the far corner of the cell. He felt abandoned, lost to the world.

"What will happen to me now?" he asked himself. And if it happens bad who will ever know? I might as well be dead. Recalling his father-in-law and wife, he could conjure neither of them close. Especially the wife. He thought of his father and mother, young people in their weedy graves, and their fate gave him no comfort. His frustrated innocence outraged him. He was unjustly accused, helpless, unable to offer proof or be believed. What horror would they accuse him of next? "If they knew me could they say such things?" He tried to comprehend what was happening and explain it to himself. After all, he was a rational being, and a man must try to reason. Yet the more he reasoned the less he understood. The familiar had become evil. What happened next was weighted with peril. That he was a Jew, willing or unwilling, was not enough to explain his fate. Remembering his life filled him with hatred for the way things went and were going. I'm a fixer but all my life I've broken more than I fix. What would they accuse him of next? How could a man defend himself against such terrible hints, insinuations, *accusations*, if no one was willing to believe him? Panic gnawed him. He was full of desperate thoughts of what to do next – somehow to sneak out of the cell and seek in the ghetto for the old man to tell the Russians that he had been hit on the head by a rock and Yakov had wiped away the blood?

The fixer goes from house to house, knocking on each thin door and asking for the tzadik but nobody knows him; then in the last house they know him, a saintly man, but he had long ago gone away. The fixer hurriedly travels on the train to Minsk and after months of desperate searching meets the old man, the moon on his rabbinic hat, coming home one evening from the synagogue.

"Please, you must go back to Kiev with me and prove my innocence. Tell the officials I didn't do what they say I did."

But the old tzadik does not recognize the fixer. He looks at him long but shakes his head. The wound on his temple has healed and he cannot now recall the night Yakov says he had spent with him in the room above the stable.

When the fixer remembered where he was he tore at his hands with his nails, and he tore at his face.

The snorer awoke with a gasp. "Akimytch," he cried out. "Formerly a tailor. I am innocent," he whimpered. "Don't beat me."

The other one snickered.

"Have you got a cigarette, Potseikin?" the former tailor asked the one on the other mattress. "A piece of butt?"

"Fuck yourself," said the blinker, a man with bloodshot eyes.

"Have you got a cigarette?" Akimytch asked Yakov.

"My bag is empty," said the fixer. He held it up.

"I'll bet you don't know why I'm here," Akimytch said.

"No."

"Neither do I. It's mistaken identity with me. I never did what they say I did, may they choke to death on their mothers' milk. They mistook me for an anarchist."

He began to weep.

"I'm here because of a pack of pamphlets or whatever you call 'em," Potseikin said. "Some poor bastard, a man with wild eyes and a thick greatcoat says to me on Institutsky Street, 'Brother,' he says, 'I have to piss, so hold my bundle a minute, and when I come back here I'll slip you a five-kopek piece, on my honour.' What can you say to a man who has to piss? Could I say no to that? Then he might piss on me. So I held on to his bundle and in two minutes a pig-eyed detective comes running across the street and jabs a gun in my gut so hard it almost busts, and then he marches me off to the Secret Police without listening to a word I say. When we get there three big ones give me a going over with fat sticks till all my bones are cracked, and they show me where the pamphlets say to overthrow the Tsar. Who wants to overthrow the Tsar? Personally, I have only the highest regard for Nicholas the Second and the royal family, especially the young princesses and the poor sick boy, who I love as my own. But nobody believed me and that's why I'm here. It's all the fault of those bastard pamphlets."

"It's mistaken identity with me," said Akimytch. "What's it with you, pal?"

"The same," said Yakov.

"What did they say you did?"

He thought he oughtn't to tell them, but it came out quickly, in accusation of the accusers.

"They say I killed a boy – it's a dirty lie."

There was a deep silence in the cell. Now I've blundered, Yakov thought. He looked for the guard but he had gone for the soup pail.

The two on the straw pallets, their heads together, whispered in each other's ears, first Akimytch whispering, then Potseikin.

"Did you?" Akimytch asked Yakov.

"No, of course not. Why would I kill an innocent child?"

They whispered once more and Potseikin said in a thick voice, "Tell us the truth, are you a Jew?"

"What difference would it make?" Yakov said, but when they were whispering again he was afraid.

"Don't try anything or I'll call the guard."

The one in rags got up and approached the fixer, sneering. "So you're the bastard Jew who killed the Christian boy and sucked the blood out of his bones? I saw it in the papers."

"Leave me in peace," Yakov said. "I've done nothing like that to anybody, not to speak of a twelve-year-old child. It's not in my nature."

"You're a stinking Jew liar."

"Think as you like but let me alone."

"Who else would do anything like that but a mother-fucking Zhid?"

Potseikin pounced on the fixer and with his rotten teeth tried to bite his neck. Yakov shoved him off but Akimytch,

116

foul-breathed, was on his back beating the fixer's head and face with his clammy bony hands.

"Christkiller!"

"Gevalt!" cried Yakov, flailing his arms. Though he whirled, ducked, and struck out with his fists, Potseikin hit him with a knee in the back as Akimytch struck him on the neck with both fists. The fixer went down, his mind darkened in pain. He lay motionless as they kicked him savagely, and felt as he passed out, a terrible rage.

Afterwards he woke on his mattress, and when he heard their snoring, retched. A rat scuttled across his genitals and he bolted up in horror. But there was a bit of horned moon at the small high barred window and he watched for a while in peace.

IV

The stable had burned to the ground in a matter of minutes, Proshko said, spitting at the fixer's feet, and it wouldn't surprise him if it were done with Jewish magic. He pointed to the blackened remains of the stalls where four maddened, rearing, trumpeting horses had died, and a crisscross pile of burnt and broken planks and timbers had fallen from the roof.

The moustached and bearded officials in the brickyard, some uniformed and booted, a few carrying umbrellas although it was no longer raining, and the Secret Police gendarmes, plainclothes detectives, and Kiev City Police – among them also an Imperial Army general with two rows of gold buttons and one of medals across his chest – looked on in silence as the foreman spoke. Grubeshov, in English bowler, mud-spattered gaiters, and rain cape, flushed at Proshko's testimony, whispered in Colonel Bodyansky's lowered ear, clutching his hand tightly, and the colonel earnestly whispered something in return as Yakov licked his dry lips. Bibikov, with small, yellow-muddy, ankle-length shoes, his winter scarf and large hat, standing behind two tight-faced Black Hundreds representatives wearing their accusatory buttons, chain-smoked cigarettes from a box he amiably offered around. Near-by, the pimply Ivan Semyon-ovitch accompanied an oldish priest of the Orthodox Church, Father Anastasy, a "specialist", Yakov had heard it whispered, "of the Jewish religion"; he was a round-shouldered man with a streaked beard, thin hands, and restless dark eyes, dressed in flowing vestments and round pot-hat which he pressed down with his palm when the wind blew. What he was expected to add to the miserable state of Yakov's affairs the fixer didn't know and was afraid to guess. Manacled, his legs chained, nervously exhausted, his body in flight though he tried with ten fingers to hold on to his mind, he stood with five armed guards at his back, apart from the rest. Though almost a month had gone by since his arrest he could still only half believe this had happened to him, someone who did not recognize himself in the dream he was dreaming; and listened stunned to Proshko, as though the accusation of the monstrous crime were both true and an irrelevancy, as though it had happened to someone he didn't know very well, in truth a stranger, although he clearly remembered fearing that something like this might happen to him.

Otherwise the brickyard was deserted on a grey and green overcast Sunday afternoon in what had been a cold May. None of the workers was around except for the drivers Richter and Serdiuk, who listened without speaking and occasionally spat, the Ukrainian holding his cap in his large red hand, ill at ease, the German staring darkly at the former overseer. Nikolai Maximovitch had been expected but Yakov knew it was too late in the day for him to leave the house sober. After a morning fog had thinned and lifted, it began to rain heavily; and it poured again in the afternoon. The horses drawing the half-dozen carriages that had left at intervals from the District Courthouse in the Plossky, and met first in the brickyard, had splashed through puddles, and the motor-car carrying Yakov, Colonel Bodyansky and the gendarmes, had got stuck in the mud on a road in the Lukianovsky, drawing several people, and irritating the Prosecuting Attorney, who made it known to the chauffeur that he didn't want "the matter getting out". Not very much about the fixer had appeared in the newspapers. All they seemed to know was that a Jew from the Podol had been arrested "as a suspicious person", but not who or why. Grubeshov had promised more information at a later date in order not, presently, to impede the investigation. Bibikov, before they left the courthouse, had managed to convey this to Yakov, but not much else.

"Start from the beginning," Grubeshov said to Proshko, dressed in his Sunday thick-trousered suit with short jacket. "– I want to hear your earliest suspicions."

The Prosecuting Attorney had planned this re-enactment, he had told the accused, "to let you know the inescapable logic of our case against you so that you may act accordingly and for your own benefit."

"But how for my benefit?"

"It will become clear to you."

The foreman blew his nose, wiped it in two strokes and thrust the handkerchief into his pants pocket.

"On one look I knew he was a Jew, even though he was faking that he was a Russian. It's easy enough to tell an onion from a radish if you're not colour blind." Proshko

laughed a little from the chest. "Yakov Ivanovitch Dologushev, he called himself, but I knew from the sound of it on
his tongue that the name didn't fit him. A name belongs to
you as your birthright, but it hung on him like a suit of
stolen clothes. I felt in my blood he was a Jew the same way
as you feel in the dark the presence of a ghost. Wait up,
little brother, I thought to myself, something smells fishy
here. Maybe it's his natural smell, or the way he talks
Russian, or maybe it's the flatfooted way he runs when he
chases young boys, but when I looked with both of my eyes
open I saw what I already knew – he was a Zhid and no
two ways about it. You can't make a gentleman out of a
toad, as the saying goes, and a born Jew can't hide the Zhid
in his face. This is a foxy bastard, I thought to myself, and
he thinks he's got it hidden because he wears a belted sheepskin coat and has shaved off his Jewish whiskers and curls,
and maybe it'll be a little slow smoking him out of his hole
now that he's fooled Nikolai Maximovitch, but smoke him
out I will, and with God's help it's what I did."

"Tell the details," said Grubeshov.

"It wasn't more than fifteen minutes after I first saw him
that I went back to the office shack and asked him for his
papers so as to hand them over to the District Police, and
right off he showed me who he was. He lied that he had
given them to the boss and he had registered them with the
police. If a man talks crooked, I thought to myself, he's
crooked elsewhere, and I'll watch out to see where else. I
didn't have long to wait. Once when he was nosing around
the kilns for purposes of his own, I sneaked into the shack
and checked up on his figures in the books. He was crooked
in his accounts and every day entered smaller amounts
than he should so he could keep some roubles for himself –
not so many, a Jew is cunning – maybe three or four or five

122

a day that Nikolai Maximovitch had no suspicions of, and he saved himself a nice little pile in a tin can in his room."

"You're a liar," Yakov said, trembling, "you're the thief and you're putting it on me. You and your drivers stole thousands of bricks from Nikolai Maximovitch, and you hated me for watching you so you couldn't steal more."

Nobody was listening.

"What did he do with the roubles you say he stole?" Bibikov asked the foreman. "There were about ninety in the tin can, if I remember correctly. If he was stealing four roubles a day, let us say, he should have had many more."

"Who knows what a Jew does with money. I've heard it said they take it to bed with them and give it a fuck once in a while. I bet he gave most of it to the Zhidy synagogue in the Podol. They have plenty of uses for a Russian rouble."

"The Secret Police confiscated altogether one hundred and five roubles," Grubeshov announced after conferring with Colonel Bodyansky. "Keep your mouth shut," he said to Yakov. "Answer when you're spoken to."

"What's more," Proshko went on, "he sneaked other Jews into the brickyard, and one was one of those Hasids with a round hat, or whatever you call them, who prayed up there in the stable with this one here. The other one came when they thought nobody was around to watch them. They both tied horns on their heads and prayed to the Jewish God. I watched them through the window and saw them praying and eating matzos. I figured they baked some in the stove up there and I was right, there was half a sack of flour hidden under the bed that the police got. I kept track of them because I had my own suspicions, like I told you. I saw this one here sneaking around like a ghost at night, his face white and eyes strange, looking for something, and I also saw him chasing the boys that I told you about. I was worried he would do them some kind of harm, little knowing how right I was. One day two or three school kids came in the yard with their book satchels. I saw him chase them but they got away over the fence. Once I asked him, 'Yakov Ivanovitch, why did you chase those young school kids, they are good boys and all they want to do is to see how we make bricks,' but he answered me, 'If they are so innocent Jesus Christ will protect them.' He thought Proshko wouldn't know what he meant by that but I did."

Yakov groaned.

"That's why I kept my eye on him and when I couldn't I told the drivers to watch him."

"That's so." Serdiuk, still smelling of horse, nodded, and Richter said yes.

"I saw them praying with their little black hats on, and I spied on them when they were baking those matzos. Then when the boy was murdered and they found him in the cave with all those wounds the morning it was snowing – when the snow came again in April – I saw this one take the other Jew with the round hat down the stairs and they left the brickyard in a hurry. I went up there, walking right in their footsteps in the snow so he wouldn't see I had been there, and that was the day I found pieces of matzos they had baked, half a bag of flour under the bed, his sack of tools, and that bloody rag I told you about. The devil scatters his dung wherever he goes.

"After that he wanted to set the stable on fire to burn the evidence but he saw I had my eye on him. When I met him in the brickyard the blood ran out of his face and he couldn't raise his eyes at me. That was after they had killed the kid.

After the funeral I went to the police, and in a week they came and arrested him. They took the matzos away and the other things that I told you about, but I went up there with Serdiuk and Richter here, to tear up the floorboards – some had certain dark stains on them that we wanted to show the police. Just then we see an old greybeard Jew run out of the stable, and the next thing the place was up in roaring flames, and the whole stable burned down in less than five minutes, so it was just by luck we saved any of the horses. We saved six and lost four. If the fire had been an ordinary kind we would've saved the whole ten, but being as it was, there was something that made it burn as if the wind was caught in it, and it cried out like people were dying and ghosts were going to meet them. They had said some magic words from a Zhidy book, I'll swear to God, and upstairs where this one here had lived before they arrested him, the flames turned an oily green such as I never saw before, and then yellow, and then almost black, and they burned twice as fast as the fire in the stalls even though the loft was full of hay. In the stalls the fire burned orange and red, and it was slower, more like an ordinary fire, so we got six horses out of the burning stalls and lost the other four."

Richter swore every word was true and Serdiuk crossed himself twice.

2

Father Anastasy stiffly embraced Marfa Golov, the haggard mother of the martyred boy, a tallish, scrawny-necked woman with red-rimmed, wet, flecked grey eyes, and dark skin drawn tautly over her face, who tried to curtsy and collapsed in the priest's arms.

"Forgive us our transgressions, Father," she wept.

"You must forgive us, my child," said the priest, in a nasal voice. "The world has sinned against you. In particular, those who sin against our Lord."

He crossed himself, his hand like a bird, and so did some of the officials.

Marfa Golov, when Yakov first saw her waiting for the officials to arrive, was standing, with a thick-shawled neighbour who quickly ran off when the carriages appeared, on the sagging steps of a two-storey wooden house with a peaked corrugated-tin roof. The house overlooked a low-walled cemetery, and in the distance the brickyard, which Bibikov stopped to stare at, its chimneys smokeless on Sunday. It was a box-like house that had once been painted white but was now weathered grey and peeling. The grass-less front yard, muddy from the rain, was surrounded by a high unpainted fence, held together horizontally on the street side by long uneven darkly weathered boards. The road in front of the house where the carriages and motor-car waited was pitted and muddy, and the carriages looked like those of a funeral party except that there was no visible hearse. Marfa, thirty-nine, the newspaper had said, and vaguely pretty, with a tense distracted manner, eyes glancing in every direction, a drawn unhappy mouth and slight chin, wore for the occasion a dark-flowered blouse, long green skirt, and pointed two-tone button shoes. She had pinned a discoloured cameo at her worn throat and thrown a light scarf over her shoulders. And she had on a new white hat topped with a bunch of bright cherries that caused some interested glances. When the fixer was led through the gate into the yard, Marfa burst into sobs. One of the officials in the Prosecuting Attorney's office and a gendarme near by cursed the prisoner under their breaths yet loud enough for him to hear.

"It's surely the one," Marfa gasped.

"Which one is that?" Bibikov asked, snapping on his silver-rimmed pince-nez and staring at her.

"The Jew Zhenia told me about, who had chased him with a long knife."

"Note the identification," said Grubeshov to Ivan Semyonovitch. The assistant hadn't his notebook with him, but he mentioned it to one of the policemen, who wrote it down.

There was a green mildewed stone well in the yard and Bibikov peered down it but could see nothing.

He dropped a small stone down the well and after a while there was a splash. The officials looked at one another but the Investigating Magistrate walked away.

"The room's upstairs, your honour," Marfa said to the Prosecuting Attorney. "It's small as you'll see, but Zhenia was small himself for a lad his age. That's not from me, you'll notice, because I don't lack size, but from his cowardly father who deserted us." She smiled nervously.

Marfa led them in and hurried upstairs to show the officials where the poor child had slept. They wiped their feet on a muddy rag at the door and went up in small hushed groups to stare into the dark tiny cubicle between a large untidy bedroom with a two-pillowed brass bed, and a room with a locked door Marfa said was a storeroom.

"What can a widow do with so many bedrooms? Generally I store things. When my aunt died she left me her furniture although I have enough of my own."

Yakov was ordered to go up after the others had seen the

boy's room. He wanted not to go but knew that if he said so they would drag him up. He went slowly up the stairs in his clanking leg chains that rubbed his ankles sore, followed by three booted gendarmes who waited for him on the landing with drawn pistols. Marfa, Father Anastasy, Grubeshov, Ivan Semyonovitch and Colonel Bodyansky were in the corridor as the Jew glanced furtively into the boy's room. They watched him intently, Grubeshov's lips pursed. The fixer had wanted to look calmly and with dignity but had been unable to. It was as though he expected a wild animal in the room to spring out at him. He glanced fearfully into the tiny cubicle with torn wallpaper and unmade cot, the crumpled bedsheet grey, soiled, the faded blanket torn. Though the room and cot were strange to him, Yakov had a momentary hallucinatory thought he had seen them before. He then recalled his cubicle in the printer's flat in the Podol. This was what he remembered but he worried they thought he was thinking of something that would surely convict him were it known what.

"My darling Zhenechka hoped to be a priest," Marfa whispered loudly to Father Anastasy, dabbing at her reddened eyes with a scented handkerchief. "He was a religious child and worshipped God."

"It was reported to me that he was being prepared for the seminary," said the priest. "One of the monks told me he was a dear boy, in some respects a saintly boy. I understand he had already had a mystical experience. I was also told he loved our priestly vestments and hoped some day to wear them. His death is God's loss."

Marfa wept miserably. Ivan Semyonovitch's eyes clouded and he turned away and wiped them on his coat sleeve. Yakov felt like crying but couldn't.

Then Father Anastasy came down and Bibikov went up

the stairs, squeezing past the gendarmes. He glanced casually into Zhenia's small room, looked around absently, then got down on his knees, and lifting the bed-sheet, peeked under the bed. He touched the floor and examined his soiled finger-tips.

"The floor may be dusty," Marfa said quickly, "but I always empty the chamber-pot."

"Never mind that," said Grubeshov distastefully. "Well, what have you discovered?" he asked Bibikov.

"Nothing."

The Investigating Magistrate glanced quickly into Marfa's bedroom and stopped at the locked door of the other room as if he were listening, but did not try the knob. He then wandered downstairs. Marfa hurriedly attempted to make the boy's bed up but Grubeshov ordered her to leave it alone.

"It will take me only a minute."

"Leave it as it is. The police prefer it that way."

They went downstairs. Although it was drizzling outside, some of the officials were gathered in the yard. The others, including the prisoner and gendarmes who guarded him, met in Marfa's dusty disordered parlour that smelled of tobacco smoke, stale sweet beer, and cabbage. At Grubeshov's request, she pulled open the window vent, and with a dirty rag hastily wiped the seats of a half-dozen chairs nobody sat down in. The prisoner was afraid to sit. Marfa tried to do something to the floor with a broom but the Prosecuting Attorney took it from her.

"This can wait, Marfa Vladimirovna. Please give us your fullest attention."

"I just thought I'd clean up a bit," she hurriedly explained. "To tell the truth, I wasn't expecting so many high officials. I thought the prisoner was coming to see what he had done and why should I clean up for a dirty Jew?"

"That'll do," Grubeshov said. "We're not interested in your household affairs. Go now into the story of what happened to your son."

"Ever since he was little he wanted to be a priest," Marfa wept, "but now he's a dead corpse in his grave."

"Yes, we all know that and it's a tragic story, but perhaps you ought to limit yourself to what you know about the details leading up to the crime."

"First shouldn't I serve tea, do you think, your honour?" she asked, distracted. "The samovar's boiling."

"No," he said. "We are very busy and have much to do before we can return to our homes. Please tell the story – specifically of Zhenia's disappearance and death – how, for instance, you learned of it."

"You," he said to Yakov, who was gazing out the window at the rain in the chestnut trees, "you know well this concerns you so pay attention." In the time the fixer had been in prison the city had turned green and there were sweet-smelling lilacs everywhere but who could enjoy them? Through the open window he could smell the wet grass and new leaves, and where the cemetery ended there were birches with silver trunks. Somewhere near by an organ-grinder was playing a waltz that Zinaida Nikolaevna had played for him once on her guitar, "Summer Is Gone Forever."

"Go on, please," Grubeshov said to Marfa.

She lifted both hands to straighten her hat, then caught his eye and dropped them.

"He was an earnest boy," Marfa quickly began, "and never gave me much trouble as boys do. As for myself I'm a widow of stainless character, pure and simple. My husband,

130

who was a telegrapher, deserted me, as I mentioned before, your honour, and a couple of years later died of galloping consumption, which served him right for the way he mistreated us. I support myself by hard work and that's why my house that you're in isn't the neatest, but my child has always had a roof over his head, and my life has been one of irreproachable toil. If you work like a horse you can't live like the gentry, if you'll pardon my frankness. We got along without the deserter. This house doesn't belong to me, I rent it and sometimes let out a room or two, though one has to be careful of riffraff, especially those not given to paying what they owe to others. I didn't want my child associating with such, so I rarely took boarders in – even though I had to work that much harder – and then only if they were genteel people. But even if he didn't have all the advantages, Zhenia had what he needed and wasn't above showing his appreciation by giving me help – not like some boys I could name you, for instance Vasya Shiskovsky in the next house from here. My own was an obedient lad, an angel. He once asked me if he should leave the ecclesiastical school and become a butcher's apprentice but I advised him, 'Zhenia, my good darling, it's best to go on with your lessons. Get an education and when you're rich some day, you can support your poor mother in her old age.' 'Mamenka,' he answered me, 'I will always take care of you even when you are old and sick.' He was a saintly child, and it didn't in the least surprise me when he came back from his Bible lesson one day and said he wanted to be a priest. My eyes were full of tears that day."

She glanced nervously at Grubeshov, who nodded slightly.

"Go on, Marfa Vladimirovna, tell now what happened towards the end of March, a few short weeks before the

Jewish Passover this year. And speak more slowly so that we can comprehend everything you say. Don't slur your words."

"Are you paying attention?" he asked Yakov.

"The closest, your honour, though I honestly don't understand what this has to do with me. It's all so strange."

"Only be patient," Grubeshov said. "It will be as familiar and close as the nose on your face."

Several of the officials, including the army general, laughed.

"On the morning in the week you mention," said Marfa, darting a glance at the Jew, "it was a Tuesday I'll never forget in my life, Zhenia woke up and got dressed in his black stockings that I had bought him for his name day and left for school as usual at six in the morning. I had to work until long after dark that day, then attend to the marketing so I naturally didn't get home until late. Zhenia wasn't in the house and after I had rested a while – I've had painful varicose veins since giving birth to my child – I went to Sofya Shiskovsky, my neighbour in the next house down a ways, whose Vasya was in Zhenia's form in school, and asked him where my boy was. Vasya said he didn't know because though he had seen Zhenia after school, Zhenia hadn't come home with him as was usual. 'Where did he go?' I said. 'I don't know,' he answered. Ach, I thought, he is at his grandmother's, I won't worry. But on the same night I caught the flu. I had the shakes and shivers for three days and stayed in bed in a weak condition for three more, only getting up, if you'll excuse me, to go to the toilet, or boil up a little rice and water to stop diarrhoea. Zhenia was missing for about a week – six or seven days to be exact, and when I made up my mind to get dressed and report it to the police he was found dead in a cave with forty-seven stabs on his

132

body. The neighbours came into my house with slow steps and sad faces – they looked like dead folk and frightened me before they spoke – then when they told me what horror had happened to me, I cried out, 'My life is over because I've lost my reason to live!'"

Marfa put her hand to her eyes and tottered. Two of the officials stepped towards her but she held on to a chair and remained upright. The men withdrew.

"Excuse me," Bibikov said gently, "but how is it you waited six or seven whole days before thinking to report that your son was missing? If it were my son I would have reported it at once – at the very latest on the night he had not yet appeared in the house. It's true that you were sick but even sick people have been known to pull themselves out of bed and act in emergencies."

"It all depends on how sick they are, if you please, your honour. Whether it's your son or mine, when you're running a high fever and are nauseous besides, your thoughts aren't always at their best. I worried about Zhenia and had terrible nightmares besides. I was afraid he was in some kind of horrible trouble, but I thought I dreamed that because I was feverish. And while I was so sick with the flu, so was my neighbour Sofya, and also Vasya. No one came to knock on my door, as usually happens two or three times during the day. And Yuri Shiskovsky, Sofya's husband, is as likely to knock on a person's door when you need him as Father Christmas. We don't get along at all but that's a story for a winter night. Anyway, if someone had come into my house during those five or six days I would have split both his ears crying out my fears for my poor child, but nobody ever did."

"Let her go on with the story," Grubeshov said to Bibikov. "If necessary you can ask questions later."

The Investigating Magistrate nodded to his colleague. "I assure you it's necessary enough, Vladislav Grigorievitch, but as you please, I'll ask later. As for what else may be necessary, or even not so necessary, for instance this entire procedure during a time of investigation, I think we ought to discuss that too, at least in principle if for no other reason."

"Tomorrow," said Grubeshov. "We'll talk over everything tomorrow."

"Come now to the point of the matter, Marfa Vladimirovna," he said. "Tell us what Zhenia and Vasya Shiskovsky told you about the Jew before the fatal incident."

Marfa had listened intently to the exchange between the men, alternating uneasiness with apparent boredom. When Bibikov was speaking she cast nervous glances around her but lowered her eyes if anyone looked at her.

"Vasya also told me what I heard Zhenia say more than once – that they were afraid of the Jew in the brickyard."

"Go on, we're listening."

"Zhenia told me that one day when he and Vasya were playing in the factory yard they saw two Jews – it was toward nightfall – sneak through the gate and go up the stairs where this one lived."

She glanced at the fixer, then averted her eyes. He was standing with his head bowed.

"Excuse me for interrupting," Bibikov said to the Prosecuting Attorney, "but I would like to understand how the boys identified the two men as Jews?"

Colonel Bodyansky guffawed and Grubeshov smiled.

"Easily, your honour," Marfa said in excitement, "they were wearing Jewish clothes and had long rough beards, not nicely trimmed ones like some of the gentlemen here.

Also the boys used to peek in the window and saw them praying. They wore black hats and robes. The boys were frightened and ran home here. I asked Vasya to stay for a cup of cocoa and slice of white bread with Zhenia, but he was scared sick and said he wanted to go home to his own house."

Grubeshov listened, standing with his thumbs locked behind him, "Please go on."

"I heard from the boys that this one here brought other Jews up in his stable. One was an old man with a black satchel that the Lord knows what they did with. Zhenia once told this one to his face that he would tell the foreman if he chased him again. 'And if you do that I'll kill you once and for all,' said the Jew. One day Zhenia saw him running after another boy in the brickyard, a lad not eight years old from the neighbourhood around here, Andriushka Khototov, whose father is a street sweeper. The boy luckily got out through the open gate, thank the Lord. Then the Jew saw my Zhenia and chased him, but my Zhenia climbed the fence and escaped that time, though he told me his heart hurt because he did not think he would get over the fence before the Jew grabbed him. One day, hiding by the kiln, Zhenia saw two of the Jews try to catch a Russian child and drag him into the stable. But the boy was a smart one and bit, clawed, and screamed so loud they got frightened and let him go. I warned Zhenia more than once not to go back there or he might get kidnapped and killed, and he promised me he wouldn't. I think he didn't for a time, then one night he came home frightened and feverish, and when I cried out, 'Zhenia, what ails you, tell me quickly what happened?' he said that the Jew had chased him with a long knife in the dark among the gravestones in the cemetery. I got down on my knees to him. 'Zhenia Golov, in the name of the Holy

Mother, promise me not to go near that evil Jew again. Don't go in that brickyard.' 'Yes, dear Mamenka,' he said, 'I will promise.' That's what he said, but he went back in there again, anyway. Boys are boys, your honour, as you already know. God knows what draws them to danger, but if I had kept him under lock and key in this house as I sometimes did when he was a little boy he'd be alive today and not a corpse in his coffin."

She fervently crossed herself.

"Marfa Vladimorovna, please tell us what else you were told by the two boys," Grubeshov said to her.

"I was told they had seen a bottle of blood on the Jew's table."

The army general gasped and the officials looked at each other in horror. Yakov stared whitely at Marfa, his lips working in agitation. "There was no bottle of blood on my table," he cried out. "If there was anything it was a jar of strawberry jam. Jam is not blood. Blood is not jam."

"Be quiet!" Grubeshov ordered. "We will inform you when it is your time to speak."

One of the gendarmes pointed his revolver at Yakov.

"Put that foolish gun away," Bibikov said. "The man is chained and manacled."

"Did you personally see 'the bottle of blood'?" he asked Marfa.

"No, but both of the boys did, and they told me about it. They could hardly talk. Their faces were green."

"Then why didn't you report that to the police? It was your duty to, as well as the other incidents you just enumerated, as for instance the suspect chasing your son with a knife. That is a criminal act. This is a civilized society. Such things must be reported to the police."

136

She answered at once: "Because I've had my fill of the police, if you won't mind me saying so, your honour, and with apologies to those of them present that never bothered me. I once complained to them that Yuri Shiskovsky, for reasons that will be kept to myself, struck me on the head with a block of wood, and all morning they kept me in the police station answering personal questions while they filled out long forms, as if I myself were the criminal and not that madman who they let go, although I had a bloody gash in my scalp, and even an idiot would know who had hit who. I can't afford to lose my time like that. I have to earn a living and that's why I didn't report what the boys told me."

"Which is understandable enough," said Grubeshov – turning to the general, who nodded – "although I agree with the Investigating Magistrate that such things should be reported at once. Now finish your story, Marfa Vladimirovna."

"I have finished, there's no more to tell."

"In that case," said the Prosecuting Attorney, addressing the officials, "it's best to move on."

He pulled a thin gold watch from his yellow waistcoat pocket and consulted it closely.

"Vladislav Grigorievitch," Bibikov said, "I must insist on my prerogative to question the witness."

Marfa's intent gaze at him changed from fear to anger.

"What have I done to you?" she cried out.

"Neither of us has done anything to the other, that's not the point. Marfa Golov, I would like to ask you a question or two. Please, Vladislav Grigorievitch, I insist. Unfortunately, I can't go into certain things just now, but one or two questions I insist on asking and I would like them answered honestly and directly. Is it true, for instance, Marfa Golov, that you receive stolen goods from a gang of thieves, one of whom is or was your lover who often visits this house?"

"You needn't bother to answer that," Grubeshov said, flushing. "It's irrelevant to the matter at issue."

"I insist it is not so irrelevant, Vladislav Grigorievitch."

"No, I don't receive such goods," said Marfa, white-lipped, her eyes darkening. "That's a filthy rumour spread by my enemies."

"Is that your response?"

"Of course it is."

"Very well, then. Is it true that a year ago last January you threw the contents of a phial of carbolic acid into the eyes of your lover and blinded him for life, a man whom you have since become reconciled with?"

"Is he the one who reported me?" she asked, enraged.

"Reported you?"

"Told you these filthy lies?"

"Boris Alexandrovitch, as your superior in rank, I forbid these questions," Grubeshov said, irritated. "If you have anything of that nature to ask, please do so in my office tomorrow morning, though I personally don't see how such irrelevancies can matter. They do not change the weight of the significant evidence. We must absolutely get on now. It's Sunday and we all have obligations to our families."

"What is the 'significant evidence' you refer to?"

"The evidence we have been engaged in collecting, including the evidence of history."

"History is not law."

"We will see about that."

"I must insist on a reply from Marfa Golov."

"I have no more to say than I've already said," Marfa answered haughtily. "He used to beat me up and I defended myself. My legs and back were black and blue for months where he beat me, and once he smashed me in the eye so hard it ran pus for three weeks."

"Is it true that he also beat your son, once so severely that the boy lost consciousness?"

"I forbid you to answer," Grubeshov shouted.

"Don't be a fool," Colonel Bodyansky said to Bibikov.

"The Jew killed my child," Marfa cried out. "Somebody ought to scratch his eyes." She ran to the window and called out of the open vent to the gravestones in the cemetery, "Zhenia, my baby, come home! Come home to your mother!"

She wept heartbrokenly.

She's insane, thought Yakov. So is her hat with the cherries.

"See how he glares at me like a starving wolf from the forest," Marfa, turning to the fixer, shouted. "Make him stop!"

There was a stir among the officials. Two of the gendarmes pinned the prisoner by his arms.

Marfa, glaring at him, attempted then to remove her hat. Her eyelids fluttered, and moaning she sank to the floor. The hat rolled off her head, but before fainting she gazed loosely around to see where it was. Father Anastasy and Colonel Bodyansky bent to assist her.

When Marfa recovered only the police and gendarmes were in the room with her and the prisoner. Bibikov, to Yakov's misery, had left first, and he saw him, through the window, walk down the muddy road and get into a carriage alone. The dead boy's mother asked for her hat, blew on it, and put it carefully away in a sideboard drawer.

She covered her head with a coarse black shawl.

3

Grubeshov, in his bowler and wet rain cape, hovered over Father Anastasy with a large black umbrella as the wet-lipped priest, standing on a low flat rock, his voice rising and falling sometimes out of context with what he was saying, nasally recited the blood guilt of the Jewish Nation.

The group of officials and police had abandoned the carriages and motor-car at the bottom of an inclined street paved with rocks, lined on one side by a row of blackened shanties from which people stared at them out of windows and doorways, but no one came out to watch. A flock of pigeons rose in the street and two small white dogs, barking shrilly, darted into the houses as the crowd of officials approached. On foot they climbed first up the steps of a terraced hill from which the winding Dnieper was visible in the distance, then descended into a muddy ravine, and along it to the bottom of an almost perpendicular rocky hill with some caves in its face, in one of which the body of Zhenia Golov had been found. This cave, minutely described in the newspapers Yakov had read on the day of the discovery of the boy's body, one of those cut into the hill by religious hermits centuries ago, was about fifteen feet up its face. To get up into it one climbed the rough steps that had been hewn into the rocky hill. On top of it was a sparse birchwood grove with thin-trunked white trees full of chirping swallows, and beyond that lay a flat section of the outskirts of the city consisting of scattered houses and empty lots, about two versts from Nikolai Maximovitch's brick factory.

"There is from here an almost straight road from the

brick factory where Zhenia was presumed to be killed," Grubeshov said.

"But, permit me, Vladislav Grigorievitch, to draw your attention to the fact that the road from Marfa Golov's house is just as straight and a little shorter," said Bibikov.

"In any case," the Prosecuting Attorney answered, "the most important evidence will be the testimony of the experts."

The priest, a long-haired, large-nosed man whose breath smelled of garlic, was standing under Grubeshov's umbrella before a loose semicircle of listeners but the Prosecuting Attorney had Yakov brought up close, the officials giving way as he was pushed forward, his chains rattling, by his guards. Bibikov, standing in the rear, looked on, impassively smoking. It was still drizzling and the fixer had lost his cap, unsettling him further, more than he thought possible in his present condition. It's only a cap, not my life; but the thought was a terrible one, because it was the first time he had admitted to himself he was afraid for his life. Fearing he was about to hear some secret fact that would absolutely condemn him once it was known, he stood inch-deep in the mud, breathing thickly, listening transfixed.

"My dear children," said the priest to the Russians, wringing his dry hands, "if the bowels of the earth were to open to reveal the population of human dead since the beginning of the world, you would be astonished to see how many innocent Christian children among them have been tortured to death by Christ-hating Jews. Throughout the ages, as described in their holy books and various commentaries, the voice of Semitic blood directs them to desecrations, unspeakable horrors — for example, the Talmud, which likens blood to water and milk, and preaches hatred of gentiles, who are characterized as being not human, no more than animals. 'Thou shalt not kill' does not apply to us, for do not they also write in their books: 'Murder the good among gentiles'? This, perfidy, too, is prescribed in their Kabbala, the book of Jewish magic and alchemy, wherein the name of Satan is invoked; hence there have been multitudes of slaughtered innocent children whose tears have not moved their murderers to mercy."

His eyes darted over the faces of the officials but no one moved.

"The ritual murder is meant to re-enact the crucifixion of our dear Lord. The murder of Christian children and the distribution of their blood among Jews are a token of their eternal enmity against Christendom, for in murdering the innocent Christian child, they repeat the martyrdom of Christ. Zhenia Golov, in the loss of his own warm blood, symbolizes to us our Lord's loss of his precious lifeblood, drop by cruel drop, as he hung in pain on the wooden cross to which the anti-Christ had nailed him. It is said that the murder of the gentile – any gentile – hastens the coming of their long-awaited Messiah, Elijah, for whom they eternally leave the doors open but who has never, during all the ages since his first coming, bothered to accept the invitation to enter and sit in the empty chair. Since the destruction of their Temple in Jerusalem by the Legions of Titus there has been no sacrificial altar for animals in their synagogues, and it has come about, therefore, that the killing of gentiles, in particular innocent children, is accepted as a fitting substitute. Even their philosopher Maimonides, whose writings were suppressed in our country in 1844, orders Jews to murder Christian children. Did I not tell you they think of us as animals?

"In the recorded past," said Father Anastasy in his nasally musical voice, "the Jew has had many uses for

142

Christian blood. He has used it for purposes of sorcery and witches' rituals, and for love potions and well poisoning, fabricating a deadly venom that spread the plague from one country to another, a mixture of Christian blood from a murdered victim, their own Jewish urine, the heads of poisonous snakes, and even the stolen mutilated host – the bleeding body of Christ himself. It is written that all Jews require some Christian blood for the prolongation of their lives else they die young. And in those days they considered our blood to be – this too is recorded – the most effective therapeutic for the cure of their diseases. They used it, according to their old medical books, to heal their women in childbirth, stop hemorrhages, cure the blindness of infants, and to alleviate the wounds of circumcision."

One of the Kiev police officials, Captain Korimzin, a man in a damp coat and muddy boots, secretly made the sign of the cross. Yakov felt faint. The priest, staring at him intently for a minute, went on, and although he spoke calmly his gestures were agitated. The Russians continued to listen with grave interest.

"There are those among us, my children, who will argue that these are superstitious tales of a past age, yet the truth of much I have revealed to you – I do not say it is all true – must be inferred from the very frequency of the accusations against the Jews. None can for ever conceal the truth. If the bellman is dead the wind will toll the bell. Perhaps in this age of science we can no longer accept every statement of accusation made against this unfortunate people; however we must ask ourselves how much truth remains despite our reluctance to believe. I do not say that all Jews are guilty of these crimes and that pogroms should therefore be instituted against them, but that there are certain sects among them, in particular the Hasidim and their leaders, the tzadikim, who commit in secret crimes such as I have described to you, which the gentile world, despite its frequent experience with them, seems to forget until, lo! another poor child disappears and is found dead in this fashion: his hands tied behind his back, and his body punctured by a sharp weapon in several places, the number of wounds according to magic numbers: 3, 7, 9, 13, in the manner of such crimes of former times. We know that their Passover, though they ascribe to it other uses, is also a celebration of the crucifixion. We know that is the time they kidnap gentiles for their religious ceremonials. Here in our Holy City, during the Polovostian raids in the year 1100, the monk Eustratios was abducted from the Pechera Monastery and sold to the Jews of Kherson, who crucified him during Passover. Since they no longer dare such open crimes they celebrate the occasion by eating matzos and unleavened cakes at the Seder service. But even this act conceals a crime because the matzos and cakes contain the blood of our martyrs, though of course the tzadikim deny this. Thus through our blood in their Passover food they again consume the agonized body of the living Christ. I give you my word, my dear children, that this is the reason why Zhenia Golov, this innocent child who wished to enter the priesthood, was destroyed!"

The priest wiped one eye, then the other, with a white handkerchief. Two of the guards standing nearest the fixer edged away from him.

But then Yakov cried out, "It's all a fairy-tale, every bit of it. Who could ever believe such a thing? Not me!" His voice quavered and his face was bloodless.

"Those who can understand will believe," said the priest.

"Be respectful if you know what's good for you," Grubeshov said heatedly in an undertone. "Listen and learn!"

"How can it be so if the opposite is true," the fixer

144

shouted, his throat thick. "It's all right to theorize with a fact or two but I don't recognize the truth in what's been said. If you please, your reverence, everybody knows the Bible forbids us to eat blood. That's all over the book, in the laws and everything. I've forgotten most of what I knew about the sacred books, but I've lived among the people and know their customs. Many an egg my own wife would throw out to the goat if it had the smallest spot of blood on the yolk. 'Raisl,' I said, 'take it easy. We can't afford to live like kings,' but there was no getting the egg back on the table, either by hook or by crook, once she took it off, even admitting anyone wanted to, which I never did – you get used to the customs. What she did was final, your reverence. I never said, 'Bring back the bloody egg,' and she would have thrown it at me if I had. She also soaked for hours the little meat or chicken we ate, to wash out every fleck of blood, and then sprinkled it with salt so as to be sure she had drained out every last drop. The rinsings with water were endless. That's the truth of it, I swear. I swear I'm innocent of this crime you say I did, not you personally, your reverence, but some of the officials here. I'm not a Hasid and I'm not a tzadik. I'm a fixer by trade, it's a poorer trade than most, and formerly for a short time I was a soldier in the Imperial Army. In fact, to tell the whole truth, I'm not a religious man, I'm a freethinker. At first my wife and I quarrelled about this but I said a man's religion is his own business, and that's all there is to it, if you'll pardon me for saying so, your reverence. Anyway, I never touched that boy or any boy in my life. I was a boy myself once and it's a time I find hard to forget. I'm affectionate to children and I would have been a happy man if my wife had given birth to a child. It's not in my nature to do anything such as has been described, and if anyone thinks so it's mistaken identity for sure."

He had turned to the officials. They had listened courteously, even the two Black Hundreds representatives, though the shorter of them could not hide the distaste he felt for the fixer. The other now walked away. One man in a round cloth cap smiled sweetly at Yakov, then gazed impassively into the far distance where the golden cupolas of a cathedral rose above the trees.

"You'd be better off confessing," Grubeshov said, "instead of raising this useless stink." He asked the priest's pardon for his language.

"Confessing what, your honour, if as I told you I didn't do it? I can confess to you some things but I can't confess this crime. You'll have to excuse me there – I didn't do it. Why would I do such a thing anyway? You're mistaken, your honour. Somebody has made a serious mistake."

But no one would admit it and a heavy sadness settled on him.

"Confessing how it was done," Grubeshov replied. "How you enticed the boy into the stable with sweets, and then two or three of you pounced on him, gagged his mouth, tied him hand and foot, and dragged him up the stairs to your habitat. There you prayed over him with those black hats and robes on, undressed the frightened child, and began to stab him in certain places, twelve stabs first, then another making thirteen wounds – thirteen each in the region of the heart, on the neck, from which most of the blood is drawn, and on the face – according to your cabalistic books. You tormented and terrified him, enjoying the full shuddering terror of the child victim and his piteous pleas for mercy, in the meanwhile collecting his dripping lifeblood into bottles until you had bled him white. The five or six litres of warm blood you put into a black satchel, and this, if I understand

146

the custom, was delivered by a hunchback Jew to the synagogue in time for making the matzos and afikomen. And when poor Zhenia Golov's heart was drained of blood and he lay on the floor lifeless, you and the tzadik Jew with the white stockings picked him up and carried him here in the dead of night and left his corpse in the cave. Then you both ate bread and salt so that his ghost would not haunt you and hurried away before the sun rose. Fearing the discovery of the bloodstains on your floor, you later sent one of your Jews to burn down Nikolai Maximovitch's stable. That is what you ought to confess."

The fixer, moaning, wrung his hands and beat them against his chest. He looked for Bibikov but the Investigating Magistrate and his assistant had disappeared.

"Take him up to the cave," Grubeshov ordered the guards.

Shutting his umbrella, he quickly preceded them, scampering up the steps, and entered the cave.

The leg chains were too short for Yakov to climb the steep steps, so he was seized under the arms by two of the gendarmes and dragged and pushed up, the other guards following directly behind. Then one guard went into the cave and the others shoved the fixer in through the narrow stone opening.

Inside the dank cave, smelling of death, in the dim light of a semicircle of dripping candles fastened on the wall, Grubeshov produced Yakov's tool sack.

"Aren't these your tools, Yakov Bok? They were found in your habitat in the stable by the driver Richter."

Yakov identified them in the candlelight.

"Yes, your honour, I've had them for years."

"Look at this rusty knife and these awls cleansed of blood with this rag, and now deny these instruments were used by you and your gang of Jews to perforate and bleed the body of a sweet and innocent Christian child!"

The fixer forced himself to look. He gazed at the gleaming point of the awl, and beyond it, into the depths of the cave which he now saw clearly, everyone present, among them Marfa Golov, her head wrapped in a black shawl, her wet eyes reflecting the candle lights, wailing on her knees at the bier of her Zhenia, disinterred from his grave for the occasion, lying naked in death, the wounds of his grey shrunken pitiful body visible in the light of two long thickly dripping white candles burning at his large head and small feet.

Yakov hastily counted the wounds on the child's bloated face, and cried out, "Fourteen!"

But the Prosecuting Attorney replied these were two magic groups of seven, and Father Anastasy, the stink of garlic rising from his head, fell on his knees and with a quiet moan began to pray.

V

The days were passing and the Russian officials were waiting impatiently for his menstrual period to begin. Grubeshov and the army general often consulted the calendar. If it didn't start soon they threatened to pump blood out of his penis with a machine they had for that purpose. The machine was a pump made of iron with a red indicator to show how much blood was being drained out. The danger of it was that it didn't always work right and sometimes sucked every drop of blood out of the body. It was used exclusively on Jews; only their penises fitted it.

In the morning the guards came into the cell and awakened him roughly. He was searched carefully and ordered to dress. Yakov was manacled and chained, then marched up two flights of stairs – he had hoped to Bibikov's office but it was to the Prosecuting Attorney's across the hall. In the anteroom, on a bench against the wall in the rear two men in threadbare suits looked up furtively at the

149

prisoner, then lowered their eyes. They are spies, he thought. Grubeshov's office was a large high-ceilinged room with a long ikon of a crucified blue-haloed Christ on the wall behind the prosecutor's desk, where he sat reading legal documents and referring to open law books. The fixer was ordered to sit in a chair facing Grubeshov, and the guards lined up behind him.

The day was uncomfortably warm, the windows shut against the heat. The prosecutor wore a light greenish suit with the same soiled yellow vest and black bow tie. His side-whiskers were brushed, and he mopped his moist face and palms and wiped the back of his heavy neck with a large handkerchief. Yakov, disturbed by his bad dream of that morning, and almost unable to look at the Prosecuting Attorney since his performance at the cave, felt he was suffocating.

"I have decided to send you to the preliminary confinement cell in the Kiev Prison to await your trial," Grubeshov said, blowing his nose and cleaning it slowly. "It is, of course, not easy to predict when it will begin, so I thought I would inquire whether you had become more co-operative? Since you have had time to reflect on your situation, perhaps you are now willing to tell the truth. What do you say? Further resistance will gain you only headaches. Co-operation will perhaps ease your situation."

"What else is there to say, your honour?" the fixer sighed sadly. "I've looked in my small bag of words and I have nothing more to say except that I'm innocent. There's no evidence against me, because I didn't do what you say I did."

"That's too bad. Your role in this murder was known to us before you were arrested. You were the only Jew living in the district, with the exceptions of Mandelbaum and

Litvinov, Merchants of the First Guild, who weren't in Russia during the time of the commission of the crime, perhaps on purpose. We suspected a Jew at once because a Russian couldn't possibly commit that kind of crime. He might cut a man's throat in a fight, or suddenly kill a person with two or three heavy blows, but no Russian would maliciously torture an innocent child by inflicting forty-seven deadly wounds on his body."

"Neither would I," said the fixer. "It's not in my nature, whatever else is."

"The weight of the evidence is against you."

"Then maybe the evidence is wrong, your honour?"

"Evidence is evidence, it can't be wrong."

Grubeshov's voice became persuasive. "Tell me the honest truth, Yakov Bok, didn't the Jewish Nation put you up to this crime? You seem like a serious person – perhaps you were unwilling to do it but they urged it on you, made threats or promises of certain sorts, and you reluctantly carried out the murder for them? To put it in other words, wasn't it their idea rather than yours? If you'll admit that, I'll tell you frankly – I'll put it this way – your life would be easier. We will not prosecute to the full extent of our powers. Perhaps after a short while you will be paroled and your sentence suspended. In other words, there are 'possibilities'. All we ask is your signature – that's not so much."

Grubeshov's face glistened, as though he were making a greater effort than was apparent.

"How could I do such a thing, your honour? I couldn't do such a thing. Why should I blame it on innocent people?"

"History has proved they are not so innocent. Besides I don't understand your false scruples. After all, you're an admitted freethinker, this admission occurred in my presence. The Jews mean very little to you. I size you up as a man who is out for himself, though I can't blame you. Come, here is an opportunity to free yourself from the confines of the net you have fallen into."

"If the Jews don't mean anything to me, then why am I here?"

"You are foolish to lend yourself to their evil aims. What have they done for you?"

"At the very least, your honour, they've let me alone. No, I couldn't sign such a thing."

"Then keep in mind that the consequences for you can be very grave. The sentence of the court will be the least of your worries."

"Please," said the fixer, breathing heavily, "do you really believe those stories about magicians stealing the blood out of a murdered Christian child to mix in with matzos? You are an educated man and would surely not believe such superstitions."

Grubeshov sat back, smiling slightly. "I believe you killed the boy Zhenia Golov for ritual purposes. When they know the true facts, all Russia will believe it. Do you believe it?" he asked the guards.

The guards swore they did.

"Of course we believe it," Grubeshov said. "A Jew is a Jew, and that's all there is to it. Their history and character are unchangeable. Their nature is constant. This has been proved in scientific studies by Gobineau, Chamberlain and others. We here in Russia are presently preparing one on Jewish facial characteristics. Our peasants have a saying that a man who steals wears a hat that burns. With a Jew it is the nose that burns and reveals the criminal he is."

He flipped open a notebook to a page of pen-and-ink sketches, turning the book so that Yakov could read the printing at the top of the page: "Jewish noses."

152

"Here, for instance, is yours." Grubeshov pointed to a thin high-bridged nose with slender nostrils.

"And this is yours," Yakov said hoarsely, pointing to a short, fleshy, broad-winged nose.

The Prosecuting Attorney, though his colour had deepened, laughed thinly. "You are a witty man," he said, "but it won't do you any good. Your fate is foreseen. Ours is a humane society but there are ways of punishing hardened criminals. Perhaps I ought to remind you – to show you how well off you are – how your fellow Jews were executed in the not too distant past. They were hanged wearing caps full of hot pitch and with a dog hanging beside them to show the world how despised they were."

"A dog hangs a dog, your honour."

"If you can't bite don't show your teeth." Grubeshov, his neck inflamed, slashed the fixer across the jaw with a ruler. Yakov cried out as the wood snapped, one piece hitting the wall. The guards began to beat his head with their fists but the Prosecuting Attorney waved them away.

"You can cry to Bibikov from now to doomsday," he shouted at the fixer, "but I'll keep you in prison till the flesh rots off your bones piece by piece. You will beg me to let you confess who compelled you to murder that innocent boy!"

2

He feared the prison would go badly for him and it went badly at once. It's my luck, he thought bitterly. What do they say? – "If I dealt in candles the sun wouldn't set." Instead, I'm Yakov Fixer and it sets each hour on the stroke. I'm the kind of man who finds it perilous to be alive. One thing I must learn is to say less – much less – much less, or I'll ruin myself. As it is I'm already ruined.

The Kiev Prison, also in the Lukianovsky, was a high-walled old grey fortress-like building with a large interior muddy yard, strewn on the iron gate side with junk piles – a broken wagon, rotting mattresses, blackened boards, barrels of rubbish, rock and sandpiles where prisoners sometimes worked with cement. A clear area between the administrative offices on the west and the main cell block was the promenade grounds. Yakov and his guards had got to the prison on a trolley, a ride of several versts from the District Courthouse where he had been in jail until then. At the prison the fixer was greeted by the cross-eyed warden, "Hello, blood-drinker, welcome to the Promised Land." The Deputy Warden, a lean, narrow-faced man with depthless eyes and a four-fingered right hand, said, "Here we'll feed you flour and blood till you shit matzos." The sub-officials and clerks rushed out of their offices to see the Jew, but Warden Grizitskoy, a man of sixty-five, with a limp yellowish grey beard, a khaki uniform with gold epaulets, and a visored cap, shoved open a door and led the fixer into an inner office, where he sat down at his desk.

"I don't want your kind here," he said, "but I have no choice in the matter. I'm the Tsar's servant and follow his orders faithfully. You are the lowest of Jewish scum – I've read of your deeds – but nevertheless a charge of his Imperial Majesty Nicholas the Second. So here you'll stay till they tell me otherwise. You'd better behave yourself. Follow the rules and regulations and do as you're told. Quickly does it. Under no circumstances are you to attempt to communicate with any person outside this prison unless I authorize it. If you make trouble you will be shot in your tracks. Understood?"

"How long must I stay here?" Yakov managed to ask. "I mean considering I haven't yet been tried."

"As long as the proper authorities deem necessary. Now keep your questions to yourself and go along with the sergeant. He will tell you what to do."

The sergeant, a man with drooping moustaches, led the fixer down the corridor past some dingy offices from whose doorways the clerks were staring out, to a long room with a counter and several benches where he was ordered to undress. Yakov changed into a sack-like white jacket, smelling of human sweat, and a pair of shapeless linen trousers. He was handed a shirt without buttons and a worn greatcoat that had once been brown and was now grey, to sleep in or under at night. As he was pulling off his boots to change into a pair of stiff prison shoes, a wave of oppressive darkness swept over him. Though he felt like fainting he wouldn't give them the satisfaction.

"Sit down in that chair for your haircut," the sergeant ordered.

Yakov sat down in a straightback chair, but as the prison barber was about to crop his hair with a pair of large clippers, the sergeant, checking his official paper, stopped him.

"Never mind that. The orders say let him keep his head of hair."

"It's always like that," said the barber, incensed. "These pricks are born with privileges."

"Cut it off!" shouted Yakov, "cut off my hair!"

"Silence!" ordered the sergeant. "Learn to follow orders! Move on!"

He unlocked a metal door with a large key and followed the fixer down a dimly lit dank corridor to a large crowded cell with a barred grating on one side, and a wall on the other containing two high small dirty windows through which little light penetrated. A smelly urinal, no more than an open drain, ran along the rear wall of the cell.

"It's the thirty-day cell," said the sergeant. "You stay here for a month and either you go on trial or they transfer you elsewhere."

"Where elsewhere?"

"You'll find out."

Wherever it is what difference does it make? the fixer thought blackly.

The noise in the cell quieted as the door clanked open, and the silence deepened as though a quilt had been thrown over the prisoners as they watched Yakov enter. After the door shut behind him they began talking and moving again. There were about twenty-five men in the room, their searing stench in the almost airless cell nauseating. Some sat on the floor playing cards, two men danced closely together, a few wrestled or sparred, fell over each other, got kicked and cursed at. An old fanatic jumped repeatedly from the seat of a broken stool. A man with a sick sunken face hammered his shoe with the heel of another. There were a few benches and tables in the cells but no cots or mattresses. The prisoners slept on a low wooden platform along the outer wall, raised a centimetre from the damp filthy floor. Yakov sat alone in the farthest corner, reflecting on his wretched fate. He would have torn out fistfuls of his hair but was afraid to be noticed.

3

A guard with a gun outside the grating shouted "Supper!" and two other guards opened the cell door and delivered three steaming wooden pails of soup. The prisoners ran with a roar to the pails, crowding around each. Yakov, who had eaten nothing that day, got up slowly. A guard handed out a wooden spoon to one prisoner in each group around the three pails. Sitting on the floor before his pail, the prisoner was allowed to eat ten spoonfuls of the watery cabbage soup, thickened with a bit of barley, then had to pass the spoon to the next one in line. Those who tried to take extra spoonfuls were beaten by the others. After each prisoner had had his quota, the first began again.

Yakov edged close to the nearest pail but the one eating the soup, a clubfoot with a scarred head, stopped spooning, reached into the pail, and with a shout of triumph plucked out half a dead mouse, its entrails hanging. The prisoner held the mouse by the tail, hastily spooning down the soup with his other hand. Two of the prisoners violently twisted the spoon out of his hand and shoved him away from the pail. The clubfoot limped over to the men at the next pail and dangled the mouse in front of their faces, but though they cursed him into the ground no one left the pail. So he clumsily danced around with his dead mouse. Yakov glanced into the second pail, already empty except for a few dead cockroaches floating at the bottom. He did not look into the third pail. Nor did he care for the colourless tea that was served in tin mugs without sugar. He had hoped for a bit of bread but was given none because his name had not been entered on the bread list by the sergeant. That night when the other prisoners were snoring side by side on the platform, the fixer, wrapped in his greatcoat, though it was not a cold night, walked back and forth the length of the cell in the thick dark until the nails in his shoes bit into his feet. When he lay down exhausted, covering his face with half a sheet of newspaper he had found in the cell, to keep off the flies, he was at once awakened by the clanging bell.

At breakfast he gulped down the weak tea that smelled like wood rotting but could not touch the watery grey gruel in the pails. He had heard the wooden pails were in use in the bathhouse when they were not filled with soup or gruel. He asked for bread but the guard said he was still not on the list.

"When will I be?"

"Fuck you," said the guard. "Don't make trouble."

The fixer noticed that the mood of the prisoners to him, neutral to begin with, had altered. The men were quieter, subdued. During the morning they congregated in groups close to the urinal, whispering, casting glances at Yakov. The clubfoot from time to time appraised him with shrewd and cunning eyes.

Yakov felt icicles sprout in his blood. Something has happened, he thought. Maybe somebody told them who I am. If they think I killed a Christian boy they might want to kill me.

In that case should he cry out to the guard and ask to be transferred to another cell before they murdered him in this? And if he did would he live long enough to get there? Suppose the prisoners rushed him and the guards made no move to defend him?

During the morning "promenade", the ten-minute exercise break when the men marched in double lines of twelve around the yard, ten paces between each group, as armed guards, some with coiled bullwhips, stood at the foot of the high thick walls, the clubfoot, who had slipped into line next to Yakov, said in a whisper, "Why isn't your head shaved like the rest of us?"

"I don't know," Yakov whispered. "I told the barber to go ahead and do it."

158

"Are you a stool pigeon or squealer? The men are suspicious of you."

"No, no, tell them I'm not."

"Then why do you sit apart from us? Who the hell do you think you are?"

"To tell the truth my feet hurt in these shoes. Also it's my first time in prison. I'm trying to get used to it but it's not so easy."

"Are you expecting any food packages?" asked the clubfoot.

"Who would send me packages? I have nobody to send me a package. My wife left me. Everyone I know is poor."

"Well, if you get one, share and share alike is my motto. That's the rule here."

"Yes, yes."

The clubfoot limped along in silence.

They don't know who I am, Yakov thought. From now on I'd better be sociable. Once they find out it will be blows, not questions.

But when the prisoners had marched back into the cell there were whispered arguments among them, and Yakov, remembering how he had been beaten in the District Courthouse cell, felt himself sweating hotly.

Afterwards, another prisoner, a tall man with humid eyes, detached himself from a group of others and approached Yakov. He was heavily built, with a pale hard intense face, an almost black neck, and thin bent legs. He walked forward slowly, oddly, as though afraid something might fall out of his clothes. The fixer, sitting on the floor with his back to the wall, scrambled up quickly.

"Listen, little brother," the other prisoner began, "I am Fetyukov. The prisoners have sent me to talk to you."

"If you're worried that I'm a stool pigeon," Yakov said hastily, "you've got the wrong worry. I'm here like everybody else, waiting for my trial. I haven't asked for any privileges, not that they would give me any. I'm not even getting a bread ration. As for my hair, I told the barber to go ahead and cut it off but the sergeant said not to, though don't ask me why."

"What are you accused of?"

The fixer touched his lips with a dry tongue. "Whatever they've accused me of I didn't do. I give you my word. It's too complicated to go into without turning it into a wearying tale, something I don't understand myself."

"I'm a murderer," said Fetyukov. "I stabbed a stranger at the inn in my village. He provoked me so I stabbed him twice, once in the chest, and when he was falling, once in the back. That was the end of him. I had had more than a drop or two, but when they told me what I had done I was greatly surprised. I'm a peaceful man, I never make trouble if you don't provoke me. Who would've thought I could murder anybody? If you had told me any such thing I would have laughed at you to your face."

The fixer, staring at the murderer, edged sideways along the wall. At the same time he saw two other prisoners sneaking up on him, one from either side. As he cried out, Fetyukov reached behind him whipping a short heavy stick out of his trousers. He struck Yakov a hard blow on the head. The fixer went down on one knee, holding both hands over his pain-racked, bloody head, then fell over.

He awoke, lying on the clammy wooden platform. His head ached sickeningly and a searing pain throbbed on the left side of his skull. His fingers sought out the wet swollen cut on his scalp. Blood dripped from it. He was anguished. Would he be beaten every time he was moved to

160

another cell and met other prisoners? The fixer dizzily sat up, blood trickling down his face.

"Wipe it off," advised an old man with cracked eye-glasses, peering down at him. It was the slop-pail man who took care of the excrement buckets, brought in drinking water, and occasionally swept the wet floor. "Use the water bucket by the door."

"Why do you hit a man who has done nothing to you? What have I done to you?"

"Listen, matey," the old man whispered, "wash the blood off before the guard comes or the men will kill you."

"Let them kill me," he shouted.

"I told you he's a shitnose squealer," the clubfoot said from the other side of the cell. "Finish him off, Fetyukov."

A nervous murmur rose among the prisoners.

Two guards came running in the corridor, one carrying a shotgun. They peered through the grating.

"What's going on here? Cut out the noise, you pigs, or you'll live on half rations for a week."

The other guard stared through the barred grating into the gloomy cell.

"Where's the Jew?" he called.

There was dead silence. The prisoners looked among themselves; some glanced furtively at Yakov.

After a while Yakov said he was there. A low murmur came from the prisoners. The guard pointed a shotgun at them and the murmur ceased.

"Where?" said the guard. "I can't see you."

"Here," said Yakov. "There's nothing to see."

"The sergeant wrote your name on the bread list. You'll get your six ounces tonight."

"In the meantime you can dream of matzos," said the

guard with the gun. "Also the blood of Christian martyrs, if you know what I mean."

When the guards left the prisoners talked excitedly among themselves. Yakov felt renewed fright.

Fetyukov, the murderer, approached again. The fixer rose tensely, his hand clawing the wall.

"Are you the Jew they say has murdered a Russian lad?"

"They lie," Yakov said hoarsely, "I'm innocent."

The mutterings of the prisoners filled the cell. One of them shouted, "Jew bastard!"

"That's not why I hit you," said Fetyukov. "Your head wasn't shaved and we thought you were a spy. We did it to see if you would report us to the guard. If you had done that it would have finished you off. The clubfoot would have knifed you. We are going on trial and don't want anybody testifying what he has heard in this cell. I didn't know you were a Jew. But if I had I wouldn't have hit you. When I was a boy I was apprenticed to a Jew blacksmith. He wouldn't have done what they say you did. If he drank blood he would have vomited it up. And he wouldn't have harmed a Christian child. I'm sorry I hit you, it was a mistake."

"It was a mistake," said the clubfoot.

Yakov went unsteadily to the water bucket. The bucket stank but he sank to his knees and poured some water over his head.

After that the prisoners lost interest in him and turned to other things. Some of them went to sleep on the platform and some played cards.

That night Fetyukov woke the fixer and gave him a piece of sausage he had saved from a package his sister had sent him. Yakov gobbled it up. The murderer also handed him a wet rag to press down the swollen cut on his head.

162

"Tell the truth," he whispered, "did you kill that lad? Maybe you did it for a different reason? You might have been drunk."

"For no other reason," Yakov said. "And I wasn't drunk. It never happened, I'm innocent."

"I wish I were innocent," sighed Fetyukov. "It was a terrible thing I did. The man was a stranger to me. One must protect strangers, it says so in the Book. I had had a drop, you understand, and the next thing I knew I grabbed up a knife and he was dead at my feet. God, who gives us life, lets it hang by a thread. One blow and it's torn away. Don't ask me why unless the devil is the stronger. If I could give that man his life again I would. I would say take your life and don't come near me again. I don't know why I did it but I don't want to be a murderer. Things are bad enough as they are, who needs worse? Now they'll pack me off to a prison camp in Siberia and if I live out my term I'll have to stay there the rest of my days.

"Little brother," he said to Yakov, making the sign of the cross over him, "don't lose hope. The stones of the bridge may crumble but the truth will come out."

"And till then," sighed the fixer, "what of my wasted youth?"

4

His youth dribbled away.

He had been imprisoned almost three months, three times longer than Bibikov had predicted and God only knew when it would end. Yakov nearly went mad trying to figure out what was happening to him. What was a poor harmless fixer doing in prison? What had he done to deserve this terrible incarceration, no end in sight? Hadn't he had more than his share of misery in a less than just world? He tried desperately to put together a comprehensible sequence of events that had led inevitably from his departure from the shtetl to a prison cell in Kiev; but to think of all these strange and unexpected experiences as meaningfully caused by related events confused him. True, the world was the kind of world it was. The rain put out fires and created floods. Yet too much had happened that didn't make sense. He had committed a few errors and paid for them in more than kind. One dark night a thick black web had fallen on him because he was standing under it, and though he ran in every direction he could not extricate himself from its sticky coils. Who was the spider if it remained invisible? He sometimes thought God was punishing him for his unbelief. He was, after all, the jealous God. "Thou shalt worship no other Gods before me," not even no Gods. He also blamed the goyim for their eternal hatred of Jews. Things go badly at a historical moment and go that way, God or no God, for ever. Did it *have* to be so? And he continued to curse himself. It could have happened to a more dedicated Jew, but it had happened instead to a recent freethinker because he was Yakov Bok. He blamed his usual mistakes – he could not always tell those of the far-off past from those that had led directly to his arrest in the brickyard. Yet he knew there was something from the outside, a quality of fate that had stalked him all his life and threatened, if he wasn't careful, his early extinction.

He hungered to explain who he was, Yakov the fixer from a small town in the Pale, an orphan boy who had married Raisl Shmuel's daughter and had been deserted by her, a curse on her soul; who had been poor all his life, had grubbed for a living, and was poor in other ways too – if he was that one what was he doing in prison? Who were they punishing if his life was punishment? Why put a harmless man into a prison with thick stone walls? He thought of begging them to let him go simply because he was not a criminal – it was a known fact – they could ask in the shtetl. If any of the officials – Grubeshov, Bodyansky, the warden – had known him before, they would never have believed he could commit such a monstrous crime. Not such as he. If only his innocence were written on a sheet of paper, he could pull it out and say, "Read, it's all here," but since it was hidden in himself they would know it only if they sought it, and they were not seeking. How could anyone look twice at Marfa Golov, note her suspicious ways and those crazy cherries on her hat, and not suspect she knew more about the murder than she was willing to admit? And what had happened to the Investigating Magistrate whom he hadn't seen now in more than a month? Was he still loyal to the law, or had he joined with the others in their vicious hunt for a guilty Jew? Or had he merely forgotten an expendable man?

During Yakov's first days in the courthouse jail the accusation had seemed to him almost an irrelevancy, nothing much to do with his life or deeds. But after the visit to the cave he had stopped thinking of relevancy, truth, or even proof. There was no "reason", there was only their plot against a Jew, any Jew; he was the accidental choice for the sacrifice. He would be tried because the accusation had been made, there didn't have to be another reason. Being born a Jew meant being vulnerable to history, including its worst errors. Accident and history had involved Yakov Bok as he had never dreamed he could be involved. The involvement was, in a way of speaking, impersonal, but the effect, his

165

misery and suffering, were not. The suffering was personal, painful, and possibly endless.

He felt entrapped, abandoned, helpless. He had disappeared from the world and nobody he could call friend knew it. Nobody. The fixer berated himself for not having listened to Shmuel's advice and staying where he belonged. He had got himself in a terrible mess, for what? Opportunity? An opportunity to destroy himself. He had fished for a herring and had been snatched by a shark. It wasn't hard to guess which of them would eat meat. And though he had now, at last, a little understanding of what was going on, or thought he had, he could of course still not resign himself to what had happened. In a philosophical moment he cursed history, anti-Semitism, fate, and even, occasionally, the Jews. "Who will help me?" he cried out in his sleep, but the other prisoners had their own anguish, their own bad dreams.

One night a new guest was let into the cell, a fattish heavy-faced young man with a blondish beard and small hands and feet, who wore his own clothes. At first his manner was morose and he returned furtive glances to anyone who looked in his direction. Yakov observed him from the distance. The young man was the only fat one in a cellful of skinny prisoners. He had money, bribed the guards for favours, lived well on packages from the outside – two large ones in a week – and wasn't stingy with food or cigarettes. "Here, boys, eat hearty," and he would hand out whatever there was to spare, yet keep himself well supplied. He even passed around green bottles of mineral water. He seemed to know how to get along, and some of the prisoners played cards with him. The clubfoot offered to be his personal servant but he waved him away. At the same time he was a worried man, muttered to himself, shook his head in disagreement, and sometimes tore at his round wrists with dirty finger-nails. One by one he pulled off the buttons of his shirt. Yakov, though wanting to talk to the man, skirted him in the beginning, possibly because he didn't know what to say to people with money, partly because the man obviously didn't want to be bothered, and partly for reasons he could not explain to himself. The new prisoner dispensed his favours with pretended cordiality, his eyes unable to conceal the fact that he was not a cordial man, and then withdrew. He sat alone often, muttering. Yakov sensed this one was aware of him. They both minded their business and looked each other over. One morning, after the promenade in the prison yard, they began to talk in a corner of the cell.

"You're a Jew?" said the fat man, in Yiddish.

Yakov admitted it.

"I, too."

"I thought so," said the fixer.

"If you thought so why didn't you come over?"

"I thought I'd wait a little."

"What's your name?"

"Yakov Bok the fixer."

"Gronfein, Gregor. Shalom. What are you in here for?"

"They say I killed a Christian child." He still couldn't say it keeping his voice steady.

Gronfein looked at him in astonishment.

"So you're the one? God, why didn't you tell me right away? I'm happy to be in the same cell with you."

"Why should you be happy?"

"I heard they had accused somebody of killing the Russian boy they found in the cave. Of course the whole thing is a manufactured fake, but there's a rumour running around in the Podol that a Jew was arrested, though nobody has seen you or knows who. Whoever he is he's a martyr for us all. Is it really you?"

"It's me, I wish it wasn't."

"I had my doubts that such a person exists."

"Only that and no more," the fixer sighed. "My worst enemies should exist like this."

"Don't grieve," said Gronfein. "God will help."

"He will or he won't as it suits him, but if he doesn't I hope somebody else will soon, or they might as well put me in the ground and cover me up with earth and grass."

"Patience," Gronfein said absently. "Patience. If there's not one way, there's another."

"Another what?"

"As long as a man stays alive he can't tell what chances will pop up next. But a dead man signs no cheques."

He began to talk about himself. "Of course I'm better off than some I can think of," Gronfein said, looking at Yakov to see if he agreed. "I have a first-class lawyer already working for me in what you could call unofficial ways, and I'm not afraid to part with a few hundred roubles if I have to, because there's more where they come from. What I do is I'm a counterfeiter. It's not honest but pays well, and so what if it takes away from Tsar Nicholas – he's got plenty he takes from the Jews. Still, if a bribe doesn't work this time I don't know what will. I've got a wife and five children and I'm getting a little worried. This is the longest I've spent in a cell. How long have you been here yourself?"

"Here about a month. Altogether three months since I was arrested."

"Whew." The counterfeiter gave Yakov two cigarettes and a piece of apple strudel from his last package, and the fixer ate and smoked gratefully.

Next time they talked, Gronfein asked Yakov questions

about his parents, family, and village. He wanted to know what he had been doing in Kiev. Yakov told him this and that but not too much. He did, however, mention Raisl, and Gronfein squirmed.

"Not so much of a Jewish daughter I'd say. My wife couldn't have such thoughts, not with a goy anyway, let alone do such a thing."

The fixer shrugged. "Some do, some don't. And some who do are Jewish."

Gronfein started to ask something, looked around cautiously, then whispered he would be interested in knowing what exactly had happened to the boy. "How did he die?"

"How did who die?" the fixer said, astonished.

"That Russian boy who was murdered."

"How would I know?" He drew away from the man. "What they say I did I didn't do. If I weren't a Jew there'd be no crime."

"Are you sure? Why don't you confide in me? We're both in the same pot."

"I have nothing to confide," said Yakov coldly. "If there was no fowl there are no feathers."

"It's tough luck," said the counterfeiter amiably, "but I'll do what I can to help you. Once they let me out of here I'll speak to my lawyer."

"For that I'll thank you."

But Gronfein had grown depressed, his eyes clouding, and said no more.

The next day he sidled up to Yakov and whispered, worried. "They say on the outside that if the government brings you up on trial they might start a pogrom at the same time. The Black Hundreds are making terrible threats. Hundreds of Jews are leaving the city as if fleeing the plague. My father-in-law is talking of selling his business and running to Warsaw."

The fixer listened in silence.

"Nobody's blaming you, you understand," Gronfein said.

"If your father-in-law wants to run away at least he can run away."

As they talked, the counterfeiter, from time to time, nervously glanced in the direction of the cell door, as if he were watching for the guard.

"Are you expecting a package?" Yakov asked.

"No no. But if they don't let me out of here I'll soon go mad. It's a stinking place and I'm worried about my family."

He drifted away, but was back in twenty minutes with the remnants of a package.

"Guard what's left here," he said to Yakov, "maybe I'm getting some action after all."

A guard opened the door and Gronfein disappeared from the cell for half an hour. When he returned he told the fixer they were letting him out that evening. He seemed satisfied but his ears were flaming, and afterwards he muttered much to himself for more than an hour. Later he was calmer.

That's how it goes with money, Yakov thought. If you've got it you've got wings.

"Something I can do for you before I go?" Gronfein whispered, slipping the fixer a ten-rouble note. "Don't worry, it's guaranteed good."

"Thanks. With this I can get myself a few things. They won't give me my own money. Maybe I can buy a better pair of shoes from one of the prisoners. These hurt my feet. Also if your lawyer can help me I'll be much obliged."

"I was thinking maybe you want to leave me a letter to

170

send to somebody?" said Gronfein. "Just write it out with this pencil and I'll mail it along. I have paper and an envelope or two in my pack. Stamps I'll paste on on the outside."

"With the greatest of thanks," Yakov said, "but who have I got to write to?"

"If you have nobody to write to," said Gronfein, "I can't manufacture you a correspondent, but what about your father-in-law that you told me about?"

"He's a poor man all his life. What can he do for me?"

"He's got a mouth, hasn't he? Let him start yelling."

"A mouth and a stomach but nothing goes in."

"They say when a Jewish rooster crows in Pinsk they hear him in Palestine."

"Maybe I'll write," said Yakov.

The more he thought about it, the more he wanted to write. He had a desperate desire to make known his fate. On the outside, as Gronfein had said, they knew somebody was in prison but not who. He wanted everyone to know it was Yakov Bok. He wanted them to know his innocence. Somebody had to know or he would never get out. Maybe a committee of some sort could be formed to help him? Maybe, if you knew the law, it was possible for a lawyer to see him before the indictment; if not that, he could at least urge them to produce the document so they could begin his defence. In another week it would be thirty days in this smelly detention cell and he had heard from no one. He considered writing to the Investigating Magistrate but didn't dare. If he should turn over the letter to the Prosecuting Attorney things might go worse. Or if he didn't maybe his assistant, Ivan Semyonovitch, might. In any case, it was too great a chance to take.

The fixer then slowly wrote two letters, one to Shmuel,

and another to Aaron Latke, the printer who had rented
him a room in his flat.

"Dear Shmuel," wrote Yakov. "As you predicted I got
myself into serious trouble and am now in the Kiev Prison
near Dorogozhitsky Street. I know it's impossible but try to
help me as soon as you can. Who else can I appeal to? Your
son-in-law, Yakov Bok. P.S. If she's back I'd rather not
know."

To Aaron Latke he wrote, "Dear friend Aaron, your
recent boarder Yakov Bok is now in the Kiev Prison, in the
thirty-day cell. After thirty days God knows what will
happen to me. What's happened already is bad enough. I
am accused of killing a Russian child by the name of Zhenia
Golov, who I swear I didn't touch. Do me a favour and take
this letter to some Jewish journalist or maybe to a sincere
philanthropist, if you happen to know of one. Tell them if
they can get me out of here I'll work hard my whole life to
pay them back. Only hurry because it's a desperate situation and getting worse. Yakov Bok."

"Good," said Gronfein, accepting the sealed letters, "that
should do it. Well, the best of luck to you, and don't worry
about the ten roubles. You can pay me when you get out.
Where there's that there's more."

The guard opened the cell door and the counterfeiter
hurriedly disappeared down the corridor, the prison guard
trotting after him.

Fifteen minutes later Yakov was called to the warden's
office. He handed the remnant of Gronfein's package to
Fetyukov to watch, promising to divide it with him.

Yakov hurried through the hall with the guard's gun at
his back. Maybe it's the indictment, he thought in excitement.

Warden Grizitskoy was in his office with the Deputy

Warden and a stern-faced inspector in a uniform like a general's. In the corner sat Gronfein, his hat on and eyes shut.

The warden waved the two letters, out of their envelopes, that the fixer had just written.

"Are these yours? Answer truthfully, you son-of-a-bitch."

The fixer froze, his heart sinking. "Yes, your honour."

The warden pointed to the Yiddish script. "Translate these bird droppings," he said to Gronfein.

The counterfeiter opened his eyes long enough to read the letters aloud in Russian, in a quick monotone.

"You Zhid bloodsucker," said the warden, "how dare you break prison regulations? I personally warned you not to try to get in touch with anybody on the outside without my express permission."

Yakov said nothing, staring, sickened to the pit of his stomach, at Gronfein.

"He turned them over to us," the Deputy Warden said to the fixer. "A law-abiding citizen."

"Don't expect a moral man," Gronfein said to nobody in particular, his eyes still clamped shut. "I'm only a counterfeiter."

"You bastard stool pigeon," Yakov shouted at him, "why did you trick an innocent man?"

"Watch your language, you," warned the warden. "A foul heart, a foul tongue."

"It's every man for himself," Gronfein muttered. "I have five small children and a nervous wife."

"What's more," said the Deputy Warden," we have it in writing that you also tried to bribe him to poison the yard-keeper who saw you attempting to kidnap the boy in the brickyard, and also to pay Marfa Golov not to testify against you. Isn't that the truth?" he asked Gronfein.

The counterfeiter, sweat trickling from under his hat down his dark lids, nodded once.

"Where would I get the money to pay for those bribes?" Yakov asked.

"The Jewish Nation would supply it," answered the inspector.

"Get him out of here," said the old warden. "The Prosecuting Attorney will call you when he needs you," he said to Gronfein.

"Stool pigeon!" Yakov shouted, "bastard traitor – it's a filthy lie!"

Gronfein, as though blind, was led out of the room by the Deputy Warden.

"This is the sort of assistance you can expect from your compatriots," the inspector said to Yakov. "It would be best for you to confess."

"We won't have our rules flouted by such as you," the warden said. "To strict confinement you go, and if you have any more letters to write you'll write them in your own blood."

5

He was being boiled alive in the smothering heat of the small solitary cell they had thrust him into, the sweat drenching his back and flowing from his armpits; but on the third night the bolt was shot back, a key grated in the lock, and the door opened.

A guard ordered him downstairs to the warden's office. "Get a move on, you fuck, you're more trouble than you're worth."

The Investigating Magistrate was there, sitting in a chair,

fanning himself with a wilted yellow straw hat. He wore a
crumpled linen suit and a white silk tie, his pallid face con-
trasting with his dark short beard as he talked earnestly with
the Deputy Warden, an uneasy-eyed man with smelly
polished boots; he was flushed and self-consciously irritated
when Yakov entered. When the prisoner, ghastly grey and
close to shock, limped into the room, the two officials
momentarily stopped talking. The Deputy Warden, gnawing his lip, remarked, "It's an irregular procedure if you
ask my opinion"; but Bibikov patiently differed. "I'm here
in the pursuit of my official duties as Investigating Magistrate,
Mr Deputy Warden, so there is nothing to fear."

"So you say, but why close to midnight when the
warden's away on vacation and the other officials are sleeping? It's a strange time to come here on business, if you ask
me."

"It's a dreadful night after a dreadfully hot day," the
magistrate said huskily, coughing into his fist, "but much
cooler at this hour. In fact there's a veritable breeze off the
Dnieper once you are in the street. To be frank, I was
already in bed, but the heat in the house was unbearable
and the bedsheets perspired more than I did. I tossed and
turned, then I thought, it's useless, I'll get up. Once I had
dressed it occurred to me it would be helpful if I got on with
official matters rather than lie around drinking cold drinks
that give me gas, and curse the heat. Fortunately, my wife
and children are at our dacha on the Black Sea, where I will
go to join them in August. Do you know the heat rose to
40·5 in the shade this afternoon, and must now be hovering
around 33·8? I assure you it was all but impossible to work
in my office today. My assistant complained of nausea and
had to be sent home."

"Go on, then, if you want to," said the Deputy Warden,

175

"but I have to insist that I stay here as a witness to your questions. The prisoner's under our jurisdiction, that's clear enough."

"May I remind you that your function is custodial and mine investigatory? The suspect has not yet been tried or sentenced. In fact there is no indictment up to now. Nor has he officially been remanded to prison by administrative decree. He is simply here as a material witness. If you will allow me, I am within my rights to question him alone. The time may be inconvenient, but it is so in a formal sense only; therefore I beg you to absent yourself for a brief period, say not more than a half-hour."

"At least I ought to know what you're going to ask him about in case the warden wants to know when he gets back. If it's about his treatment in this prison, I warn you flatly the warden will be annoyed if you ask about that. The Jew hasn't been made any exception of. If he follows the rules and regulations he gets the same treatment as everybody else. If he doesn't he's in for trouble."

"My questions will not refer to his prison treatment, although I hope it is always humane. You may tell Warden Grizitskoy that I was checking some testimony of the accused made before me at a previous date. If he would like more precise information, let him telephone me."

The Deputy Warden withdrew, casting a sullen glance at the prisoner.

Bibikov, after sitting a minute with two fingers pressed to his lips, moved quickly to the door, listened intently, then carried his chair and one for Yakov to the windowless far corner of the office, and motioned him to sit down.

"My friend," he said hurriedly in a low voice, "I can see from your appearance what you have been through, and I beg you not to think me remiss or without feeling if I do not comment on it. I have promised the Deputy Warden to confine myself to other matters, and besides our time is short and I have much to say."

"That's fine with me, your honour," muttered Yakov, struggling with his emotions, "but I would like to know if you could get me a different pair of shoes. The nails in these hurt my feet though nobody believes me. Either let them give me a different pair or lend me a hammer and pliers so I can fix them myself."

He sucked in his breath and wiped an eye with his sleeve. "Excuse me for being out of order, your honour."

"I see we're wearing similar linen garments," Bibikov joked, fanning himself slowly with his limp hat. He remarked in an undertone, "Tell me your size and I'll send you a pair of shoes."

"Maybe it's better not to," Yakov whispered, "or the Deputy Warden would know I complained to you."

"You understand it wasn't I but the Prosecuting Attorney who ordered your imprisonment?"

The fixer nodded.

"Would you care for a cigarette? You know my Turkish beauties?"

He lit one for him but after a few puffs Yakov had to put it out. "Excuse me for wasting it," he coughed, "but it's hard to breathe in this heat."

The magistrate put away his cigarette-box. He reached into his breast pocket for his pince-nez, blew on them, and settled the glasses on his perspiring nose. "I would like you to know, Yakov Shepsovitch – if I may – that your case holds an extraordinary interest for me, and only last week I returned in a beastly stuffy, crowded train from St Petersburg, where I had consulted the Minister of Justice, Count Odoevsky."

M

He leaned forward and said quietly, "I went there to submit the evidence I had already gathered, and to request that the charge against you be limited, as I had already suggested to the Prosecuting Attorney, strictly to the matter of your residing illegally in the Lukianovsky District, or perhaps even dropped altogether if you left Kiev and returned to your native village. Instead I was expressly directed to continue my investigation beyond the slightest shadow of a doubt. I will tell you in the strictest confidence what most troubled me is that although the Minister of Justice listened courteously and with obvious interest, I left with the unmistakable impression that he expects the evidence to confirm your guilt."

"Vey iz mir."

"This was not stated so specifically, you must understand – it was an impression and I may possibly be misinterpreting, although I don't think so. Frankly, the matter seemed to revolve around an imprecise use of language, further confused by hints, hesitations, odd questions I did not fully understand, shadowy remarks, and so forth. Nothing – even now – is said absolutely directly, yet I am under pressure, as it were, to uncover evidence close to the prevailing belief. The Minister of Interior also has been telephoning me regularly. I will admit these pressures have made me nervous. My wife tells me I am more difficult than usual to live with, and there are signs of gastric disturbances. In her letter today she urged me to see a doctor. And tonight," he went on, lowering his voice to the dimmest whisper, "I had the impression on my way here that my carriage was being followed by another, though no doubt I am suggestible in my present state of nerves."

He thrust his pallid face close to Yakov's, continuing to whisper: "But that's neither here nor there. To return then

to the facts: Count Odoevsky at one point offered to relieve
me of the 'burden' of this case if I felt 'pressed or unwell', or
the work had become 'distasteful' or seemed to go against
what he referred to as 'your creed'. And I believe I caught a
clear hint that the purposes of justice might better be served
by an indictment of murder for ritual reasons, an accusation
which is of course poppycock."

"As for the murder," said Yakov, "if I had a hand in it
let me live for ever a cripple in hell."

The Investigating Magistrate fanned himself slowly with
his hat. After again glancing at the door he said, "When I
told the Minister of Justice – quite directly told him, nothing
minced or hedged, shadowy remarks do not explicate or uphold the law – that my evidence pointed in the opposite
direction, towards acquittal of the major charge, he shrugged
his shoulders – the count is an imposing man, handsome,
well-spoken, discreetly perfumed – as though perhaps to
indicate I had not yet achieved true wisdom. And that's
apparently where we left it, with a shrug that may mean
much or little, but in any case a doubt. I can say in his
favour that he is a gentleman. But I will tell you frankly that
with the Prosecuting Attorney, my colleague Grubeshov,
there are not even the slightest doubts. He has, I would say,
convinced himself, perhaps almost before the fact. I say this
after careful consideration. Grubeshov has more than once
emphatically requested from me – in fact he has insisted on
it – a severe indictment of you, mincing no words – for
Zhenia Golov's murder, and I have categorically refused.
Of course that adds to my nervousness. Yet for all practical
purposes you should know this matter can't go on in such a
way much longer. If I don't draw up the indictment someone else will. They will get rid of me, if they possibly can,
and then I'll be of no use to you whatever. Therefore I will

pretend to co-operate with them while I continue my investigation, until I have a foolproof case. I will then once more submit the evidence to the Ministry of Justice, and if they insist on a prosecution, I may reveal my findings to the Press, which could conceivably cause a scandal. I would hope so. In fact I am already planning anonymously to give out selected information to one or two highly placed journalists as to the true state of affairs regarding the nature of the evidence against you, which up to now consists in nothing more than anonymous accusations and provocative articles published by the reactionary Press. I decided this as I lay awake tonight. My visit to you, which I decided on impulsively, is to inform you of my plans so that you will not think you are without a friend in the world. I know you are falsely accused. I am determined to continue this investigation to the best of my ability and powers in order to discover, and if necessary, publish the whole truth. I am doing this for Russia as well as for your sake and mine. I therefore request, Yakov Shepsovitch, though I understand how difficult your trials are, your confidence and patience."

"Thanks, your honour," said Yakov with a tremor in his voice. "If you're used to stepping out of the hut once in a while to take a breath of fresh air in your lungs while you look at the sky to see if it's going to rain tomorrow – not that it makes any difference – it's hard to go on living in a small dark solitary cell; still now I know there's somebody who knows what I did and what I didn't do, and who I trust, though I would like to hear what you mean about 'the true state of affairs' that you mentioned before when you were talking about the journalists."

Bibikov went again to the door, opened it softly, peered out, closed it carefully and returned to his chair, once more bringing his face close to Yakov's.

"My theory is that the murder was committed by Marfa Golov's gang of criminals and housebreakers, in particular her blinded lover, one Stepan Bulkin, who, thus, perhaps, revenged himself on her for the loss of his eyesight. The boy was grossly neglected by his mother. She is a wicked woman, stupid yet cunning, with the morals of a hardened prostitute. Zhenia had apparently threatened, possibly more than once, to expose their criminal activities to the District Police, and it is possible that the lover convinced her the child had to be done away with. Perhaps the incident occurred during a time of general drunkenness. The boy was killed, I am all but certain, in his mother's house, Bulkin taking the leading role in the beastly sacrifice. They obviously tortured the poor child, inflicting a large number of wounds on his body and soaking up the blood as it spurted forth, in order not to leave any telltale stains on the floor – I would imagine they burned the bloody rags – and finally plunging the knife deep into the child's heart. I have not been able to determine whether Marfa witnessed his death or had passed out drunk."

The fixer shuddered. "How did you find out about that, your honour?"

"I can't tell you except to say generally that thieves quarrel, and as I said before, Marfa is stupid, canny as she is. The true story will come out in time if we work patiently. We have reason to believe she kept her son's body in the bathtub for a week before it was removed to the cave. We are searching for one of the neighbours who is believed to have seen it there and soon thereafter moved out of the vicinity, frightened out of her wits I would guess, by Marfa's threats. To save their own necks, naturally the thieves are going along with the blood ritual accusation against you. How that originated we are not exactly sure. We suspect

Marfa herself wrote an anonymous letter suggesting that Jews did the evil work. The original letter to the police was signed 'A Christian'. I know that, though I have not been able to put my hands on the document yet. At any rate the thieves will do whatever they can to uphold the charge, even if it means testifying against you as eyewitnesses to your 'crime'. They are frightened and dangerous men. And my assistant, Ivan Semyonovitch, has ascertained that Proshko and Richter burned down Nikolai Maximovitch's stable, though without the help of any Jewish demons."

"So that's how it is," sighed Yakov. "Behind the world lies another world. Excuse me, but does the Prosecuting Attorney also know what you just told me?"

Bibikov fanned himself leisurely with his hat.

"To be absolutely truthful I don't know what he knows or doesn't. I am not one of his confidants – but I suspect he knows more than he admits. I also know he is an ambitious and opportunistic man, a restless careerist. In his youthful days he was a strong Ukrainophil, but since attaining public office he has become more Russian than the Tsar. Someday, if God's mercy does not intervene, he will be a justice of our Supreme Court – it is without a doubt what he wants most. If that should happen there will be 'justice' without justice." The magistrate caught himself and paused. "I will be grateful to you if you do not repeat this, Yakov Shepsovitch, or my other remarks to you, to anyone. Like most Russians I talk too much; however, I wanted in particular to ease your mind a bit. I ask this for our mutual protection."

"Who would I repeat it to even if there was somebody here who wasn't my enemy? But what I want to ask is, does the Prosecuting Attorney truly think I killed the boy, and does he really believe those things the priest said at the cave?"

"As to his true beliefs I must again confess my ignorance

182

although I see him often in the course of official business. He tends to believe, in my opinion, what those around him believe. I don't pretend to know how much claptrap and superstition there is in his soul or what purpose it serves. But he is not a fool, I assure you. He knows our history and is quite familiar with the law though not greatly responsive to its spirit. He surely knows that Alexander I, in 1817, and Nicholas I, in 1835, by official ukase prohibited blood libels against Jews living on Russian soil, although it is quite true that these libels have been revived within the last generation to provoke pogroms, for political purposes. I do not have to tell you there has been a disappointing retreat of progress in recent times, whatever it is we call progress, especially disappointing because of the little we have had since the Emancipation. There's something cursed, it seems to me, about a country where men have owned men as property. The stink of that corruption never escapes the soul, and it is the stink of future evil. Still, the original decrees have not been withdrawn and are therefore the law. If Grubeshov has at all looked into this subject, as I have recently, he will also know, for instance, that certain Roman Catholic Popes, including an Innocent, a Paul, a Gregory, and a Clement, whose numerical designations I have forgotten, issued certain interdictions against this accusation. I believe one of them called it 'a baseless and wicked invention'. Interestingly, I learned that this very same blood accusation made against the Jews was used by pagans of the first century to justify the oppression and slaughter of the early Christians. They too were called 'blood drinkers', for reasons you would understand if you knew the Catholic mass. The blood mystique arose in a belief of primitive people that there is a miraculous power in blood. It is, of course, a most dramatic substance in colour and composition."

"So if the Pope said no, why does the priest say yes?"

"Father Anastasy is a charlatan. He has written a stupid anti-Semitic brochure in Latin which brought him to the attention of the United Nobility, who have urged him to testify against you. Around him much of the pogrom agitation is centred. It is interesting to me that quite shortly after the appearance of his brochure, Zhenia Golov was murdered. He is a defrocked Catholic priest, for some disgraceful act, we think an embezzlement of church funds, who only latterly came from Poland and joined the Orthodox Church, whose Synod, incidentally, does not support the accusation against you, although it does not deny it. The Metropolitan of Kiev has informed me he will not issue a statement."

"That won't keep the water from boiling," the fixer muttered.

"I'm afraid not. Do you know any French, Yakov Shepsovitch?" Bibikov asked.

"Not that I can think of, your honour."

"The French have a saying, 'The more it changes, the more it remains the same.' You must admit there may be a certain truth to that, especially with reference to what we call 'society'. In effect it has not changed in its essentials from what it was in the dim past, even though we tend loosely to think of civilization as progress. I frankly no longer believe in that concept. I respect man for what he has to go through in life, and sometimes for how he does it, but he has changed little since he began to pretend he was civilized, and the same thing may be said about our society. That is how I feel, but having made that confession let me say, as you may have guessed, that I am somewhat of a meliorist. That is to say, I act as an optimist because I find

184

I cannot act at all, as a pessimist. One often feels helpless in the face of the confusion of these times, such a mass of apparently uncontrollable events and experiences to live through, attempt to understand, and if at all possible, give order to; but one must not withdraw from the task if he has some small thing to offer – he does so at the risk of diminishing his humanity.

"Be that as it may," he went on, "if the Prosecuting Attorney had indulged in a bit of Old Testament research he would, I am sure, be familiar with the prohibitions in Leviticus that Jews may not eat any manner of blood. I can't quote it exactly – my notes are on my desk at home – but the Lord warned that whoever ate blood, Israelite or stranger, He would cut him off from his people. Nor would He afterwards allow King David to raise a temple to Him, because he had fought in many wars and spilled much blood. He is a consistent God, if not gentle. I have also learned from certain Russian authorities of the Old Testament and other Jewish sacred texts that there does not exist in those writings a record of any law or custom which permits a Jew to use blood, or specifically Christian blood, for religious purposes. According to those I have consulted – secretly, you understand – the prohibition against using any blood whatsoever for whatever purpose was never retracted or altered in later Jewish writings of law, literature, or medicine. There is not, for instance, any record of a prescription of blood for use in medicine, internal or external. Et cetera, et cetera. There are many such facts that Grubeshov ought to have familiarized himself with – and I assure you I am strongly contemplating submitting him a summary of my researches for his reflection. Frankly, Yakov Shepsovitch, I am embarrassed to belittle a colleague to you in this manner but I have come to the unhappy conclusion

that whatever he knows, or may know through my intervention, that might be helpful to you in establishing your
innocence is, if not actually useless, then at least antithetical
to his aims and purposes. He also would like to have you
convicted."

Yakov wrung his hands. "If so what am I to do,
your honour? Will I be abandoned to die in this
prison?"

"Who has abandoned you?" the Investigating Magistrate
asked, looking at him gently.

"Not you, of course, and I thank what little luck I have
for that. But if Mr Grubeshov has no use for your evidence
I might rot here for years. After all, how long are our lives?
Couldn't you put out an indictment of some small sort
against me so that I could at least see a lawyer?"

"No, that wouldn't work at all. Murder is what I would
be compelled to charge you with. I'm afraid to start off that
way. Your lawyer will appear in due course. But at present
no lawyer can do as much for you as I, Yakov Shepsovitch.
And when the time comes that he can, I'll see to it that you
have a good one. I already have in mind someone who is a
vigorous and courageous man of the most excellent reputation. I will sound him out in the near future, and I am sure
he will agree to represent you."

The fixer thanked him.

Bibikov, after looking at his watch, suddenly rose. "Yakov
Shepsovitch, what more can I tell you? Take heart in the
truth and endure your trials. Sustain yourself in your
innocence."

"It's not so easy, your honour. I'm not suited for this kind
of life. I find it hard to imitate a dog. That's not exactly
what I mean but turned around a bit it is. What I mean is
that I'm sick of prison, also I'm not a brave man. To tell the

186

truth I have terrible fears that never leave me, day or night."

"No one says it's easy. Still, you are not alone."

"In my cell I'm alone. In my thoughts I'm alone. I don't want to sound bitter to you because I'm thankful for your help —"

"My dear friend," said Bibikov gravely, "your bitterness doesn't offend me. My worry is not to fail you."

"Why should you fail me?" the fixer said, anxiously rising.

"Who can say?" Bibikov put on his limp hat. "Partly it is our situation in this unfortunate country that causes me doubt. Russia is such a complex, long-suffering, ignorant, torn and helpless nation. In one sense we are all prisoners here." He paused, combed his beard with his fingers, then said, "There is so much to be done that demands the full capacities of our hearts and souls, but, truly, where shall we begin? Perhaps I will begin with you? Keep in mind, Yakov Shepsovitch, that if your life is without value, so is mine. If the law does not protect you, it will not, in the end, protect me. Therefore I dare not fail you, and that is what causes me anxiety – that I must not fail you. Now permit me to say good night. Let us both somehow try to sleep and perhaps tomorrow will be better. Thank God for tomorrow."

Yakov tried to seize his hand to press to his lips but Bibikov had gone.

6

A prisoner, an anguished and desperate man, was locked in the next cell. The minute in, he began to pound with his shoe, or both shoes, against the wall. The noise came through distantly and Yakov pounded back with his shoe. But when the man shouted he could somehow be heard, though not his words. They shouted to each other at various times of the day and night as loudly as they could – it sounded to the fixer as though someone was trying to tell him a heartbreaking tale, and he wanted with all his heart to hear and then tell his own; but the man's shouts, cries, questions, were muffled, indistinguishable. So were his, the fixer knew.

The isolation cells were rectangular cubicles, the walls of brick and cement, the outer wall containing a single three-barred window a half metre above the prisoner's head. The door was made of solid iron with a peephole at eye level, through which the guard, when he was there, peered; and though Yakov could understand what was yelled at him from the corridor, when either prisoner shouted at the other through the spy hole, neither could understand. The openings were small, and reverberations in the corridor muffled the words and turned them into noise.

Once a guard with a dark face and stupid eyes, appearing in the cell block, heard them shouting to each other and cursed them both. He ordered the other prisoner to shut up or he would beat his head to a pulp, and to Yakov he said, "No more noise out of you or I'll shoot your Jew cock off." When he was gone both men resumed beating on the wall. The guard came once a day with a bowl of watery, insect-ridden soup, and a slice of stale black bread; he also checked the cells at unpredictable intervals. Yakov would be sleeping on the floor, or pacing back and forth the meagre distance of the cell; or sitting with his back to the wall, his knees drawn up, lost in despondent thought, when he became aware of a malevolent eye staring at him, which was at once

188

withdrawn. From the number of doors opening in the morning when the guard and his assistant delivered the food, the fixer knew there were only two prisoners in that wing of cells. The other prisoner was on his left, and on the right the guards retreated fifty steps to another door which they opened with a key, then shut with a terrible thump and locked from the other side. Sometimes in the early morning hours, when the huge prison was steeped in darkness and silence although hundreds of men, more likely thousands, dreamed, moaned, snored and farted in their sleep, the prisoner in the next cell woke and began beating on the wall between them. He did this in quick bursts of sound, then slowly, as though he were trying to teach the fixer a code, and though Yakov counted the beats and tried to translate them into letters of the Russian alphabet, the words he put together made no sense and he cursed himself for his stupidity. He banged but what did it mean? Sometimes they uselessly banged on the wall at the same time.

To be imprisoned alone was the greatest desperation the fixer had known. He hadn't the wit, he told himself, to be this much alone. When the guards came with his bread and soup on his twelfth morning of solitary confinement, Yakov begged for relief. He had learned his lesson and would uphold every regulation if they kindly returned him to the common cell, where there were, at least, other faces and some human activity. "If you will tell this to the warden I'll thank you with my whole heart. It's hard to live without a little conversation once in a while." But neither of the guards answered a word. It wouldn't have cost them a kopek to give his message to the warden, but they never did. Yakov sank into silence, sometimes imagining himself in the Podol, talking casually to someone. He would stand under a tree in the tenement courtyard with Aaron Latke and say how badly things were going. (How bad was bad if you were free?) Just a homey few words, better in Yiddish, but good enough in Russian. Or since freedom, at the moment, was out of the question, if he had his tools he could, after a morning's work, break a small hole through the wall and talk with the other prisoner, maybe even see his face if he stepped back a little. They could tell each other the story of their lives and stretch it out for months, then start over again if necessary. But the other prisoner, either because he was disheartened or sick, had stopped beating on the wall, and neither of them shouted to the other.

If he had forgotten the man he suddenly remembered him. One night a distant moaning broke into his sleep. He awoke and heard nothing. The fixer beat on the wall with his heavy shoe but there was no response. He dreamed he heard footsteps in the corridor, then a smothered cry awakened him again, terrified. Something's wrong, he thought, I must hide. A cell door clanged and there were steps of more than one man in the corridor. Yakov waited tensely in the pitch gloom, about to cry out if his door moved, but the steps went past his cell. The heavy door at the end of the corridor thumped shut, a key turned in the lock, and that was the end of the noise. In the terrible silence that followed, he could not get back to sleep. He beat on the wall with both broken shoes, shouting until he was hoarse, but could rouse no response. The next morning he was not brought food. They are leaving me to die, he thought. But at noon, a drunken guard came in with his soup and bread, muttering to himself. He spilled half the soup over Yakov before the prisoner could grab the bowl.

"Here he kills a Russian child and lords it over us," the guard muttered, his breath thick with alcohol.

When he had gone it came to the fixer, as he was very slowly chewing his black bread, that the guard had not locked and bolted the door. The hair on the back of his neck prickled. He got up in excitement, thrust two fingers through the peephole and almost fainted as the door slowly opened inward.

Yakov was overwhelmed in confusion and fright. If I step out they'll kill me for sure. Someone must be waiting on the outside. He peered through the hole but could see no one. Then he shut the door softly and waited.

An hour, if not longer, went by. Again he opened the creaking door and this time quickly looked into the hall. To the right, at the end of the cell block the concrete door stood ajar. Had the drunken guard forgotten to lock that too? Yakov slunk along the corridor, stopped a few feet from the door and at once hurried back. Yet he did not go into his cell. Once more he approached the heavy door and was about to pull it open when it came to him thunderously that he was acting faster than he could think. So he ran back to his cell, entered, and slammed the door shut. There he waited, his flesh freezing, his heart a growing pain. No one came. But the fixer had thought it out and was certain the guard had left the door open on purpose. If he went through it and sneaked down the stairs, at the bottom another guard would confront him, the one with the stupid eyes. He would look at Yakov and slowly raise his pistol. In the prison log the warden would write: "The prisoner Yakov Bok shot in the stomach while attempting to escape."

But he slid out into the corridor again, his thoughts flooded with freedom, this time going the other way, astonished he hadn't thought of that before. He looked cautiously to the left and right, then peered through the peephole into the other prisoner's cell. A bearded man, swinging gently, hung from a leather belt tied to the middle bar of the open window, a fallen stool near by. He was staring down where his pince-nez lay smashed on the floor under his small dangling feet.

It took the fixer an age to admit it was Bibikov.

VI

In the luminous dark the ghost of Bibikov appeared wearing a large white hat. He had no glasses pinched to his nose, they were gone, and he rubbed the bridge in embarrassment.

"A terrible thing has happened. Yakov Shepsovitch. These men are without morality. I fear they will kill you, too."

"No, no," cried Yakov. "I don't believe in superstition."

The Investigating Magistrate lit a rose-papered cigarette and sat silent; then tried to say something and began to fade. He slowly disappeared in the dark, his white self dimming, as though evening had come and then night; and the soft glow of the cigarette diminished until it was out. All that remained was the dark memory of him hanging from the window, his bulbous eyes staring at his smashed glasses on the floor.

All night the fixer sat huddled in the corner of the cell,

filled with the dread of dying. If he slept a minute his sleep was steeped in the taste, smell, horror of dying. He lay motionless in a graveyard, rigid, terrified. In the black sky were black stars. If he stirred he would topple into an open grave, amid the rotting dead, their dead flesh and putrefying bones. But more than death he feared torture. He feared being torn and broken before he died. He saw them dragging into the cell terrible instruments, monstrous wooden machines that racked and crushed the body; they hung his remains from a window bar. At dawn, when the dirty eye staring through the hole in the door touched him, he woke from shadowy sleep begging for his life. As the door creaked open he cried out; but the guards did not strangle him. One of them, with his foot, shoved in a bowl of gruel without a cockroach in it.

All day the fixer walked in his cell, sometimes he ran, five steps, three, five, three, breaking the circuit to hurl himself against the wall, or smash his fists against the metal door with prolonged cries of grief. He mourned Bibikov with great sorrow, great bitterness. For weeks he had lived with this potential saviour in his thoughts, this just and gentle man; depended on him somehow to free him from prison, the trap laid for him, from the crime itself, the horrifying accusation. His only peace had come from these thoughts, that a good man was assisting him, and because of him, when the trial came, he would be judged not guilty. He had pictured himself freed, hurrying back to the shtetl, or running off to America if he could raise the funds. But now these hopes and expectations, these reveries on which he had lived, were gone, snatched from him without warning. Who would help him now, what could he hope for? Where Bibikov had lived in his mind was a hopeless hole. Who would now expose the murderess, Marfa Golov, and her accomplices, and proclaim his innocence to the newspapers? Suppose she left Kiev, fled to another city – or country – would they ever lay eyes on her again? How would the world ever learn about the injustice that had been committed against an innocent man? Who could help him if no one but his jailers knew where he was? For aught he meant to anyone, Yakov Bok did not exist. If they had no plans to kill him outright, then they would kill him slowly by burying him alive in prison for ever.

"Mama-Papa," he cried out, "save me! Shmuel, Raisl – anybody – save me! Somebody save me!" He walked in circles, forgetting he was walking, inventing fantastic plans to escape, each making his heart ache because each was impossible. He walked all day and into the night, until his shoes fell apart, and then walked in his bare feet on the lacerating floor. He walked in almost liquid heat with nowhere to go but his circular entrapment, striking himself on his journey – his chest, face, head, tearing his flesh, lamenting his life.

His crooked feet hurt unbearably. Yakov lay down in exhaustion on the floor. Torture by his own instrument – pain of body on deep depression. His pulpy feet, the soles covered with live scabs and red pussing sores, were like bags blown up about to burst. Then the ankles disappeared as the swelling moved up his legs. The fixer lay on his back, breathing badly, noisily. At least if it were cooler. How long can I stand this? His feet felt as though they were bound in chains and laid on fire. Both legs bulged to the knees. He lay on his back wishing for death. A cold eye stared at him. Ultimately he placed it at the peephole, an eye gazing at his suppurating feet, but the one who looked had nothing to say; and said nothing. "Help my poor feet," Yakov cried out, "it's a terrible pain." Whoever he was, if he heard, said

195

nothing. Then the eye in the hole was gone. The fixer, feverishly shivering, his clothes wet, moaned through another night of pain. In the morning a key turned in the door and Warden Grizitskoy entered. Thinking of Bibikov, Yakov shrank from him. But the cross-eyed warden looked real and even human, and what he had seen in the next cell, dreamlike, unreal; he was at times not sure he had seen it. He didn't dare ask about the Investigating Magistrate. If they knew he knew they might kill him at once.

"What tricks are you up to now?" the warden demanded.

"Please," Yakov said, "my feet are infected from the nails in my shoes. I need a doctor."

"There are no doctors for the likes of you."

The fixer wearily shut his eyes.

The warden left. In the afternoon he returned with an aide from the prison infirmary.

"He's poisoned his feet," said the aide.

"Is it serious?" said the warden, "or will it go away by itself?"

"Both feet are full of pus. It might become gangrene."

"It would serve the bastard right," said the warden.

"All right," he said to Yakov, "go down to the infirmary. I'd let you rot here but I don't want the cell to stink any more than it does, or it will get infected from your germs. Move quickly now."

"How can I walk?" said Yakov. "Could Fetyukov or somebody help me?"

"Perfect company for a fellow-murderer," said the warden. "Fetyukov is no longer present. He was shot for disobeying orders and resisting a guard."

"Shot?" said the stunned fixer.

"For insubordination. He insulted a guard. Let that be a lesson to you. Now move along quickly."

196

"I can't walk. How can I go if I can't walk?"

"If you can't walk, crawl. The devil take you."

Like a dog, thought Yakov. On his hands and knees he moved out into the corridor, then painfully towards the door leading to the stairs. Though he crawled slowly the pressure hurt his knees and he could not keep his battered feet from scraping the floor. But he forced himself not to cry out. The warden and infirmary aide had left, and a guard with a shotgun followed the fixer as he moved towards the concrete door. Going down the steep wooden steps, he had the weight of his body on his trembling arms, his feet bumping each step, and he more than once almost fell headlong down the stairs. When he paused, the guard prodded him with the butt of his gun. By the time Yakov reached the bottom of the stairs both his hands were scraped raw, and both knees bled. His back was black with sweat and the veins bulged on his neck as he crawled forward along the corridor and out of the prison door into the yard.

The infirmary was in the administration section, on the other side of the quadrangle from the prison cells. It was the time of the ten-minute afternoon promenade, and the prisoners opened their double files for the fixer as they watched him haltingly crawling across the dirt yard.

"Five kopeks on the Zhid mule," shouted the clubfoot. A prisoner in a torn greatcoat turned and struck him across the mouth. A guard beat the prisoner.

If I live will I make it? Yakov, nauseated, was close to fainting. Half-way across the yard his trembling arms gave out and he collapsed. Several prisoners broke from their lines, but the guard with the whip shouted it was forbidden. The sentries patrolling the yard pointed their rifles at the prisoners and they returned to the lines, but not the slop-pail man, the one with the cracked eyeglasses. He fished some burlap rags from a garbage pile in the corner of the yard and ran towards Yakov. Hurriedly he wound the rags around the fixer's hands and knees. The guard cursed but looked on. When the rags were tied he prodded Yakov with his foot.

The fixer got up on his raw hands and bleeding knees and went on, blindly crawling across the yard. He climbed up the stone steps into the infirmary.

The surgeon, a bald-headed man in a soiled white linen coat that smelled of carbolic acid and tobacco, inspected Yakov's feet, smeared them with a thick yellow acrid salve out of a can, and after bandaging both feet with dirty bandages and swabbing his hands and knees with alcohol, ordered the fixer into bed. This was the first bed he had been in since his arrest. He slept for a day and a half. When he awoke, the surgeon, smoking a cigar, unwound the bandages and operated on his feet. He cut into the pussing sores with a scalpel, without anaesthetic. The prisoner, biting his lips to be silent, cried out at each cut.

"This is good for you, Bok," said the surgeon. "Now you know how poor Zhenia felt when you were stabbing him and draining his blood, all for the sake of your Jewish religion."

That night as he lay in bed in the infirmary Yakov had trouble breathing. Though he took in great gulping hot breaths through his mouth, the air seemed thin and insufficient. He did not at first fear asthma because he had often had trouble breathing under stress yet had not been seriously sick for years. But then the air turned heavy and stale. It was like trying to breathe metal. His chest heaved. His lungs weighed like rock, his breathing turned heavily raspy and he felt sick. The fixer clawed the mattress. "Please, who needs more? I have enough." He sat up,

198

gasping for help but none came. Yakov got out of bed, his bandaged feet oozing blood, and tottered to the barred window. He lay under it, wheezing as he fought to draw into his lungs a few drops of air. In the midst of his exertions he fell into an exhausted and perilous half-sleep, dreaming he was expiring in a windowless cell, seeing in his drowning dreams the miserable orphans' home, a crumbling tilted shack he had spent his childhood in; Raisl running from him in terror as though he had threatened her with a meat cleaver; and his imprisonment for a lifetime in Siberia for the murder of a boy whose suffering dead face haunted him still. He dreamed he had come upon him in the woods, a child carrying his schoolbooks, and had grabbed and choked him unconscious on impulse; then with Proshko's help, as the boy lay on the ground still twitching, he stabbed him thirteen times in the chest and drained five litres of his bright blood, a magnificent liquid. All night Grubeshov, standing with both yellow gaitered feet on Yakov's chest, harangued the victim in a thick-voiced tirade, and though the fixer frantically implored Bibikov's help, the Investigating Magistrate, at his desk in another room, would or could not be disturbed.

2

The warden assigned him to a new cell, a large dampish one on the ground floor of the solitary block of the south building of the prison, to the right of the administrative section and infirmary.

"It's just to keep you close to my eye," he said. "There's talk you might try to escape with the assistance of your

Jewish cohorts, which I strongly warn you against, because if you attempt it you're sure to get shot."

He pointed to the notice on the wall:

Obey all rules and regulations without question. If the prisoner is insurbordinate or insulting to a guard or prison official, or he attempts in any way to breach the security of this prison, he will be executed on the spot.

"Furthermore," said the old warden, "the guard receives a monetary commendation for defending the regulations, so watch yourself. A smart dog recognizes the whip and avoids the lash."

He helped himself to a pinch of snuff and sneezed twice.

Yakov asked if he could have another prisoner, some decent person, for company. "It's hard to live without another soul to talk to, your honour. How is one to ease his heart a little?"

"That's the least of my worries," said the warden.

"Then could I have some kind of an animal to keep, either a cat or maybe a bird?"

"A cat out of your rations? – you'd both starve. Either he'd eat you or you'd eat him. Anyway, this is a prison for criminals, and not a tea-parlour or clubhouse. You're not here for comforts or coddling but for strict punishment for the mean murder you committed against a harmless child. Only you Jew prisoners have the nerve to make such requests. I've had enough of it."

In the fall the weather was bad, rainy and cold, and Yakov could see his breath in the cell. The asthma was not bothersome until he caught a cold, then it came on again, usually badly. Some mornings the outer wall of the cell, fronting the prison yard, was covered with lacy areas of frost. The inside walls, a foot thick, of brick, broken stone and cement, were scabby and cracked. After a heavy rain the

200

greater part of the stone-paved floor was moist with seepage from the earth. Part of the ceiling above the window dripped. On fair days the small barred window, about a metre above the fixer's head, though dirty, let in light. The light was dim and on rainy days disappeared in the dark. After supper Yakov was given a small smelly kerosene lamp without its glass chimney, that burned until morning and was then removed. But one night the lamp was not given to him because, the Deputy Warden said, kerosene cost money. The fixer asked for a candle instead, and the Deputy Warden said he would see about that, but the fixer never got the candle. The cell was pitch black all night. I'll get the candle when I get the indictment, Yakov thought.

When the wind was strong on the outside, cold air floated through the cracked window into the cell. Yakov offered to fix it if they would let him have a little putty and a ladder, but no one was interested. The cell was cold but at least he had a mattress, a thin lumpy straw pallet whose last occupant – Zhitnyak, the small-eyed, black-fingered day guard, told him – had died of jail fever. The fixer kept the mattress on the dry part of the floor. There were bedbugs in it but he managed to beat out and kill some. His back ached after he had slept on it, and the straw in the sacking stank of mould, but it was better than sleeping on the stone floor. In November they gave him a ragged blanket. He also had a three-legged stool in the cell and a greasy small wooden table, one leg shorter than the other three. He had a jug of water in one corner of the cell; and in the opposite corner he kept the smelly can he urinated and defecated in, when there was something to defecate. Once a day he was allowed to empty the slop can into one of the barrels that were trundled past the cells by another prisoner, who wasn't allowed to speak to the fixer and whom Yakov was forbidden to address. He could tell from where the trundle stopped in the corridor that the cells on both sides of him were empty. It was a solitary solitary.

The bolted cell door was made of three sheets of iron, once painted black but now largely rusted; it had a peephole at eye level covered by a metal disk that the guard slipped aside to look in. Once every hour or so during the day a single eye roamed the cell. Zhitnyak was usually there in the daytime and Kogin at night; some days their times overlapped, and occasionally they exchanged shifts. When Yakov secretly pushed aside the disk and looked through the peephole, he could see Zhitnyak sitting in a large chair against the wall, hacking with his pocket knife at a stick, looking at pictures in a magazine, or dozing. He was a heavy-shouldered man with hairy nostrils and blackened stubby fingers, as though he had once worked with grease or lampblack that he had never got off. When he stepped into the cell he smelled of sweat and cabbage. Zhitnyak had a pockmarked face and an impatient manner. He was surly and unpredictable and sometimes struck the fixer.

Kogin, the night guard, was a tall man with a gaunt face and watery eyes, worn with worry. He spoke in a deep voice that seemed to rise from the ground. Even his whisper was low and heavy. Often he paced the corridor as if he were the prisoner; Yakov could hear his boots going back and forth on the concrete floor. At night Kogin opened the spy hole and listened to the fixer's asthmatic breathing and when he talked or shouted in his sleep. Yakov knew he was there, because when his nightmares or sleep-shouting woke him, he saw the dim light from the hall through the hole, and he saw the disk slowly moved back into place. Sometimes he woke up as Kogin was shining a torch through the peephole. Sometimes he could hear the guard's heavy breathing at the cell door.

Zhitnyak was the more talkative of the two, though he said little enough. Kogin at first did not speak to the fixer, but once after he had been drinking he complained that his son had come to nothing. "He does no steady work," the guard said in his deep voice. "When will he get himself a job? I've waited thirty years for him to become a man and I'm still waiting. 'Wait,' I tell myself, 'he will change. He will become a man,' but he never does. He even steals from me and I am his father. My wife says it's my fault for not hitting him when he was a child and up to bad tricks, but that's not my nature. I had enough of that from my own father, may he rot in his grave. What's more, the daughter doesn't behave well either, but I won't go into that. The son will one day end up in prison the same as you, and it will serve him right. That's all that comes from a father's love."

In October Yakov had begged the guards to light the brick stove in the cell, but the Deputy Warden at first refused to spare the wood. Then one day in November Zhitnyak opened the door and two close-cropped prisoners, who sneaked looks at Yakov, brought the fixer a small load of wood tied in bundles. He had had a cold and asthma, and maybe one of the guards had reported it to the warden, who perhaps felt he had to keep the prisoner alive. The warden, as Yakov saw him, was not a vicious man. He was at best a disciplinarian, at worst, stupid. The Deputy Warden was something else. The fixer shuddered at the man's depthless eyes, narrow face, and four-fingered hand. Whatever he looked at he seemed to gnaw a little. His small mouth was crafty and hiddenly hungry. His boots stank of dog turd or whatever he used to polish them with. The guards wore guns in their holsters, but the Deputy Warden had a large gun on each hip. He had taken his time giving his permission for Yakov to have wood. The fixer disliked and feared him more than anyone in the prison.

The tall upright yellow brick stove leaked smoke at the top through a cracked brick, but Yakov preferred the smoke to the cold. He asked for the stove to be lit in the early morning, to get the frost off the wall although a small puddle formed on the floor when the cell warmed up; and he asked for a lit stove before supper so that he could eat in comfort. If the cell was too cold he could not taste the few bits of cabbage in his soup. If the cell was warm he tasted each morsel. To save wood he let the stove go out in the late morning. Afterwards, with his fingers he scraped the cold ashes out of the pit under the grate, put in a little kindling and some pieces of wood, then before supper, Zhitnyak came in to relight it. He did not seem to mind doing that, though he would sometimes curse as he was doing it. Yakov's hair was still not cropped but once was clipped a little by the prison barber; he was not permitted to shave, and his beard was growing long.

"That's to keep you looking more like a Jew," Zhitnyak said through the peephole. "They say the warden is going to make you wear a Zhid caftan and a rabbi's round hat, and they're going to twist earlocks out of your hair over your ears so you'll look kosher. That's what the Deputy Warden said they'll do."

The prisoners in the other solitary cells down the hall were served their meagre food by other prisoners who were not allowed to serve the Jew. In Yakov's case they had to give the food to Zhitnyak, or Kogin, and he handed it to the fixer. This annoyed Zhitnyak, and sometimes when he brought Yakov's gruel or cabbage soup and bread, he said, "Here's your bowl of Christ's blood, drink hearty, mate."

To enter the cell, the guard on duty, sometimes backed up by another guard in the hall holding a shotgun, more often alone, unlocked the six three-ringed bolts that had been attached on the door the day Yakov had been put into this cell. Hearing the six bolts being snapped back one by one, four or five times a day, put the fixer on edge.

During the late autumn Yakov did not see the warden, then one day he appeared in the cell "for purposes of official business".

"They've found a finger-print on Zheniushka's belt buckle so we'd better take yours."

A detective appeared with an ink-pad and paper and took Yakov's finger-prints.

A week later the warden entered the cell with a large pair of scissors.

"They've found some hairs on the boy's body, and we want to compare them with yours."

Yakov uneasily gave him permission to cut his hair.

"You cut it," said Warden Grizitskoy. "Cut off six or eight hairs and put them in this envelope." He handed Yakov the scissors and envelope.

The fixer snipped off several of his hairs. "How do I know you won't take these hairs and put them on the boy's corpse and then say you found them there in the first place?"

"You are a suspicious type," said the warden. "That's true of all your race."

"Excuse me, but why should the warden of a prison look for evidence of a crime? Is he a policeman?"

"That's none of your damn business," said the warden. "If you're so innocent let's have the proof of it."

A louse fell into the envelope with the hairs but Yakov let it stay.

One morning the warden entered the cell with a pen,

bottle of black ink, and several sheets of foolscap paper for some samples of Yakov's handwriting. He ordered him to write in Russian, "My name is Yakov Shepsovitch Bok. It is true that I am a Jew."

Later the warden returned and asked the fixer to write the same words, lying on the floor. Then he had Zhitnyak hold the prisoner's legs as he stood on his head while writing his name.

"What's this for?" asked Yakov.

"To see if the change in position changes your writing any. We want all possible samples."

And twice a day since he had been in this cell there were inspections of the fixer's body; "searches" they were called. The bolts of the door were shot back, and Zhitnyak and the Deputy Warden, with his smelly boots, came into the cell and ordered the fixer to undress. Yakov had to remove his clothes – the greatcoat, prison jacket, buttonless shirt, which were never washed though he had asked that he be allowed to wash them; and then he dropped his trousers and long drawers. He was allowed to keep on his threadbare under-shirt, possibly so he wouldn't freeze to death. They also made him remove the torn socks and wooden clogs he had worn since the time the surgeon had lanced the sores on his feet, and to spread his toes apart so that Zhitnyak could inspect between them.

"Why do you do this?" Yakov had asked at the time of the first search.

"Shut your trap," said Zhitnyak.

"It's to see you haven't hidden any kind of weapon up your arse or in your clothes," said the Deputy Warden. "We have to protect you."

"What weapons could I hide? Everything was taken from me."

206

"You're a foxy sort but we've dealt with your kind before. You could be hiding small files, nails, pins, matches or such; or maybe even poison pills the Jews gave you to commit suicide with."

"I have none of those things."

"Spread your arse," said the Deputy Warden.

Yakov had first to raise his arms and spread his legs. The Deputy Warden probed with his four fingers in Yakov's armpits and around his testicles. The fixer then had to open his mouth and raise his tongue; he stretched both cheeks with his fingers as Zhitnyak peered into his mouth. At the end he had to bend over and pull apart his buttocks.

"Use more newspaper on your arse," said Zhitnyak.

"To use you have to have."

After his clothes were searched he was permitted to dress. It was the worst thing that happened to him and it happened twice a day.

3

He sank into deep gloom. I'll be here for ever. The indictment will never come. I can beg on both broken knees but they won't give it to me. They will never bring me to trial.

In December, frost appeared on the four walls in the morning. Once he awoke with his hand stuck to the wall. The air was dead icy air. The fixer walked all day to keep from freezing. His asthma was worse. At night he lay on the straw mattress in his greatcoat, covered with the blanket, gasping, snoring thickly, wheezing as he desperately fought to breathe. The one listening at the peephole shut it and moved away. One morning Zhitnyak helped Yakov pile up a new load of bundles of wood almost chest high against the outer wall. And in the evening there were pieces of meat floating in the cabbage soup, and some round flecks of fat.

"What's happened?" the fixer asked.

The guard shrugged. "The higher-ups don't want you dying on them. You can't try a corpse in court, as the saying goes." He winked and laughed a little.

Maybe this means the indictment is coming, Yakov thought in excitement. They don't want me looking like a skeleton in the court.

Not only was the food better, there was more of it. In the morning there were two extra ounces of bread and the gruel was thicker, barley with watery hot milk. And there was a half lump of sugar for the tea, which diluted the rotten taste a little. The fixer chewed slowly, savouring what he was eating. A cockroach in the bowl no longer bothered him. He plucked it out and ate, afterwards licking the bowl with his tongue. Zhitnyak brought the food into the cell and left at once. But he sometimes watched Yakov eat, through the spy hole, although the prisoner as he ate usually sat on the stool with his back to the iron door.

"How's the soup?" Zhitnyak asked through the hole.

"Fine."

"Eat hearty." When Yakov had finished the guard was gone.

Though there was more to eat, the fixer hungered for more. The minute after he had eaten he was hungry. He had visions of Zhitnyak appearing one day with a huge plate of well-seasoned chicken soup, thick with broad yellow noodles, a platter of meat kreplach, and half a haleh loaf from which

208

he would tear hunks of sweet foamy bread that melted on the tongue. He dreamed of rice and noodle pudding with raisins and cinnamon, as Raisl had deliciously baked it; and of anything that went with sour cream – blintzes, cheese kreplach, boiled potatoes, radishes, scallions, sliced crisp cucumbers. Also of juicy tomatoes of tremendous size that he had seen in Viscover's kitchen. He sucked a ripe tomato till it dribbled from his mouth, then, to get to sleep, finally had to finish it off, thickly salted, with a piece of white bread. After such fantasies he could hardly wait for the guard to come with his breakfast; yet when it came at last he restrained himself, eating very slowly. First he chewed the bread until its hard texture and grain flavour were gone, then bit by bit swallowed it down. Usually he saved part of his ration for night-time, in bed, when he got ravenously hungry thinking of food. After the bread he ate the gruel, sucking each barley grain as it melted in his mouth. At night he worked every spoonful of soup over his tongue, each pulpy cabbage bit and thread of meat, taking it in very small sips and swallows, at the end scraping the bowl with his blackened spoon. He was grateful for the somewhat more satisfying portions he was getting, and although he was never not hungry, after this somewhat better, more plentiful food, he was a little less hungry than he had been.

But in a week his hunger was gone. He awoke nauseated one morning and waited a long day for it to go away but only felt worse. He felt sick in his mouth, eyes, and in the pit of his bowel. It's not asthma, he thought, then if so what's wrong with me? His armpits and crotch itched, he was cold inside himself and his feet were ice. He also had diarrhoea.

"What's going on here?" said Zhitnyak when he entered the cell in the morning. "You didn't eat your last night's soup."

o   209

"I'm sick," said the fixer, lying in his greatcoat on the straw mattress.

"Well," said the guard as he scrutinized the prisoner's face, "maybe you might have jail fever."

"Couldn't I go to the infirmary?"

"No, you had your turn already but maybe I'll tell the warden if I see him. In the meantime you better eat this barley gruel. It's got hot milk in with the barley, and that's good for sickness."

"Couldn't I get out in the yard for a breath of air? The cell stinks and I've had no exercise for a long time. Maybe I would feel better outside."

"The cell stinks because you do. You can't go out in the yard because that's against the regulations when you're in strict confinement."

"How long will I be kept that way?"

"You'd better shut up your questions. That's for the higher-ups to say."

Yakov ate the gruel and threw it up. He sweated violently, the mattress soaked. In the evening a doctor came into the cell, a young man with a sparse beard and brown fedora. He took the prisoner's temperature, examined his body, and felt his pulse.

"There is no fever," he said. "It's some kind of harmless stomach complaint. You also have a rash. Drink your tea and never mind the solid food for a day or two, then you can go back on regular fare."

He left quickly.

After fasting two days the fixer felt better and went back to gruel and cabbage soup, though not to black bread. He hadn't the energy to chew it. When he touched his head hairs came off on his fingers. He felt listless, despondent. Zhitnyak watched him through the hole, peeking in from the side. The diarrhoea occurred more frequently, and after it Yakov lay, enervated and panting, on the mattress. Though he was very weak he kept up the fire in the stove all day and Zhitnyak did not say no. The fixer still felt cold and nothing seemed to warm him. The one good thing was that there were now no searches.

He asked again to be sent to the infirmary but when the Deputy Warden came into the cell, he said, "Eat your food and cut out malingering. Starving is what makes you sick."

Yakov forced himself to eat and after a few spoonfuls it was not too bad. Later he vomited. He vomited repeatedly although there was nothing left in his stomach. And at night he had terrible dreams, visions of mass slaughter that left him sleepless, moaning. When he dozed again people were being cut down by Cossacks with sabres. Yakov was shot running into the woods. Yakov, hiding under a table in his hut, was dragged forth and beheaded. Yakov, fleeing along a rutted road, had lost an arm, an eye, his bloody balls; Raisl, lying on the sanded floor, had been raped beyond caring, her fruitless guts were eviscerated. Shmuel's split and broken body hung from a window. The fixer awoke in nausea, afraid to sleep although when he was awake the thick foul-smelling sickness was worse to bear than his nightmares. He often wished for death.

One night he dreamed of Bibikov hanging over his head and awoke with a heavy taste in his mouth, as if his tongue had turned to brass.

He sat up in fright. "Poison! My God, they're poisoning me!"

He wept for a while.

In the morning he would not touch the food Zhitnyak had brought in, nor drink the tea.

"Eat," ordered the guard, "or you'll stay sick."

"Why don't you shoot me?" the fixer said bitterly. "It would be easier for both of us than this bastard poison."

Zhitnyak turned pale and hurriedly left the cell.

He returned with the Deputy Warden.

"Why do I have to spend so much time on one goddamned Jew?" said the Deputy Warden.

"You're poisoning me," Yakov said hoarsely. "You have no true evidence against me so you're poisoning my food to kill me off."

"It's a lie," said the Deputy Warden, "you're out of your head."

"I won't eat what you give me," Yakov cried. "I'll fast."

"Fast your arse off, it'll kill you just the same."

"Then it's your murder."

"Look who's accusing other people of murder," said the Deputy Warden, "the blood killer of a twelve-year-old Christian lad."

"You shithead," he said to Zhitnyak as they left the cell.

The warden soon hastily came in. "What are you complaining about now, Bok? It's against the prison regulations to refuse food. I warn you that any more unorthodox behaviour will be severely punished."

"You're poisoning me here," Yakov shouted.

"I know of no poison," the warden said sternly. "You're inventing this tale to make us look ridiculous. The doctor reported you had a stomach cold."

"It's poison. I can feel it in me. My body is sick and shrunken and my hair is falling out. You're trying to kill me."

"To hell with you," said the cross-eyed warden as he left the cell.

In a half-hour he was back. "It's not my doing," he said.

"I never gave such orders. If there's any poisoning done it's on the part of your fellow-Jews who are the most notorious well-poisoners of all time. And don't think I've forgotten your attempt, in this prison, to bribe Gronfein to poison or kill Marfa Golov so that she couldn't testify against you in court. Now your Jewish compatriots are trying to poison you out of fear you will confess your true guilt and implicate the whole nation. We just found out that one of the cook's assistants was a disguised Jew and packed him off to the police. He's the one who was poisoning your food."

"I don't believe it," said Yakov.

"Why would we want you to die? We want you sentenced to a severe life imprisonment as a lesson for all to see of Jewish perfidy."

"I won't eat what you give me. You can shoot me but I won't eat."

"If you expect to eat, eat what you get. If not you'll starve."

For the next five days Yakov starved. He exchanged the sickness of poisoning for the sickness of starving. He lay on the mattress, sleeping fitfully. Zhitnyak threatened him with a whipping but nothing came of it. On the sixth day the warden returned to the cell, his cross-eye watering and face flushed. "I command you to eat."

"Only out of the common pot," Yakov said weakly. "What the other prisoners eat I will eat. Let me go to the kitchen and take my gruel and soup out of the common pot."

"It cannot be allowed," said the warden. "You mustn't leave your cell. You are under strict confinement. Other prisoners are not allowed to look at you. It's all in the regulations."

"They can turn their heads while I draw my rations."

213

"No," said the warden. But after Yakov had fasted another day he consented. Twice a day the fixer, accompanied by Zhitnyak holding his drawn pistol, went to the prison kitchen in the west wing. Yakov drew his bread rations in the morning and filled his bowl from the common pot as the prisoners working in the kitchen momentarily faced the wall. He did not fill the bowl too full because if he did Zhitnyak poured some of it back.

He returned to half starvation.

4

He begged for something to do. His hands ached of emptiness, but he got nothing. The fixer offered to repair furniture, build tables, chairs, other pieces they might need – all he asked for was a few boards and his sack of tools. He missed his crosscut saw with the taped handle, his small German plane, the hammer and tri-square. He could still feel each tool with his fingers and remembered how each worked. The sharp saw could rip through a six-inch board in ten seconds. He liked the touch and smell of wood shavings. There were times he heard in his thoughts the two-toned buzz of the crosscut and the responsible knock of the hammer. He remembered things he had built with his tools, and sometimes in his thoughts he built them again. If he had the tools – if not his own, any tools – and some pieces of wood, he might earn himself a few kopeks to buy underdrawers, a wool vest, a warm pair of socks – other things he needed. If he earned a little money he secretly hoped he might pay someone to smuggle out a letter; or if not a letter then a message to Aaron Latke. But the tools and wood were refused him, and he cracked his knuckles constantly to do something with his hands.

He asked for a newspaper, a book of some sort, anything he could read to forget the tedium. Zhitnyak said the Deputy Warden had told him reading matter was forbidden to prisoners who had violated the regulations. So were paper and pencil. "If you hadn't written those sneaky letters you wrote, you wouldn't be in strict confinement now." "Where would I be then?" Yakov asked. "Better off. You might still be in the common cell." "Do you know when my indictment is supposed to come?" "No, and neither does anybody else, so don't ask me." Once Yakov said, "Why did you try to poison me, Zhitnyak, what did I do to you?" "Nobody said there was poison in that food," the guard said uneasily. "All they told me was to give it to you." Later he said, "It wasn't my fault. Nobody wanted to hurt you. The Deputy Warden thought you might confess faster if you got sick. The warden gave him a tongue lashing." The next morning Zhitnyak brought the prisoner a birch twig broom. "If you want to have it here, then keep your mouth shut from now on. The Deputy Warden says he's fed up of you talking to me. I'm not supposed to listen any more."

The broom was a stick with a bunch of thin birch twigs tied to it with cord. Yakov used it to sweep the cell every morning, working not too hard at first because he still felt weak from his sickness; yet he needed exercise to keep his strength up. He had again asked to be let out in the yard once in a while but, as he expected, the request was denied. Every day he thoroughly swept the stone floor, the wet parts and the dry. He swept in the corners of the cell, lifted his mattress and swept under that. He swept in the crevices between stones and once uncovered a centipede. He saw it escape under the door and the thought of that gave him a

215

headache. He also used the broom handle to beat the mattress, its covering threadbare and split on both sides, the discoloured straw visible so that he stopped beating it lest it fall apart. And when he beat it the mattress gave off a stench. Yakov patted it with his hands each morning as though to freshen it.

As much as he could he tried to arrange things so as to break the monotony of long stretches of time. When the bell rang in the corridor at 5 a.m. he arose in the cold dark, quickly cleaned the ashes out of the stove with his hand, raising dust he could smell, sweeping the small pile of ashes into a box they had given him for the purpose. Then he filled the stove with kindling, dry twigs, and some larger pieces of wood and waited for Zhitnyak, sometimes Kogin, to come in and light it. Formerly, the guard lit the stove when he brought in the prisoner's breakfast, and now that Yakov went to the kitchen for it, he lit the fire after the fixer returned with his food. Twice a day Yakov was permitted to go to the kitchen, not willing, when the warden suggested it, to give up the privilege of leaving the cell for a few minutes, although the warden gave his personal assurance that the food would be "perfectly healthful" if it were once again brought from the kitchen by the prisoners who delivered it to the guards.

"You have nothing to fear from us, Bok," he said. "I can assure you that the Prosecuting Attorney is most eager, as are all the other officials, to bring you to trial. No one would want to kill you off. We have other plans."

"When will my trial be?"

"I can't say," said Warden Grizitskoy. "They're still collecting evidence. It takes time."

"Then if you don't mind I'd rather keep on going to the kitchen."

As long as I can, he thought. I've paid for the privilege. He thought they were letting him continue to go only because they knew he knew they had tried to poison him.

After that the number of searches of Yakov's person was increased to three a day. His heart raced after these experiences, hatred thickened in it, and it took him a while to calm down. Sometimes after a search, to get the vile taste of it out of him, he swept the cell a second and third time. Or he collected the ashes out of the pit and had the wood ready for lighting long before Zhitnyak came in to take him to the kitchen to draw his supper rations. Though the stove was smoky the fixer ate near it, and after he had drunk the last of his tea, he threw in another stick or two of wood and lay down on the mattress with a sigh, hoping he could fall asleep before the stove went out and the cell became freezing. Sometimes the drinking water was ice in the morning and he had to melt it.

Passing water was another way to pass time. He urinated often, listening to the noise as the water rose in the tin can. Sometimes he held his water until it came forth with such heat and force his teeth hurt. When the can was collected was another momentary diversion. And every second day one of the guards filled the jug of water from which he drank and washed. There were no towels and he dried his hands on his ragged coat, or at the stove, rubbing them till they were dry. Fetyukov had given him a broken comb with which the fixer combed his hair and beard. Twice, thus far, he had been allowed into the bathhouse in the presence of a guard, when none of the other prisoners was there, and was permitted to wash his naked body with tepid water from a wooden bucket. He was worried to see how thin he had become. They would not touch his hair but once when his head was very lousy, the prison barber doused it with kerosene and let him comb the dead lice out with a fine comb. His beard went uncut though nobody objected that he kept it combed. Occasionally when Yakov complained that his nails were too long, Zhitnyak cut them for him. He would not allow the fixer to hold the scissors. Afterwards the guard collected the nail parings and put them into an oilskin pouch.

"What's that for?" asked Yakov.

"For an analysis they want to make," said the guard.

One morning something new appeared in Yakov's cell. An old prayer shawl and a pair of phylacteries had been left there after he had gone to the kitchen for his food. He examined the phylacteries, then put them aside, but he wore the prayer shawl under his greatcoat to help keep him warm. He was wearing a heavier prison suit than the one he had first got, though much used by other prisoners in the past and already falling apart. He also had a small cap with ear flaps that did not fit him, which he wore with the flaps down. The seams of his greatcoat had split in places. Zhitnyak loaned him a darning needle and some thread to sew them with; and Yakov received a blow in the face from the guard when he told him, afterwards, that he had lost the needle. He really hadn't; he had hidden it inside the stove. But the coat seams opened again and there was no thread. His wooden clogs had been taken from him and he now wore bast shoes without laces; he was not allowed to have a belt. When Yakov put the prayer shawl on, Zhitnyak watched through the spy hole, often looking in unexpectedly as though hoping to catch the fixer at prayer. He never did.

Yakov spent hours pacing in the cell. He walked to Siberia and back. Six or eight times a day he read the prison regulations. Sometimes he sat at the shaky table. He could eat at the table but there was nothing else to do at it that he

218

could think of. If he only had some paper and pencil he might write something down. With a knife he could whittle a piece of firewood, but who would give him a knife? He blew on his hands constantly. He feared he might go crazy doing nothing. If only there were a book to read. He remembered how he had studied and written in his stable room in the brickyard, at the table he had built himself with his tools. Once, just after Zhitnyak had peeked in, the fixer quickly piled up the loose wood at the wall and climbed up on top of the pile to see if he could look out the window into the prison yard. He thought the prisoners might be there on their promenade. He wondered whether any of those he knew were still in prison, or had they got out. But he could not reach the window bars with his hands, and all he saw out of it was a piece of leaden sky.

5

The newspaper strips he was given to clean himself with Zhitnyak forbade him to read, though Yakov managed to read some of them anyway.

"It's because you're an enemy of the state," the guard said through the peephole. "They're not allowed to read anything."

During the endless empty days, to forget his misery a little, the fixer tried to remember things he had read. He remembered incidents from Spinoza's life: how the Jews had cursed him in the synagogue; how an assassin had tried to kill him in the street, for his ideas; how he lived and died in his tiny room, studying, writing, grinding lenses for a living until his lungs had turned to glass. He had died young, poor and persecuted, yet one of the freest of men. He was free in his thoughts, his understanding of Necessity, and in the construction of his philosophy. The fixer's thoughts added nothing to his freedom; it was nil. He was imprisoned in a cell, and even in memory because so much that had happened to him during a life that had perhaps, at times, seemed free, now seemed designed to lead to this imprisonment. Necessity freed Spinoza and imprisoned Yakov. Spinoza thought himself into the universe but Yakov's poor thoughts were enclosed in a cell.

Who am I to compare myself?

He tried to recall the biology he had studied, and reflected on as much of history as he could bring to mind. They say God appeared in history and used it for his purposes, but if that was so he had no pity for men. God cried mercy and smote his chest, but there was no mercy because there was no pity. Pity, in lightning? You could not pity anything if you weren't a man; pity was a surprise to God. It was not his invention. And Yakov also recalled tales by Peretz, and some pieces he had read in the papers by Sholem Aleichem, and a few little stories he had read in Russian by Chekhov. He recalled things from the Scriptures, in particular, fragments of psalms he had read in Hebrew on old parchment. He could, in a sense, smell the Psalms as well as hear them. They were sung weekly in the synagogue to glorify God and protect the shtetl from harm, which they never did. Yakov had chanted them, or heard them chanted, many times, and now in a period of remembrance he uttered verses, stanzas that he did not think he knew. He could not recall a whole psalm, but from fragments he put together one that he recited aloud in the cell in order not to forget it, so that he could have it to say. In the morning he said it in Hebrew, and in the dark as he lay on his mattress, he tried to trans-

late the verses into Russian. He knew Kogin listened when
he said them aloud at night.

"Behold, he travaileth with iniquity;
Yea, he conceiveth mischief, and bringeth forth falsehood.
He hath digged a pit, and hollowed it,
And is fallen into the ditch which he made."

"I am weary with my groaning;
Every night make I my bed to swim;
I melt away my couch with my tears."

"For my days are consumed like smoke,
And my bones are burned as a hearth.
My heart is smitten like grass, and withered;
For I forget to eat my bread."

"Unrighteous witnesses rise up;
They ask me things that I know not."

"For I have heard the whispering of many,
Terror on every side;
While they took counsel together against me,
They devised to take away my life."

"Arise, O Lord; O God, lift up Thy hand;
Forget not the humble."

"Break Thou the arm of the wicked."

"Thou shalt make them as a fiery furnace in the time
of Thine anger."

"He bowed the heavens also, and came down;
And thick darkness was under His feet."

"And He sent out His arrows, and scattered them;
And He shot forth lightnings, and discomfited them."

"I have pursued my enemies, and overtaken them;
Neither did I turn back till they were consumed."

He thought of himself pursuing his enemies with God at
his side, but when he looked at God all he saw or heard was
a loud Ha Ha. It was his own imprisoned laughter.

6

I scratch at memory. I think of Raisl. I'm in prison so what
difference does it make? The first time I saw her she was
riding in her father's rickety wagon, drawn by the bony nag
of late memory. She sat with the sick mother amid their few
shreds of household goods. Shmuel was on the seat talking
to himself, or the horse's tail, or God; he went where the nag
pulled, but wherever he went he was going backward. They
were coming from some place, where I don't know. Where
can you come from in the Pale that's so different from where
you're going? Everywhere he tried to make a better living,
and everywhere he couldn't so he tried some place else. He
came to our town, and the mother, fed up with adventure,
died on the spot. After that her grave kept him in one place.
Also from such a hard-luck father what kind of daughter
could you expect, so I stayed away from her. Naturally I
stayed away for the months I was in the army, but I also
stayed away from her when I got back, though not for long.
(She would have done me a favour to have got married
while I was gone.) Anyway, she was a pretty girl, intelligent
and dissatisfied, with even then a sad face. At least the right
eye was sad; the left was neutral, it reflected me. I saw her
many times in the market before I got up the nerve to talk to

her. She scared me, I wasn't sure I had what she wanted. I was afraid she would rub my nose in my future. Anyway I saw the other young men looking at her and I looked too. She was a thin lanky girl with small breasts. I remember her dark hair in braids, deep eyes, and a long neck. She wore in the morning what she had washed out at night; sometimes the clothes were damp. The father wanted her to work as a servant girl but she wouldn't. She bought a few eggs from a peasant woman and set up a little stall in the market. Whenever I could I bought an egg from her. She lived with Shmuel in a hut off the road near the bathhouse stream. When I came for a visit they seemed glad to see me, especially the father. He was looking for a husband for her and a dowry didn't exist. If it existed it was a cherry pit. But he knew my type, that I wouldn't ask questions and he wouldn't mention it.

We walked together in the woods by the water, she and I. I showed her my tools and once cut down a small tree with my saw. I fixed up their hut a little, made a bench, a cupboard, and a few shelves out of some boards I was saving. If there was a little chicken to eat I came also on Friday nights. Raisl blessed the candles and served the food, it was very nice. We liked each other but both had doubts. I think she thought, He won't move, he isn't ambitious, he'll stay here for ever. What kind of future is that? I thought to myself, She's a complicated girl and won't be easy to satisfy. What she wants she'll drive me wild to get. Still, I liked to be with her. One day in the woods we became man and wife. She said no but took a chance. Later it bothered her. She was afraid for her child once she had one, that it would be born crippled or with seven fingers. "Don't be superstitious," I said. "If you want to be free, first be free in your mind." Instead she began to cry. After a while I said, "All right, you've cried enough, so before it happens again let's get married. I need a wife and you need a husband." At this her eyes got big and once again were full of tears. She didn't answer me. "Why don't you talk?" I said. "Say yes or no." "Why don't you say love?" she said. "Who talks about love in the shtetl?" I asked her. "What are we, millionaires?" I didn't say so but it's a word that makes me nervous. What does a man like me know about love? "If you don't love me I can't marry you," she answered me. But by then the father had his nose in my ear. "She's a doll, a marvellous girl, you can't go wrong. She'll work hard and both together you'll make a living." So I said love and she said yes. Maybe my poor future looked better than her own.

After we were married, all she talked about was we must get out of Russia, including the father, because things were getting worse, not better. Worse for us and worse for the Russians. "Let's sell everything and leave while we can." I answered her. "Even if we sell everything we'll have nothing. Believe me, there's no shortage of places to go to in this wide world, but first I'll work hard and we'll save a few roubles, and in that case who knows where we'll get to. Maybe it'll take a year or two and then we'll leave." She looked at me with a tight face. "After another year you'll never go; you're afraid to leave." Maybe she was right but I said, "Your father changed places every time he breathed and all he's collected is air. I'll stay in one place and build up a little capital, and then I'll think of leaving." That wasn't strictly the truth. I was in no hurry to run to another country. Some men are by nature explorers; my nature is to stay under the same moon and stars, and if the weather is wet, under the same roof. It's a strange world, why make it stranger? When I was in the Tsar's army I was less afraid of the world but once I got home again enough was enough.

In other words, in those days to make me move, somebody had to push. So she pushed. But we didn't get along so badly until another year or two went by and we still had no capital, and we had no children. Raisl was depressed and either said nothing, or wept, and never left off complaining. Our hut was divided into two small rooms. At night she stayed in bed while I sat in the kitchen. It was at this time that I began to read more. I picked up books here and there, a few I stole, and read by the lamp. Many times after I read I slept on the kitchen bench. When I was reading Spinoza I stayed up night after night. I was by now excited by ideas and I tried to collect a few of my own. It was the beginning of a different Yakov. I thought of things I had never thought of before, and then when I began to read a little history and also a pamphlet about Nicholas I, the Tsar's father, I said to myself, "She's right, we ought to get out of here and the sooner the better."

But without a living where can you go? We went nowhere. By now it was coming to six years that we were married and still had no children. I said nothing but I was, in my heart, a disappointed man. Who could I look in the face? In her heart Raisl was frantic. She blamed it on her sins. Maybe on my sins. She was running again, in her big wig, to the rabbis, who had never helped her, if not in our town, then in the others. She tried magic and she tried spells. She recited verses from the Scriptures and drank potions squeezed out of parts of fish and hares. I don't believe in this kind of business. Anyway, as one might expect, nothing happened. "Why has God cursed me?" she cried. "What God?" I said. She was a desperate woman. "Will I be just like my father, will I always have *nothing*? Will I have less than my father?" By this time I was worn out living in a storm. She ran this way and that, she wept, she cursed her life. I said less and read more though the books didn't bring me a kopek unless I sold them. I thought I would take her to a big doctor in Kiev, but who would pay for it? So nothing happened. She stayed barren and I stayed poor. Every day she begged me to leave so our luck would change. "Leave," I said, "on whose wings?" Then I said, "Like your father's luck changed." So she looked at me with hatred. I began to stay away from the house. When I came in at night I slept in the kitchen. The next thing I knew they were talking about her in the taverns. Then one day she was gone. I opened the door and the house was empty. At first I cursed her like somebody in the Bible curses his whorish wife. "May she keep her miscarrying womb and dry breasts." But now I look at it like this: She had tied herself to the wrong future.

7

You wait. You wait in minutes of hope and days of hopelessness. Sometimes you just wait, there's no greater insult. You sink into your thoughts and try to blot out the prison cell. If you're lucky it dissolves and you spend a half-hour out in the open, beyond the doors and walls and the hatred of yourself. If you're not lucky your thoughts can poison you. If you're lucky and get out to the shtetl you might call on a friend, or if he's out, sit alone on a bench in front of his hut. You can smell the grass and the flowers and look at the girls, if one or two happen to be passing by along the road. You can also do a day's work if there's work to do. Today there's a little carpentering job. You work up a sweat sawing wood apart and hammering it together. When it's time to eat you open your food parcel – not bad. The thing about food is to have a little when you want it. A hard-boiled egg with a pinch of salt is delicious. Also some sour cream with a cut-up potato. If you dip bread into fresh milk and suck before swallowing, it tastes like a feast. And hot tea with lemon and a lump of sugar. In the evening you go across the wet grass to the edge of the wood. You stare at the moon in the milky sky. You breathe in the fresh air. An ambition teases you, there's still the future. After all, you're alive and free. Even if you're not so free, you think you are. The worst thing about such thoughts is when they leave you and you're back in the cell. The cell is your woods and sky.

Yakov counted. He counted time though he tried not to. Counting presupposed an end to counting, at least for a man who used only small numbers. How many times had he counted up to a hundred in his life? Who could count for ever? – it piled time on. The fixer had torn some splinters off sticks of firewood. The long splinters were months, the short, days. A day was a bad enough burden of time but within the day even minutes could do damage as they piled up. When one had nothing to do the worst thing to have was an endless supply of minutes. It was like pouring nothing into a million little bottles.

At five in the morning the day began and never ended. In the early evening dark he was already lying on his mattress trying to sleep. Sometimes he tried all night. During the day there were the regular checks through the spy hole, and three depressing searches of his body. There was cleaning out ashes, and making and lighting the stove. There was the sweeping of the cell to do, urinating in the can, walking back and forth until one began to count; or sitting at the table with nothing to do. There was the going for, and eating of, his meagre meals. There was trying to remember and trying to forget. There was the counting of each day; there was reciting the psalm he had put together. He also watched the light and dark change. The morning dark was different from the night dark. The morning dark had a little freshness, a little anticipation in it, though what he anticipated he could not say. The night dark was heavy with thickened and compounded shadows. In the morning the shadows unfurled until only one was left, that which lingered in the cell all day. It was gone for a minute near eleven he guessed, when a beam of sunlight, on days the sun appeared, touched the corroded inner wall a foot above his mattress, a beam of golden light gone in a few minutes. Once he kissed it on the wall. Once he licked it with his tongue. After the sun had gone, light from the window descended more darkly. When he stole a newspaper strip to read, the darkness was on the paper. It was night at half past three in the afternoon in December. Yakov put wood in the stove and Zhitnyak, after they had gone for the night rations, lit it. He ate in the dark or by the light through the stove door left ajar. There was still no lamp, no candle. The fixer set a small splinter aside to mark the lost day and crawled on to his mattress.

The long splinters were months. He figured it was January. Zhitnyak wouldn't tell him, nor would Kogin. They said they were forbidden to answer such questions. He had been arrested in the brickyard in mid-April and had served in the District Courthouse jail for two months. He figured he had been in this prison another seven months, a total of nine, if not more. It would soon – soon? – be a full year of prison. He did not, could not, think past a year. He could not foresee any future in the future. When he thought about the future all he thought about was the indictment. He imagined the warden snapping back the six bolts and bringing in the indictment in a thick brown envelope. But in this thought, after the warden had left, the indictment had still not come and he was still counting time. How long would he wait? He waited with months, days, minutes on his heavy head, and with the repetitive cycles of light and dark piled on top of the long and short pieces of time. He waited with boredom sticking its fingers down his throat. He waited for an unknown time, a time different from all the time on his head. It was unending waiting for something that might never happen. In the winter, time fell like hissing snow through the crack in the barred window, and never stopped snowing. He stood in it as it piled up around him and there was no end to drowning.

One wintry day, sickened of time, he tore off his clothes. The rags fell apart in his hands.

"Bastards!" he shouted through the peephole at the guards, prison officials, Grubeshov, and the Black Hundreds. "Anti-Semites! Murderers!"

They let him stay naked. Zhitnyak would not light the stove. The fixer's body turned blue as he walked frantically in the freezing cell. He shivered on the mattress, shook, with the prayer shawl and ragged blanket wrapped around him.

"By morning," the Deputy Warden said when he came in with the guard for the last search of the day, "you won't need clothes. You'll be frozen stiff. Spread your filthy arse."

But the warden entered before nightfall and said it was indecent to have a naked Jew parading around in the cell. "You could have been shot for less than this."

He flung at Yakov another threadbare suit of prison clothes, and another ragged greatcoat. Zhitnyak then lit the stove, but it took the fixer a week to get the ice out of his spine, and the cold hurt worse than before.

Then he began to wait again.

He waits.

8

The warden, in full uniform, delivered a message from Prosecuting Attorney Grubeshov to Yakov in his solitary cell.

"You're to get dressed in your street clothes and go to the Plossky Courthouse. Your indictment is ready."

The fixer, stunned, shut his eyes. When he opened them the warden was still there.

"How shall I go, your honour?" His voice broke.

"A detective will accompany you. Since it's a short distance you can go by streetcar. You will be allowed out for no more than an hour and a half. That is the time the Prosecuting Attorney requisitioned you for."

"Must my legs be chained again?"

The warden scratched in his beard. "No, but you'll be handcuffed and there'll be strict orders to shoot you dead if you try anything in the least irregular. Furthermore, two Secret Police officers will be following you and the detective in case any of your cohorts attempt to communicate with you."

In half an hour Yakov was outside the prison, waiting with the detective for a trolley. Though the day was dreary and cold, the streets white in every direction, the leafless trees black against the frozen sky, everywhere he looked brought tears to the fixer's eyes. It seemed to him he was seeing for the first time how the world was knit together.

On the trolley he watched the shops and passers-by in the street as though he were in a foreign country. How moving it was that a peasant entered a store. The detective sat next to him, one hand in his overcoat pocket. He was a heavy-bellied man with eyeglasses and a grey fur cap, who sat silent. All the way to the courthouse the fixer worried what the indictment would say. Would it accuse him simply of murder, or of murder "for ritual purposes"? The evidence was non-existent, "circumstantial" at best, but he feared their ingenuity. When the purpose was frame-up, the evidence could be arranged. Yet whatever the indictment said, the important thing to him now was getting it so that he could talk to a lawyer. Once he had done that maybe they would not keep him in solitary confinement. Even if they put him in with a murderer it would be better than being so desperately alone. The lawyer would tell everyone who he was. He would say, "This is a decent man, he could never have killed a child." The fixer worried about getting the proper lawyer, wondering who Bibikov had had in mind, "a vigorous and courageous man of excellent reputation". Would Ivan Semyonovitch know, if he were permitted to ask him? Was the lawyer a Russian or a Jew? Which was best? And how would he pay him? Could a lawyer advise him if he had no money to give him? And even if he had a good lawyer, would he be able to defend him if Bibikov's files had fallen into the hands of the Black Hundreds?

Despite these worries, and though he was tightly handcuffed, a prisoner out of jail for a few minutes, Yakov enjoyed the trolley ride. The people around him and the movement of the car created an illusion of freedom.

At the next stop two men boarded the streetcar, and passing the fixer, saw his manacled hands. They whispered to each other, and when they sat down, whispered to others. Some of the passengers turned their heads to stare at him. Noticing this he shut his eyes.

"It's that bastard killer of a Christian child," a man in a

knitted wool hat said. "I saw him once in a motor-car in front of Marfa Golov's house after they arrested him."

Some of the men in the car began to mutter among themselves.

Then the detective spoke calmly. "Everything is in good order, my friends. Don't excite yourselves for nothing. I am accompanying the prisoner to the courthouse, where he will be indicted for his crime."

Two bearded Jews wearing large hats hastily got off the trolley at the next stop. A third tried to speak to the prisoner but the detective waved him away.

"If they convict you," the Jew shouted at Yakov, "cry, 'Sh'ma, Yisroël, the Lord our God, the Lord is One!'" He jumped off the moving trolley, and the two secret police, who had risen, sat down.

A woman in a hat with velvet flowers, when she went by, spat at the fixer. Her spittle dribbled from his beard. Soon the detective nudged him and they left the trolley at the next stop. They were trudging along on the snowy sidewalk when the detective stopped to buy an apple from a street vendor. He handed it to the fixer, who gobbled it down in three bites.

In the courthouse building Grubeshov had moved into a larger office with six desks in the anteroom. Yakov waited with the detective, nervously impatient to see the indictment. It's strange, he thought, that an indictment of murder should be so precious, yet without it he could not make the first move to defend himself.

He was summoned into the inner office. The detective, hat in his hand, followed him in and stationed himself at attention behind the prisoner but Grubeshov dismissed him with a nod. The Prosecuting Attorney sat stolidly at a new desk regarding the prisoner with squinting eyes. Little had changed but his appearance. He looked older and if that was so, how much older did Yakov look? He saw himself as bushy-haired, bearded, swimming in his clothes, and frightened to death.

Grubeshov coughed seriously and glanced away. Yakov saw no papers on his desk. Though he had made up his mind to be controlled before this archanti-Semite, he could not help himself and began to shiver. He had been trembling within and had suppressed it, but when he thought of what had happened to Bibikov, and how he himself had been treated and what he had endured because of Grubeshov, a bone of hatred thickened in his throat and his body shook. It trembled violently as though it were trying to expel a poisonous substance. And though he was ashamed to be shivering as though feverish or freezing in front of this man, he could not stop it.

The Prosecuting Attorney looked on in puzzlement for a minute. "Are you suffering a chill, Bok?" The slightly thick voice attempted sympathy.

The fixer, still uncontrollably shaking, said he was.

"Have you been ill?"

Yakov nodded, trying to mask his contempt for the man.

"A pity," said the prosecutor. "Well, sit down and try to control yourself. Let's get on with other matters."

Unlocking his desk drawer, he took out a pack of closely typewritten long sheets of blue paper. There were about twenty pages.

My God, so many? Yakov thought. His trembling subsided and he sat forward anxiously.

"So," said Grubeshov, smiling as though he understood the matter for the first time, "you have come for the indictment?" He fingered the papers.

The fixer, staring at them, wet his lips.

"I suppose you find incarceration a not very pleasant experience?"

Though moved to shriek, Yakov nodded.

"Has it altered your thinking, yet?"

"Not of my innocence."

Grubeshov laughed a little, pushing his chair away from the desk. "A stubborn man walks with both feet tied. I am surprised at you, Bok. I wouldn't exactly have called you stupid. I think you know your future is nil if you continue to be stubborn."

"Please, when can I see a lawyer?"

"A lawyer won't do you the least good. You may take my word for it."

The fixer sat tensely, silent but wary.

Grubeshov began to walk on his oriental rug. "Even with six or seven lawyers you will be convicted and sentenced to total solitary confinement for the rest of your life. Do you think a jury of patriotic Russians will believe what some shyster concocts for you to say?"

"I will tell them the truth."

"If the 'truth' is what you have told us, no sane Russian will believe you."

"I thought you might, your honour, since you know the evidence."

Grubeshov paused in his pacing to clear his throat. "I least of all, though I have given thought to the possibility that you were once a virtuous man who became the expiatory victim of his co-religionists. Would it interest you to know that the Tsar himself is convinced you committed the crime?"

"The Tsar?" said Yakov in astonishment. "Does he know about me? How could he think such a thing?" His heart sank heavily.

234

"His Majesty has taken an active interest in this case since he read of Zhenia's murder in the newspapers. He at once sat down at his desk and wrote me in his own hand the following: 'I hope you will spare no pains to unearth and bring to justice the despicable Jewish murderer of that lad.' I quote from memory. His Majesty is a most sensitive person and some of his intuitions are extraordinary. Since then I've kept him informed of the progress of the investigation. It is conducted with his full knowledge and approval."

Ah, it's bad luck, the fixer thought. After a while he said, "But why should the Tsar believe what isn't true?"

Grubeshov quickly returned to his desk and sat down. "He is convinced, as we all are, by the accumulative evidence conveyed in the testimony of the witnesses."

"What witnesses?"

"You know very well which witnesses," Grubeshov said impatiently. "By Nikolai Maximovitch Lebedev, for instance, and his daughter, refined and genteel people. By Marfa Golov, the long-suffering mother of an unfortunate son, a tragic but pure woman. By the foreman Proshko and the two drivers. By the janitor Skobeliev, who saw you offering sweets to Zhenia, and will testify in court that you chased the boy several times in the brickyard. It was through your intervention, Nikolai Maximovitch tells us, that the man was discharged from his job."

"I never knew he was discharged."

"There's a lot you don't know that you will find out."

Grubeshov went on naming witnesses. "I shall also cite testimony by your Jewish cellmate, Gronfein, whom you urged, as a favour to the Jewish community, to bribe Marfa Vladimirovna so she wouldn't testify against you. By a beggar woman who once asked you for alms, which you refused her, and who saw you enter a shop where knives are sharpened. By the proprietor of that establishment and his assistant, who will say two of your knives were sharpened to the highest pitch and then returned to you. By certain religious figures, scientists of Jewish history and theology, and alienists who are authorities on the Jewish mind. We have already gathered more than thirty reliable witnesses. His Majesty has read all the relevant testimony. When he last visited Kiev shortly after your arrest, I had the honour to inform him, 'Sire, I am happy to report that the guilty culprit in Zhenia Golov's murder has been apprehended and is now in prison. He is Yakov Bok, a member of one of the Jewish fanatic groups, the Hasidim.' I assure you His Majesty bared his head in the rain and made the sign of the cross to express his thanks to the Lord for your apprehension."

The fixer could see the Tsar crossing himself, bare-headed in the rain. For the first time he wondered if it were a matter of mistaken identity. Could they have confused him with someone else?

The prosecutor opened a side drawer of his desk and took out a folder of newspaper clippings. He read from one: "'His Majesty expressed himself as justified in his belief that the crime was the dastardly work of a Jewish criminal who must be properly punished for his barbaric deed. "We shall do whatever is necessary to protect our innocent Russian children and their anxious mothers. When I think of my own wife and children I think of them."' If the ruler of the Russian State and its people is wholeheartedly convinced of your guilt, what chance do you think you will have for a verdict of not guilty? None, I assure you. No Russian jury will free you."

"Still," said the fixer, sighing brokenly, "the question is of the worth of the evidence."

"I have no doubts of its worth. Do you have any better evidence?"

"What if certain anti-Semitic groups committed the murder to cast suspicion on the Jews?"

Grubeshov banged his fist on the desk. "What a monstrous canard! It takes a Jew to shift the blame of his crime on to his accusers. You are apparently unaware of your own admissions, yes, confessions of guilt." He had begun to sweat and his breath whistled in his nose.

"Mine?" said Yakov, on the verge of panic. "What admissions? I have made none."

"You may think not but there is already a record of more than one confession you have made in your sleep. The guard Kogin has compiled it in his notebooks, and the Deputy Warden also heard you when he listened at the cell door at night. It's obvious that your conscience is heavily burdened, Yakov Bok, and for good and sufficient reason. There is much crying out against the abhorrent nature of your crime, sighs, ejaculations, grunts, even sobs of remorse. It is because you obviously feel some sorrow for what you have done that I am willing to talk to you in this kindly way."

Yakov's eyes again crept to the papers on the desk.

"Could I see the indictment, your honour?"

"My advice to you," Grubeshov said, wiping his neck with a handkerchief, "is to sign a confession saying you committed the murder unwillingly, under the influence of your religious cohorts. Once that's done, as I informed you the last time I talked to you, something to your advantage may be arranged."

"I have nothing to confess. What can I confess to you? I can only confess my miseries. I can't confess the murder of Zhenia Golov."

237

"Listen, Bok, I speak to you for your own good. Your position otherwise is hopeless. A confession by you will have more than one beneficial effect. For your fellow-Jews it may prevent reprisals. Do you know that at the time of your arrest Kiev was on the verge of a massive pogrom? It was only the fortuitous appearance of the Tsar to dedicate a statue to one of his ancestors that prevented it. That won't happen a second time, I assure you. Think it over, there are strong advantages for you. I am willing to see to it that you are secreted out of prison and taken to Podovoloshchisk on the Austrian border. You will have a Russian passport in your pocket and the means of transportation to some country outside of Europe. This includes Palestine, America, or even Australia, if you choose to go there. I advise you to consider this most carefully. The alternative is to spend your lifetime in prison under circumstances much less favourable than those you are presently enjoying."

"Excuse me, but how will you then explain to the Tsar that you let a confessed murderer of a Christian child go?"

"That part doesn't concern you," said Grubeshov.

The fixer didn't believe him. A confession, he knew, would doom him for ever. He was already doomed.

"The warden said you would give me the indictment."

Grubeshov uneasily studied the top sheet of the paper, then put it down. "The indictment requires the signature of the Investigating Magistrate. He is away on official business and has not yet returned to his office. In the meantime I want to know what your response is to my more than reasonable proposal?"

"I have enough to confess but not that crime."

"Ach, you are a stupid Jew."

Yakov readily agreed.

238

"If you have hopes of the sympathy and perhaps assistance of Magistrate Bibikov, you had better give them up. He has been replaced by another."

The fixer clamped his teeth tight to keep from going into shudders again.

"Where is Mr Bibikov?"

Grubeshov spoke restlessly. "He was arrested for peculating from official funds. While awaiting trial, overwhelmed by his disgrace, he committed suicide."

The fixer shut his eyes.

When he opened them he said, "Could I speak to his assistant, Mr Ivan Semyonovitch?"

"Ivan Semyonovitch Kuzminsky," said the Prosecuting Attorney coldly, "was taken into custody at the Agricultural Fair last September. He did not remove his hat when the band played 'God Save the Tsar'. If my memory is correct he was sentenced to a year in the Petropavelsky Fortress."

The fixer gasped silently.

"Do you get the point?" Grubeshov's face was taut, sweaty.

"I am innocent," the fixer shouted hoarsely.

"No Jew is innocent, least of all a ritual assassin. Furthermore, it is known you are an agent of the Jewish Kahal, the secret Jewish international government which is engaged in a subterranean conspiracy with the World Zionist Organization, the Alliance of Herzl, and the Russian Freemasons. We also have reason to believe that your masters are dickering with the British to help you overthrow the legitimate Russian government and make yourselves rulers of our land and people. We are not exactly naïve. We know your purposes. We have read the 'Protocols of the Elders of Zion', and the 'Communist Manifesto', and fully understand your revolutionary intentions!"

"I am not a revolutionist. I am an inexperienced man. Who knows about such things? I am a fixer."

"You can deny it all you want, we know the truth," Grubeshov shouted. "The Jews dominate the world and we feel ourselves under their yoke. I personally consider myself under the power of the Jews; under the power of Jewish thought, under the power of the Jewish Press. To speak against the crimes of the Jews means to evoke the charge that one is either a Black Hundred, an obscurantist, or a reactionary. I am none of these things. I am a Russian patriot! I love the Russian Tsar!"

Yakov stared miserably at the indictment papers.

Grubeshov grabbed them and locked them in the drawer.

"If you come to your senses, let me know through the warden. Until then you will continue to give off your stink in prison."

Before Yakov was permitted to leave the office, the Prosecuting Attorney, his face darkened by blood, reading from his notebook, asked the prisoner if he was related to Baal Shem Tov or Rabbi Zalman Schneur of Ladi, and whether there had ever been a shochet in his family. To each question Yakov, shivering uncontrollably, replied no, and Grubeshov painstakingly recorded his answers.

9

He sat in his prison clothes in the dark cell, his beard tormented, eyes red, head burning, the acid cold cracking his bones. The snow hissed on the window. The wind seeping through the split glass sank on him like an evil bird, gnawing his head and hands. He ran in the cell, his breath visible,

beating his chest, waving his arms, slapping blue hands together, crying anguish. He sighed, he wailed, called to the
sky for help, until Zhitnyak, one nervous eye at the spy
hole, ordered him to shut up. When the guard lit the evening fire the fixer sat at the smoky stove with its door open,
the collar of his greatcoat raised above his ears, the light of
the flames heatless on his face. Except for the glowing,
crackling, moaning fire the cell was black, dank, heavy with
wet stink. He could smell the rotten odour of himself in the
enduring stench of all the prisoners who had lived and died
in this miserable cell.

The fixer shivered for hours, plunged in the deepest
gloom. Who would believe it? The Tsar himself knew of
him. The Tsar was convinced of his guilt. The Tsar wanted
him convicted and punished. Yakov saw himself locked in
combat with the Russian Emperor. They wrestled, beard to
beard, in the dark until Nicholas proclaimed himself an
angel of God and ascended into the sky.

"It's all a fantasy," the fixer muttered. "He doesn't need
me and I don't need him. Why don't they let me alone?
What have I truly done to them?"

His fate nauseated him. Escaping from the Pale he had at
once been entrapped in prison. From birth a black horse
had followed him, a Jewish nightmare. What was being a
Jew but an everlasting curse? He was sick of their history,
destiny, blood guilt.

VII

He waits.

The snow turned to rain.

Nothing happened.

Nothing but the long winter; not the indictment.

He felt the change of weather in his head. Spring came but stayed outside the bars. Through the window he heard the shrilling of swallows.

The seasons came faster than the indictment. The indictment was very slow. The thought that it might sometime come made it so slow.

In the spring it rained heavily. He listened to the sound of the rain and liked the thought of the outside wet, but he didn't like the inside wet. Water seeped through the wall on the prison yard side. Lines of wet formed on the cement between the exposed bricks. From an eroded part of the ceiling above the window, water dripped after the rain had stopped. After the rain there was always a puddle on the floor. Sometimes the dripping went on for days. He awakened at night listening to it. Sometimes it stopped for a few minutes and he slept. When the dripping began again he awoke.

I used to sleep through thunder.

He was so nervous, irritable, so oppressed by imprisonment he feared for his sanity. What will I confess to them if I go mad? Each day's oppressive boredom terrified him. The boredom and the nervousness made him think he might go insane.

One day, out of hunger for something to do, for a word to read, he cracked open one of the phylacteries that had been left in the cell. Holding it by the thongs he hit the box against the wall till it burst with a puff of dust. The inside of the phylactery box smelled of old parchment and leather, yet there was a curious human odour to it. It smelled a little like the sweat of the body. The fixer held the broken phylactery to his nose and greedily sucked in the smell. The small black box was divided into four compartments, each containing a tightly rolled little scroll, two with verses from Exodus and two from Deuteronomy. Yakov puzzled out the script, remembering the words faster than he could read. The bondage in Egypt was over, and in one scroll Moses proclaimed the celebration of Passover. Another scroll was the Sh'ma Yisroël. Another enumerated the rewards for loving and serving God and the punishment for not: the loss of heaven, rain, and the fruit of that rain; even life. In each of the four scrolls the people were commanded to obey God and teach his words. "Therefore you shall lay up these my words in your heart and in your soul, and bind them for a sign upon your hand, that they may be frontlets between your eyes." The sign was the phylactery and it was the phylactery that Yakov had broken. He read the scrolls with excitement and sadness and hid them deep in the mattress

244

straw. But one day Zhitnyak, his eye roving at the peephole, caught the fixer absorbed in reading them. He entered the cell and forced him to give them up. The appearance of the four scrolls puzzled the guard, although Yakov showed him the broken phylactery; and Zhitnyak turned them over to the Deputy Warden, who was greatly excited to have this "new evidence".

A few weeks later, Zhitnyak, while in the cell, sneaked the fixer a small green paper-covered New Testament in Russian. The pages were worn and soiled with use. "It's from my old woman," Zhitnyak whispered. "She said to give it to you so you could repent for the wrong you did. Besides, you're always complaining you have nothing to read. Take it but don't tell anyone who gave it to you or I will break your arse. If they ask you say that one of the prisoners in the kitchen slipped it in your pocket without you knowing it, or maybe one of those who empty the shit cans."

"But why the New Testament, why not the Old?" Yakov said.

"The Old won't do you any good at all," Zhitnyak said. "It's long been worn out and full of old greybeard Jews crawling around from one mess to the other. Also there's a lot of fucking in the Old Testament, so how is that religious? If you want to read the true word of God, read the gospels. My old woman told me to tell you that."

Yakov would at first not open the book, having from childhood feared Jesus Christ, as stranger, apostate, mysterious enemy of the Jews. But with the book there his boredom grew deeper and his curiosity stronger. At last he opened it and began to read. He sat at the table reading through the darkness on the page, though not for long periods because he found it hard to concentrate. Yet the story of Jesus fascinated him and he read it in the four

245

gospels. He was a strange Jew, humourless and fanatic, but the fixer liked the teachings and read with pleasure of the healing of lame, blind, and of the epileptics who fell into fire and water. He enjoyed the loaves and fishes and the raising of the dead. In the end he was deeply moved when he read how they spat on him and beat him with sticks; and how he hung on the cross at night. Jesus cried out help to God but God gave no help. There was a man crying out in anguish in the dark, but God was on the other side of his mountain. He heard but he had heard everything. What was there to hear that he hadn't heard before? Christ died and they took him down. The fixer wiped his eyes. Afterwards he thought if that's how it happened and it's part of the Christian religion, and they believe it, how can they keep me in prison, knowing I am innocent? Why don't they have pity and let me go?

Though his memory gave him trouble he tried to learn by heart some of the verses he liked in the gospels. It was a way to keep his mind occupied and his memory alert. Then he would recite to himself what he had learned. One day he began to say verses aloud through the peephole. Zhitnyak, sitting in his chair in the corridor, hacking at a stick with his knife, heard the fixer recite the Beatitudes, listened to the end, then told him to shut his mouth. When Yakov could not sleep at night; or when he had slept a little and was waked by some dream or noise, he passed part of his waking time reciting in the cell, and Kogin as usual kept his ear to the spy hole, breathing audibly. One night, the guard, lately morose with worry, remarked through the door in his deep voice, "How is it that a Jew who killed a Christian child goes around reciting the words of Christ?"

"I never even touched that boy," said the fixer.

"Everybody says you did. They say you had a secret dispensation from a rabbi to go ahead and do it and your con-science wouldn't hurt you. I've heard it said you were a hardworking man, Yakov Bok, but you still could have committed the crime because in your thinking it was no crime to murder a Christian. All that blood and matzo business is an old part of your religion. I've heard about it ever since I was a small boy."

"In the Old Testament we're not allowed to eat blood. It's forbidden," said Yakov. "But what about these words: 'Truly, truly, I say to you, unless you eat the flesh of the Son of man and drink his blood, you have no life in you; he who eats my flesh and drinks my blood has eternal life, and I will raise him up on the last day. For my flesh is food indeed, and my blood is drink indeed. He who eats my flesh and drinks my blood, abides in me, and I in him.'"

"Ah, that's a different load of fish altogether," said Kogin. "It means the bread and wine and not the real flesh and blood. Besides, how do you know those words that you just said? When the Devil teaches scripture to a Jew they both get it wrong."

"Blood is blood. I said it the way it was written."

"How do you know it?"

"I read it in the Gospel of John."

"What's a Jew doing reading the gospels?"

"I read them to find out what a Christian is."

"A Christian is a man who loves Christ."

"How can anyone love Christ and keep an innocent man suffering in prison?"

"There is no innocent Christ-killer," Kogin said, shutting the disk over the spy hole.

But the next night as the rain droned steadily in the prison yard and drops of water dripped from the ceiling, the guard came to hear what else Yakov had memorized.

"I haven't been in a church in years," Kogin said. "I'm not much of a body for incense and priests but I like to hear the words of Christ."

"'Which of you convicts me of sin?'" said Yakov. "'If I tell the truth, why do you not believe me?'"

"Did he say that?"

"Yes."

"Go on to another one."

"'But it is easier for heaven and earth to pass away, than for one dot of the law to become void.'"

"When you say the words they sound different than I remember them."

"They're the same words."

"Go on to another one."

"'Judge not, that you be not judged. For with the judgement you pronounce you will be judged and the measure you give will be the measure you get.'"

"That's enough," said Kogin. "I've had enough."

But the next night he brought a candle stub and match.

"Look, Yakov Bok, I know you're hiding a book of the gospels in your cell. How did you get it?"

Yakov said someone had slipped it into his pocket when he went to get his rations in the kitchen.

"Well, maybe, and maybe not," said Kogin, "but since you have the book in there you might as well read me something. I'm bored to my arse out here all alone night after night. What I really am is a family man."

Yakov lit the candle and read to Kogin through the hole in the door. He read him of the trial and suffering of Christ, as the yellow candle flame dipped and sputtered in the damp cell. When he came to where the soldiers pressed a crown of thorns on Jesus' head, the guard sighed.

Then the fixer spoke in an anxious whisper. "Listen,

248

Kogin, could I ask you for a small favour? It isn't much of one. I would like a piece of paper and a pencil stub to write a few words to an acquaintance of mine. Could you lend them to me?"

"You better go fuck yourself, Bok," said Kogin. "I'm on to your Jew tricks."

He took the candle, blew it out, and did not again come to hear the verses of the gospels.

2

Sometimes he caught the scent of spring through the broken window when a breeze that had passed through the flowering bushes and trees left him with a remembrance of green things growing on earth, and his heart ached beyond belief.

One late afternoon in May, or possibly June, after the fixer had been imprisoned more than a year, a priest in grey vestments and a black hat appeared in the dark cell, a pale-faced young man with stringy hair, wet lips, and haunted, dark eyes.

Yakov, thinking himself hallucinated, retreated to the wall.

"Who are you? Where do you come from?"

"Your guard opened the door for me," said the priest, nodding, blinking. He coughed, a complex fit it took him a while to get through. "I've been ill," he said, "and once as I lay in bed in a fever I had an extraordinary vision of a man suffering in this prison. Who can it be? I thought, and at once it came to me, it must be the Jew who was arrested for killing the Christian child. I was covered with perspiration and cried out, 'Heavenly Father, I thank you for this sign, for I understand you wish me to be of service to the imprisoned Jew.' When I had recovered from my illness, I wrote at once to your warden asking him to permit me to see you. At first it seemed impossible, but after I had prayed and fasted, it was finally arranged with the Metropolitan's assistance."

Seeing the ragged, bearded fixer in the gloom, standing with his back to the sweating wall, the priest fell to his knees.

"Dear Lord," he prayed, "forgive this poor Hebrew for his sins, and let him forgive us for sinning against him. 'For if you forgive men their trespasses, your heavenly father also will forgive you; but if you do not forgive men their trespasses, neither will your father forgive your trespasses.'"

"I forgive no one."

Approaching the prisoner on his knees, the priest tried to kiss his hand but the fixer snatched it away and retreated into the shadows of the cell.

Groaning, the priest rose, breathing heavily.

"I beg you to listen to me, Yakov Shepsovitch Bok," he wheezed. "I am told by the guard Zhitnyak that you religiously read the gospels. And the guard Kogin says that you have memorized many passages of the words of the true Christ. This is an excellent sign, for if you embrace Christ, you will have truly repented. He will save you from damnation. And if you are converted to the Orthodox faith, your captors will be compelled to reconsider their accusations and ultimately to release you as one of our brothers. Believe me, there is none so dear in the eyes of God as a Jew who admits he is in error and comes willingly to the true faith. If you agree I will begin to instruct you in the Orthodox dogma. The warden has given his permission. He is a broad-minded man."

The fixer stood mute.

"Are you there?" said the priest, peering into the shadows. "Where are you?" he called, blinking uneasily. He coughed with a heavy rasp.

Yakov stood in the dim light, motionless at the table, the prayer shawl covering his head, the phylactery for the arm bound to his brow.

The priest, coughing thickly, his handkerchief held to his mouth, retreated to the metal door and banged on it with his fist. It was quickly opened and he hurried out.

"You'll get yours," said Zhitnyak to the fixer, from the hall.

Afterwards a lamp was brought into the cell and Yakov was stripped of his clothes and searched for the fourth time that day. The Deputy Warden, in a foul mood, kicked at the mattress and found the New Testament in the straw.

"Where the hell did you get this?"

"Somebody must've slipped it to him in the kitchen," said Zhitnyak.

The Deputy Warden floored the fixer with a blow.

He confiscated the phylacteries and Zhitnyak's New Testament but returned in the morning and flung at Yakov a handful of pages that flew all over the cell. They were pages from the Old Testament in Hebrew, and Yakov collected them and patiently put them together. Half the book was missing and some of the pages were covered with muddy brown stains that looked like dry blood.

3

The birch twig broom came apart. He had used it for months and the twigs had worn out on the stone floor. Some had snapped off in the sweeping and he was given nothing to replace them with. Then the frayed cord that bound the twigs wore away and that was the end of the broom. Zhitnyak would not supply twigs or a new cord. Yakov had asked for them, but he took the broomstick away instead.

"That's so you won't hurt yourself, Bok, or try any more of your dirty tricks on anybody else. Some say you clubbed the poor boy unconscious before you stuck him with your knife."

The fixer talked less with the guards, it was less wearying; they said little to him, once in a while a gruff command, or a curse if he was slow. Without the broom his thin routine began to collapse. He tried to hang on to it but now there was no stove to make or tend, or wait to be lit, and he was no longer permitted to go to the kitchen to get his rations. The food was brought to him in the cell, as it had been before. They said he had stolen things from the kitchen. The New Testament Bible, for instance. And a knife had been "found" during an inspection of his cell. That ended the excursions he had looked forward to, sometimes with excited eagerness, twice a day. "It's only right," said the warden. "We can't have a Jew going around flouting the rules. There have been mutterings among some of the other prisoners." What was left of the routine was to be waked by the prison bell in the morning, to eat meagrely not once but twice a day, and three times each day to be searched to desperation.

He had stopped keeping track of time with the long and short splinters. Beyond a year he couldn't go. Time was summer now, when the hot cell stank heavily and the walls sweated. There were mosquitoes, and bugs hitting the walls. Yet, better summer; he feared another winter. And if there was a spring after the winter it would mean two years in prison. And after that? Time blew like a steppe wind into an empty future. There was no end, no event, indictment, trial. The waiting withered him. He was worn thin by the struggle to wait, by the knowledge of his innocence against the fact of his imprisonment; that nothing had been done in a whole year to free him. He was stricken to be so absolutely alone. Oppressed by the heat, eaten by damp cold, eroded by the expectation of an indictment that never came, were his grey bones visible through his skin? His nerves were threads stretched to the instant before snapping. He cried out of the deepest part of him, a narrow pit, but no one appeared or answered, or looked at him or spoke to him, neither friend nor stranger. Nothing changed but his age. If he were tried, convicted, and sentenced to Siberia, that at least would be something to do. He combed his hair and beard until the teeth of the comb fell out. No one would give him another although he begged, wheedled; so he combed with his fingers. He picked his nose obsessively. His flesh, containing girls who had never become women, tempted him, but that upset his stomach. He tried unsuccessfully to keep himself clean.

Yakov read the Old Testament through the stained and muddied pages, chapter by fragmentary chapter. He read each squat letter with care, although often the words were incomprehensible to him. He had forgotten many he once knew, but in the reading and rereading some came back; some were lost for ever. The passages he could not understand and the missing pages of the book did not bother him; he knew the sense of the story. What wasn't there he guessed at, or afterwards recalled. At first he read only for a few minutes at a time. The light was bad. His eyes watered and head swam. Then he read longer and faster, gripped by the narrative of the joyous and frenzied Hebrews, doing business, fighting wars, sinning and worshipping – whatever they were doing always engaged in talk with the huffing-puffing God who tried to sound, maybe out of envy, like a human being.

God talks. He has chosen, he says, the Hebrews to preserve him. He covenants, therefore he is. He offers and Israel accepts, or when will history begin? Abraham, Moses, Noah, Jeremiah, Hosea, Ezra, even Job, make their personal covenant with the talking God. But Israel accepts the covenant in order to break it. That's the mysterious purpose: they need the experience. So they worship false Gods; and this brings Yahweh up out of his golden throne with a flaming sword in both hands. When he talks loud history boils. Assyria, Babylonia, Greece, Rome, become the rod of his anger, the rod that breaks the heads of the Chosen People. Having betrayed the covenant with God they have to pay: war, destruction, death, exile – and they take what goes with it. Suffering, they say, awakens repentance, at least in those who can repent. Thus the people of the covenant wear out their sins against the Lord. He then forgives them and offers a new covenant. Why not? This is his nature, everything must begin again, don't ask him why. Israel, changed yet unchanged, accepts the new covenant in order to break it by worshipping false gods so that they will ultimately suffer and repent, which they do endlessly. The purpose of the covenant, Yakov thinks, is to create human experience, although human experience baffles God. God is after all God; what he is is what he is: God. What does he know about such things? Has he ever worshipped God? Has he ever suffered? How much, after all, has he experienced? God envies the Jews: it's a rich life. Maybe he would like to be human, it's possible, nobody knows. That's this God, Yahweh, the one who appears out of clouds, cyclones, burning bushes; talking. With Spinoza's God it's different. He is the eternal infinite idea of God as discovered in all of Nature. This one says nothing; either he can't talk or has no need to. If you're an idea what can you say? One has to find him in the machinations of his own mind. Spinoza had reasoned him out but Yakov Bok can't. He is, after all, no philosopher. So he suffers without either the intellectual idea of God, or the God of the covenant; he had broken the phylactery. Nobody suffers for him and he suffers for no one except himself. The rod of God's anger against the fixer is Nicholas II, the Russian Tsar. He punishes the suffering servant for being godless.

It's a hard life.

Zhitnyak watched him as he read. "Rock back and forth like they do in the synagogue," he said through the spy hole. The fixer rocked back and forth. The Deputy Warden was called to see. "What else would you expect?" he said as he spat.

Sometimes Yakov lost sight of the words. They were black birds with white wings, white birds with black wings. He was falling in thoughtless thought, a stupefying whiteness. The fixer lost track of where he was, a forgetting so profound he ached on coming out of it. This occurred often now and went on for hours. Once he fell into this state in the morning, sitting at the table reading the Old Testament, and came back to the present in the late afternoon, standing naked in the cell, being searched by the Deputy Warden and Zhitnyak. And he sometimes walked across Russia without knowing it. It was hard on the feet and had to be controlled because he wore out the soles of his bast shoes and nobody wanted to give him another pair. He walked in his bare feet over a long rocky road and afterwards found both feet battered and blistered. He awoke to find himself walking and it frightened him when he recalled the pain of the surgeon's scalpel. He willed himself to attention when he began to walk. He took a step or two on the long road and awoke in fright.

Yakov reveried the past; the shtetl, the mistakes and failures of his life. One white-mooned night, after a bitter quarrel about something he couldn't remember now, Raisl had left the hut and run in the dark to her father. The fixer, sitting alone, thinking over his bitterness and the falseness of his accusations, had thought of going after her but had gone to sleep instead. After all, he was dead tired doing nothing. The next year the accusation against her had come true, although it wasn't true then. Who had made it come true? If he had run after her then, would he be sitting here now?

He turned often to pages of Hosea and read with fascination the story of this man God had commanded to marry a harlot. The harlot, he had heard it said, was Israel, but the jealousy and anguish Hosea felt was that of a man whose wife had left his bed and board and gone whoring after strangers.

"And let her put away her harlotries from her face,
    and her adulteries from between her breasts;
Lest I strip her naked,
And set her as in the day that she was born,
And make her as the wilderness,
And set her like dry land,
And slay her with thirst.
And I will not have compassion on her children;
For they are the children of harlotry.
For their mother hath played the harlot,
She that conceived them hath done shamefully;

For she said: 'I will go after my lovers,
That give me bread and my water.
My wool and my flax, mine oil and my drink!'
Therefore, behold, I will hedge up thy way with thorns,
And I will make a wall against her,
That she will not find her paths.
And she shall run after her lovers,
    but she shall not overtake them,
And she shall seek them, but shall not find them;
Then shall she say: 'I will go and return to my first
    husband:
For then was it better with me than now.'"

4

One morning Zhitnyak brought the prisoner a thick letter
in a soiled white envelope with a long row of red stamps.
The stamps were portraits of the Tsar in military tunic,
wearing a medallion of the royal coat of arms, the double-
headed eagle. The letter had been opened by the censor and
resealed with a strip of gummed paper. It was addressed to
"The Murderer of Zhenia Golov" and sent in care of the
Prosecuting Attorney of the Superior Court, Plossky
District, Kiev.

Yakov's heart palpitated when he took the letter. "Who
is it from?"

"The Queen of Sheba," said the guard. "Open and see."

The fixer waited until the guard had gone. He put the
letter down on the table to get it out of his hand. He stared
at it for five minutes. Could it be the indictment? Would
they address it like that? Yakov clumsily ripped open the

envelope, tearing it across, and found in it a sixteen-page letter written in Russian in a woman's spidery handwriting. There were blots of ink on every page, many words misspelled, and some heavily crossed out and rewritten.

"Sir," it began, "I am the bereaved and unfortunate mother of the martyred Zhenia Golov, and I take my pen in my hand to beg you to do the right and decent thing. In God's name give an ear to a mother's pleas. I am worn out by the wicked insults and insinuations that have been wrongfully cast on myself by certain worthless people – including certain neighbours I have now cut myself off from, without any proof whatsoever. *On the contrary* with all the proof directed against you, and I beg you to clear the air up by a complete and candid confession. Although I admit your face, when I saw it in my household, didn't look too Jewish, and maybe you really wouldn't commit such a dreadful crime murdering a child and taking out his precious lifeblood if you hadn't been egged on to do it by fanatical Jews – you know the kind I mean. Still you probably did it because they threatened you with death, although maybe you didn't want to, I don't know. But now I know for a certainty that it was these old Jews with long black coats and nasty beards that warned you you had to make the kill and they would hide my child's corpse in the cave when you did. Just the same night before Zheniushka disappeared I dreamed of one of them carrying a satchel, with wild glaring eyes and bright red spots in his beard, and my former neighbour Sofya Shiskovsky told me she had dreamed the same dream that I had on the same night.

"I am asking you to own up because the evidence is all against you. One thing you might not know is that after Zheniushka confided to me you had chased him with a knife in the cemetery, I had you followed by a gentleman

258

friend of mine to find out what other criminal activities you were engaged in. It is a known fact that you were involved in certain illegal acts in secretly dealing with other Jews in the brickyard who pretended they were not Jews, and also in the cellar of the synagogue, where you all met in the Podol District. You smuggled, robbed, and traded in goods that didn't belong to you. Zheniushka found out all about this and other of your illegalities, and that's another reason why you bore him such a violent hatred, and why you had him in your mind as the victim as soon as you were chosen to find one and drain his blood for the Jewish Easter. You also acted as a fence for this gang of Jews who broke into the homes of the Gentry as well as in certain commercial stores, and houses in the Lipki District, where the aristocratic houses are, and took out all sorts of loot in money, furs and jewels, not to mention other precious objects of different kinds. Also you paid your gang only a part of the real price the goods were worth because as the saying is, each Jew cheats the other. Which is nothing new to anybody because the whole world knows they are born criminals. A Jew wanted to lend a friend of mine money to build a house, but she went to the priest for advice and he began to tremble and advised her to take nothing from a cursed Jew, in Christ's name, because they will defraud and cheat you because it is their nature and they can't do otherwise. This priest said their Jewish blood itches when they aren't engaged in evil. If it weren't for that maybe you would have resisted the murder of a saintly boy when they egged you to do it. And I suppose you know there have been attempts to bribe me not to testify against you when your trial comes. One fat Jew in silk clothes offered me the sum of 40,000 roubles to leave Russia and he would pay me the sum of another 10,000 roubles, on arriving in Austria, but even if he and your

259

fellow-Jews had offered me 400,000 roubles, I would still spit in their faces and say *absolutely no* because I prefer the honour of my good name to 400,000 roubles of Jewish blood money.

"My gentleman friend also saw you spit on the ground one day when you walked around on the outside of St Sophia's Cathedral after spying out the school in the courtyard where Zhenia went. He saw you turn your head as though you might go blind if you didn't, when you looked up on the golden crosses on top of the green domes, and you spat fast so no one should see you, but my friend saw you. I was also told you practise black magic religious ceremonies and certain cabalistic superstitions.

"Also, don't think I don't know the sordid part of the story. Zhenia told me about the times you enticed him to come to your room in the stable and there with the promise of bonbons and sweets you got him to open the buttons of his trousers and with your hand caused him intense excitement. There were other lewd things you performed which I can't even write because I get very faint. He told me that after you did those awful things you were afraid he would tell me and I would denounce you to the police, so you used to give him ten kopeks not to say anything to anybody. He never did at the time this all happened, although once he told me about what went on up there, because he was worried and frightened, but I haven't breathed a word of it to anyone, not even to my closest neighbours because I was ashamed to say anything, and also because your crime of murder is enough to answer for, and you will probably suffer the tortures of the cursed for that alone. Yet I will honestly and frankly tell you that if people go on making suspicious and vile remarks about me behind my back, I will tell all the facts of the case whether I blush or not to the

Prosecuting Attorney who is first of all a gentleman. I will also tell everybody the sordid things you did to my child.

"I will petition the Tsar to defend my good name. Besides losing my child I have led an irreproachable life of toil. I have been an honest person and a pure woman. I have been the best of mothers even though I was a working woman with no time to herself and two people to support. Those who say I didn't weep for my poor boy at his funeral are saying a filthy lie and I will some day sue someone for libel and character assassination. I looked after my Zhenia as though he were a prince. I attended to his clothes and all of his other needs. I cooked special dishes that he liked most of all, all sorts of pastries and expensive treats. I was a mother and also a father to him since his own weakling of a father deserted me. I helped him with his lessons where I could and encouraged him and said yes when he wanted to be a priest. He was already in a preparatory church school to prepare for the priesthood when he was murdered. He felt to me the way I felt to him – he loved me passionately. Rest assured of that. Mamashka, he said, I only love you. Please, Zheniush-ka, I begged him, stay away from those evil Jews. To my sorrow he did not follow his mother's advice. You are my son's murderer. I urge you as the martyred mother of a martyred child to confess *the whole truth* at once and clear the evil out of the air so that we can breathe again. If you do, at least you won't have to suffer so much in the afterworld.

"Marfa Vladimirovna Golov"

The excitement of receiving the letter had increased in the reading and Yakov's head throbbed at the questions that ran through his mind. Was the trial she had mentioned already on its way or only assumed to be by her? Probably assumed, yet how could he be sure? Anyway the indictment would still have to come, and where was the indictment? What had caused her to write the letter? What were the "wicked insults and insinuations", and the "suspicious and vile remarks" she referred to? And who was making them? Could it be she was being investigated, yet by whom if not Bibikov? Certainly not Grubeshov, yet why had he let the letter, mad as it was, go through to him? Had she written it with his help? Was it to demonstrate the quality of the witness, to show Yakov what he was up against and thus again to warn or threaten him? To say we assure you she will say these things and more you can never guess, and she will convince a jury of people like her, so why not confess now? They were multiplying the accusations and disgusting motives, and would not rest until they had trapped him like a fly in a gluepot; therefore he had better confess before other means of escape were impossible.

Whatever her reason for sending it the letter seemed close to a confession by her, maybe a sign something else was going on. Would he ever know what? The fixer felt his heart-beat in his ears. He looked around for a place to hide the letter, hoping to pass it on to the lawyer, if he ever had one. But the next morning after he had finished eating, the letter was missing from his coat pocket and he suspected he had been doped, or they had got it some other way, possibly while he was being searched. Anyway the letter was gone.

"Can't I send her an answer?" he asked the Deputy Warden before the next search, and the Deputy Warden said he could if he was willing to admit the wrongs he had done.

That night the fixer saw Marfa, a tallish, scrawny-necked woman with a figure something like Raisl's, enter the cell and without so much as a word begin to undress – the white hat with cherries, the red rose scarf, green skirt, flowery

262

blouse, cotton petticoat, pointed button shoes, red garters, black stockings and soiled frilly drawers. Lying naked on the fixer's mattress, her legs spread apart, she promised many goyish delights if he would confess to the priest at the peephole.

5

One night he awoke hearing someone singing in the cell and when he listened with his whole being the song was in a boy's high sweet voice. Yakov got up to see where the singing was coming from. The child's pale, shrunken, bony face, corroded copper and black, shone from a pit in the corner of the cell. He was dead yet sang how he had been murdered by a black-bearded Jew. He had gone on an errand for his mother and was on his way home through the Jewish section when this hairy, bent-back rabbi caught up with him and offered him a lozenge. The instant the boy put the candy into his mouth he fell to the ground. The Jew lifted him on to his shoulder and hurried to the brickworks. There the boy was laid on the stable floor, tied up, and stabbed until the blood spouted from the orifices of his body. Yakov listened to the end of the song and cried, "Again! Sing it again!" Again he heard the same sweet song the dead child was singing in his grave.

Afterwards the boy, appearing to him naked, his stigmata brightly bleeding, begged, "Please give me back my clothes."

They're trying to unhinge me, the fixer thought, and then they'll say I went mad because I committed the crime. He feared what he might confess if he went crazy; his suffering to defend his innocence would come to nothing as he babbled his guilt and the blood guilt of those who had put him up to it. He strove with himself, struggled, shouted at him to hold tight to sanity, to keep in the dark unsettled centre of the mind a candle burning.

A bloody horse with frantic eyes appeared: Shmuel's nag. "Murderer!" the horse neighed. "Horsekiller! Child-killer! You deserve what you get!"

He beat the nag's head with a log.

Yakov slept often during the day but badly. Sleep left him limp, depressed. He was being watched by many eyes through the spy hole for the minute he went mad. The air throbbed with voices from afar. There was a plot afoot to save him. He had visions of being rescued by the International Jewish Army. They were laying seige to the outer walls. Among the familiar faces he recognized Berele Margolis, Leib Rosenbach, Dudye Bont, Itzik Shulman, Kalman Kohler, Shloime Pincus, Yose-Moishe Magadov, Pinye Apfelbaum, and Benya Merpetz, all from the orphans' home, although it seemed to him they were long since gone, some dead, some fled – he should have gone with them.

"Wait," he shouted. "Wait."

Then the streets around the prison were noisy, the crowds roaring, chanting, wailing; animals mooing, clucking, grunting. Everyone ran in several directions, feathers floating in the air, *gevalt* they were killing the Jews! A horde of thick-booted, baggy-trousered, sword-swinging Cossacks were galloping in on small ferocious ponies. In the yard the double-eagle banners were unfurled and fluttered in the wind. Nicholas the Second drove in in a coach drawn by six white horses, saluting from both sides the hundreds of Black Hundreds aching to get at the prisoner and hammer nails into his head. Yakov hid in his cell with chest pains and heartburn. The guards were planning to murder him with rat poison. He planned to murder them first. A Zhid shits on Zhitnyak. Kog on Kogin. He barricaded the door with the table and stool, then smashed them against the wall. While they were battering the door down to get at him he sat cross-legged on the floor, mixing blood with unleavened flour. He kicked savagely as the guards lugged him through the corridor, raining blows on his head.

The fixer crouched in a dark place trying to hold his mind together with a piece of string so he wouldn't confess. But it exploded into a fountain of rotting fruit, one-eyed herrings, birds of Paradise. It exploded into a million stinking words but when he confessed he confessed in Yiddish so the goyim couldn't understand. In Hebrew he recited the Psalms. In Russian he was silent. He slept in fear and waked in fright. In dreams he heard the voices of screaming children. Dressed in a long caftan and round fur hat he hid behind trees, and when a Christian child approached, compulsively chased him. One small-faced boy, a consumptive type, ran from him frantically, his eyes rolling in fright.

"Stop, I love you," the fixer called to him, but the child never looked back.

"Once is enough, Yakov Bok."

Nicholas II appeared, in the white uniform of an admiral of the Russian Navy.

"Little Father," said the fixer on both knees, "you'll never meet a more patriotic Jew. Tears fill my eyes when I see the flag. Also I'm not interested in politics, I want to make a living. Those accusations are all wrong or you've got the wrong man. Live and let live, if you don't mind me saying so. It's a short life when you think of it."

"My dear fellow," said the blue-eyed, pale-faced Tsar in a gentle voice, "don't envy me my throne. Uneasy lies the et cetera. The Zhidy would do well to understand and stop complaining in a whining tongue. The simple fact is there are too many Jews – my how you procreate! Why should Russia be burdened with teeming millions of you? You yourselves are to blame for your troubles, and the pogroms of 1905–6 *outside* the Pale of Settlement, mind you, were proof positive, if proof is needed, that you aren't staying where you were put. The ingestion of this tribe has poisoned Russia. Who ever wanted it? Our revered ancestor Peter the Great, when asked to admit them into Russia, said, 'They are rogues and cheats. I am trying to eradicate evil, not increase it." Our revered ancestor, the Tsarina Elizabeth Petrovna, said, 'From the enemies of Christ I wish neither gain nor profit.' Hordes of Jews were expelled from one or another part of the Motherland in 1727, 1739, 1742, but still they crawled back and we have been unable to delouse ourselves of them. The worst of it happened, our greatest error, when Catherine the Great took over half of Poland and inherited the whole filthy lot, a million poisoners of wells, spies against us all, cowardly traitors. I always said it was the Poles' plot to ruin Russia."

"Have mercy on me, your Majesty. So far as I'm concerned, I am an innocent man. What have I seen of the world? Please have mercy."

"The Tsar's heart is in God's hands." He stepped into his white sailboat and sailed away on the Black Sea.

Nikolai Maximovitch had lost weight, the girl limped badly and would not look at the fixer. Proshko, Serdiuk and Richter came in on three skittish horses whose droppings were full of oats he longed to get at. Father Anastasy sought to convert him to Roman Catholicism. Marfa Golov, wept dry-eyed and haggard, offered him a bribe to testify against himself; and the Deputy Warden, in the uniform of a naval officer, for personal reasons insisted on continuing the searches. The guards promised the fixer anything if he would open up and name names, and Yakov said he might for a heated cell in wintertime, a daily bowl of noodles and cheese, and a firm clean hair mattress.

Shots were fired.

He passed through time he had no memory of and one day awoke to find himself in the same cell, not a new one with six doors and windows he had dreamed of. It was still hot but he couldn't be sure it was the same summer. The cell seemed the same, possibly a bit smaller, with the same scabby sweating walls. The same wet stone floor. The same stinking straw mattress; its smell had never killed the bugs. The table and three-legged stool were gone. Scattered over the wet floor were pages of the Old Testament, stained and muddied. He could not find the phylacteries but still wore the ragged prayer shawl. And the last of the firewood had been removed and the cell hosed down as though to make it fit for him to stay for ever.

"How long was I gone?" he asked Zhitnyak.

"You weren't gone. Who says you were gone?"

"Was I sick then?"

"They say you ran a fever."

"What did I say when I ranted and raved?" he asked uneasily.

"Who the hell knows," said the guard impatiently. "I have my own troubles. Try and live on the lousy wages they pay you here. The Deputy Warden listened to you twice a day but couldn't make out heads or tails. He says you have a filthy mind but nobody expected otherwise."

"Am I better now?"

"That's up to you, but if you break another piece of furniture, we'll smash your head."

Though his legs trembled, he stood at the peephole, looking out. Moving the disk aside with his finger, he stared out into the corridor. A yellow bulb lit the windowless wall. The cells on both sides of him, he remembered, were empty. He had more than once hit a log against the walls but there was never any response. Once an official passing by in the corridor saw his eye staring out and ordered him to shut the hole and move away from the door. After the man had gone Yakov looked out again. All he could see on the left was the chair the guards sat on, Zhitnyak whittling a stick, Kogin sighing, worrying. The other way a dusty bulb lit up a broken barrel against the wall. The fixer stood for hours staring into the corridor. When Zhitnyak came over to look in, he saw the fixer's eye staring out.

6

One midsummer night, long past midnight, Yakov, too long imprisoned to sleep, was staring out of the peephole when his eye throbbed as if it had been touched, and slowly filled with the pained sight of Shmuel.

The fixer cursed himself, withdrew his eye, and tried the other. Whether vision or visitor it looked like Shmuel, though older, shrunken, greyer, a scarecrow with a frightened beard.

The prisoner, in disbelief, heard a whisper. "Yakov, it's you? Here is Shmuel, your father-in-law."

First the Tsar and now Shmuel. Either I'm still crazy or it's another mad dream. Next comes the Prophet Elijah or Jesus Christ.

But the figure of the fragile old man in shirt-sleeves and a

268

hard hat, standing in the yellow light, his fringed garment
hanging out under his shirt, persisted.

"Shmuel, don't lie, is it really you?"

"Who else?" said the pedlar hoarsely.

"God forbid you're not a prisoner, are you?" the fixer
asked in anguish.

"God forbid. I came to see you though I almost didn't.
It's erev shabbos but God will forgive me."

Yakov wiped his eyes. "I've dreamed of everybody so why
not you? But how did you get in? How did you come here?"

The old man shrugged his thin shoulders.

"We came in circles. I did what they told me. Yakov, for
more than a year I tried to find you but nobody knew
where. I thought to myself he's gone for good, I'll never see
him again. Then one day I bought for a few kopeks a hill of
rotting sugar beets from a sick Russian. Don't ask me why
but for the first time in my life what I bought for rotten was
not all rotten. More than half the beets turned out good,
God's gift to a poor man. The sugar company sent some
wagons and took them away. Anyway, I sold the beets for
forty roubles, my biggest profit since I'm in business. Also I
met Fyodor Zhitnyak, the brother of the one here – he
peddles in the Kiev market. We got to talking and he knew
your name. He told me that for forty roubles he could
arrange it so I could speak to you. He spoke to the brother
and the brother said yes if I came late at night and wasn't
too ambitious. Who's ambitious, so here I am. For forty
roubles they will let me stand here just ten minutes, so we
must talk fast. Time I've had like dirt my whole life but now
it's worth money. Zhitnyak, the brother who's the guard
here, changed shifts with another one who took the night
off because his son got arrested. That's how it goes, I wish
him luck. Anyway, Zhitnyak will wait for ten minutes down

269

the hall by the outside door but he warned me if somebody comes he might have to shoot. He might as well, if they see me I'm lost."

"Shmuel, before I faint from excitement, how did you know I was in prison?"

Shmuel moved his feet restlessly. It wasn't a dance though it looked like one.

"How I know, he asks. I knew because I knew. I know. When it came out in the Yiddish papers last year that a Jew was arrested in Kiev for murdering a Christian child, I thought to myself who can this poor Jew be, it must be my son-in-law Yakov. Then after a year I saw your name in the newspaper. A counterfeiter by the name of Gronfein got sick from his nerves and went around saying that Yakov Bok was in the Kiev prison for killing a Russian child. He saw him there. I tried to find this man but he disappeared and those who are hopeful hope he's alive. Maybe he went to America, that's what they hope. Yakov, maybe you don't know, it's a terrible tumult now all over Russia, and to tell you the truth, the Jews are frightened to death. Only a few know who you are, and some say it's a fake, there's nobody by that name, the goyim made it up to cast suspicion on the Jews. In the shtetl those who never liked you say it serves you right. Some have pity and would like to help you but we can't do a thing till they give you an indictment. When I saw your name in the Jewish paper I wrote you right away a letter and they sent it back – 'No such prisoner.' I also sent you a little package, not much in it, just a few little things, but did you ever get it?"

"Poison I got but no package."

"I tried to get in here to see you and nobody would let me till I made my profit on the sugar beets and I met the brother Zhitnyak."

"Shmuel, I'm sorry for your forty roubles. It's a lot of money and what are you getting for it?"

"Money is nothing. I came to see you, but if it paves my way a foot into Paradise it's a fine investment."

"Run, Shmuel," the fixer said, agitated, "get out while you can or they'll shoot you in cold blood and call it a Jewish conspiracy. If that happens I'm doomed forever."

"I'm running," said Shmuel, cracking his knuckles against his bony chest, "but tell me first why they blame you for this terrible crime?"

"Why they blame me? Because I was a stupid ass. I worked for a Russian factory owner in a forbidden district. Also I lived there without telling him my papers were Jewish."

"You see, Yakov, what happens when you shave your beard and forget your God?"

"Don't talk to me about God," Yakov said bitterly. "I want no part of God. When you need him most he's farthest away. Enough is enough. My past I don't have to tell you, but if you knew what I've lived through since I saw you last." He began to say but his voice cracked.

"Yakov," said Shmuel, clasping and unclasping his excitable hands, "we're not Jews for nothing. Without God we can't live. Without the covenant we would have disappeared out of history. Let that be a lesson to you. He's all we have but who wants more?"

"Me. I'll take misery but not for ever."

"For misery don't blame God. He gives the food but we cook it."

"I blame him for not existing. Or if he does it's on the moon or stars but not here. The thing is not to believe or the waiting becomes unbearable. I can't hear his voice and never have. I don't need him unless he appears."

271

"Who are you, Yakov, Moses himself? If you don't hear his voice so let him hear yours. 'When prayers go up blessings descend.'"

"Scorpions descend, hail, fire, sharp rocks, excrement. For that I don't need God's help, the Russians are enough. All right, once I used to talk to him and answer myself, but what good does it do if I know so little in the first place? I used to mention once in a while the conditions of my life, my struggles, misfortunes, mistakes. On rare occasions I gave him a little good news, but whatever I said he never answered me. Silence I now give back."

"A proud man is deaf and blind. How can he hear God? How can he see him?"

"Who's proud if I ever was? What have I got to be proud of? That I was born without parents? I never made a decent living? My barren wife ran off with a goy? When a boy was murdered in Kiev, out of three million Jews in Russia they arrested me? So I'm not proud. If God exists I'll gladly listen to him. If he doesn't feel like talking let him open the door so I can walk out. I have nothing. From nothing you get nothing. If he wants from me he has to give first. If not a favour at least a sign."

"Don't ask for signs, ask for mercy."

"I've asked for everything and got nothing." The fixer, after a sigh, spoke close to the peephole. "'In the beginning was the word,' but it wasn't his. That's the way I look at it now. Nature invented itself and also man. Whatever was there was there to begin with. Spinoza said so. It sounds fantastic but it must be true. When it comes down to basic facts, either God is our invention and can't do anything about it, or he's a force in Nature but not in history. A force is not a father. He's a cold wind and try and keep warm. To tell the truth, I've written him off as a dead loss."

272

"Yakov," said Shmuel, squeezing both hands, "don't talk so fast. Don't look for God in the wrong place, look in the Torah, the law. That's where to look, not in bad books that poison your thoughts."

"As for the law it was invented by man, is far from perfect, and what good is it to me if the Tsar has no use for it? If God can't give me simple respect I'll settle for justice. Uphold the Law! Destroy the Tsar with a thunderbolt! Free me from prison!"

"God's justice is for the end of time."

"I'm not so young any more, I can't wait that long. Neither can the Jews running from pogroms. We're dealing nowadays with the slaughter of large numbers and it's getting worse. God counts in astronomy but where men are concerned all I know is one plus one. Shmuel, let's drop this useless subject. What's the sense of arguing through a little hole where you can barely see part of my face in the dark. Besides, it's a short visit and we're eating up time."

"Yakov," said Shmuel, "He invented light. He created the world. He made us both. The true miracle is belief. I believe in him. Job said, 'Though he slay me, yet will I trust in him.' He said more but that's enough."

"To win a lousy bet with the devil he killed off all the servants and innocent children of Job. For that alone I hate him, not to mention ten thousand pogroms. Ach, why do you make me talk fairy-tales? Job is an invention and so is God. Let's let it go at that." He stared at the pedlar with one eye. "I'm sorry I'm making you feel bad on your expensive time, Shmuel, but take my word for it, it's not easy to be a freethinker in this terrible cell. I say this without pride or joy. Still, whatever reason a man has, he's got to depend on."

"Yakov," said Shmuel, mopping his face with his blue

handkerchief, "do me a favour, don't close your heart. Nobody is lost to God if his heart is open."

"What's left of my heart is pure rock."

"Also don't forget repentance," said Shmuel. "This comes first."

Zhitnyak appeared in a great hurry. "That's enough now, it's time to go. Ten minutes is up but you talked longer."

"It felt like two," Shmuel said. "I was just about to say what's on my heart."

"Run, Shmuel," Yakov urged, his mouth pressed to the peephole. "Do whatever you can to help me. Run to the newspapers and tell them the police have imprisoned an innocent man. Run to the rich Jews, to Rothschild if necessary. Ask for help, money, mercy, a good lawyer to defend me. Get me out of here before they lay me in my grave."

Shmuel pulled a cucumber out of his trouser pocket. "Here's a little pickle I brought you." He attempted to thrust it through the spy hole but Zhitnyak grabbed it.

"None of that," the guard loudly whispered. "Don't try any Jew tricks on me. Also you shut up," he said to Yakov. "You've had your say and that's enough now."

He grabbed Shmuel by the arm. "Hurry up, it's getting towards morning."

"Good-bye, Yakov, remember what I told you."

"Raisl," Yakov called after him. "I forgot to ask. Whatever happened to her?"

"I'm running," said Shmuel, holding on to his hat.

VIII

Shmuel's visit left the fixer with a heavy burden of excitement. Something must happen now, he thought. He will run to people on my behalf. He will say this is my son-in-law Yakov and look what happened to him. He will tell them I'm in prison in Kiev and what for. He will cry out my innocence and beg for help. Maybe a lawyer will then go to Grubeshov and ask for the indictment. He will say, "You must give it to us before this man dies in his cell." Maybe he will even petition the Minister of Justice. If he's a good lawyer he will think of other things to do. He won't neglect me here.

Instead the warden appeared in the cell, tense and agitated. His good eye gleamed. His mouth was loose with anger. "We'll give you escape, you bastard. We'll give you conspiracy."

A prisoner in strict confinement nearby had heard voices that night and had informed on Zhitnyak. The guard was arrested and after a while confessed that he had let an old Jew in to talk to the murderer.

"This time you overreached yourself, Bok. You'll wish you had never laid eyes on this other conspirator. We'll show you what good outside agitation will do. You'll wish you had never been born."

He demanded to know who the conspirator was, and the fixer excitedly answered, "Nobody. He was a stranger to me. He didn't tell me his name. A poor man. He met Zhitnyak by accident."

"What did he say to you? Come out with it."

"He asked me if I was hungry."

"What did you answer?"

"I said yes."

"We'll give you hunger," shouted the warden.

Early the next day two workmen entered the cell with boxes of tools, and after labouring all morning with steel hammers and long metal spikes, drilled four deep holes in the inner wall, in which they cemented heavy bolts with attached rings. The workmen also constructed a bed-size platform with four short wooden legs. The foot of the "bed" was a stock for enclosing the prisoner's legs, that would be padlocked at night. The window-bars were strengthened and two more were added, reducing the meagre light in the cell. But the cracked window was left cracked, and six additional bolts were fastened to the outside of the iron door, making twelve altogether, plus the lock that had to be opened by key. There was a rumour, the Deputy Warden said, that the Jews were planning a ruse to free him. He warned the fixer a lookout tower was being constructed on the high wall directly opposite his cell, and the number of guards patrolling the yard had been increased.

"If you try to escape out of this prison we'll slaughter

the whole goddamn gang of you. We'll get every last one."

In Zhitnyak's place a new guard was stationed at the cell door during the day, Berezhinsky, an ex-soldier, a dark-faced man with pouched, expressionless eyes, swollen knuckles and a broken nose. There were patches of hair on his cheekbones and neck even after he had shaved. At times, out of boredom, he thrust a rifle-barrel through the spy hole and sighted along it at the prisoner's heart.

"Bang!"

The fixer was chained to the wall all day, and at night he lay on the bedplank, his legs locked in the stocks. The leg holes were tight and chafed his flesh if he tried to turn a little. The straw mattress had been removed from the cell. At least that smell was gone, and the bedbugs, though some still inhabited his clothes. Since the fixer slept on his side when he slept, it took a while before he could begin to fall asleep on his back. He lay awake until he could no longer stand it, then seemed to faint into sleep. He slept heavily for an hour or two and woke. If he slept again the slightest movement of his body awakened him.

Now in chains, he thought the searches of his body might end, but they were increased to six a day, three in the morning and three in the afternoon. If the Deputy Warden went off duty early, the six searches were carried out in the morning. Berezhinsky went in with him in place of Zhitnyak. Six times a day his key grated in the lock, and one by one the twelve bolts were snapped back, each with a noise like a pistol-shot. Yakov put his hands to his head, obsessed by the thought that someone was hitting him repeatedly. When the searchers appeared he was unchained and ordered to strip quickly. Though he tried to hurry, his fingers were like lead;

277

he could not open his few buttons, and the guard booted him for not moving fast enough. He begged them to examine half his body at a time, with his jacket and shirt on and trousers off; then with his trousers on and the other clothes off, but they wouldn't. All he was allowed to keep on was his undershirt. It was as though, if that was not removed the search could not be such a bad thing whatever else they did to him. During the search Berezhinsky grabbed the fixer's beard in his fist and tugged. When Yakov complained, he yanked his penis.

"Ding-dong, giddyap. A Jew's cock's in the devil's hock."

The Deputy Warden's colour heightened. He laughed with a gasp and during the search his mouth wore a smile.

After each search. Yakov, exhausted, bleak, fell into depression. At first he had waited with hope that *anyway* something might come of Shmuel's visit. Then he began to fear that the pedlar had been arrested. At times he wondered whether Shmuel had really come to see him, and if he had, he now wished he hadn't. If he had not come, there would now be no chains. For the chains he cursed him.

The second winter in prison was worse than the first. The outside weather was worse, less snow and sleet but more clear freezing days, especially cold when a wind was blowing. The wind bayed at the window like starving wolves. And the inside weather was worse. The cold glowed in the cell. It sometimes struck him with pain, pressing his chest so hard it hurt to breathe. He wore his cap with earflaps, the ragged prayer shawl looped around it, twice around the head, and knotted on top. He wore it until it fell apart and then kept a piece of it for a handkerchief. He tried to get his coat-sleeves under the manacles but couldn't. The icy shackles encircled his bare legs. They threw him a horse blanket which he wore over his head and shoulders in the

278

worst of winter, for though there were now a few bundles of wood in the cell, Berezhinsky was never in a hurry to light the stove, and most of the day the fixer's bones were like ice-covered branches of a tree in the winter woods. The searches in the freezing cold were terrible; the cold plunged knives into his chest, armpits, anus. His body shrivelled and teeth chattered. But when Kogin came in, in the late afternoon, he built a fire. Sometimes he lit one late at night. Since the arrest of his son, the guard's eyes were almost glazed. He usually said nothing, puffed on a dead butt. After Yakov had cleaned out his supper bowl and lain down, Kogin locked his feet in the bed stocks and left.

During the day the fixer sat in chains on a low stool they had given him. The Old Testament pages had been taken from the cell the day he was chained to the wall, and the Deputy Warden said they had been burned. "They went up like a fart in the breeze." Yakov had nothing to do but sit and not think. To keep his blood from freezing he would often get up, move one step to the right, then two to the left; or one to the left and two to the right. He could also move a step back to the frozen wall, then one step forward. This was as far as he could go, and whichever way he moved he dragged the clanking chains with him. He did this for hours during the day. Sometimes he sobbed as he strained to pull the chains out of their sockets.

He was allowed to do nothing for himself. To urinate he had to call the guard and ask for the can. If Berezhinsky was not at the door, or was too lazy to hear, or Yakov could not stand the sound of the bolts hitting his head, he held his water till it cut like a knife. When he could no longer hold it he pissed on the floor. Once he held it so long the stream burst forth, wetting his pants and shoes. When Berezhinsky came in and saw what had happened he slapped the fixer's face with one hand, then with the other until the day blotted out.

"You cocksucker Zhid, I ought to make you lick it up off the floor."

When Berezhinsky delivered the gruel, Yakov often begged him to remove the manacles for a few minutes while he ate, but the guard refused. Once after eating, while the guard was gone, Yakov turned sideways, used the spoon handle to dig a little at the cement around one of the bolts. But the guard saw this through the spy hole, entered the cell, and bloodied the prisoner's mouth. After that Berezhinsky had the cell searched by a detail of five guards. Nothing was turned up at first, but they came again later in the week and found the blackened needle Yakov had long ago borrowed from Zhitnyak and carefully hidden in a crevice in the stove. To punish the fixer, his stool was removed for a week. He stood in chains all day and at night slept the sleep of the dead.

Thus the days went by. Each day went by alone. It crawled along like a dying thing. Sometimes, if he thought about it, three days went by, but the third was the same as the first. It was the first day because he could not say that three single days, counted, came to something they did not come to if they were not counted. One day crawled by. Then one day. Then one day. Never three. Nor five or seven. There was no such thing as a week if there was no end to his time in prison. If he were in Siberia serving twenty years at hard labour, a week might mean something. It would be twenty years less a week. But for a man who might be in prison for countless days, there were only first days following one another. The third was the first, the fourth was the first, the seventy-first was the first. The first day was the three thousandth.

Yakov thought how it used to be before he was chained to the wall. He remembered sweeping the floor with the birch broom. He remembered reading Zhitnyak's gospels, and the Old Testament pages. He had saved and counted the wood splinters and kept track of the days and months when it seemed a sort of reward to add up time. He thought of the minutes of light on the scabby wall. He thought of the table he had once had to sit at reading before he smashed it in a fit of madness. He thought of being free to walk back and forth in the cell, or in circles, until he was too tired to think. He thought of being able to urinate without having to call the guard; and of only two searches a day instead of a terrifying six. He thought of lying down on the straw mattress any time he wanted to; but now he could not even lie down on the wooden bed except when they released him to. And he also thought of the time he was allowed to go to the kitchen to fill his bowl; and also of tending the stove in winter, and Zhitnyak, who was not too bad, coming in twice a day to light it. The guard had permitted him a good fire. He allowed Yakov to put in plenty of wood; then before leaving the cell he lit it with a match and watched until it really blazed. Yakov thought he would be glad if things went back to how they had once been. He wished he had enjoyed the bit of comfort, in a way of freedom, he had had then. In chains all that was left of freedom was life, just existence; but to exist without choice was the same as death.

He had secret, almost pleasurable thoughts of death, had had from the time he had stolen Zhitnyak's needle. He had thought, if I want to die sometime I can use the needle to cut my veins. He could do it after Kogin left, and bleed all night. In the morning they would find a corpse. He had these thoughts more intensely now. After a while all he

281

thought of was death. He was terribly weary, hungry to rid himself of the hard chains and the devilishly freezing cell. He hoped to die quickly, to end his suffering for once and all, to get rid of all he was and had been. His death would mean there was one last choice, there always is, and he had taken it. He had taken his fate in his hands. How will I do it? He thought of a hunger strike but that would take too long, slowly starving. He had no belt but could tear up his clothes and the blanket, braid the strips together, and if he did not first freeze to death, hang himself from the window-bars. But he couldn't reach the window-bars, and even if he found some way to get the rope behind them and down to him, hanging himself was not what he wanted. It would leave them out of it. He wanted them involved. He thought of Fetyukov shot by the guard. That's how I have to do it. They want me to die but not directly by their hand. They'll keep me in chains, making searches until my heart gives out. Then they can say I died of natural causes "while awaiting trial". I'll make it unnatural causes. I'll make it by their hand. I'll provoke them to kill me. He had made up his mind. He planned to do it during the sixth search of the next day, when they were at their most irritable, so they would react without thought, mechanically, instantly. He would refuse to undress, and when they ordered him to, he would spit into the Deputy Warden's eye. If he were not at once shot he would try to wrestle a gun out of one of his holsters. By then Berezhinsky would have shot him through the head. It would be over in minutes, and the guard would later receive five or ten roubles for meritorious service. The Tsar would read about it in the St Petersburg newspapers and at once sit down at his desk to write out a telegram to Grubeshov. "I heartily congratulate you for paying back in his own coin the Jewish murderer of Zhenia Golov. You

will hear from me soon regarding advancement. Nicholas."
But then the officials would have to explain his death, and
whatever they said, they could never say they had proved
his guilt. Who would believe them? It might even create a
tumult on the outside.

Let the Tsar jig on his polished floor. I shit my death on
him.

2

It is later afternoon. The sun is sinking behind the cold
treetops. A black carriage appears in the distance (coming
from what city?) drawn by four black horses. He loses it
amid traffic on the Kreshchatik, among other carriages,
droshkies, trolleys, wagon-trucks, a few motor-cars. The
trees are now black. It is night again. Kogin is restlessly
pacing back and forth in the corridor. He has often stood
by Yakov's cell door, the spy hole open, listening to his
noisy wheezing, the guard's breathing audible as he wets
his pencil and writes in the notebook what Yakov cries
out in his sleep. But tonight, a blizzarding night, the snow
swirling thickly around the prison, after hours of walking
back and forth past Yakov's cell door, knowing the
prisoner is awake, the guard stops and sighs through the spy
hole, "Ah, Yakov Bok, don't think you're the only one
with troubles. They're piled on my head like snows on a
mountain-top."

He walks away and then returns to say that his son
Trofim has murdered an old man while robbing a house in
the Podol. "That's what it comes to, you see."

After a long silence he says, "I had trouble enough with

my daughter, who got herself pregnant by a man of my age, a goddamn drunk, but no sooner do I get her married off to someone," Kogin says through the spy hole, "than the boy takes to robbing a house, a thing that never entered his mind before. He stole from me but never from anybody else until this night he went into a house by the Dnieper, and while he was in there, killed the old man who lived in it. He was a harmless old man, and anyone in his right mind could see from the outside of the house that there wasn't likely to be anything of any value in it, not a thing. He knew it, but in that case why did he do it, Yakov Bok? Was there anything on his mind but to pay me back with worries for the years of love I gave him? When the old man caught him in his house he grabbed Trofim's coat and hung on to it, and he, in fright, he says, beat the old man on the head with his fists until he let go, but by that time it was too late – the old man had had some kind of stroke and died. That was the end of him. Trofim came in, as you might say, to partake of his hospitality, and he stayed on there to light the funeral candles and maybe say a prayer over the remains. He returned to the house that morning as I was taking my boots off after a night's work and told me what he had done. So I put my boots on again, and we went together to the District Police and there inscribed him for murder. A few months ago he was tried in court and sentenced to the highest penalty, twenty years at forced labour in Siberia. He's on his way there now. They started out across the Nicholas Bridge on a freezing day in December, and God only knows where they are now in all this snow and wind. Just imagine, twenty years – it's a lifetime."

"It's only twenty years," says Yakov.

"I won't see him, if we both live that long, till he's fifty-two, which is the age I am now."

284

The guard's low voice rumbles in the cell so he goes on in a thick whisper.

"I asked him why he had done that thing, and he said he had no particular reason. Can you imagine a more ridiculous statement, Bok? He came to the end I had predicted for him, all of a father's love gone for nothing. That's how it goes. You plan one thing and get another. Life plays no favourites and what's the use of hoping for it? The children were ruined by their mother, a woman of unsettled character and lax ways. My son was always hard to control because of her ways with him, and I thought for a time he would murder one of us in spite of all the love I had for him, but it turned out that he murdered somebody else."

Kogin sighs, pauses a minute, and asks Yakov if he wants a cigarette.

Yakov says no. He breathes deeply so the guard can hear the whine in his chest. A cigarette would make him sick.

"But if you open the stocks for a minute," he says, "it would ease my stiff legs."

Kogin says he can't do that. He stands silently at the spy hole for a few minutes, then whispers heavily, "Don't think I am not aware of your misfortunes, Bok, because I am. It's a terrible thing to see a man in chains, whoever he is, and have to lock his feet in stocks every night, but to be frank with you I don't allow myself to dwell on it much. I try not to think of you there in chains all day long. The nerves can take just so much, and I already have all the worry I can stand. I think you know what I mean by that.

Yakov says he does.

"You're sure about a cigarette? It's a small infraction of the rules. Some of the guards sell them to prisoners here, and if you ask me the warden knows it. But if I opened your stocks I could get myself shot."

After a while Yakov thinks the guard has gone away but he hasn't.

"Do you still have the gospels in there?" Kogin asks.

"No, they're gone."

"What about the sayings you used to say by memory? Why don't you say any of them any more?"

"I've forgotten them."

"This is one I remember," says the guard. "'But he who endures to the end will be saved.' It's either from Matthew or Luke, one or the other."

Yakov is moved so deeply he laughs.

The guard walks away. Tonight he is restless and in a half-hour returns to the cell door, holding a lamp to the hole, peering above it to see what he can see. The light falls on the fixer's imprisoned feet, waking him again. Kogin is about to say something but doesn't. The light goes out. Yakov moves restlessly, lying awake listening to the guard walking back and forth in the corridor as though he were walking to Siberia along with his son. The prisoner listens until exhaustion overtakes him, then goes on with the dream he was having.

He locates the black carriage once again, only it is a rickety wagon coming from the provinces, carrying a coffin made of weatherbeaten pine boards. For me or who else? he thinks. Afraid to name names he struggles to wake up and instead finds himself in an empty room standing by a small black coffin, like a trunk locked with chains.

It's Zhenia's coffin, he thinks. Marfa Golov has sent it to me as a present. But when he unlocks the rusty chains and raises the coffin lid, there lies Shmuel, his father-in-law, with a prayer shawl covering his head, a purple hole in his forehead and one eye still wet with blood.

286

"Shmuel, are you dead?" the fixer cries, and the old man, if not in peace, at least in repose, for once has nothing to say.

The fixer awakens, grieving, his beard damp with salt tears.

"Live, Shmuel," he sighs, "live. Let me die for you."

Then he thinks in the dark, how can I die for him if I take my life? If I die I die to fuck them and end my suffering. As for Shmuel, he's already out in the cold. He may even die for my death if they work up a pogrom in celebration of it. If so what do I get by dying, outside of release from pain? What have I earned if a single Jew dies because I did? Suffering I can gladly live without, I hate the taste of it, but if I must suffer let it be for something. Let it be for Shmuel.

The next day he is searched six times in the bitterly cold cell, standing barefoot on the floor, each stone like a block of ice, as they poke their filthy fingers into his private parts. The sixth search, when he has planned to die, is the most dreadful of all. He struggles with himself to keep from leaping on the Deputy Warden, to murder him a little with his bare hands before he is shot to death.

He tells himself he mustn't die. Why should I take from myself what they are destroying me to take? Why should I help them kill me?

Who, for instance, would know if he dies now? They'll sweep his remains off the bloody floor and throw them into a wet hole. A year or two later they'd say he died attempting to escape. Who would question it after a year or two? It was a natural thing for prisoners to die in prison. They died like flies all over Russia. It was a vast country and there were many prisons. There were more prisoners than there were Jews. And what difference if the Jews said they didn't believe he had died naturally? They would have other headaches then.

Not that he is afraid to die because he is afraid of suicide, but because there is no way of keeping the consequences of his death to himself. To the goyim what one Jew is is what they all are. If the fixer stands accused of murdering one of their children, so does the rest of the tribe. Since the crucifixion the crime of the Christ-killer is the crime of all Jews. "His blood be on us and our children."

He pities their fate in history. After a short time of sunlight you awake in a black and bloody world. Overnight a madman is born who thinks Jewish blood is water. Overnight life becomes worthless. The innocent are born without innocence. The human body is worth less than its substance. A person is shit. Those Jews who escape with their lives live in memory's eternal pain. So what can Yakov Bok do about it? All he can do is not make things worse. He's half a Jew himself, yet enough of one to protect them. After all, he knows the people; and he believes in their right to be Jews and live in the world like men. He is against those who are against them. He will protect them to the extent that he can. This is his covenant with himself. If God's not a man he has to be. Therefore he must endure to the trial and let them confirm his innocence by their lies. He has no future but to hold on, wait it out.

He is enraged by what has happened – is happening to him – a whole society has set itself against Yakov Bok, a poor man with a few grains of education, but in any case innocent of the crime they accuse him of. What a strange and extraordinary thing for someone like himself, a fixer by trade, who had never in his life done a thing to them but live for a few months in a forbidden district, to have as his sworn and bitter enemies the Russian State, through its officials and Tsar, for no better reason than that he was born a Jew, therefore their appointed enemy, though the truth of it is he is in his heart no one's enemy but his own.

Where's reason? Where's justice? What does Spinoza say – that it's the purpose of the State to preserve a man's peace and security so he can do his day's work. To help him live out his few poor years, against circumstance, sickness, the frights of the universe. So at least don't make it any worse than it is. But the Russian State denies Yakov Bok the most elemental justice, and to show its fear and contempt of humankind, has chained him to the wall like an animal.

"Dogs," he cries out.

He beats his chains against the wall, his neck cords thick. He is in a rage to be free, has at times glimmerings of hope, as though imagining creates it, thinks of it as close by, about to happen if he breathes right, or thinks the one right thought. Maybe a wall will collapse, or sunrise burn through it and make an opening as large as a man's body. Or he will remember where he has hidden a book that will tell him how to walk with ease through a locked-and-twelve-times-bolted door.

"I'll live," he shouts in his cell, "I'll wait, I'll come to my trial."

Berezhinsky opens the spy hole, inserts his rifle, and sights along the barrel at the fixer's genitals.

Yakov sits in the pit. An angelic voice, or so he thinks, calls his name, but he isn't sure he has heard right; his hearing is dulled in the right ear since Berezhinsky hit him there. The sky rains and snows on him. Or it may be bits of wood or frozen time. He doesn't reply. His hair is matted and long. His nails grow until they break. He has dysentery, dirties himself, stinks.

T

Berezhinsky douses him with a bucket of cold water. "It's no secret why Jews won't eat pig. You're blood brothers and both live on shit."

He sits on the grass under a leafy tree. The fields are full of flowers. He talks to himself not to forget. Some things he remembers astonish him. Are they memories or thoughts of things he had hoped to do? He is shrouded in thick clouds of yellow fog. Sometimes in painful stretches of light. Memories thin out and fall away. Events of the past he has difficulty recalling. He remembers having gone mad once. Where do you look if you lose your mind? That's the end of it. He would, in his mind, be forever locked in prison, no longer knowing why or what he is locked in. Locked in his final fate, the last unknowing.

"Die," says Berenzhinsky. "For Christ's sake, die."

He dies. He dies.

Kogin says he has received a letter that his son is dead. He has drowned himself in a river in Irkutsk on the way to Novorosiisk.

3

"Remove your cap," said the warden, standing in his cell.

He removed his cap, and the warden handed him a sheaf of papers.

"It's your indictment, Bok, but that doesn't mean your trial is necessarily on its way."

Afterwards, crouched on his stool in chains, Yakov very slowly read the papers. His heart raced as he read but the mind ran ahead of the heart; this Jew they were talking about had committed a terrible crime and then stepped into a trap, and at once the prisoner saw him dead and buried in a thin grave. Sometimes the words on the paper grew blurred and disappeared under water. When they rose to the surface he read them one by one, saying each aloud. After reading three pages he hadn't the strength to concentrate longer. The papers weighed like oakwood and he had to put them down. Soon, though the barred window was still lit, it was too dark to read. At night he awoke famished to devour the words. He thought of begging Kogin for a candle but had visions of the paper catching fire and burning. So he waited for morning, once dreaming he was trying to read the indictment but the language was Turkish. Then he awoke and frantically felt for the papers. They were in his greatcoat pocket. He waited impatiently for daylight. In the morning, when there was enough light the fixer avidly read through the whole document. It seemed to him that the story had changed from how he read it yesterday, but then he realized it had changed from how he knew it as he had pieced it together from the questions he had been asked, and the accusations that had been made. The crime was the same but there were details that he had not heard before, some fantastic ones; and some of the old ones had been altered and a new mystery created. Yakov read, straining to find a combination of facts that would make them, by virtue of this arrangement, truer than they were when he first heard them; or as though, if he comprehended them in some way others did not, he would at once establish his innocence. And once he established it they would have to release him from his chains and open the prison doors.

This "Court Indictment", typed on long sheets of blue paper, retold the murder of Zhenia Golov, much as Yakov knew it, but now the number of wounds was unaccountably forty-five, "3 groups of 13, plus 2 additional groups of 3". There were wounds, the paper said, on the boy's chest, throat, face, and skull – "around the ears"; and the autopsy performed by Professor M. Zagreb of the Medical Faculty of Kiev University, indicated that all the wounds had been inflicted on the body when the boy's heart was still strong. "But those in the principal veins of the neck had been inflicted when the heart was weakening."

On the day the boy was found murdered in the cave, his mother, when she heard the news, fainted. This had been noted on the police record of the case. Then came some details Yakov read quickly but had to go back and read slowly. The collapse of Marfa Golov, the indictment said, "was noted here with particular interest" because it was later observed that she was composed at the funeral and did not weep at her son's burial, although others, "mere strangers", had wept without restraint. Some "well-meaning spectators" and others "perhaps not so well-meaning", were disturbed by this, and "foolish rumours" began at once to circulate "concerning the possible involvement of this good woman, through a former and seriously incapacitated friend, in the murder of her own child". Because of this baseless rumour, but in the interests of arriving at the truth, she was arrested and thoroughly investigated by the police. They searched her house more than once and found "nothing in the least incriminating". Thus, after days of painstaking investigation she was released with the apologies of the police and other officials. The Chief of Police concluded that the rumours previously referred to were false and unfounded, "probably the invention of the enemies of Marfa Golov, or possibly of certain sinister forces", for Marfa Golov was a devoted mother, "blameless of any crime against her child". Such suspicion was con-

292

temptible. Her composed behaviour at her son's funeral was the "behaviour of a dignified person in control of her sentiments although involved in a profound personal loss". For "not all who are sad, weep" and "guilt is not a matter of facial expression but of evidence". "How much this unfortunate woman had mourned and endured *prior* to the child's funeral no one had inquired." However, witnesses had testified that Marfa Golov had been a more than ordinarily conscientious mother, and a "hardworking virtuous woman of unstained character, who without any assistance to speak of, had provided for her child since the desertion and death of the irresponsible father". It was therefore concluded that the attempts to destroy her reputation were "the work of unknown subversive alien groups" for the purpose of "concealing the guilt of one of its members, the true murderer of Zhenia Golov, the jack-of-all-trades, Yakov Bok".

"Vey is mir," said Yakov.

The fixer had been suspected from the beginning. Even before the funeral, rumours had begun to fly through the city that "the real culprit responsible for the murder of the boy was a member of the Hebrew faith". Then came a summary of reasons why Bok had come to the attention of the police "as a suspicious person": First, because it had come out he was a Hebrew using a false name and living in the Lukianovsky District, a district forbidden by special law to all members of his faith except Merchants of the First Guild and some professionals. Second, while representing himself as a Russian, one Yakov Ivanovitch Dologushev, this same Yakov Bok had made improper advances, and even attempted physical assault of Zinaida Nikolaevna, the daughter of Bok's employer, Nikolai Maximovitch Lebedev. "By good fortune she thwarted his nefarious purposes."

Third, Yakov Bok was suspected by certain of his fellow employees at the brickworks, in particular "the observant foreman Proshko", of systematically peculating from funds belonging to the business enterprise of Nikolai Maximovitch Lebedev. Fourth, he was seen on certain occasions by the yardkeeper Skobeliev, the foreman Proshko, and "other witnesses", chasing boys in the brickyard, near the kilns. These were Vasya Shiskovsky, Andrei Khototov, the deceased Zhenia Golov, and other even younger children, all of them boys. And fifth, Zhenia Golov had one night been pursued among the tombstones in the cemetery close to the brickyard by the same Yakov Bok "clasping in his hand a long thin carpenter's knife". The frightened boy had related this to his mother. In Bok's living quarters in the stable the police had unearthed his bag of tools, which included "certain bloodstained awls and knives". Some bloody rags also were recovered in this room.

The fixer sighed and went on reading.

"In addition to the above-listed evidence, Marfa Golov has testified that Zhenia complained Yakov Bok had interfered with him sexually and had feared the boy would expose him to the authorities." "Zhenia, a bright and perceptive lad," had "on certain occasions" followed Bok and discovered that he sometimes met "with a group of other Hebrews, suspected smugglers, housebreakers, and other criminal elements, in the cellar of the synagogue." Her son, according to the mother, threatened to report these illegal activities to the police. Furthermore, Vasya Shiskovsky and Zhenia Golov had once or twice "in the manner of boys", angered Bok by flinging rocks at him and taunting him about his race, and he was determined to take revenge on them. "Zhenia Golov, to his great misfortune, was the one who had fallen into Bok's evil hands, but by great good luck Vasya Shiskovsky had escaped his poor friend's fate."

He read quickly through the section where he had killed the boy. ("Skobeliev testified that he had seen Bok carrying something heavy in his arms, a large squirming package of some sort that resembled a human body, up the stairs to his quarters. There, the evidence is clear, the boy was tortured and then murdered by Yakov Bok, probably with the assistance of one or two of his co-religionists.") "While in prison," the indictment went on, "the said Yakov Bok had attempted to influence the counterfeiter Gronfein, a friend and fellow-religionist, to bribe Marfa Golov not to testify against him. The sum of money for that purpose was to be raised by subscription in the Hebrew communities of the Jewish Pale of Settlement. Another bribe was offered to Marfa Golov herself at a later date, the large sum of 40,000 roubles if she would flee across the Austrian border, but she indignantly refused."

The last paragraph read: "It is therefore the fully considered opinion of the Investigating Magistrate, the Prosecuting Attorney, and the President of the Superior Court of the Kiev Province, where the Court Indictment is this day filed, that Yakov Bok, an admitted Hebrew, had with premeditation, and for purposes of torture and murder, stabbed to death Yevgeny Golov, age 12, the beloved son of Marfa Vladimirovna Golov, for the reasons stated above; in sum, an overweening and abnormal desire for revenge against an innocent child who had discovered his participation in criminal activities. However, the crime was so wicked and debased that an additional element may be said to have been present. Only a criminal of the worst sadistic instincts could have engaged in such an unnatural act of unprovoked hostility and degraded bestiality."

The indictment was signed by Yefim Balik, Investigating Magistrate; V. G. Grubeshov, Prosecuting Attorney; and P. F. Furmanov, President of the Superior Court.

Yakov squeezed his throbbing head after reading the papers. Though his eyes ached – he felt as though he had read the words through sand and glue – he at once re-read them, and again, in increasing astonishment and disbelief. What had happened to the charge of ritual murder? Holding each sheet up for better light he searched it in vain. There was no such charge. Every reference to a religious crime, though hinted at, led up to, had in the end been omitted. The Jews had become Hebrews. Why? The only reason he could think of was that they could not prove a charge of ritual murder. And if they couldn't prove that, what could they prove? Not these stupid lies, vile, ridiculous, some snipped directly out of Marfa's insane letter. They can't prove a thing, he thought, that's why they've kept me in solitary imprisonment for almost two years. They know the mother and her lover murdered the boy. He fought a deepening depression. With this "evidence" they'll never bring me to trial. The weakness of the indictment showed they had no intention to.

Still it was an indictment and he was wondering if they would now let him see a lawyer, when the warden appeared again in the cell and ordered him to hand over the papers.

"You may not believe this, Bok, but they were issued through an administrative error. I was supposed to look them over but not give them to you."

They're afraid of the trial, the fixer thought bitterly, after the warden had left. Maybe people are asking when it will begin. Maybe this has them worried. If I live, sooner or later they'll have to bring me to trial. If not Nicholas the Second, then Nicholas the Third will.

4

When his chains were unlocked and he was permitted to lie on his bedbench as long as he liked with his legs free, or to walk around, he could not comprehend what had happened and for a while suffered from excitement. Yakov limped around the cell but mostly lay, breathing through his mouth, on the wooden bed. "Is it another indictment, or maybe is the trial coming?" he asked Berezhinsky, but the guard wouldn't say. One day the fixer's hair was trimmed a bit and the beard combed. The barber, glancing stealthily at a yellowed photograph in his tunic pocket, combed out curls over his ears. He was then given another suit of prison clothes, permitted to wash his hands and face with soap, and called to the warden's office.

Berezhinsky pushed him out into the hall and commanded him to move along, but the prisoner limped slowly, stopping often to recover his breath. The guard prodded him with his rifle-butt, then the fixer ran a step and limped two. He worried how he would make it back to the cell.

"Your wife is here," said Warden Grizitskoy, in his office. "You can see her in the visitors' room. There'll be a guard present, so don't presume any privileges."

He felt, in towering astonishment, this could not be true, they were deceiving him to extend the torture. And when, as he watched the warden and guard, he believed it, the fixer gasped as though fire had scorched his lungs. When he could breathe he was frightened.

"My wife?"

"Raisl Bok?"

"It's true."

"You'll be allowed to speak to her for several minutes in the visitors' room, but watch your step."

"Please, not now," said Yakov wearily. "Some other time."

"That'll do," said the warden.

The fixer, shaken, upset, his thoughts in turmoil, was led in a limping trot by Berezhinsky through a series of narrow corridors to the prisoners' pen in the visitors' room. At the door Yakov tried to straighten himself, entered, and was locked in. It's a trick, he thought, it's not her, it's a spy. I must be careful.

She sat on a bench, separated from him by a heavy wire grating. On the far side of the bare-walled boxlike room, a uniformed guard stood behind her, his rifle resting against the wall, slowly rolling a cigarette.

Yakov sat stiffly opposite her, hunched cold, his throat aching, palms clammy. He felt a dread of cracking up, going mad in front of her – of will failing him once they talked and how would he go on after that?

"Get along with your business," said the guard in Russian.

Though the visitors' room was dimly lit it was brighter than his cell, and the light hurt his eyes before he could get used to it. The woman sat motionless, her coat threadbare, a wool shawl covering her head, her fingers clasped like spikes in her lap. She was watching him mutely, eyes stricken. He had expected a hag, but though she was worn, tensely embarrassed, and had abandoned the wig she had never liked to wear, she looked otherwise the same, surprising how young though he knew she was thirty, and not bad as a woman. It's at my expense, he thought bitterly.

"Yakov?"

"Raisl?"

298

"Yes."

As she unwound her shawl – her own dark hair cut short, the hairline damp – and he looked fully into her face, at the long exposed neck, both eyes sad, she was staring at him with fright and feeling. He tried twice to speak and could not. His face ached and mouth trembled.

"I know, Yakov," Raisl said. "What more can I say? I know."

Emotion blinded him.

My God, what have I forgotten? I've forgotten nothing. He experienced a depth of loss and shame, overwhelming – that the feelings of the past could still be alive after so long and terrible an imprisonment. The deepest wounds never die.

"Yakov, is it really you?"

He shook away the beginning of tears and turned his good ear to her.

"It's me. Who else could it be?"

"How strange you look in earlocks and long beard."

"That's their evidence against me."

"How thin you are, how withered."

"I'm thin," he said, "I'm withered. What do you want from me?"

"They forbade me to ask you any questions about your conditions in this prison," Raisl said in Yiddish, "and I promised not to but who has to ask? I have eyes and can see. I wish I couldn't. Oh, Yakov, what have they done to you? What did you do to yourself? How did such a terrible thing happen?"

"You stinking whore, what did *you* do to me? It wasn't enough we were poor as dirt and childless. On top of that you had to be a whore."

She said tonelessly, "It's not what I alone did, it's what

we did to each other. Did you love me? Did I love you? I say yes and I say no. As for being a whore, if I was I'm not. I've had my ups and downs, the same as you, Yakov, but if you're going to judge me you'll have to judge me as I am."

"What are you?"

"Whatever I am I'm not what I was."

"Why did you marry me for I'd like to know? 'Love', she says. If you didn't love me why didn't you leave me alone?"

"You can believe me I was afraid to marry you, but you were affectionate then, and when a person is lonely it's easy to lean towards a tender word. Also I thought you loved me although you found it hard to say so."

"What can a man say if he's afraid of a trap? I was afraid of you. I never met anybody so dissatisfied. I am a limited man. What could I promise you? Besides that, your father was behind me, pushing with both hands: If I married you the world would change, everyday a rainbow. Then you got me in the woods that day."

"We were to the woods more than once. You wanted what I wanted. It takes two to lie down, one on top of the other."

"So we got married," he said bitterly. "Still, we had a chance. Once we were married you should have been faithful. A contract is a contract. A wife is a wife. Married is married."

"Were you such a fine husband?" Raisl said. "Yes, you always tried to make a living, I won't say no, though you never did. And if you wanted to stay up all night reading Spinoza I had nothing against that either, though it wasn't Torah, except when it was at my expense, and you know what I mean. What bothered me most were the curses and dirty names. Because I slept with you before we were

300

married you were convinced I was sleeping with the world. I slept with no one but you until you stopped sleeping with me. At twenty-eight I was too young for the grave. So, as you advised, I stopped being superstitious and at last took a chance. Otherwise I would soon have been dead. I was barren. I ran in every direction. I flung myself against trees. I tore at my dry breasts and cursed my empty womb. Whether I stayed or left I was useless to you, so I decided to leave. You wouldn't so I had to. I left in desperation to change my life. I got out the only way I could. It was either that or death, one sin or worse. I chose the lesser sin. If you want to know the truth, Yakov, one reason I left was to make you move. Whoever thought it would come to this?"

She cracked her white knuckles against her chest. "Yakov, I didn't come here to fight about the past. Forgive me, forgive the past."

"Why did you come?"

"Papa said he saw you in prison, it's all he talks about. I went back to the shtetl last November. I was first in Kharkov, then in Moscow, but couldn't get along any more, so I had to go back. When I found out you were in Kiev Prison I came to see you but they wouldn't let me in. Then I went to the Prosecuting Attorney and showed him the papers that I was your wife. He said I couldn't see you except under the most extraordinary circumstances, and I said the circumstances were extraordinary enough when an innocent man is kept in prison. I went to see him at least five times and finally he said he would let me in if I brought you a paper to sign. He told me to urge you to sign it."

"A black year on his papers to sign. A black year on you for bringing it."

"Yakov, if you sign you can go free tomorrow. It's at least something to think about."

"I've thought," he shouted. "It's nothing to think about. I'm innocent."

Raisl stared at him mutely.

The guard came over with his rifle. "Nobody's supposed to be talking Yiddish here," he said. "You're supposed to be talking Russian. This prison is a Russian institution."

"It takes longer in Russian," she said. "I speak very slowly in Russian."

"Hurry up with the paper you're supposed to give him."

"The paper has to be explained. There are advantages but there are also disadvantages. I have to tell him what the Prosecuting Attorney said."

"Then tell him, for Christ's sake, and be done with it."

Taking a small key out of his trouser pocket, he unlocked a small wire door in the grating.

"Don't try to pass anything but the paper he has to sign or it'll go hard on you both. I've got my eyes wide open."

Raisl unclasped a greyed cloth handbag and took out a folded envelope.

"This is the paper I promised I would give you," she said in Russian to Yakov. "The Prosecuting Attorney says it's your last chance."

"So that's why you came," he said in vehement Yiddish, "to get me to confess lies I've resisted for two years. To betray me again."

"It was the only way I could get in," Raisl said. "But it's not why I came, I came to cry." She gasped a little. Her mouth fell open, the lips contorted; she wept. Tears flowed through her fingers as she pressed them to her eyes. Her shoulders shook.

He felt, as he watched her, the weight of the blood in his heart.

The guard rolled another cigarette, lit it, and smoked slowly.

This is where we left off, thought Yakov. The last time I saw her she was crying like this, and here she is still crying. In the meantime I've been two years in prison without cause, in solitary confinement, and chains. I've suffered freezing cold, filth, lice, the degradation of those searches, and she's still crying.

"What are you crying for?" he asked.

"For you, for me, for the world."

She was as she wept, a frail woman, lanky, small-breasted, worn and sad. Who would have thought so frail? As she wept she moved him. He had learned about tears.

"What's there to do here but think, so I've thought," Yakov said after a while. "I've thought about our life from beginning to end and I can't blame you for more than I blame myself. If you give little you get less, though of some things I got more than I deserved. Also, it takes me a long time to learn. Some people have to make the same mistake seven times before they know they've made it. That's my type and I'm sorry. I'm also sorry I stopped sleeping with you. I was out to stab myself, so I stabbed you. Who else was so close to me? Still I've suffered in this prison and I'm not the same man I once was. What more can I say, Raisl? If I had my life to live over, you'd have less to cry about, so stop crying."

"Yakov," she said, when she had wiped her eyes with her fingers, "I brought this confession paper here so they would let me talk to you, not because I want you to sign it. I don't. Still, if you wanted to what could I say? Should I say stay in prison? What I also came to tell you is maybe not such good news. I came to say I've given birth to a child. After I ran away I found out I was pregnant. I was ashamed and frightened, but at the same time I was happy I was no longer barren and could have a baby."

There's no bottom to my bitterness, he thought.

He flailed at the wooden walls of the pen with both fists. The guard sternly ordered him to stop, so he beat himself instead, his face and head. She looked on with shut eyes.

Afterwards, when it was over, except what was left of his anguish, he said, "So if you weren't barren, what was the matter?"

She looked away, then at him. "Who knows? Some women conceive late. With conception you need luck."

Luck I was short of, he thought, so I blamed her.

"Boy or girl?" Yakov asked.

She smiled at her hands. "A boy, Chaiml, after my grand-father."

"How old now?"

"Almost a year and a half."

"It couldn't be mine?"

"How could it be?"

"Too bad," he sighed. "Where is he now?"

"With Papa. That's why I went back, I couldn't take care of him alone any more. Ah, Yakov, it's not all raisins and almonds. I've gone back to the shtetl but they blame me for your fate. I tried to take up my little dairy business but I might just as well be selling pork. The rabbi calls me to my face, pariah. The child will think his name is bastard."

"So what do you want from me?"

"Yakov," she said, "I'm sorry for what you're suffering. When I heard it was you I tore my hair; but I figured you'd also be sorry for me. Please, it might make things easier if

304

you wouldn't mind saying you are my son's father. Still, if you can't you can't. I don't want to add to your burdens."

"Who's the father, some goy I'll bet."

"If it makes you feel better he was a Jew, a musician. He came, he went, I forgot him. He fathered the child but he's not his father. Whoever acts the father is the father. My father's the father but he's only two steps from death's door. One knock and I'm twice widowed."

"What's the matter with him?"

"Diabetes, though he drags himself around. He worried about you, he worries about me and the child. He wakes up cursing himself for not having been born rich. He prays every time he thinks of it. I take care of him the best I can. He sleeps on a bag of rags pushed to the wall. He needs food, rest, medicine. The little we get comes from charity. One or two of the rich send their servants over with this or that, but when they see me they hold their noses."

"Has he talked to anybody about me?"

"To everybody. He runs everywhere, sick as he is."

"What do they say?"

"They tear their hair. They beat their chests. They thank God it wasn't them. Some collect money. Some say they will make protests. Some are afraid to do anything because it may annoy the Christians and make things worse. Some are pessimistic but a few have hope. Still, there's more going on than I know."

"If it doesn't go faster I won't be here to find out what."

"Don't say that, Yakov. I went myself to see some lawyers in Kiev. Two of them swear they will help you but nobody can move without an indictment."

"So I'll wait," said Yakov. Before her eyes he shrank in size.

"I've brought you some haleh and cheese and an apple

in a little pack," Raisl said, "but they made me leave it at the warden's office. Don't forget to ask for it. It's goat's cheese but I don't think you'll notice."

"Thanks," said Yakov wearily. He said, after a sigh, "Listen, Raisl, I'll write you a paper that the child's mine."

Her eyes glistened. "God will bless you."

"Never mind God. Have you got a piece of paper, I'll write something down. Show it to the rabbi's father, the old melamed. He knows my handwriting and he's a kinder man than his son."

"I have paper and pencil," she whispered nervously, "but I'm afraid to give them to you with this guard in the room. They warned me not to hand you anything but the confession and to take nothing but that from you or they would arrest me for attempting to help you escape."

The guard was restless and again came forward. "There's nothing more to talk about. Either sign the paper or go back to your cell."

"Have you got a pencil?" the fixer asked.

The guard took a fat fountain-pen from his tunic pocket, and gave it to him through the opening in the grating.

He stayed to watch but Yakov waited until he had withdrawn.

"Give me the confession," he said to Raisl in Russian.

Raisl handed him the envelope. Yakov removed the paper, unfolded it, and read: "I, Yakov Bok, confess that I witnessed the murder of Zhenia Golov, the son of Marfa Golov, by my Jewish compatriots. They killed him on the night of March 20, 1911, upstairs in the stable in the brickyard belonging to Nikolai Maximovitch Lebedev, merchant of the Lukianovsky District."

Under that a heavy line was drawn on which to sign his name.

306

Yakov placed the paper on the shelf before him and wrote in Russian on the line for his name: "Every word is a lie."

On the envelope, pausing between words to remember the letters for the next, he wrote in Yiddish, "I declare myself to be the father of Chaim, the infant son of my wife, Raisl Bok. He was conceived before she left me. Please help the mother and child, and for this, amid all my troubles, I'll be grateful. Yakov Bok."

She told him the date and he wrote it down, "February 27, 1913." Yakov passed it to her through the opening in the grating.

Raisl slipped the envelope into her coat sleeve and handed the guard the confession paper. He folded it at once, and thrust it into his tunic pocket. After examining the contents of Raisl's handbag and tapping her coat pockets he told her to go.

"Yakov," she wept, "come home."

IX

He was chained to the wall again. Things went badly.
Better not have been unchained, the getting back was so
bad. He beat the clanking chains against the wall until it
was scarred white where he stood. They let him beat the
wall. Otherwise he slept. But for the searches he would have
slept through the day. He slept the sleep of the dead with his
feet in stocks. He slept through the end of winter and into
spring. Kogin said it was April. Two years. The searches
went on except when he was sick with dysentery. The Deputy
Warden did not come near him then, though Berezhinsky
sometimes searched him alone. Once after the fixer was sick
the cell was hosed down and a fire started in the stove. An
old pink-faced man came into the cell dressed in winter
clothes. He wore a black cape and black gaiters and grasped
a gnarled cane. Berezhinsky followed him in, carrying a
slender chair with a delicate back, and the old man sat in it
erectly, several feet from the fixer, holding the cane with
grey-mittened hands. His watery eyes wandered. He told

Yakov he was a former jurist of high repute, and that he came with good news. An excitement so thick it felt like sickness surged through the fixer. He asked what good news. The former jurist said this was the year of the three-hundredth anniversary of the rule of the House of Romanov and that the Tsar, in celebration, would issue a ukase amnestying certain classes of criminals. Yakov's name would be listed among them. He was to be pardoned and permitted to return to his village. The old man's face flushed with pleasure. The prisoner clung to the wall, too burdened to speak. Then he asked, Pardoned as a criminal or pardoned as innocent? The former jurist testily said what difference did it make so long as he was let out of prison. It was impossible to erase the sins of the past, but it was not impossible for a humane ruler, a Christian gentleman, to forgive an evil act. The old man sneezed without snuff and peered at his silver watch. Yakov said he wanted a fair trial, not a pardon. If they ordered him to leave the prison without a trial they would have to shoot him first. Don't be foolish, said the former jurist, how can you go on suffering like this, caked in filth? The fixer moved his chains restlessly. I have no choice, he said. I have just offered you one. That's not choice, said Yakov. The former jurist tried to convince the prisoner, then gave up in irritation. It's easier to reason with a peasant. He rose and shook his cane at the fixer. How can we help you, he shouted, if you are so pigheaded? Berezhinsky, who had been listening at the spy hole, opened the door and the old man left the cell. The guard came in for the chair but before taking it, he let Yakov urinate in the can, then dumped the contents on his head. The fixer was left in chains that night. He thought that whenever he had been through the worst, there was always worse.

One day, during Yakov's third summer in prison, his

manacles and shackles were unlocked. Immediately his heart beat heavily and when he touched it with his hand the hand beat like his heart. In an hour the warden, who had aged since the fixer had last seen him and walked with shorter steps, brought in a new indictment in a brown envelope, a sheaf of papers twice thicker than the last. The fixer took the papers and read them slowly and frantically, fearing he would never get to the end of them; but he had discovered at once what he had expected: that the blood murder charge had been violently revived. Now they are serious again, he thought. The reference to sexual experiences with the boy, and to activities with a gang of Jewish housebreakers and smugglers operating out of the cellar of the Kiev synagogue – all the insane lies from Marfa Golov's letter – were omitted. Once again Yakov Bok was accused of murdering the innocent boy in order to drain his body of blood necessary for the baking of Passover matzos and cakes.

This was affirmed by Professor Manilius Zagreb, who with his distinguished colleague, the surgeon Dr Sergei Bul, had twice performed the autopsy of Zhenia's remains. Both categorically stated that the vicious wounds had been inflicted in prearranged clusters with a time interval between each cluster in order to prolong the torture and facilitate the bleeding. It was estimated that one litre of blood was collected from each set of wounds, and that a total of five litres of blood was collected in bottles. Such was also the conclusion of Father Anastasy, the well-known specialist in Jewish affairs, who had made a close study of the Talmud, his reasons given in minute detail for eight single-spaced pages. And it was also the conclusion of Yefim Balik, the Investigating Magistrate. He had carefully reviewed the entire evidence and agreed with its "direction and findings".

How the bloodthirsty crime was committed was described

in this indictment much as it had been by Grubeshov at the cave, more than two years ago, "with careful note taken of the fanatic Hasidic tsadik, seen in the brickyard by the foreman Proshko; who had no doubt helped the accused drain the necessary blood from the boy's still living body, and also assisted him in transporting the corpse to the cave where two horrified boys had found it". And related evidence omitted from the previous indictment was included in this. It was stated that half a bag of matzo flour was "hidden away" in Yakov Bok's stable room, together with certain hard pieces of already baked matzo no doubt containing the innocent blood, which both the Jews "in all probability" had eaten. And the usual bloodstained rag, "admitted by the accused to be a piece of his shirt" had been uncovered in the same room. According to the testimony of Vasya Shiskovsky, a bottle of bright-red blood was seen by him and Zhenia on a table in Bok's stable room, but it had disappeared when the police searched for it. And a sack of carpenter's tools containing bloodstained awls and knives had been found in the same room after the fixer's arrest, "despite a plot later carried out by Jewish co-conspirators to destroy this and other significant evidence by burning down the brickyard stable, a plot which they ultimately achieved."

Towards the end of this wearying, terrifying document a new subject was introduced, "the matter of Yakov Bok's self-proclaimed atheism". It was noted that although the accused, when first examined by the authorities, had confessed he was a Jew "by birth and nationality", he had, however, claimed for himself "an atheistic status; to wit, that he was a freethinker and not a religious Jew". Why he should make "such an odious self-description" was understandable to anyone who reflected for a moment on the matter. It was done to create "extenuating circumstances" and "obfuscating details" in order "to deflect the legal investigation by hiding the motive for this dastardly crime". However, this assertion of atheism could not be defended, for it was observed by reliable witnesses, including prison guards and officials, that Yakov Bok, while incarcerated and awaiting trial, "though persisting in his false claim of irreligion, had in his cell secretly prayed daily in the manner of Orthodox Jews, wrapped in a prayer shawl, with black phylacteries entwined around his brow and left arm". He was also seen piously reading an Old Testament Bible, "which, like the previously mentioned Orthodox religious instruments, had been smuggled into his cell by fellow-Jews of the synagogue". It was clear to all who observed him that he was engaged in the performance of a devout religious rite. He had continued to use the prayer shawl until he had worn it out, and "even now he kept a remnant of this sacred garment in his coat pocket".

It was the opinion of investigators and other officials that this self-incriminating atheism "was a fabrication of Yakov Bok's, in order to hide from the legal authorities that he had committed a vile religious murder of a child for the sole and evil purpose of providing his Hasidic compatriots with the uncorrupted human blood needed to bake the Passover matzos and unleavened cakes".

After he had finished reading the document the fixer, in exhaustion, thought, there's no getting rid of the blood any more. It's stained every word of the indictment and can't be washed out. When they try me it will be for the crucifixion.

The fixer grew more intensely worried. Now that he had this paper would they withdraw it and later issue another? Was this the newest torture? Would they hand him indictments, time after time, for the next twenty years? Would he read them till he died of frustration or his dry brain exploded? Or would they, after this indictment, or the third, seventh, or thirteenth *at last* bring him to trial? Could they make a strong enough circumstantial case against him? He hoped they could. Anyway, just barely. If not, would they keep him in chains for ever? Or were they planning a worse fate? One day as he was about to clean himself with a scrap of newspaper he read on it, "THE JEW IS DOOMED." Yakov frantically read on to find out why, but that part was torn off.

2

He had been told a lawyer was on his way to the prison, but when the cell door was opened on a hot July night, it was not the lawyer, it was Grubeshov, in evening dress. The fixer awoke when Kogin, holding a dripping candle, unlocked his feet. "Wake up," said the guard, shaking him, "his honour is here." Yakov awoke as though coming up out of deep dirty water. He beheld Grubeshov's moist fleshy face, his side-whiskers limp, his red-shot eyes, lit, restless. The public prosecutor's chest rose and fell. He began pacing in the cell, unsteadily, then sat down on the stool, one hand on the table, an enormous shadow on the wall behind him. He stared for a moment at the lamp, blinked at it, and gazed at Yakov. When he talked, the stink of rich food and alcohol on his breath drifted across to the fixer, nauseating him.

"I am on my way home from a civic banquet in honour of the Tsar," Grubeshov, breathing with a whistle, said to the prisoner. "Since my motor-car happened to be in this district, I ordered the driver to go on to the prison. I thought I would speak to you. You are a stubborn man, Bok, but perhaps not yet beyond reason. I thought I would talk to you one last time. Please stand up while I am speaking."

Yakov, sitting on the wooden bed with his bony bare feet on the clammy floor, slowly got up. Grubeshov, gazing at his face, shuddered. The fixer felt a violent hatred of him.

"First of all," said Grubeshov, patting the back of his flushed neck with a large humid handkerchief, "you oughtn't to let your expectations rise too high, Yakov Bok. You will be disappointed if they do. Don't think just because an indictment has been issued that your worries are over. On the contrary – now begin your worst troubles. I warn you, you will be publicly unmasked and seen for what you are."

"What do you want from me here, Mr Grubeshov? It's late at night. I need my little rest for the chains in the morning."

"As for the chains, that's your fault; learn to follow orders. It's none of my affair, I came on other business. Marfa Golov, the victim's mother, visited me in my office today. She knelt before me with holy tears streaming from her eyes, and swore before God that she had told the absolute truth regarding Zhenia and his experiences with you that led to the murder. She is a totally sincere woman and I was deeply affected by her. I am more than ever convinced that a jury will believe what she says, and so much the worse for you. Her testimony and the sincerity of her appearance will demolish whatever case you think you can make."

"Then let her give her testimony," Yakov said. "Why don't you begin the trial?"

Grubeshov, who squirmed on the stool as though it were the top of a hot stove, answered, "I have no intention of engaging in an argument with a criminal. I came to tell you that if you and your fellow-Jews continue to press me to bring you to trial before I have gathered every last grain of evidence, or investigated all courses of action, then you ought to know what dangers you are creating for yourself. There can be too much of a good thing, Bok, if you understand my meaning. The kettle may steam but don't be surprised if the water is boiled off."

"Mr Grubeshov," said Yakov, "I can't stand up any more. I'm tired and must sit down. If you want to shoot me call the guard, he has a gun."

Yakov sat down on the bedplank.

"You're a cheeky one," Grubeshov said, his voice emotional. "The Russian people are sick to their souls of your Jewish tricks and deceptions. That holds also for your investigators, your complaints, your libels from all over. What is happening, Bok, obviously reveals the underground involvement of the Jewish conspiracy in Russian affairs, and I warn you to take rational notice that there is bound to be a tumultuous reprisal against the enemies of the State. Even if by some trickery you were to succeed in swaying a jury to render a judgement against the weight of the true evidence, then you can believe me that the Russian people in justifiable wrath will avenge this poor Zhenia for the pain and torture that you inflicted on him. You may wish for the trial now, but remember this: even the judgement that you are guilty will set off a bloodbath in this city that will outdo the ferocity of the so-called Kishinev massacres. A trial will not save you nor your fellow-Jews. You would be better off confessing, and after a period of time when the public has settled down, we could announce your death in prison, or something of the sort, and spirit you out of Russia. If you insist on the trial, then don't be surprised if bearded heads roll in the street. Feathers fly. Cossack steel invades the tender flesh of young Jewesses."

316

Grubeshov had risen from the hot stool and was pacing again, his shadow going one way on the wall as he went the other.

"A government has to protect itself from subversion, by force if it can't persuade."

Yakov stared at his white crooked feet.

The public prosecutor, in the grip of his excitement, went on: "My father once described to me an incident involving a synagogue cellar full of Jews, men and women, who attempted to hide from the Cossacks during a raid on their village. The sergeant ordered them to come up one by one and at first none of them stirred, but then a few came up the steps holding their arms over their heads. This did do them not the least good as they were clubbed to death with rifle-butts. The rest of them, though they were like herrings stuck together in a stinking barrel, would not move although they had been warned it would go worse with them. And so it did. The impatient Cossacks rushed into the cellar, bayoneting and shooting every last Jew. Those who were dragged out still alive were later thrown from speeding trains. A few, beginning with their benzine-soaked beards, were burned alive, and some of the women were dropped in their underclothes into wells to drown. You can take my word for it that in less than a week after your trial, there will be a quarter-million fewer Zhidy in the Pale."

He paused to breathe, then went on thickly. "Don't think we don't know that you wish to provoke just such a pogrom. We know from Secret Police reports that you are plotting to bring down on yourselves a violent reaction for revolutionary purposes – to stimulate active subversion among Socialist revolutionaries. The Tsar is informed of this, you can be sure, and is prepared to give you increased doses of the medicine I have described if you persist in trying to destroy his authority. I warn you, there is already a detachment of Ural Cossacks quartered in Kiev."

Yakov spat on the floor.

Either Grubeshov did not see or pretended he hadn't. Now, as though he had spent his anger, his voice became calm. "I am here to tell you this for your own good, Yakov Bok, and for the ultimate good of your fellow-Jews. It's all I will say now, absolutely all. I leave the rest to your contemplation and judgement. Have you any suggestions on how to forestall such an appalling, catastrophic – and I say frankly – useless tragedy? I appeal to your humanitarian impulses. One can imagine all sorts of compromises a person in your situation might be willing to make to tip the balance against disaster. I'm very serious. Have you something to say? If so, speak up."

"Mr Grubeshov, bring me to trial. I will wait for the trial, even to my death."

"And death is what you will get. It's on your head, Bok."

"On yours," said Yakov. "And for what you did to Bibikov."

Grubeshov stared at the fixer with white eyes. The shadow of a huge bird flew off the wall. The lamps went out and the cell door clanged.

Kogin, in a foul mood, slammed the stocks on the fixer's feet.

3

The lawyer had come and gone, Julius Ostrovsky.

He had appeared one day a few weeks after the Prosecuting Attorney's visit, whispered with the prisoner an hour,

318

filling his ear with what was going on, some that the fixer already had guessed, much that astonished him. He was astonished that strangers knew more than he of the public cause of his suffering and that the complications were so fantastic and endless.

"Tell me the worst," Yakov had begged, "do you think I will ever get out of here?"

"The worst is that we don't know the worst," Ostrovsky had answered. "We know you didn't do it, the worst is they know it too but say you did. This is the worst."

"Do you know when my trial is coming – if ever?"

"What can I answer you? They won't tell us what's happening today, so what can we expect to find out about tomorrow? Tomorrow they also hide from us. They hide even the most basic facts. They're afraid that anything we might know is a Jewish trick. What else can you expect if you are fighting a deadly war and everybody pretends, who's fighting? it's peace. It's a war, believe me."

The lawyer had risen when Yakov had limped into the room. This time there was no screen separating the prisoner from his visitor. Ostrovsky had at once cautioned him with a gesture, then whispered in his ear. "Speak quietly – to the floor. They say there's no guard outside the door but speak as if Grubeshov stands there if not the devil."

He was past sixty, a stocky man with a lined face and baldish head from which a few grey hairs rose like stubble. He had bent legs, wore two-toned button shoes, a black cravat and a short beard.

He had, when the prisoner appeared, stared at Yakov as though unable to believe this was the one. Finally he believed and his eyes changed from surprise to concern. He spoke in intense whispered Yiddish with more than one emotion. "I will introduce myself, Mr Bok, Julius Ostrovsky

319

of the Kiev bar. I'm glad I'm here at last but don't cheer yet, it's a long way to go. Anyway, some friends sent me."

"I'm thankful."

"You have friends though not all Jews, I'm sorry to say, are your friends. What I mean is that if a man hides his head in a bucket, whose friend is he? To my great regret some of our people shiver in every weather. We have organized a committee to help you but their caution is excessive. They're afraid to 'meddle' or there'll be another calamity. That's in itself a calamity. They shoot with popguns and run from the noise. Still, who has all friends?"

"Then who are my friends?"

"I am one and there are others. Take my word, you're not alone."

"Can you do anything for me? I'm sick of prison."

"What we can do we'll do. It's a long fight, I don't have to tell you, and the odds are against us. Still, anyway, calm, calm, calm. As the sages say, there are always two possibilities. One we know from too long experience; the other – the miracle – we will hope for. It's easy to hope, it's the waiting that spoils it. But two possibilities make the odds even. So enough philosophy. At this minute there's not much good news; finally we squeezed out an indictment, which means they will now have to schedule the case for trial, though when I leave to Rashi. But first, if you'll excuse me, I'll give you the bad news." Ostrovsky sighed. "I'm sorry that your father-in-law, Shmuel Rabinovitch, who I had the pleasure to meet and talk to last summer – a gifted man – is now, I'm sorry to tell you, dead from diabetes. This your wife wrote me in a letter."

"Ah," said Yakov.

Death had preceded itself. Poor Shmuel, the fixer thought, now I'll never see him again. That's what happens when you say good-bye to a friend and ride out into the world.

He covered his face with his hands and wept.

"He was a good man, he tried to educate me."

"The thing about life is how fast it goes," Ostrovsky said.

"Faster than that."

"You suffer for us all," the lawyer said huskily. "I would be honoured to be in your place."

"It's without honour," Yakov said, wiping his eyes with his fingers, and rubbing his hands together. "It's a dirty suffering."

"You've got my respect."

"If you don't mind tell me how my case stands. Tell me the truth."

"The truth is that things are bad though how bad I don't know myself. The case is clear enough – it's a bad joke from top to bottom – but it's mixed up in the worst way with the political situation. Kiev, you understand, is a medieval city full of wild superstition and mysticism. It has always been the heart of Russian reaction. The Black Hundreds, may they sink into their graves, have aroused against you the most ignorant and brutal of the masses. They are deathly afraid of Jews and at the same time frighten them to death. This reveals to you something about the human condition. Rich or poor, those of our brethren who can run out of here are running. Some who can't are already mourning. They sniff at the air and it stinks of pogrom. What's going on, as I say, nobody can say precisely. There's on the one hand a rumour that everything that happens, including your indictment, is another delay, and your trial, if you'll excuse me for saying it, will never take place; but on the other hand we hear it might start right after the Duma elections in September. Yes or no, they have no case against you. The civilized world knows this, including the Pope and his cardinals. If Grubeshov 'proves' anything it will be by the lies of 'the experts'. But we have our experts against them, for instance a Russian professor of theology, and I've written to Pavlov, the Tsar's surgeon, to testify on the medical report of the boy's autopsy and he hasn't said no yet. Grubeshov knows who the real murderers are but he shuts both eyes and stares at you. He went to law school with my oldest son and was famous for his socks and vests. Now he's famous for his anti-Semitic socks and vests. Out of Marfa Golov, that piece of trash, he tries to make if not a new saint, at least a persecuted heroine. Her blind lover tried last week to take his life but thank God, he's still alive. Also a clever journalist – may the Lord make more like him! – Pitirim Mirsky, discovered recently that Zhenia's father left him a life insurance legacy of five hundred roubles that the two murderers coveted, got, and at once spent. Two hogs, as they say, are worse than one. Mirsky printed this last week in *Poslednie Novosti*, and for that the publisher was fined and the press shut down by the police for three months. They must now discontinue all items about Golov. This is black reaction, but I'm not here to frighten you. You have enough to worry about."

"What else can frighten me?"

"If you feel bad think of Dreyfus. He went through the same thing with the script in French. We're persecuted in the most civilized languages."

"I've thought of him. It doesn't help."

"He was in prison many years, much longer than you."

"So far."

Ostrovsky, nodding absently as he gazed at the door, softened his whisper. "We also have an affidavit from Sofya Shiskovsky. One night she went into the toilet in Marfa's

322

house to relieve herself, and there in the bath-tub lay the naked corpse covered with wounds. So she screamed and ran out of the house. Marfa, who had gone for a minute upstairs to get a letter to prove a lie, ran after her and caught her in the street. That one – a mad woman of the First Guild – threatened to murder the whole Shiskovsky family if they breathed a word to anybody. They were afraid for Vasya, so they packed the furniture and moved out. When we finally located them, in a log hut in a back street in Moscow, she threatened to kill herself if we interfered with her, but with luck we got at least a short affidavit. She wouldn't let us question Vasya but we will try to have them both in court when the trial starts, if they aren't by that time in Asia. So this is another reason why the prosecution drags its feet: they can't prove a ritual murder but they won't stop trying, and the longer they take the more dangerous the situation becomes. It's dangerous because it's irrational, complex, secret. And it grows more dangerous as they get more desperate."

"Then what will I do?" said Yakov in despair. "How much more can I stand if I'm already half dead?"

"Patience, calm, calm, calm," Ostrovsky counselled, clasping his hands and squeezing. Then he looked at the fixer in a new light and struck his head with his palm.

"For God's sake, why are we standing yet? Come sit down. Forgive me, I'm blind in both eyes."

They sat then on a narrow bench in the far corner of the room away from the door, the lawyer still whispering. "Your case is tied up with the frustrations of recent Russian history. The Russo-Japanese War, I don't have to tell you, was a terrible disaster but it brought on the Revolution of 1905, which was coming anyway. 'War,' as Marx says, 'is the locomotive of history.' This was good for Russia but bad

323

for the Jews. The government, as usual, blamed us for their troubles and not more than one day after the Tsar's concessions pogroms started simultaneously in three hundred towns. Of course you know this, what Jew doesn't?"

"Tell me anyway, what harm can it do?"

"The Tsar was frightened by the rising agitation – strikes, riots, assassinations. The country was paralysed. After the Winter Palace massacre he reluctantly gave out a ukase promising the basic freedoms. He granted a Constitution, the Imperial Duma was established, and for a short time it looked – for Russia, you understand – like the beginning of a liberal period. The Jews cried hurray for the Tsar and wished him luck. Imagine, in the first Duma we had twelve deputies! Right away they brought up the question of equal rights for all and the abolition of the Pale of Settlement. Like a new world, no?"

"Yes, but go on."

"I'll go on but what can I say? In a sick country every step to health is an insult to those who live on its sickness. The imperial absolutists, the rightist elements, warned the Tsar his crown was slipping. He was already regretting the concessions and began to try to cancel them. In other words, for ten minutes he put on the lights and what he saw frightened him so much, since then he has been putting them out one by one so nobody will notice. As much as he could he changed back to an autocratic régime. The reactionary groups – the Union of Russian People, the Society of the Double-headed Eagle, the Union of the Archangel Michael – oppose worker and peasant movements, liberalism, socialism, any kind of reform, which also meant, naturally, the common enemy, the Jews. At the thought of a constitutional monarch their bones rattled. Organized together, they became the Black Hundreds, which means in gangs of a hundred for what disgusting purposes I don't have to tell you. They gnaw like rats to destroy the independence of the courts, the liberal press, the prestige of the Duma. To distract popular attention from the breaches of the Russian Constitution they incite nationalism against non-Orthodox Russians. They persecute every minority – Poles, Finns, Germans, us – but especially us. Popular discontent they divert into anti-Semitic outbreaks. It's a simple solution to their problems. Also they enjoy themselves because with the government's help they murder Jews and it's good for business."

"I'm only one man, what do they want from me?"

"One man is all they need so long as they can hold him up as an example of Jewish bloodthirst and criminality. To prove a point it's best to have a victim. In 1905 and 1906 thousands of innocent people were butchered, property damage in the millions of roubles. These pogroms were planned in the office of the Minister of Interior. We know that the anti-Jewish proclamations were printed on Police Department presses. And there are rumours that the Tsar himself contributes from the royal treasury for anti-Semitic books and pamphlets. We got all we need to frighten us but we're also frightened by rumours."

"By the wind," said Yakov.

"If you're frightened everything frightens you," Ostrovsky said. "Anyway, it's a long story but I'm making it short. Now I come direct to your door. When Premier Stolypin, no friend of ours, wanted, before the election of the second Duma, to throw a few bones to the Jews, a few little rights to stop their big complaints, the reactionaries ran to the Tsar and right away he changed the Electoral Laws, taking away the vote from a large part of the population to reduce Jewish and liberal representation in the Duma and

325

cut down opposition to the government. We now have maybe three deputies for three and a half million Jews and these too they want to get rid of. A year ago they assassinated one right in the street. But now I come to you. An atmosphere of hysteria developed all over the country. Still, there was some progress, don't ask me how, and the Imperial Duma was once more discussing whether, yes or no, to abolish the Pale of Jewish Settlement when right at this minute, when the Black Hundreds were frantic, one day a Christian boy was found dead in a cave and there appeared on the scene, Yakov Bok."

The fixer sat numbed. He waited for Ostrovsky to spit, but the lawyer sighed deeply and went on talking. "Where you came from nobody knew, or who you were, but you came just in time. I understand you came on a horse. When they saw you they pounced, and that's why we're sitting here now. But don't feel too bad, if it weren't you there'd be another in your place."

"Yes," said Yakov. "Somebody like me. I've thought it all out."

"So that's your bag of history," Ostrovsky said.

"In that case, what difference does it make if my trial comes or it doesn't?"

Ostrovsky got up, tiptoed to the door and abruptly opened it. Then he returned to the bench. "No one there but this way they'll know we're alert to them. I told you the worst," he said as he sat down, "now I'll tell you the best: You have a chance. What kind of chance? A chance. A chance is a chance, it's better than no chance. Anyway, hear me out so I can stop talking. First of all, not every Russian is your enemy. God forbid. The intelligentsia is disturbed by this case. Many luminaries of literature, science, and the professions have objected against the blood ritual slander.

Not so long ago the Kharkov Medical Society passed a resolution protesting your imprisonment, and the next thing that happened the society was dissolved by the government authorities. I told you already about *Poslednie Novosti*. Other newspapers have been fined for their probing articles and editorials. I know members of the bar who openly say that Marfa Golov and her lover committed the murder. Some say she wrote the original letter to the Black Hundreds, accusing the Jews of the crime. My theory is they came to her and asked her to write such a letter. Anyway, an opposition exists, which is good and it's bad. Where there's opposition to reaction there's also repression; but better repression than public sanction of injustice. So a chance you've got."

"Not more?"

"More. Freedom exists in the cracks of the state. Even in Russia a little justice can be found. It's a strange world. On the one hand we have the strictest autocracy; on the other we are approaching anarchy; in between courts exist and justice is possible. The law lives in the minds of men. If a judge is honest the law is protected. If that's the case, so are you. Also a jury is a jury – human beings – they could free you in five minutes."

"Should I hope?" said the fixer.

"If it doesn't hurt, hope. Still, since I'm telling the truth let me tell it all. Once we're on trial some witnesses will lie because they're frightened, and others because they're liars. Also you can expect that the Minister of Justice will appoint a presiding judge who is favourable to the prosecution. If the verdict is guilty his career will advance. And we also suspect that intellectuals and liberals will be eliminated from the jury lists and there's nothing we can do about it. With those that are left we will have to contend. So if you must hope,

327

hope. I'm sure Grubeshov isn't confident of his case. What's more important he's not confident of himself. He's ambitious but limited. In the end he will need better evidence than he has now. The trouble with resting your case on experts is that there are other experts. So I come back to the jury. In our favour is that although they may be ignorant peasants and shopkeepers, simple folk, as a rule they have little love for state officials, and when it comes to facts they can smell when they stink. For instance they know that Jewish roosters don't lay eggs. If Grubeshov strains he will make serious mistakes and your lawyer will know how to take advantage of them. He's an outstanding man from Moscow, Suslov-Smirnov, a Ukrainian by birth."

"Not you?" said Yakov in astonishment. "You aren't my lawyer."

"I was," said Ostrovsky with an apologetic smile, "but not any more. Now I'm a witness."

"What kind of witness?"

"They accuse me of attempting to bribe Marfa Golov not to testify against you. Of course she swears to it. I talked to her, naturally, but the accusation is ridiculous, it's to keep me from defending you. I don't know if you've heard my name before, Mr Bok? Probably not," he sighed, "but I have a little reputation in criminal cases. Still I don't want you to worry. Suslov-Smirnov I would use myself if I were in your place. He will be chief of your defence. He was in his youth anti-Semitic but he has now become a vigorous defender of the rights of Jews."

Yakov groaned. "Who needs a former anti-Semite?"

"You can take my word," Ostrovsky said quickly. "He is a brilliant lawyer, and his conversion is sincere. Next time I come I will bring him to you. Believe me, he will know how to deal with these people."

328

He glanced at his ticking watch, tucked it into his vest pocket, then hurried to the door and opened it. A guard with a rifle was standing there. Without surprise the lawyer shut the door and returned to the prisoner.

"I will speak what's on my mind," he said in Russian. "I say this against my will, Mr Bok, and with a heavy heart. You have suffered much and I don't want to add to your burdens, but the prosecution is desperate and this makes me fear your life. If you should die, naturally an unproved case will help the government more than a verdict against them, no matter how much they are suspected of or criticized for your death. I think you know what I mean. So all I will say to you is be careful. Don't allow yourself to be provoked. Remember – patience, calm, you have a few friends."

Yakov said he wanted to live.

"Please," said Ostrovsky.

4

He was not, on his return to the cell, locked in chains. They had been torn out of the wall and the holes cemented. The fixer, all but weightless, sat on the edge of the wooden bed, his head in rarefied air, his body roaring with excitement. He listened to the noise for half an hour before he knew he was listening to his swarming clanking thoughts. Shmuel was dead, let him rest in peace. He had deserved better than he had got. A lawyer, Ostrovsky, had been to see him. He had spoken of the trial; there was a chance. Another lawyer, a reformed Ukrainian anti-Semite, would defend him in court before a prejudiced judge and ignorant jury. But that was all in the future, when, nobody could say. Now he was at least no longer anonymous to all but his prosecutors and jailers. He was not unknown. There had blown up from somewhere a public opinion. Not every Russian believed him guilty. The fog was thinning a little. Newspapers were printing articles casting doubt on the accusation. Some lawyers were openly blaming Marfa Golov. A doctor's society had protested his imprisonment. He had become – who would have thought it? – a public person. Yakov laughed and wept a little. It was fantastic to believe. He tried to be hopeful but was immersed in fears of all there was still to live through.

"Why me?" he asked himself for the ten thousandth time. Why did it have to happen to a poor, half-ignorant fixer? Who needed this kind of education? Education he would have been satisfied to get from books. Each time he answered his question he answered it differently. He saw it as part personal fate – his various shortcomings and mistakes – but also as force of circumstances, though how you separated one from the other – if one really could – was beyond him. Who, for instance, *had* to go find Nikolai Maximovitch lying drunk in the snow and drag him home to start off an endless series of miserable events? Was that the word of God, inexorable Necessity? Go find your fate – try first the fat Russian with his face in the snow. Go be kind to an anti-Semite and suffer for it. And from him to his daughter with the crippled leg was only one crippled step, and then another into the brickyard. And a crippled hop into prison. If he had stayed in the shtetl it would never have happened. At least not this. Something else would have happened, better not think what.

Once you leave you're out in the open; it rains and snows. It snows history, which means what happens to somebody starts in a web of events outside the personal. It starts of course before he gets there. We're all in history, that's sure, but some are more than others, Jews more than some. If it snows not everybody is out in it getting wet. He had been doused. He had to his painful surprise, stepped into history more deeply than others – it had worked out so. Why he would never know. Because he had taken to reading Spinoza? An idea makes you adventurous? Maybe, who knows? Anyway, if he hadn't been Yakov Bok, a born Jew, he would not have been, to start with, an outlaw in the Lukianovsky when they were looking for one; he would never have been arrested. They might still be looking. It was, you could say, history's doing, it was full of all sorts of barriers and limitations, as though certain doors had been boarded up in a house and to get out you had to jump out of a window. If you jumped you might land on your head. In history, thicker at times than at others, too much happens. Ostrovsky had explained this to him. If conditions were ripe whatever was likely to happen was waiting for you to come along so it could happen. With less history around you might walk by or through it: it looked like rain but the sun was shining. In the snow he had once come upon Nikolai Maximovitch Lebedev wearing his Black Hundreds button. Nobody lived in Eden any more.

Yet though his young mother and father had remained all their poor lives in the shtetl, the historical evil had galloped in to murder them there. So the "open", he thought, was anywhere. In or out, it was history that counted – the world's bad memory. It remembered the wrong things. So for a Jew it was the same wherever he went, he carried a remembered pack on his back – a condition of servitude, diminished opportunity, vulnerability. No, there was no need to go to Kiev, or Moscow, or any place else. You could stay in the shtetl and trade in air or beans, dance at weddings or funerals, spend your life in the synagogue, die in bed and pretend you had died in peace, but a Jew wasn't free. Because the government destroyed his freedom by reducing his worth. Therefore wherever he was or went and whatever happened was perilous. A door swung open at his approach. A hand reached forth and plucked him in by his Jewish beard – Yakov Bok, a freethinking Jew in a brick factory in Kiev, yet any Jew, any plausible Jew – to be the Tsar's adversary and victim; chosen to murder the corpse His Majesty had furnished free; to be imprisoned, starved, degraded, chained like an animal to a wall although he was innocent. Why? because no Jew was innocent in a corrupt state, the most visible sign of its corruption its fear and hatred of those it persecuted. Ostrovsky had reminded him that there was much more wrong with Russia than its anti-Semitism. Those who persecute the innocent were themselves never free. Instead of satisfying him this thought filled him with rage.

It had happened – he was back to this again – because he was Yakov Bok and had an extraordinary amount to learn. He had learned, it wasn't easy; the experience was his; it was worse than that, it was he. He was the experience. It also meant that now he was somebody else than he had been, who would have thought it? So I learned a little, he thought, I learned this but what good will it do me? Will it open the prison doors? Will it allow me to go out and take up my poor life again? Will it free me a little once I am free? Or have I only learned to know what my condition is – that the ocean is salty as you are drowning, and though you know it you are drowned? Still, it was better than not knowing. A man had to learn, it was his nature.

Being without chains goaded impatience, what could he do with himself? Time began to move again, like a loco-

332

motive with two cars, three cars, four cars, a cluster of days, then two weeks gone, and to his horror, another season. It was autumn and he trembled at the thought of winter. The cold thought hurt his head. Suslov-Smirnov, an excitable, loose-boned long man with thick-lensed eyeglasses on a thin nose, and a bushy head of blond hair, had come four times to ask questions and take voluminous notes on thin sheets of paper – Ostrovsky had been forbidden to return. The lawyer had embraced the prisoner and promised – "Although we are hindered by stupid officials dragging their feet" – to move with all possible dispatch. "But in the meantime you must be careful of every step you take. Walk, as they say, on eggs, Mr Bok. On eggs." He nodded, winked with both eyes, and pressed four fingers to his lips.

"Do you know," Yakov said, "that they killed Bibikov?"

"We know," whispered Suslov-Smirnov, looking around in fright, "but we can't prove it. Say nothing or you'll make your situation worse."

"I've already said it," the fixer said, "to Grubeshov."

Suslov-Smirnov wrote it down quickly, then erased it and left. He said he would return but didn't, and no one would tell the fixer why. Have I made still another mistake? Again the indictment withdrawn? Yakov slowly tore at his flesh with his nails. The rest of another month leaked by. He again kept count of the days with bits of paper torn from the toilet paper strips. He weighed, he thought, a ton, all grief. His little hope – the hope he had foolishly dared – flickered, waned, withered. His legs were swollen and his back teeth loose. He was at the lowest ebb of his life when the warden appeared with an immaculate paper, saluted, and said his trial was about to begin.

5

All night the cell was crowded with prisoners who had lived and died there. They were broken-faced, greenish-grey men, with haunted eyes, scarred shaved heads and ragged bodies, crowding the cell. Many stared wordlessly at the fixer and he at them, their eyes lit with longing for life. If one disappeared two appeared in his place. So many prisoners, thought the prisoner, it's a country of prisoners. They've freed the serfs, or so they say, but not the innocent prisoners. He beheld long lines of them, gaunt-eyed men with starved mouths, lines stretching through the thick walls to impoverished cities, the vast empty steppe, great snowy virgin forests, to the shabby wooden work camps in Siberia. Trofim Kogin was among them. He had broken his leg and lay in the snow as the long lines slowly moved past him. He lay with his eyes shut and mouth twitching but did not call for help.

"Help!" cried Yakov in the dark.

This night before his trial, the fixer was oppressed by fear of death and though he was deathly sleepy he would not sleep. When his heavy eyes shut momentarily he saw someone standing over him with a knife raised to rip his throat. So the fixer forced himself to stay awake. He threw aside his blanket to make it too cold to sleep. Yakov pinched his arms and thighs. If anyone attempted to sneak into the cell he would shout when the door opened. To cry out was his only defence. It might scare the assassins if they thought any of the prisoners in the cells down the corridor would hear, and guess the Jew was being murdered. If they heard, after a while it would get to the outside that the officials had assassinated him rather than bring him to trial.

The wind wailed mutely in the prison yard. His heart was like a rusted chain, his muscles taut, as though each had been bound with wire. Even in the cold air he sweated. Amid the darkly luminous prisoners he saw spies waiting to kill him. One was the grey-haired warden with a gleaming two-headed axe. He tried to hide his crossed eye behind his hand but it shone like a jewel through his fingers. The Deputy Warden, his fly open, held a black bullwhip behind his back. And though the Tsar wore a white mask over his face and a black on the back of his head, Yakov recognized him standing in the far corner of the cell, dropping green drops into a glass of hot milk.

"It will make you sleep, Yakov Shepsovitch."

"After you, Your Majesty."

The Tsar faded in the dark. The spies disappeared but the lines of prisoners were endless.

What's next, the fixer thought, and when will it happen? Will the trial begin, or will they call it off at the last minute? Suppose they withdraw the Act of Indictment in the morning, hoping I collapse or go insane before they give me another. Many men have lived in prison longer and some under worse conditions, but if I have to live another year in this cell I would rather die. Then the sad-eyed prisoners who crowded the cell began to disappear. First those who were standing around the wooden bed, then those squeezed together in the centre, then those at the walls, and finally the long lines of sunken-faced men, moaning women, and ghostly children with glazed eyes in purple sockets, extending through the prison walls into the snowy distance.

"Are you Jews or Russians?" the fixer asked them.

"We are Russian prisoners."

"You look like Jews," he said.

Yakov fell asleep. Knowing he had, he frantically strove

335

to awake, hearing himself sob as he slept, but it was growing lighter in the cell and he soon saw Bibikov sitting at a table in his white summer suit, stirring a spoonful of strawberry jelly in his tea.

"This would hardly be the time for them to kill you, Yakov Shepsovitch," he said. "Anyone would know it was a put-up job, and it would arouse an outcry. What you must watch out for is the sudden and unexpected peril, the apparently accidental. So sleep now, without fear for your life, and if you should ever manage to get out of prison, keep in mind that the purpose of freedom is to create it for others."

"Your honour," said Yakov, "I've had an extraordinary insight."

"You don't say? What is it?"

"Something in myself has changed. I'm not the same man I was. I fear less and hate more."

Before daylight Zhenia came to him with his punctured face and bleeding chest and begged for the return of his life. Yakov laid both hands on the boy and tried to raise him from the dead but it wouldn't work.

In the morning the fixer was still alive. He had wakened in astonishment, his mood mixed, anticipation with depression. It was the end of October, two and a half years after his arrest in Nikolai Maximovitch's brickyard. Kogin told him the date when he came in with the prisoner's breakfast. This morning the gruel was boiled rice in hot milk, eight ounces of black bread, a yellow piece of butter, and an enamel pot of sweet-smelling tea, with a chunk of lemon and two lumps of sugar. There was also a cucumber and a small onion to chew on to strengthen his teeth and reduce the swelling of his legs. Kogin wasn't feeling well. His hands trembled when he put down the food. He looked flushed and said he wanted to get home to bed but the warden had ordered him to stay on till the prisoner had left for the courthouse.

"Full security regulations, the warden said."

Yakov did not touch the food.

"You'd better eat it," Kogin said.

"I'm not hungry."

"Eat anyway, it'll be a long day in court."

"I'm too nervous. If I ate now I'd vomit."

Berezhinsky entered the cell. He seemed uneasy, not knowing whether to smile or mourn. He smiled uneasily.

"Well, your day has come. Here's the trial now."

"What about my clothes?" Yakov asked. "Will I have to wear the prison ones or can I have my own?"

He wondered whether they were going to hand him a silken caftan and a round Hasidic fur hat.

"You'll find out about that," said Berezhinsky.

Both guards accompanied the prisoner to the bathhouse. He undressed and was allowed to soap and wash himself from a bucket of warm water. The warmth of the water brought secret tears to his eyes. He washed slowly with handfuls of water from the bucket. He washed the smells and dirt away.

Yakov was given a comb and carefully combed his long hair and beard, but then the prison barber appeared and said he must shave his head.

"No," the fixer shouted. "Why should I look like a prisoner now when I didn't before?"

"Because you are a prisoner," said Berezhinsky. "The gate's not open yet."

"Why now and not before?"

"Orders," said the prison barber, "so sit still and keep your mouth shut."

"Why does he cut my hair?" Yakov, angered, asked Kogin. He felt, then, the pangs of hunger.

"Orders must be obeyed," said the guard. "It's to show you had no special privileges and were treated like the others."

"I was treated worse than the others."

"If you know all the answers, then don't ask any questions," Kogin said in irritation.

"That's right," said Berezhinsky. "Keep your mouth shut."

When the hair clipping was done, Kogin went out and returned with the fixer's own clothes and told him to put them on.

Yakov got dressed in the bathhouse. He blessed his clothes though they hung on his bony body loosely and limply. The baggy pants were held up by a thin cord. The dank sheepskin coat hung almost to his knees. But the boots, though stiff, were comfortable.

Back in the cell, strangely lit in the light of two lamps, Kogin said, "Listen, Bok, I advise you to eat. I give you my word there's nothing to be afraid of in that food. You better eat."

"That's right," said Berezhinsky. "Do what you're told."

"I don't want to eat," said the fixer, "I want to fast."

"What the hell for?" said Kogin.

"For God's world."

"I thought you didn't believe in God."

"I don't."

"The hell with you," said Kogin.

"Well, good luck and no hard feelings," Berezhinsky said uneasily. "Duty is duty. The prisoner's the prisoner, the guard's the guard."

338

From the window came the sound of a troop of horses clattering into the prison yard.

"It's the Cossacks," said Berezhinsky.

"Will I have to walk in the middle of the street?"

"You'll find that out. The warden's waiting so hurry up or it will go hard on you."

As Yakov came out of the cell an escort of six Cossack guards with crossed bandoliers were lined up in the corridor. The captain, a burly man with a black moustache, ordered the guard to surround the prisoner.

"Forward march," commanded the escort captain.

The Cossacks marched the prisoner along the corridor towards the warden's office. Though Yakov tried to straighten his leg he walked with a limp. He went as quickly as he could to keep up with the guard. Kogin and Berezhinsky remained behind.

In the warden's inner office the captain carefully searched the prisoner; he wrote out a receipt for him and handed it to the warden.

"Just a minute, young man," said the warden. "I want to have a word of my own with the prisoner."

The captain saluted. "We leave at 8 a.m., sir." He went to wait in the outer office.

The old man wiped the corners of his mouth with a handkerchief. His eye was tearing so he wiped that too. He took out his snuffbox, then put it away.

Yakov watched him nervously. If he withdraws the indictment now I'll choke him to death.

"Well, Bok," said Warden Grizitskoy, "if you had had the sense to follow the Prosecuting Attorney's advice you'd be a free man today and out of the country. As it is now, you'll probably be convicted on the evidence and will spend the rest of your natural life in the strictest confinement."

The fixer scratched his palms.

The warden got his glasses out of a drawer, adjusted them on his nose, and read aloud an item from a newspaper lying on his desk. It was about a tailor in Odessa, Markovitch, a Jew, the father of five children, accused by the police of murdering a nine-year-old boy in a waterfront street late at night. He had then carried the child's body to his tailor shop and drained the still-warm corpse of its lifeblood. The police, suspicious of the tailor, who walked alone in the streets at night, had discovered bloodstains on the floor and had at once arrested him.

The warden put down the newspaper and removed his glasses.

"I'll tell you this, Bok: if we don't convict one of you we'll convict the other. We'll teach you all a lesson."

The fixer remained mute.

The warden, his mouth wet with anger, threw open the door and signalled the escort captain.

But then the Deputy Warden entered from the hall. He came in a hurry, paying no attention to the escort captain.

"Warden," he said, "I have here a telegram that forbids special privileges for the Jewish prisoner Bok just because he happens to be going on trial. He hasn't been searched this morning through no fault of mine. Please have him returned to his cell to be searched in the usual way."

A sick pressure burdened the fixer's chest.

"Why should I be searched now? What will you find if you search me? Only my miseries. This man doesn't know where to stop."

"I've already searched him," said the Cossack captain to the Deputy Warden. "The prisoner is now in my custody. I've given the warden my personal receipt."

"It's on my desk," said the warden.

The Deputy Warden drew a folded white paper out of his tunic pocket. "This telegram is from his Imperial Majesty in St Petersburg. It orders us to search the Jew most carefully to prevent any possible dangerous incident."

"Why wasn't the telegram sent to me?" asked the warden.

"I notified you it might come," said the Deputy Warden.

"That's right," said the warden, flustered.

"Why should I be insulted again?" Yakov shouted, the blood burning in his face. "The guards saw me naked in the bathhouse and watched me dress. Also this captain searched me a few minutes ago in front of the warden. Why should I be further humiliated on the day of my trial?"

The warden banged his fist on the desk. "That will do. Be still, I warn you."

"No one wants your opinion," said the black-moustached captain coldly. "Forward march. Back to the cell."

There's more to this than it says in the telegram, Yakov thought. If they're trying to provoke me I'd better be careful.

Sick to his soul, he was marched to the cell by the Cossack guard.

"Welcome home," Berezhinsky laughed.

Kogin stared at the fixer in frightened surprise.

"Hurry it up," said the Cossack captain to the Deputy Warden.

"Please, friend, don't tell me how to do my job and I won't tell you how to do yours," said the Deputy Warden, coldly. His boots smelled as though he had freshly stepped in excrement.

"Inside and undress," he ordered Yakov.

The prisoner, the Deputy Warden, and the two guards entered the cell, leaving the captain and the escort guard waiting in the corridor. The Deputy Warden slammed the cell door shut.

Inside the cell Kogin crossed himself.

Yakov slowly undressed, shivering. He stood there naked, except for his undershirt. I must be careful, he thought, or it will go hard on me. Ostrovsky warned me. Yet as he told himself this he felt his rage growing. The blood roared in his ears. It was as though he had dug a hole, then put the shovel aside but the hole was still growing. It grew into a grave. He imagined himself tearing the Deputy Warden's face apart and kicking him to death.

"Open your mouth," Berezhinsky ran a dirty finger under his tongue.

"Now spread your arse apart."

Kogin stared at the wall.

"Take off that stinking undershirt," ordered the Deputy Warden.

I must calm my anger, thought the fixer, seeing the world black. Instead, his anger grew.

"Why should I?" he shouted. "I have never taken it off before. Why should I take it off now? Why do you insult me?"

"Take it off before I tear it off."

Yakov felt the cell tremble and dip. I should have eaten, he thought. It was a mistake not to. He saw a bald-headed thin naked man in a freezing prison cell ripping off his undershirt and to his horror watched him fling it into the face of the Deputy Warden.

A solemn silence filled the cell.

Though his wet eyes were lit, murderous, the Deputy Warden spoke calmly. "I am within my rights to punish you for interfering with and insulting a prison official in the performance of his duty."

342

He drew his revolver.

My dirty luck. Yakov thought of the way his life had gone. Now Shmuel is dead and Raisl has nothing to eat. I've never been of use to anybody and I'll never be.

"Hold on a minute, your honour," said Kogin to the Deputy Warden. His deep voice broke. "I've listened to this man night after night, I know his sorrows. Enough is enough, and anyway it's time for his trial to begin."

"Get out of my way or I'll cite you for insubordination, you son-of-a-bitch."

Kogin pressed the muzzle of his revolver against the Deputy Warden's neck.

Berezhinsky reached for his gun but before he could draw, Kogin fired.

He fired at the ceiling and after a while dust drifted to the floor.

A whistle sounded shrilly in the corridor. The prison bell clanged. The iron cell door was slammed open and the white-faced captain and his Cossack guards rushed into the cell.

"I've given my personal receipt," he roared.

"My head aches," Kogin muttered. He sank to his knees with blood on his face. The Deputy Warden had shot him.

6

A church bell tolled.

A black bird flew out of the sky. Crow? Hawk? Or the black egg of a black eagle falling towards the carriage? If it isn't that what is it? If it's a bomb, thought Yakov, what can I do? I'll duck, what else can I do? If it's a bomb why was I ever born?

The prisoner, watched in silence by a crowd of officials, guests, and the mounted Cossacks in the yard, had limped amid the guard from the prison door to the massive black armoured carriage drawn by four thick-necked, heavy-rumped horses at the gate. On the driver's seat sat a hawk-eyed coachman in a long coat and visored cap, whip in his hand.

The fixer was boosted up the metal step by two Cossacks and locked in the large-wheeled coach by the Chief of Police and his assistant. Inside it was dark and musty. An unlit lamp hung in the corner; the windows were round and small. Yakov put his eye to one of them, saw nothing he wanted to see – Warden Grizitskoy in military cap and coat rubbing a bloodshot eye – and sat back in the gloom.

The coachman shouted to the horses; a whip snapped and the huge carriage with its escort of fur-capped, grey-coated Cossack riders, a platoon in front with glittering lances, another in the rear with swords unsheathed, lumbered through the gate and rattled out on the cobblestone street. The coach moved quickly up the street, turned a corner and then went along an avenue with fields on one side and occasional factories and houses on the other.

I'm off, thought the fixer, for better or worse, and if it's worse it'll be worse than it was.

He sat for a while shrunken in loneliness, then through a window saw a bird in the sky and watched with emotion until he could no longer see it. The weak sun stained the thin drifting clouds and for a minute snow flurried in different directions. In a wood not far from the road the oaks retained their bronze leaves but the large chestnut trees were black and barren. Yakov, seeing them in memory in full bloom, regretted the seasons he had missed and the years of his youth lost in prison.

Though still stunned by Kogin's death he felt, finally, the relief of motion, though to what fate who could say? Yet on the move at last to the courthouse, his trial about to take place, they said, a full three years from the time he had left the shtetl and ridden to Kiev. Then as they passed the brick wall of a factory, its chimneys pouring out coal smoke whipped by the wind into the sky, he caught a reflected glimpse of a faded shrunken Jew in the circle of window and hid from him, but could not, a minute later, from the memory of his gaunt face, its darkened stringy beard white around the bitter mouth, and though he would not weep for himself, his palms, when he rubbed his eyes, were wet.

At the factory gate five or six workers had turned to watch the procession; but when it had gone a verst into the business district, the fixer looked up in astonishment at the masses of people gathered on both sides of the street. Though it was early morning the crowds stretched along, five and six deep, labourers and civil servants on their way to work, shopkeepers, peasants in sheepskin coats, women in shawls and a few in hats, a scattering of military cadets and soldiers, and here and there a grey-robed monk or priest staring at the carriage. The trolleys were stopped, passengers rising from their seats to look out the windows as the Cossack riders and lumbering coach passed by. In the side-streets the police held up carriages and motor-cars, and bullock carts from the provinces, piled high with vegetables and grains, or loaded with cans of milk. Along the route to the courthouse mounted police were stationed at intervals to keep order. Yakov moved from one window to another to see the crowds.

"Yakov Bok!" he called out. "Yakov Bok!"

The Cossack riding on the left side of the carriage, a thick-shouldered man with overhanging brows and a moustache turning grey, gazed impassively ahead; but the rider cantering along on the door side, a youth of twenty or so on a grey mare, from time to time stole a glance at Yakov when he was staring out the window, as though trying to measure his guilt or innocence.

"Innocent!" the fixer cried out to him. "Innocent!" And though he had no reason to, he smiled a little at the Cossack for his youth and good looks, and for being, as such things go, a free man, give or take a little. The Cossack then rode forward as the mare, raising her tail, dropped a steaming load on the street at which a schoolboy pointed.

Amid the crowd were a few Jews watching with commiseration or fear. Most of the Russian faces were impassive, though some showed hostility and some loathing. A shopkeeper in a smock spat at the carriage. Two boys hooted. Some of the men in the crowd wore Black Hundreds buttons and when Yakov, out of one window then quickly the other, saw how many of them there were at this place, he grew apprehensive. Where there was one there were a hundred. A man with a strained face and deadly eyes threw his hand into the air as though it had caught on fire. The fixer's scrotum shrank painfully and he tore at his chest with his fingers as a black bird seemed to fly out of the white hand clawing the air.

Yakov frantically ducked. If this is my death I've endured for nothing.

"You might have waited a bit, Yakov Bok," the chairman of the jury said. "None of us are gentry or educated folk, but neither are we without a bit of experience in the world. A man learns to recognize the truth even if he doesn't always

346

live by it. And there are times he does that if it suits his fancy. The officials may not want us to know what the truth is but it comes in, you might say, through the chinks in the walls. They may try to deceive us, as they do often enough, but we will sift the evidence and if the facts are not as they say, then let them look to their consciences."

"They have none."

"So much the worse for them, in that case. You aren't born human for nothing, I say."

"I'm innocent," said Yakov, "you can look at me and see. Look in my face and say whether a man like me, whatever else he might do, could kill a boy and drain the blood out of his body. If I have any humanity in my heart and you are men you must know it. Tell me do I look like a murderer?"

The chairman was about to say but a violent explosion rocked the coach.

Yakov waited for death. He wandered for a while in a cemetery reading the names on the tombstones. Then he ran from grave to grave, searching them frantically, one after another, but could not find his name. After a while he stopped looking. He had waited a long time but maybe he had longer to wait. If you were a certain type death stayed its distance. Your afflictions were from life – a poor living, mistakes with people, the blows of fate. You lived, you suffered, but you lived.

He heard screams, shouts, commotion, the frightened whinnying of horses. The carriages rattled and seemed to leap up, then struck the ground and stopped dead, shuddering, but remained upright. The stench of gunpowder bored through his nostrils. A door lock snapped and the door fell ajar. He felt an overwhelming hunger to be back home, to see Raisl and set things straight, to decide what to do.

347

"Raisl," he said, "dress the boy and pack the few things we need, we'll have to hide." He was about to kick the door open but warned himself not to. Through the cracked right window he saw people on the run. A squad of Cossacks with lances raised galloped away from the carriage. A squad with uplifted sabres galloped towards it, risen in their saddles. The grey mare lay dead on the cobblestones. Three policemen were lifting the young Cossack rider. His foot had been torn off by the bomb. The boot had been blown away and his leg was shattered and bloody. As they carried him past the carriage his eyes opened and he looked in horror and anguish at Yakov as though to say, "What has my foot got to do with it?"

The fixer shrank from the sight. The Cossack had fainted but his torn leg shook, spattering blood on the policemen. Then a Cossack colonel galloped up to the carriage, holding a sword aloft, shouting to the coachman, "Go on, go on!" He dismounted and tried to slam the door shut but it wouldn't lock. "Go on, go on!" he shouted. The carriage rumbled on, the horses picked up speed and broke into a fast trot. The colonel, on a white horse, cantered along beside the coach in place of the wounded Cossack.

Yakov sat in the gloomy coach overcome by hatred so intense his chest heaved as though the carriage were airless. He saw himself, after a while, sitting at a table somewhere, opposite the Tsar, a lit candle between them, in a cell or cellar, whatever it was. Nicholas the Second, of medium height, with frank blue eyes and neatly trimmed beard a little too large for his face, sat there naked, holding in his hand a small silver ikon of the Virgin Mary. Though distraught and pale, afflicted with a bad cough he had recently developed, he spoke in a gentle voice and with moving eloquence.

348

"Though you have me at a disadvantage, Yakov Shepsovitch, I will speak the truth to you. It isn't only that the
Jews are freemasons and revolutionaries who make a
shambles of our laws and demoralize our police by syste-
matic bribery for social exemptions – I can forgive that a bit
but not the other things, in particular the terrible crime you
are accused of, which is so repellent to me personally. I refer
to the draining of his lifeblood out of Zhenia Golov's body. I
don't know whether you are aware that my own child, the
Tsarevitch Alexis, is a haemophiliac? The newspapers, out
of courtesy to the royal family, and the Tsarina in particular,
do not, of course, mention it. We are fortunate in having
four healthy daughters, the princess Olga, the studious one;
Tatyana, the prettiest, and something of a coquette – I say
this with amusement; Maria, shy and sweet-tempered; and
Anastasya, the youngest and liveliest of them; but when
after many prayers an heir to the throne was born at last –
it pleased God to make this joy our greatest trial – his blood
unfortunately was deficient in that substance which is
necessary for coagulation and healing. A small cut, the most
trivial, and he may bleed to death. We look after him,
as you can expect, with the greatest care, on tenterhooks
every minute because even a quite ordinary fall may
mean extreme peril. Alexei's veins are fragile, brittle,
and in the slightest mishap internal bleeding causes him
unbearable pain and torment. My dear wife and I – and
I may add, the girls – live through death with this poor
child. Permit me to ask, Yakov Shepsovitch, are you a
father?"

"With all my heart."

"Then you can imagine our anguish," sighed the sad-
eyed Tsar.

His hands trembled a little as he lit a green-papered

Turkish cigarette from an enamelled box on the table. He offered the box to Yakov but the fixer shook his head.

"I never wanted the crown, it kept me from being my true self, but I was not permitted to refuse. To rule is to bear a heavy cross. I've made mistakes, but not, I assure you, out of malice to anyone. My nature is not resolute, not like my late father's – we lived in terror of him – but what can a man do beyond the best he can? One is born as he is born and that's all there is to it. I thank God for my good qualities. To tell you the truth, Yakov Shepsovitch, I don't like to dwell on these things. But I am – I can truthfully say – a kind person and love my people. Though the Jews cause me a great deal of trouble, and we must sometimes suppress them to maintain order, believe me, I wish them well. As for you, if you permit me, I consider you a decent but mistaken man – I insist on honesty – and I must ask you to take note of my obligations and burdens. After all, it isn't as though you yourself are unaware of what suffering is. Surely it has taught you the meaning of mercy?"

He was coughing insistently now and his voice, when he finished, was unsteady.

Yakov moved uneasily in his chair. "Excuse me, Your Majesty, but what suffering has taught me is the uselessness of suffering, if you don't mind me saying so. Anyway, there's enough of that to live with naturally without piling a mountain of injustice on top. Rachmones, we say in Hebrew – mercy, one oughtn't to forget it, but one must also think how oppressed, ignorant and miserable most of us are in this country, gentiles as well as Jews, under your government and ministers. What it amounts to, Little Father, is that whether you wanted it or not you had your chance; in fact many chances, but the best you could give us with all good intentions is the poorest and most reactionary state in

350

Europe. In other words, you've made out of this country a valley of bones. You had your chances and pissed them away. There's no argument against that. It's not easy to twist events by the tail but you might have done something for a better life for us all – for the future of Russia, one might say, but you didn't."

The Tsar rose, his phallus meagre, coughing still, disturbed and angered. "I'm only one man though ruler yet you blame me for our whole history."

"For what you don't know, Your Majesty, and what you haven't learned. Your poor boy is a haemophiliac, something missing in the blood. In you, in spite of certain sentimental feelings, it is missing somewhere else – the sort of insight, you might call it, that creates in a man charity, respect for the most miserable. You say you are kind and prove it with pogroms."

"As for those," said the Tsar, "don't blame me. Water can't be prevented from flowing. They are a genuine expression of the will of the people."

"Then in that case there's no more to say." On the table at the fixer's hand lay a revolver. Yakov pushed a bullet into the rusty cylinder chamber.

The Tsar sat down, watching without apparent emotion, though his face had grown white and his beard darker. "I am the victim, the sufferer for my poor people. What will be will be." He stubbed out his cigarette in the candle saucer. The light flickered but burnt on.

"Don't expect me to beg."

"This is also for the prison, the poison, the six daily searches. It's for Bibikov and Kogin and for a lot more that I won't even mention."

Pointing the gun at the Tsar's heart (though Bibikov, flailing his white arms, cried no no no no), Yakov pressed

351

the trigger. Nicholas, in the act of crossing himself, over-turned his chair, and fell, to his surprise, to the floor, the stain spreading on his breast.

The horses clopped on over the cobblestones.

As for history, Yakov thought, there are ways to reverse it. What the Tsar deserves is a bullet in the gut. Better him than us.

The left rear wheel of the carriage seemed to be wobbling.

One thing I've learned, he thought, there's no such thing as an unpolitical man, especially a Jew. You can't be one without the other, that's clear enough. You can't sit still and see yourself destroyed.

Afterwards he thought, Where there's no fight for it there's no freedom. What is it Spinoza says? If the state acts in ways that are abhorrent to human nature it's the lesser evil to destroy it. Death to the anti-Semites! Long live revolution! Long live liberty!

The crowds lining both sides of the streets were dense again, packed tight between kerb and housefront. There were faces at every window and people standing on rooftops along the way. Among those in the street were Jews of the Plossky District. Some, as the carriage clattered by and they glimpsed the fixer, were openly weeping, wringing their hands. One thinly bearded man clawed his face. One or two waved at Yakov. Some shouted his name.